Andrew Hammond began his working life in a cheap suit, sitting in the bowels of York Magistrates' Court, interviewing repeat offenders who always said they 'didn't do it'. After three years in the legal profession, Andrew re-trained as an English teacher. CRYPT is Andrew's first fictional series but he has written over forty English textbooks for schools and he can spot the difference between an adjectival and adverbial phrase at fifty paces (if only someone would ask him to). He now works as a headmaster in Hampshire with his wife Andie and their four angels – Henry, Edward, Eleanor and Katherine – none of whom are old enough yet to read 'Daddy's scary books'. But one day . . .

By Andrew Hammond

CRYPT: *The Gallows Curse*
CRYPT: *Traitor's Revenge*
CRYPT: *Mask of Death*
CRYPT: *Blood Eagle Tortures*

CRYPT

COVERT RESPONSE YOUTH PARANORMAL TEAM

BLOOD EAGLE
TORTURES

ANDREW HAMMOND

headline

First published in 2013 by
HEADLINE PUBLISHING GROUP

2

Cataloguing in Publication Data is available from the British Library

ISBN 978 0 7553 7824 1

Typeset in Goudy Old Style by Avon DataSet Ltd, Bidford-on-Avon,
Warwickshire

Printed and bound in Great Britain by Clays Ltd, St Ives plc

Headline's policy is to use papers that are natural, renewable and recyclable
products and made from wood grown in sustainable forests. The logging and
manufacturing processes are expected to conform to the environmental
regulations of the country of origin.

HEADLINE PUBLISHING GROUP
An Hachette UK company
338 Euston Road
London NW1 3BH

www.headline.co.uk
www.hachette.co.uk

For Bear

GHOSTS ARE THE STUFF OF FICTION, RIGHT?

WRONG.

THE GOVERNMENT JUST DOESN'T WANT YOU TO KNOW ABOUT THEM . . .

THIS IS THE TOP SECRET CLASSIFIED HISTORY OF CRYPT.

In 2007, American billionaire and IT guru Jason Goode bought himself an English castle; it's what every rich man needs. He commissioned a new skyscraper too, to be built right in the heart of London. A futuristic cone-shaped building with thirty-eight floors and a revolving penthouse, it would be the new headquarters for his global enterprise, Goode Technology PLC.

He and his wife Tara were looking forward to their first Christmas at the castle with Jamie, their thirteen-year-old son, home from boarding school. It all seemed so perfect.

Six weeks later Goode returned home one night to find a horror scene: the castle lit up with blue flashing lights, police everywhere.

His wife was dead. His staff were out for the night; his son was the only suspect.

Jamie was taken into custody and eventually found guilty of killing his mother. They said he'd pushed her from the battlements during a heated argument. He was sent away to a young offenders' institution.

But throughout the trial, his claims about what really happened never changed:

'The ghosts did it, Dad.'

His father had to believe him. From that day on, Jason Goode vowed to prove the existence of ghosts and clear his son's name.

They said Goode was mad – driven to obsession by the grief of losing his family. Plans for the new London headquarters were put on hold. He lost interest in work. People said he'd given up on life.

But one man stood by him – lifelong friend and eminent scientist Professor Giles Bonati. Friends since their student days at Cambridge, Bonati knew Goode hadn't lost his mind. They began researching the science of disembodied spirits.

Not only did they prove scientifically how ghosts can access our world, they uncovered a startling truth too: that some teenagers have stronger connections to ghosts than any other age group. They have high extrasensory perception (ESP), which means they can see ghosts where others can't.

So was Jamie telling the truth after all?

Goode and Bonati set up the Paranormal Investigation Team (PIT), based in the cellars of Goode's private castle. It was a small experimental project at first, but it grew. Requests came in for its teenage agents to visit hauntings across the region.

But fear of the paranormal was building thanks to the PIT. Hoax calls were coming in whenever people heard a creak in the attic. Amateur ghost hunters began to follow the teenagers and interfere with their work. But it didn't stop there. Goode and Bonati quickly discovered a further truth – something which even they had not bargained for. As more and more people pitched up at hauntings to watch the agents in action, so the ghosts became stronger. It seemed as though the greater the panic and hysteria at a scene, the more powerful the paranormal activity became. There was no denying it: the ghosts fed off human fear.

So where would this lead?

To prevent the situation from escalating out of control, Goode was ordered to disband the PIT and stop frightening people. Reporters tried to expose the team as a fraud. People could rest easy in their beds – there was no such thing as ghosts. Goode had to face the awful truth that his son was a liar – and a murderer. The alternative was too frightening for the public to accept.

So that's what they were told.

But in private, things were quite different. Goode had been approached by MI5.

The British security services had been secretly investigating paranormal incidents for years. When crimes are reported without any rational human explanation, MI5 must explore all other possibilities, including the paranormal. But funding was tight and results were limited.

Maybe teenagers were the answer.

So they proposed a deal. Goode could continue his paranormal investigations, but to prevent more hoax calls and widespread panic, he had to do so under the cover and protection of MI5.

They suggested the perfect venue for this joint operation – Goode's London headquarters. The skyscraper was not yet finished. There was still time. A subterranean suite of hi-tech laboratories could be built in the foundations. A new, covert organisation could be established – bigger and better than before, a joint enterprise between Goode Technology and the British security services.

But before Jason Goode agreed to the plan, he made a special request of his own. He would finish the building, convert the underground car park into a suite of laboratories and living accommodation, allow MI5 to control operations, help them recruit the best teenage investigators they could find and finance any future plans they had for the organisation – all in return for one thing.

He wanted his son back.

After weeks of intense secret negotiations, the security services finally managed to broker the deal: provided he was monitored closely by the Covert Policing Command at Scotland Yard, and, for his own protection, was given a new identity, Jamie could be released. For now.

The deal was sealed. The Goode Tower was finished – a landmark piece of modern architecture, soaring above the Thames. And buried discreetly beneath its thirty-eight floors was the Covert Response Youth Paranormal Team.

The CRYPT. Its motto: *EXSPECTA INEXSPECTATA*. Expect the unexpected.

Jamie Goode was released from custody and is now the CRYPT's most respected agent.

And his new identity?

Meet Jud Lester, paranormal investigator.

CRYPT

COVERT RESPONSE YOUTH PARANORMAL TEAM

BLOOD EAGLE
TORTURES

CHAPTER 1

TUESDAY, 7.14 A.M.

DUNWICH BEACH, SUFFOLK

The dawn mist hung low over the icy waters of the North Sea as they ripped into the pebble beach. The pale stones tumbled helplessly towards the soapy froth. Another gust and the tide crept further still up the shifting sands, depositing its unwelcome gift of flotsam before retreating again beneath its foggy shroud.

There was no horizon; the thick, white cloud extended forwards, upwards, all around.

A lone gull swooped from nowhere to investigate a discarded, rusty Coke can left by the last riptide, flipped it eagerly with its sharp beak, then took off in disappointment, vanishing into the nothingness.

Another gust of wind bit through the mist, sending swirls of cloud rolling across the rippling grey waves and allowing a small light to become visible about a mile out to sea. Just a faint yellow light, winking at no one, and the faint trace of a mast, rising and tumbling and swaying with every wave that rocked the little vessel.

Dan Summers was not on his boat.

But it remained anchored and it had, so far at least, resisted the lashing waves that had been crashing into its dirty hull since the small hours.

Dan was several metres beneath the surface – just where he liked to be. Though he'd been diving for years, this was his first foray into these cold, eerie waters.

The landlord of the little hotel had boasted to Dan how it was a common occurrence to see a skull wash up on the beach, or a thigh bone, or a foot. As a child (so he'd said), he would often find human bones whilst playing on the beach with his brothers and sister. There was, after all, a whole graveyard beneath the waves. And the sea doesn't respect a dead man's privacy, as he kept saying. 'It'll turn you into driftwood if it so wishes.'

And now the sunken village of Dunwich, hidden beneath the waves for more than a century, was exceeding even Dan's inflated expectations.

Scrabbling around on the seabed among the debris of fallen buildings and walls and gravestones, he'd found more than some divers before him had found after years of diving here.

There had been plenty of similar expeditions to this particular edge of Suffolk. They knew it wasn't every day that a whole town was claimed by the ocean. And plenty of historians and authors too had written of the place that dwelled beneath the waves – 'England's own Atlantis,' some called it. In its history, Dunwich had been a Roman fort, a thriving port – the envy of all coastal towns in the East – and even the capital city of a Saxon kingdom. At one stage, Dunwich had a population the size of half of London.

But the ripping tides had shown no mercy over the years and now the only evidence you could find on land of this ghost city was the ruins of the Franciscan friary, still clinging to the cliffs. Everything else had slipped, like the pebbles on the beach, into the ravaging jaws of the North Sea. And though this deserted edge of Suffolk had seen more than its fair share of invaders from Europe over the centuries, no army was so destructive as nature itself.

On quiet nights, when at last the wind abated in this wild stretch of coastline and the air was still, save for the gulls' cries, locals said they heard the desperate peels from the bells of St Mary's Church, from its own watery grave.

The landlord said, if you wanted 'a wild, remote, spooky adventure of a holiday, then come to Dunwich beach.' But then, he would.

As a diver, Dan was no stranger to adventure; in fact, it took much to impress him after the exploits he'd enjoyed over the years.

But here, right now, beneath the freezing waters, he'd found something that had made the journey – and the expense, and the sleepless night on the rickety bed, and the almost impossible navigation to get here – worthwhile.

CHAPTER 2

TUESDAY, 8.41 A.M.

CRYPT, LONDON

Jud Lester edged closer to the battlements. The wind was racing around the top of the tower, brushing his hair in every direction and battering his cold cheeks. He tiptoed on, closer and closer to the plunging descent into darkness. He imagined the feel of the hard, unforgiving tarmac at the bottom and felt a shudder inside.

As he gazed over the edge into blackness, a tear fell from his cheek and landed on his boot. Then another.

He wiped his eyes, sniffed and stiffened his body.

'Come on,' he said aloud. 'Think. *Remember*.'

The roar of the wind rose again and there was a thunderclap that shook him, shook the very foundations of the building.

He looked skywards and closed his eyes.

'Talk to me!' he shouted out. 'Say something. *Anything!*'

'Where the hell is Jud?' Bex asked Luc as they passed in the corridor on Sector One.

He shrugged. 'Search me. Still in bed, I s'pose.'

'He's not. That's just the point. I've tried his room. He's gone, Luc.'

'What do you mean, *gone?*'

'His bed's not even been slept in. I'm telling you, he's not here.'

'I'm sure he hasn't vanished, Bex. Chill out. Look, I'm sorry I can't help you,' Luc replied. 'I've got to get down to the briefing room. Vorzek's demonstrating some equipment. In fact, I thought you were supposed to be there too.'

'I am!' said Bex. 'And so is Jud. That's why I went to check he was up. I've been calling him on his mobile too. No answer. I'm worried, Luc. Something's up. I can feel it.' Bex found Luc's laid-back attitude irritating. He was so cool, so unflappable – which was great in times of crisis, but frustrating at other moments when she found it difficult to prompt him into action. And if he told her to 'chill out' one more time, she'd go mad. Was she the only one in the CRYPT who cared about Jud Lester? Sometimes it felt like that.

But irritation didn't suit Bex. She too was cool and classy and at times just as bomb-proof as Luc. When it came to paranormal investigations, there were few agents in the whole enterprise with the same gutsy courage as Bex De Verre. Her auburn hair and huge dark eyes, combined with her pale complexion, made her stand out from the crowd and there were very few male agents in the place who didn't hold a soft spot for Bex, albeit a secret one – there was no point in allowing their feelings to grow; everyone knew she only had eyes for one agent.

And it was the self-same agent who, for some reason, possessed this uncanny knack of disappearing suddenly from view. He was slippery, elusive – like a fox but, unluckily for Bex, with the same alluring charm. How many hours had she spent searching the long corridors and empty labs 'fox hunting'? And here she was, at it again. But Jud's disappearance troubled her. Yes, he was brave, strong, scarily intelligent, but he was vulnerable too. Only Bex knew that. And he possessed a temper that was as volatile as mercury. She *had* to find him; he was a law unto himself sometimes.

'Look, I can't miss this briefing,' said Luc. 'And neither should you, Bex. Jud's probably in there by now, wondering where we are.'

'So why was his bed not slept in, huh?'

'I dunno. Don't much care, either. Maybe he's suddenly decided to start making it every morning, like a good boy,' said Luc, smirking. His dark skin, his bright shining eyes and his beautiful white teeth made him no less alluring than Jud. And when he smiled, as he was doing now, his face lit up. But Bex was not in the mood to be charmed, at least not by Luc.

She raised an eyebrow as if to say, *You don't believe that either, do you?*

'Look, I've got to go, Bex. If he's not with Vorzek, we'll search later, OK? He can't have gone far. He always tells me when he's going out. Come on, let's not be late or Vorzek will kill us.'

She shook her head. 'I'm going to see Bonati. I'm not convinced, Luc. Something's up.'

He shrugged. 'OK. Whatever. I'll help you later, if he really has gone – but I bet he hasn't. You know what he's like, Bex. You worry too much about that guy. Anyone would think . . .' he raised his eyebrows cheekily and an endearing grin returned to his face as he trailed off and left her alone. He made off in the direction of the lifts.

A few minutes later, Bex found the professor in his office, on the telephone. She waited patiently for him to end his call and look up in her direction. She watched his piercing eyes behind those rimless specs as they flickered across the computer screen to his left. He leaned back in his chair and ran a hand through his impressive shock of grey hair – 'the silver fox,' they sometimes called him, though Bex didn't need another fox in the place. He was good looking in an intellectual way – like a dashing surgeon or the barrister in court whom the jurors always fall for. It always puzzled Bex why he'd never married – he must have had plenty of offers. But he was wedded to the CRYPT.

He soon finished his phone call and looked up.

'Morning, Rebecca. Problem?'

'I can't find Jud, sir. He's meant to be attending Dr Vorzek's meeting and I was hoping to catch him first to discuss a case we're on. You know, the Old Bailey ghost? I wanted to run some theories past him before the briefing. We were supposed to be meeting for breakfast. But I can't find him anywhere.'

Bonati was as calm and measured as ever. He removed his glasses, rubbed his eyes – already tired from staring at a computer screen since the early hours – and took a sip from the lukewarm coffee on his desk.

'If I had a pound for every time that boy vanished . . . He won't have gone far, Bex. Tried the SPA rooms?'

'Why? He's not due a session today is he?'

The professor laughed. 'I wish I could restrict our Jud Lester to scheduled sessions only. You know how much he likes it in there. We've tried changing the access codes, but he always cracks them. It's his playground. Probably been there all night.'

They both knew that the CRYPT's SPA rooms held an intoxicating allure for Jud Lester. The Simulated Paranormal Activity rooms were filled with the very latest technology, allowing agents to conjure up 'real-life' hauntings in which they could test their extrasensory perception (and their courage). But access to the SPA rooms was strictly limited to official training sessions only, arranged by Professor Bonati or Dr Vorzek.

However, they both knew it was as difficult to keep Jud out of there as it is to prevent a rat from entering a chicken coop. He always found a way in.

'OK, thank you, sir. I'll go and look.'

'Wait,' said Bonati, rising from his desk. 'I'll come with you. If he *has* been down there all night then it's high time I had a word with him. That boy needs sleep like everyone else does. He's not as superhuman as he thinks, you know. Besides, those damn SPA simulations are a drain on resources. If he thinks it's a playground, it's a bloody expensive one.' He made for the door and shut it quickly behind them. 'Let's go and surprise him, shall we? Then I want to catch some of Vorzek's seminar too.'

They moved swiftly to the lifts and descended to Sector Three. Bex was relieved to have convinced at least one person to join her on her hunt.

SPA-1 was unoccupied. The doors slid open and the place was empty. SPA-2 was in use – they could see from the small screen to the left of the door that a training session was already underway. The agents' names and the start and expected finish time were shown on the LED screen. It was possible that Jud had faked their names, but the professor remembered he had scheduled those agents to be in there, so there was no need to check.

They moved on to SPA-3. The small screen read, 'Occupied – routine operational maintenance.'

'Jud!' they said, almost in unison.

Bonati keyed in the pass code and the first electric door slid smoothly to the left before sweeping shut behind them again, enclosing them in the small space between doors. That was always when your adrenalin started to run. Agents rarely knew what was to be found on the other side of those internal doors. The technology inside the SPA rooms allowed for all manner of scenes to be conjured up. It was like walking inside an Xbox game, quite literally. With hi-tech projectors everywhere, booming sound systems, holographic images and sudden temperature drops, you never knew what to expect.

Two seconds later, the internal doors slid open and they were inside.

'What the—' said Bonati, stopping in his tracks.

Bex stared in silent shock.

It was like opening a door and finding a fifty-foot drop on the other side. Jud was at the opposite end of the room and between them there seemed to lie a great abyss – like the giant mouth of a stone well.

The room was dimly lit, save for sporadic lightning flashes that illuminated the space, each one followed by deafening thunder rolls, resembling cannon fire. But they could see Jud through the gloom – and the strange platform he appeared to be standing on. He was at their level – he must have been – but it looked for all the world like he'd climbed to the top of some vast tower or stone keep – and was now standing perilously close to the edge.

His face looked horror struck. As the lightning flashed again, they could see the whites of his eyes and the red rings around them, giving the distinct impression that he'd been crying.

No, thought Bex. Jud – crying? It wasn't possible; there was some other explanation.

His legs and feet were hidden from view – obscured by what looked like crenulations, resembling the stone battlements you see at the top of a castle.

And just what was he looking at?

They followed his line of sight and gazed downwards, through the gloom.

'Look, Professor!' shouted Bex. 'Over there.'

They peered at the floor – it had the impression it was many metres below them. There was definitely something visible at the bottom.

Was it the outline of a body? It was possible.

Ignoring the simulated drop, Bonati marched right across the floor, a furious expression on his face. He made for the computer panels in the corner of the room. Within seconds he'd keyed in the pass code, pressed 'ABORT' and the entire holographic scene had begun to fade. The dimensions of the room slowly returned – the white walls, the tiled floor.

As the lights rose, Bex could see Jud was slumped on the floor, his back resting against the far wall. He didn't even look up.

'Hey, Jud?' said Bex.

'Out!' the professor shouted.

Bex didn't move. He was shouting at Jud, surely.

'I said *out*, Rebecca. Now!'

'What, me? Why? But sir, I—'

'That's an order! Leave us!'

She frowned in disbelief, shrugged and then turned towards the exit. She pressed the silver button and the internal door slid to one side. She stepped into the foyer but was able to steal a quick glance behind her just before the door swung shut again. She saw Bonati grab a defeated-looking Jud, haul him to his feet, push him against the wall and begin jabbing his finger angrily into his chest.

She'd never seen him that angry before.

CHAPTER 3

TUESDAY, 9.11 A.M.

CLIFF TOP, DUNWICH

Jürgen Møller walked to the bench at the furthest end of the cliff-top path and sat down. He lit up a cigarette, closed his eyes and felt the bracing wind against his face.

His shock of closely cropped, blond hair stood proud against the breeze. Though it was freezing, he didn't feel especially cold in his thin shirt and jeans. He was used to conditions far worse than this. This was nothing. If anything, it made him feel more at home.

He fished around inside his bag for the binoculars, then turned to face the sea and lifted them up to his eyes. A thin trail of smoke rose from the cigarette in his right hand, like a miniature chimney, swirling skywards before dispersing when the next gust took hold.

A few seconds of focusing and Møller had the little boat in his sights. It was making for the coastline. Perfect timing, he thought.

He watched it head inland; he was unable to make out the identity of the man at the helm from this distance, but then he didn't need to. He'd studied the boat for some time and knew exactly who was on it.

His hands were chapped and blistered from the cold air but

his skin was so leathery he felt no pain. His pale face wore a thin beard of blond stubble and his teeth were stained yellow with nicotine.

He took a last, long drag of the cigarette and hurled it to the floor before returning to the binoculars again. The little boat had nearly reached the jetty now.

A few more minutes and it was moored. Møller watched the man leap from its deck and fasten the boat to the pontoon with red ropes.

The man disappeared inside again but returned a moment later with a small knapsack slung over his shoulder. He checked the moorings were secure and then headed along the jetty towards the beach.

Møller placed the binoculars back in his bag and took out his mobile phone. He dialled a number and waited.

'Lars?'

'Yes, Jürgen.'

'It's here. Get going.'

'On my way.'

Møller glanced at his watch. 'I'll be at the rendezvous at eleven o'clock. OK? Don't be late.'

He ended the call before Lars even had a chance to reply and then placed the phone into his bag, sat back against the damp bench and lit up another cigarette. The cold wind rattled through his shirt but failed to bring a chill to his steely bones. There wasn't a goose bump on his body.

CHAPTER 4

TUESDAY, 9.55 A.M.

DUNWICH BEACH, SUFFOLK

A pungent, salty smell of bacon filled the deserted café. Outside, the mist had subsided, giving way to a blanket of grey cloud. The windows in the restaurant rattled as the pitter-patter of silver globules grew stronger. Soon, rain was pelting against the steamy glass and Dan felt a shiver run through him. He held the warm mug as though it were a precious chalice and lowered his head over it, allowing the revitalising aroma of coffee to fill his nostrils.

'Bacon and egg sandwich, sir?' the young chef shouted, putting the plate of food on the counter.

Dan rose slowly and made his way across the room, which was furnished with plastic red chairs and small, metal tables, each one laid with cheap knives and forks, tarnished salt and pepper pots and plastic ketchup dispensers in the shape of giant tomatoes. His legs felt stiff from the cold that had been seeping into him since his early-morning dive. His mop of tousled blond hair was still matted from the driving rain but it framed his weather-beaten face well. He had freckles across his nose and piercing blue eyes. It rarely surprised people to learn that, when he wasn't diving, Dan was a keen surfer – he had that kind of look: sun-bleached and adventurous. But he preferred warmer conditions than the frozen chill of the North Sea that morning.

'Thanks, mate,' he said. 'Just what I need.'

He returned to his table, nodding to the only other customer in the place, a thin, middle-aged man with a worn, stubbly face, seated by a window in the far corner, bent over a steaming cup of hot tea. The man nodded politely back in Dan's direction but showed no interest in starting a conversation.

Licking his lips as he sat down, Dan lifted one slice of bread, picked up the red tomato, and squeezed hard. A giant dollop of ketchup plopped on to the runny egg and bacon. He closed the sandwich again and patted the bread down hard. Ketchup oozed slowly out of the sides of the sandwich, like blood from a wound, mixing with the yellow yoke and forming an orange goo on the plate.

It tasted good and Dan polished it off in just a few gluttonous bites; indigestion would soon come calling but he didn't care. He was ravenous and could have eaten another three of these little babies.

As the last morsel of bread dislodged itself from his throat under a torrent of warm coffee, Dan glanced down at the package on the plastic chair next to him. He felt that surge of excitement again – the same feeling he'd experienced down on the murky seabed.

He picked it up and slowly unwrapped it, as a child unwraps a longed-for present on Christmas morning.

There were three different items inside, each one intriguing for its own reasons.

The first was a coin – not easily identifiable as such, encrusted as it was with all manner of minerals and salts dredged up from the sand, but undeniably some kind of money. He picked it up and scratched the less worn side gently with his fingernail. He could see three words written on three separate lines, right across the middle of the coin: DOR – ESTΛT – FIT. It meant nothing to him. He flipped it over. The reverse side was more decayed – presumably this side had been exposed, rather than buried and better preserved in the sea bottom. There was some kind of cross in the centre of the coin with perhaps more lettering around its edge, but the letters were worn and encrusted with debris so they were impossible to read. He twirled the coin between his fingertips, puzzled by its origin. Suddenly he caught sight of the young chef gazing in his direction, and quickly placed it back inside the tissue.

He waited for the young man to busy himself in the kitchen again and then removed the second item from the crumpled tissue. It didn't look much – just a piece of broken stone – but it was just as intriguing to Dan. Granite, perhaps? Small enough to fit in his palm, there was a jagged edge on one side, suggesting it had once formed part of a larger piece and, judging by its thickness, quite a large piece too.

But it wasn't so much its shape or texture that had excited Dan during his dive. It was the fact that there were letters – or symbols of some kind – running across it from left to right. They ended abruptly at the point where the stone had fractured. He'd not been able to make out any identifiable wording, but the letters or shapes were definitely there – etched into the stone with some kind of sharp knife or engraving tool, perhaps? He gazed at it, tracing the weird shapes with his finger. What language was this?

And below the markings there was some kind of drawing visible – faint and barely traceable, but something was carved into the stone. The front part of a horse, perhaps? he thought. It seemed like there were too many legs for that – he could count four just at the front of the animal, suggesting it might have had as many as eight in total – but it certainly looked like the head of a horse. If this was part of a gravestone, it was unlike any he'd seen before.

'Finished, 'ave you, my darling?' said a middle-aged woman, as she approached Dan from behind and made straight for his plate. The congealed egg and ketchup had now set in a strange whirling pattern.

'Oh, er . . . yes, thank you,' he muttered, moving quickly to try and cover up his find. The other items were safely beneath the tissue.

'First time in Dunwich?'

He nodded.

'Whatcha got there then, my lovely?' The lady had been waiting for an excuse to talk to this welcome stranger. She'd noticed him the day before, when he'd come in. Although she was old enough to be his mother, she knew a good-looking lad when she saw one and couldn't resist gazing at that handsome, weather-beaten face.

'What? Oh, nothing,' said Dan, dismissively. 'Just a few bits of rubbish, you know. I found them on the dive this morning. It's nothing really.'

'Oh, so you're a diver, are you? Well I never! You've come to the right place, my darlin'.'

'Yeah, it's a decent spot. I've dived in Suffolk before, years ago, but further up, near Southwold.'

'Oh, no, you want Dunwich, my lovely. This is the best place anywhere. So you been out, 'ave you? You're a brave one, so you are! It looked 'orrible out there this mornin'. You must be freezin'. All wet. You got some dry clothes, 'ave you, my love? You need warmin' up, so you do!'

'No, I'm fine. Really. But thank you.'

She looked inquisitively at his hand, now covering something.

'Piece of gravestone, is it, eh?' she said, uninspired. She had eyes like a hawk and had already clocked it, well before he'd covered it up.

'Oh, erm, yes. Well, it may be.'

'There's lots of graves beneath the ocean out there, my love – from all the churches and graveyards that slipped into the sea over the years. But I don't need to tell you that, eh? I s'pose you knows all about the history round 'ere.'

Dan nodded, as he placed the packages back into his rucksack on the chair. The third and most intriguing find of all would have to wait for now. Too risky to take it out here.

'Yes, it's sad, isn't it? All those bodies claimed by the sea. And their gravestones too. It's a gloomy place.'

'Not always,' said the woman. 'But listen to you! Oh, you are a sad soul. Good lookin' lad like you shouldn't be worryin' about sad things like dead people an' all. Life's too short, eh, my dear? You need to enjoy yourself! Got a girlfriend, 'ave you?'

Dan raised an eyebrow. Strange question for a middle-aged woman like her to be asking, he thought. *And no, I'm not enjoying myself with you, if that's what you're thinking*, he wanted to say out loud – but he was too polite, and the bacon and egg sandwich had been so good. This woman was getting flirty, but it was comical really. The young man in the kitchen had now made himself scarce – probably embarrassed, thought Dan.

She bent over and began wiping the table in front of him with a vigorous action that shook the salt and pepper pots in their little metal tray and made the plastic tomato wobble. 'Best left be, those bodies, that's what I say. They don't need disturbin' down there. Listen, can I top you up, love?'

'What?'

'Your coffee. Do you want a top up?'

'Oh, er . . . no, thanks. I'm great.'

'Oh, that you are!'

'What? Oh, erm . . . can I just have the bill, if you don't mind?' asked Dan, quickly. She was getting annoying now.

'OK,' she replied sulkily, and trudged off towards the kitchen, her open-toed sandals flip-flopping on the linoleum floor, newly mopped that morning.

Dan stared out of the steamy window and wiped a small area clear with his fingertips. The rain was still thrashing down on to the gravel car park, which looked desolate with only a couple of cars huddled close to the café and a Land Rover in the far corner, near the dunes, beyond which he could just make out the grey waves rising and falling.

This was a desolate place and no mistake. Yet the café looked large enough to seat a great number of visitors. Given the size of the fat fryers and saucepans and the number of little metal tea pots and jugs stacked up by the cash till, Dan assumed they received vast numbers of tourists in the summer months.

But this was mid-January and a very different place in winter. He'd been surprised to find the café open at all, in fact. He gazed around the walls, bedecked with cheap tea towels for sale and nautical pictures in pine frames. There were flags and buckets and spades and the usual plastic flowers on sticks that you hold up against the wind and watch their petals whirl around like spokes on a watermill.

Dan's hostess lived above the shop all year round – 'So why should I close?' she often said to her friends. She was the owner of the establishment, and mother to the young man in the kitchen who called himself chef. Life was better all round when they both found distraction in the café; the flat seemed too small now her son had grown up.

She soon returned with a small strip of till roll on a plastic plate and another renewed smile for Dan. He quickly paid in cash.

As he stood up, a flash of lightning penetrated into the room and caused the lights to buzz and flicker briefly, followed by the inevitable rumble of thunder outside.

'Goin' to be another wild one,' the woman warned, as Dan opened the door and let a gust of wind inside. 'Mind 'ow you go, young man. Oh, keep that door shut, won't you!'

He smiled politely and left the building, nodding again to the customer in the corner who was still sipping his tea. Pulling the collar of his raincoat up to his neck, Dan walked back down the long path towards the dunes and the jetty beyond, to which his little boat was still desperately clinging.

CHAPTER 5

TUESDAY, 10.39 A.M.

DUNWICH BEACH, SUFFOLK

'He's a brave one, eh?' the woman shouted over to her first customer of the day.

'I'm sorry?' he said from across the room.

'The young man who just left. I say, he's a brave one to be diving in these conditions, don't you think?'

'Oh, yes. Quite. Still, we all have our hobbies, I suppose.' The man returned to his teacup, uninterested, and quickly drained it.

The wind rose again to a tempestuous level, shaking the windows and clanking the metal roofs of the little winch sheds up on the beach.

The weather was anything but the sort you'd want for a holiday.

But this customer didn't care.

It felt good just to be away from the city for a short while. His doctor, and the few people he counted as friends, had all joined forces and told him to get away for a rest. They'd said he looked like he needed it.

But then DCI Khan had never looked especially healthy. He survived, rather than thrived, in life. He lived for work, and worked in order to live, but even then only frugally. He had no extravagant tastes, no hobbies to speak of and no great social calendar. He liked it that way.

He had sat late one evening, in his usual chair, with the usual glass of whisky in his hand and a road atlas on his lap, and stared blankly at the UK, wondering where on earth he was supposed to escape to in cold, wintery January? What did his friends suppose he should do for this so called 'rest'?

He'd resolved that nowhere could guarantee sunshine, or even just dry, cloudy conditions, so he'd decided to go for a different tactic altogether. Where did he remember holidaying as a child? Where did he last feel relaxed, regardless of the weather? Where would herald the most memories he could escape into again and bring the place to life, if only for a short while?

And then the idea came. The Suffolk coast: big skies, deserted beaches, crumbling cliffs, acres of heathland. It's where his parents took him every Easter – though no one really knew how or why such a tradition had grown. Maybe it was just because it was uncomplicated – it made no demands on you. He recalled a desolate wilderness that seemed so appealing now, away from the hubbub of London.

And somehow the strong winds helped to blow the clutter and cobwebs away, for now. Let the Suffolk sky chuck everything it has at him, he thought, nothing could be as bad as delving into murder investigations in smog-filled London. And the sky was obliging. It was tempestuous out there right now – the wind was rattling around the thin windowpanes of the small café like a wild animal, intent on entering. Hailstones beat a regular rhythm on the roof and it was rapidly descending into the kind of weather that made you grip your mug of tea extra close to drive out the shivers.

He gazed at the rain-soaked, steamy window and rubbed a small circle in the centre of it with the palm of his hand.

Outside, the car park was deserted, save for a sturdy-looking Land Rover Defender seemingly abandoned at the far end, nearest the sand dunes, whose long grass was being battered around like hair in the wind.

He let his eyes glaze, the way they do when you lose focus for a while and just think about nothing in particular.

But after a few seconds of gawping something attracted his attention and brought him out of his gaze.

There was a man walking over the dunes towards the car park, his head bent low against the wind and rain, with his collar pulled up to his neck. But Khan could see it wasn't the same man who'd just left the café. He was long gone.

He soon realised it was just the owner of the Land Rover – out for a walk, perhaps. But no dog, which seemed odd. And in weather like this?

You can take a break from policing, but you can't stop being a policeman, he thought to himself. He just couldn't stop noticing odd situations when they arose. Why was this man here at this time, in this storm, if not for the obligatory exercising of a dog?

But then here was Khan too, out on his own, enjoying the remoteness of it all. And with no dog. So, was that odd? Why shouldn't others do the same?

He watched the man walk closer to his car, his coat flapping in the wind. He heard a very faint beep and the car's warning lights flashed simultaneously.

Then Khan watched as, without warning, the figure fell to the ground – a sharp, sudden fall that looked painful, even from this distance, his head meeting brutal stones and squelchy mud.

Had he tripped over? Surely it was too brutal a fall for that? Too forced.

The man remained on the gravel, lying awkwardly. He wasn't moving. There was a sinking feeling growing inside Khan's stomach.

He leaned closer to the window, his breath steaming the glass again and causing him to wipe it away with his hand once more.

As the steam vanished, he saw the man still hadn't got to his feet. But he was moving now. In fact, he was writhing around on the stones.

Was this an epileptic fit? Khan thought.

He stood up abruptly and ran towards the café door.

'Call for an ambulance!' he shouted as he went past the open kitchen where the owner and her son were chatting.

'You what?' a shout came back.

'An ambulance. Quick. There's a man in difficulty outside. Just do it.'

Khan opened the door and ran down the steps.

He stopped and stared across the car park.

'What the hell—'

He could hardly believe what he was seeing. There, at the other side of the car park, the man had now ceased writhing around. His body had fallen limp. But it looked for all the world like he was being dragged – literally – away from his car, towards the sand dunes.

He wasn't propelling himself along the ground. His legs and boots lay still and his arms were limp. But his shoulders seemed hunched together and his coat was gathered around his neck.

Someone was dragging this man over the stony ground.

But what startled Khan most, and caused an ache to throb in his stomach and a prickly shiver to shoot up his spine, was that he could see no one else there.

No one at all.

But the body of the man was still shifting, no mistake. It had moved a few feet now, and continued to slide along the ground.

The café door behind him opened. 'I've called for an ambulance. So what's happened, then?' said the café owner. 'And who *are* you, anyway?'

Khan spun round and faced her. 'Back inside, quick.'

'What? Why? Eh, don't you push me, love. This is my place.'

'Just get back inside, will you – please? Look, it's OK. I'm a police officer. You must do what I say, *please*. Go and wait inside. You don't need to come out. I'll explain everything later. Now *go!*'

Fortunately for Khan, she closed the door again. The last thing he needed was for her to see the sight he'd just witnessed. He knew only too well how quickly fear could spread among the public. There'd be crowds here watching this, if he wasn't careful.

He turned around. The body was just disappearing over the sand dunes at the far end of the car park. He took off after it.

The stony ground was uneven. Puddles lay strewn across the entire space, hiding the giant potholes that lurked beneath some of them, like mantraps. You never knew which one was going to be firm or which one hid a crater in the ground.

Within seconds, Khan's left ankle sank unexpectedly and gave way. He toppled over and grimaced with pain.

'Shit!'

He tried desperately to stagger to his feet but a sharp, stabbing pain deep inside his left ankle caused him to hit the deck again. It was agony. He couldn't even support his own body weight. He looked up in the direction of the dunes. Now the figure had disappeared altogether – dragged out of sight, it seemed.

'Oh, great,' he said sardonically, slapping his leg and rubbing his ankle in frustration. 'Some holiday.'

CHAPTER 6

TUESDAY, 10.49 A.M.

DUNWICH BEACH, SUFFOLK

Dan stood, surrounded by mess: a table overturned, windows smashed, books and charts ripped up, screwed up and strewn across the linoleum floor, glasses and crockery in pieces and the sofa bed slashed.

It looked unpleasant – a violation even – but it hadn't angered Dan half as much as what he'd found up at the helm. His diving suit was slashed; totally wrecked. He couldn't believe it. His aqualungs were gone (thrown over the side, he presumed) and his entire collection of highly expensive search equipment had been smashed to pieces – the side scan sonar, the magnetometer, the video camera and the very latest metal detector he'd had for Christmas. All useless.

'Why?' he shouted to no one in particular. 'Why me?'

His heart was racing as he ran up on to the deck and scanned the area like a hawk. He saw no one, heard nothing, save for the cries from the gulls high overhead and the crash of the waves breaking on the pebble beach. Suddenly this place seemed remote. He was exposed. A chill ran up his spine as he contemplated the thought that the perpetrator was still right here, on his boat, hiding somewhere. He didn't move for a second or two;

just stood there, taking deep breaths and letting the anger seep through him. He gathered himself together and reminded himself this was *his* boat – no one else's. If someone had invaded his space, he'd bloody well find him and throw him overboard – whoever he was. He could take him on.

He ran back down to the cabin and flung open every cupboard door, even to the spaces no one could possibly fit into. The place was empty – the burglar was long gone.

He went to grab the boat's radio system to call for help but soon slammed the hand piece down – destroyed along with everything else. He fished inside his pocket for his mobile phone. Useless – no signal in this God forsaken place.

He wanted to shout and scream and punch something hard – preferably the person who did this – but there was nothing on which he could take his temper out. The place was already smashed up.

He resolved to run back to the café and ask to use their phone to call the police. It was his only option.

Stumbling over the mess on the floor, he returned to the little flight of wooden steps, grabbed his knapsack, vaulted the staircase and ran on to the deck. He jumped off and began running along the pontoon to the shore. The pebbles crunched under his boots as he set out towards the café once again. The biting winds blew right into his face, through his blond hair, and caused his ears to sting with the cold as he kept running.

The beach was anything but a flat sandy stretch and was tedious to run over. His boots sank into the undulating mounds of stones that rose and dipped like dunes. As he approached the tufts of real sand dunes that provided a breakwater for the car park and café up ahead, he stopped in his tracks.

What the hell was that on the floor?

Was it a body? Or a collection of bags?

He could see something was spread out over the pebbles about fifty yards up ahead. It looked more like a long trail of fishing nets than a single mass. And it looked like something – or someone – was caught inside them. He thought he could see flesh. Was this some kind of fisherman's catch that had been abandoned on the beach? Why would anyone leave it here like that?

He began walking slowly towards it, a sinking feeling in the pit of his stomach. This didn't look right.

As Dan kept walking and approached the mess on the ground, it dawned on him what he had been gazing on all along.

He couldn't help but scream – an agonising kind of cry, like he himself was in pain. He was a tough guy: never cried, never complained, despite all the physical stresses and strains diving and surfing often brought; he was a rock. But this – this was different. The sight had shocked him to his core, assaulted his senses. The pain in his stomach swelled; he stooped to cough and then promptly wretched. The regurgitated egg and bacon sandwich slopped on to the pebbles and ran into the cracks between them, as more gunk poured out of his dribbling mouth. Long globules of vomit and spit swung from his lip like pendulums. He wiped his face with a sleeve.

'Oh, Jesus!' he cried. 'What the hell . . . ?'

He was staring at the mutilated body of a man, lying face down in the stones, his limbs twisted and contorted. His shirt had been ripped from his body and there was a gaping wound in the middle of his back, from which blood was still pouring – so much blood. The pebbles around him were solid red, like someone had dropped a giant tin of dark red paint. It looked so incongruous – a sharp, disturbing contrast to the pale, sandy-coloured stones.

Dan could see through to the man's spine – right through the fleshy walls of skin to the white bones. His ribs had been split open. Actually forced open, like railings attacked with a crowbar. And there, fanning across the man's open back like wings on a bird, were his lungs. Soft, pulpy sacks, with long sinews and veins attached, like two pieces of raw liver stretched across hard bone.

Dan wretched again. He'd never seen a dead body, let alone one that had been so savagely cut.

The stretch of beach where he was standing was awash with blood, and it continued to ooze from the man's gaping wound.

Dan felt faint. He turned away from the corpse and tried to gulp in large breaths of sea air. Blood was draining from his face and the whole beach now began to spin. He lost his balance and was about to keel over when he felt a firm grip on his arm.

'It's OK; I've got you.'

He'd spent so much time stooped over, vomiting or stealing surreptitious glances at the ugly corpse, that he'd failed to notice the man hobbling over the dunes towards him.

He told him to sit down and place his head between his knees.

The inspector turned back to steal his own glance at the body, wincing at the pain still throbbing in his ankle. There was no doubt this was the same man he'd seen through the window of the café. Same trousers. Same hair. The same man he'd foolishly thought was having an epileptic fit.

So many questions whizzed through Khan's head. How the hell did he get here? Who on earth could have done this? And why?

He'd seen many bodies in his career – some brutally dispatched – but rarely had he seen something so mutilated. This was macabre. And so quickly, too. How could anyone – anything – have done this in such a short time? He knew he'd stumbled in the car park and had not even been able to walk for the first few minutes, but he'd got up eventually and limped right over. So how could this have happened? There must have been a gang of them. But where were they now? He scanned the beach area, just as Dan had done on the boat, and saw no one. Not even in the distance. Foolishly, he looked out to sea – as if someone could have come from there! – and still saw no one.

It couldn't have been the terrified man sitting on the ground beside him who'd done it. There was no blood on his hands and, besides, Khan knew the scream must have come from him, not the victim. The man had not looked capable of screaming in the car park once his body had gone limp and the mysterious dragging had started. No, the scream was from this guy, who was now whimpering like a kid.

'You've just found him, yes?' he asked.

Dan nodded solemnly, his eyes still fixed firmly on the ground, trying desperately to resist the temptation to take another morbid peek at the dead flesh. He couldn't stop the tears now. It was an assault on his senses and not even he could hold the emotion back.

'See anyone nearby?'

He shook his head and sniffed hard.

'Hear anything?'

'No.'

Khan placed a hand on his shoulder. 'Look, I'm a police officer – Detective Chief Inspector Khan. I need to ask you these questions. And you are?'

'Dan Summers.'

'So what brings you here, Mr Summers? You were in the café just now, weren't you?'

Dan looked up, still keeping his gaze above the mess on the ground. 'Yes. My boat is moored down on the jetty – you can see it over there. I've been diving off the coast here for a few days.'

'OK. But you saw no one who could have done this?'

'No. Honest to God. Nobody. There was no one around . . . just me.' He realised what he was saying and his voice choked with emotion again. 'Oh, Christ. Hang on; that doesn't mean that—'

'Calm yourself,' said Khan. 'I saw this man collapse in the car park. You weren't there. Quite how he got here, of course, who knows? But I don't believe you could have done this to him in the time it took me to get from the car park to here.' He saw Dan's face ease slightly. 'But don't leave Dunwich just yet, Mr Summers. I'll have many more questions for you in time.'

'Look, there's something else, Inspector,' said Dan, nervously. 'I returned from the café to my boat just now and found it's been, well . . . messed up. Everything's wrecked. My diving equipment, the sonar, the radio system – everything. You can come and see it.'

'You mean someone's been in and ransacked it?'

Summers nodded.

'And this is the man who did it, huh?' There was something in Khan's tone that sounded ominously suspicious.

'What? Erm . . . I dunno. Could be. Wait a minute.' There was panic in Dan's voice and Khan detected it. 'I didn't come after him. I've already said I didn't do this. Even if it *was* him who wrecked my boat, I wouldn't do this. I mean I couldn't—'

'And was it?'

'What?' Dan was getting confused.

'You said, "even if it was him," just then. So, was it?'

'No! I mean, I dunno. But I didn't kill him! Oh my God. I'm tellin' you, I never—'

'Calm down, sir,' said Khan. 'It's true that two crimes in a short space of time in a deserted place like this are likely to be connected – your burglary and this killing. But I haven't accused you of some kind of revenge. Keep calm. We need a clear head here.'

'Keep calm?' said Dan, incredulously.

Khan spoke sternly: 'Yes!'

Dan nodded obediently.

'So you *do* think this might be the same man who broke into your boat? I mean, if there was no one else around?'

'Yes, it could be. But the dunes can hide anyone, you know. There could have been others around here – they've just disappeared.'

'Would have to have done that bloody quickly, I'd say,' said Khan.

'But I didn't do it!'

'Please, that's enough, sir.' Khan glanced around again, up at the dunes on the fringe of the pebble beach and the roof of the café beyond. Then he looked down at the mutilated body on the ground between them. He was trying desperately to keep up with the pace of things here.

'Do you have some kind of tarpaulin or plastic sheeting on your boat, Mr Summers?'

'Why?' Dan snapped, guiltily. 'What am I supposed to have done now?'

'I need something to cover the body.'

'Er . . . yes, OK, I can probably find something.'

'Good. Now go and fetch it, please. As quickly as you can. I'll be watching you – you're safe now. Whoever did this won't have hung around, I can assure you of that. They'll be long gone by now. And I can see the boat from here, anyway. I'll be watching.'

Dan nodded and rose to his feet, not sure whether Khan had meant he would be watching to protect him or to make sure he didn't flee from the scene. Either way, he was relieved to get going. The soles of his deck shoes were now soaked in red, and blood was creeping up the sides too. He welcomed the chance to get some distance between him and the body.

'Thank you. Bring it back as soon as you can. I'll make sure it's replaced with a new one, of course. You won't want it back again afterwards, believe me.'

Dan sloped off towards his boat.

'Quickly, please, sir!' shouted Khan. 'We don't want anyone else to see this, do we?'

Dan nodded and broke into a gentle run. He still felt queasy from the shock.

So the man in the café was a detective chief inspector? Why was he here, in Dunwich? Seemed weird that he just appeared like that, Dan thought.

And who the hell wrecked his boat? he wondered. If it was the man now lying dead on the beach then that meant he was a suspect for a revenge killing, for sure. The inspector had told him not to leave Dunwich, after all.

He glanced over his shoulder. DCI Khan was still watching him, his body fixed perpendicular to the vast expanse of flat beach, and his gaze set in his direction. Dan suddenly became aware he was staring back at him, which looked even more suspicious. He quickly turned round and headed towards the boat.

Khan watched him go and then fished out his mobile phone and checked the reception. One bar only – one bloody bar! What was it with these damn phones? Why did they never work properly?

He hoped it would be enough. He couldn't leave the body and return to the café. He had to stay rooted to the spot. Hopefully the ambulance would be here soon. He'd look out for the blue flashing lights from the car park and call over to them, if Summers wasn't back by then. He'd need the police too.

But he had to make a different call first.

He typed in the number – he knew it by heart.

A hundred miles away, in central London, buried deep in the subterranean headquarters of the CRYPT, Bonati's phone began ringing.

CHAPTER 7

TUESDAY, 11.12 A.M.

GREYFRIARS ABBEY, DUNWICH

Mist was drifting over the rain-soaked hill upon which the old ruins of the abbey stood proudly. Centuries of wind and rain had taken their toll. Now all that remained were the remnants of a monastic refectory – its two-storey wall resisting the elements – and a few foundations scattered around the place, giving the impression of a giant campus, long gone. Set into the remaining solitary wall were several arched windows, now empty, and above one of these was the shocking face of a gargoyle, staring wide-eyed out to sea. Its nose and mouth were barely traceable now, but its eyeballs were still intact and the startled expression across its ugly face had not changed for eight hundred years.

The gargoyle had unsettled Jürgen Møller, so he'd trudged over the muddy field to wait on the opposite side, out of the stone monster's view.

Where the hell was Lars?

He knew he'd done the job – Møller had stayed on the cliff top, watching the boat. He'd seen Summers leave his boat and had then watched Lars running along the pontoon to board it. A few minutes later, he had reappeared on deck and fled from the jetty, at which point Møller had packed up his binoculars and headed straight for the abbey. Job done.

So why had Lars not shown? Had something happened? Car trouble, perhaps? But the team had provided a new Land Rover for him to do the job – he'd picked it up at the airport on arrival. Perhaps the damn fool had got lost on his way to the abbey grounds? But how was that possible? It was only a short drive away!

There was the roar of a car engine in the distance, hurtling at a fast pace by the sounds of it. At last! he thought.

He walked briskly towards the perimeter stone wall and the gateway that led on to the small road. The engine was approaching but then he heard the sudden sound of a siren accompanying it. Police?

Had someone seen Lars leave the boat? He'd better not have squealed! He would have his revenge, if Lars had implicated him in any way.

As the noise of the engine rose, Møller ducked behind a section of overgrown wall and waited for the vehicle to pass. A row of nettles clawed at his face and he felt a sharp stinging sensation on his cheek as he crouched to keep out of sight. The long grass here was soaked and an unwelcome dampness was rising up his trouser legs from his sodden boots.

It was an ambulance that eventually hurtled past. He saw the white roof and the yellow and green squares as the vehicle headed straight down the hill towards Dunwich.

So where the hell was Lars? Møller had a strange feeling that something had gone wrong. He rose up and approached the gateway that led out on to the road. The rickety gate swung shut after him and the wind took up once again, blowing around the empty shell of the abbey behind him as its resident warden, the stone gargoyle, continued to stare ominously out to sea.

CHAPTER 8

TUESDAY, 11.29 A.M.

CRYPT, LONDON

Bonati was pacing the floor of his office. He looked anxious.

A brief knock on the door and Bex entered. She could see Bonati was agitated. She could always tell: he wouldn't sit still, wouldn't sit down at all whenever he was nervous. And she could see he was clenching his fists, which was unlike him. She couldn't see his eyes – the light from the fluorescent spots above reflected brightly off his rimless glasses, but there was a tell-tale frown that ran across his lined forehead. Jud was averting his gaze, preferring to bend and sculpt a paper clip out of all recognition, which he'd taken from the professor's desk. She could see his knuckles were white with tension as he twisted the thin metal arms around his fingers.

What the hell has happened here? she thought. And why was no one talking about the SPA session?

Bex assumed Bonati was still angry with Jud, though she'd still not been able to find out why. The scene in SPA-3 had been significant, anyone could see that, but neither of them wanted to discuss the matter, despite her repeated attempts to find out more. Jud had sloped off to his room and was not accepting calls.

Bonati remained tight-lipped and had just said, 'I'm dealing with it, Rebecca. Let it go.'

And now here the three of them were again, an awkward silence lingering in the room like a curse.

Bonati had asked them both to report to his office. Bex had naturally assumed it was to discuss the earlier incident in SPA-3, but she could tell already that was wrong.

'Thank you for coming so quickly, Bex,' said the professor after what seemed like an age. 'Please, sit down.'

She took the other vacant chair adjacent to his desk, pulling it slightly further away from Jud, who still hadn't looked up yet.

'There is a reason I've called you both here,' he began. 'I've had a call about an incident that's just happened.'

'Yeah?' said Jud, looking up slowly. 'Where?' Bex could see there were still stains around his eyes. Had he *really* been crying? What the hell had gone on in that room?

'Suffolk,' said the professor sharply, encouraging Bex to look in his direction instead.

'Oh, yes?' she said, trying to sound a little more eager than her fellow agent and partner. She could see the professor's mood had soured and she was keen to inject some positive energy into the room. Why was it Jud was always so cool and laid back when it came to being given a new mission, when everyone knew that he was just as eager as anyone else, even more so, perhaps? He thrived on keeping busy. Bex often likened him to a Border collie sheepdog – sleek, fit and strong, loyal and highly intelligent, but, without hard work, liable to go crazy and self-destruct. You had to keep Jud busy, that was the key. Without the distraction of a case, he was more prone to self-doubt and a withdrawn disposition than any other agent – and that was saying something, since most of the agents at the CRYPT could be self-critical and over-analytical. They were intelligent and thought too much, you might say, about everything. It kind of went with the job. And when not applying their voracious appetites for investigating and thinking and processing their observations, inevitably these reflective skills turned inwards, towards themselves. And that was bad news, especially for Jud, it seemed.

He could be *so* infuriating. But he was also addictive, and Bex knew she was hooked. She didn't even try to deny it to herself now.

Working on assignments with him was a privilege and one she clung on to defensively. Whenever Bonati or Vorzek suggested a different pairing for a particular case, she fought vociferously to remain with Jud, saying that their skills complemented one another and that they had an 'understanding' which would be wasted if Jud was paired up with someone else. Bonati knew what that special 'understanding' meant, though he couldn't argue with the fact that they made a very good team.

'There's been a killing,' he said in a matter of fact tone. 'A badly mutilated body has been found on the beach at a place called Dunwich. It's right out on the east coast.'

'So?' said Jud despondently. 'Why have we been contacted?'

'Because an eyewitness saw something which he was apparently unable to explain, that's why,' Bonati said calmly, ignoring Jud's sulky tone. 'The witness saw the body move by itself – like it was being . . . somehow dragged. At least, that's what was reported.'

'*Dragged?*' said Bex.

'Yes. Though, by all accounts, there was no one there to be doing the dragging.'

'What do you mean?' Bex screwed her face up in puzzlement.

'Look, I know this sounds strange. But reports that come to us always do, don't they? That's just the point. Sometimes there is no rational explanation available – you know that, Rebecca. After this mysterious dragging – by some invisible force – the body was then found minutes later in a dreadful state of mutilation.'

Jud's face showed no emotion. 'Is this a reliable source, sir? I mean, is the eyewitness a credible one? Suffolk is a long way for us to go, if it's just a hoax call, surely. And it does sound a bit odd, this one.'

The professor was unimpressed with this uncharacteristically cautious approach from Jud; he was always pretty laid back, Bonati knew that, but behind the cool attitude lay an impatience to get on with the job and a tendency to dive in first and ask questions later. Bonati could recall the Tyburn case, when Jud was so quick to get to the haunted railway station at Holborn, he almost got himself run over by a bloody train. Or the case at Westminster, where his impatience to get down into the haunted basements landed him accused of all manner of crimes. He just didn't think sometimes. Too brave, that was his trouble. But this time Bonati detected a resistance to help – and he knew very well what was causing it. He'd caught him red-handed in the SPA room and, when he'd found out just what he'd been recreating in there, the professor had good reason to explode at him the way he did. And, boy, had he shouted. Jud knew he'd overstepped the mark this time, and there would be repercussions. No wonder he was sulking now.

'Oh, I think we can rely on the credibility of the eyewitness, Jud,' Bonati replied, curtly. He stared him down, for the second time that morning.

'How come you're so sure, sir?' Jud was in no mood to be talked to so stiffly, especially in front of Bex.

'Because the eyewitness in question is Detective Chief Inspector Khan, that's why, Lester. So start packing, both of you.' He stood up to signify the meeting was at an end. 'And be at the helipad in Battersea by twelve. That's all for now. You're dismissed.'

CHAPTER 9

TUESDAY, 12.49 P.M.

DUNWICH BEACH, SUFFOLK

The usually deserted pebble beach at Dunwich had become a hive of activity. Khan often thought how surprising – and disturbing – it was to see the effect that the presence of a dead body had on a place. It brought out a macabre curiosity in people – a blood-thirsty legacy left over perhaps from the days when people flocked to watch executions at the gallows. It had taken all his time – and the efforts of the hapless and dazed local coppers who'd joined him – to prevent visitors from leaving the car park and entering this stretch of beach.

News travels fast in rural parts, and bad news even faster. It seemed amazing to Khan how many people had come to walk their dogs on Dunwich beach that day.

This was, of course, good news for the owner of the café. The little metal teapots and milk jugs were being filled constantly.

Khan had roped off the section of the beach from the car park all the way down to the sea's edge, assisted by two dazed-looking paramedics. They had also seen their fair share of accidents and fatalities, but this was something else. When they had come from the ambulance with a stretcher, Khan had said categorically they wouldn't be needing it. 'No one moves the body. Not yet,' he'd said, in a tone which suggested there was no point in arguing. Then, luckily, Summers had returned with the tarpaulin and Khan was able to cover the corpse before anyone else saw it. Not even the policemen who soon pitched up were allowed to view it. Khan was already thinking ahead about what the hell he was going to tell the public – what would his press statement be? – and so the fewer people who saw the body the better. He was pulling rank on these local coppers, and they weren't appreciating it.

And now here they were, waiting for what Khan had described as 'crime scene investigators'. Bonati had advised even Khan not to touch the corpse – not even to roll it over to identify it – until his CRYPT agents had attended.

Bonati had told him it was essential to obtain accurate readings of any possible electromagnetic radiation left as a residue on the body, which might point to paranormal activity. Therefore the body must remain untouched – at least for now.

The car park was lit up with blue flashing lights – which only attracted yet more interest from locals, who continued to trickle into the edge of the car park at the far side, nearest the road. The police were on hand to turn them away as quickly as they'd arrived – although they were at liberty to call into the café if they so wished, which they promptly did, primarily to find out anything they could about what was happening, and to drink tea, of course.

'Why can't we examine the body?' whispered one of the junior officers in the car park. 'I mean, why the secrecy?'

'Dunno,' said another. 'You'd expect forensics to have been all over the body by now. But, no. There was one, but I think she just headed off towards some boat or other, over by the jetty.'

'Yeah, I saw her. What's all that about then?'

'The Sarge said there's been a break-in on the boat, apparently.'

'Oh, right. And did he tell you anything about this body? The one directing the operation, I mean. Who is he to tell us what we can and can't see? It's ridiculous.'

'Sarge says he's a DCI. From London, I think.'

'*London?* What the hell is he doing in Suffolk then, eh?'

His partner just shrugged and kept waving to the oncoming cars, beckoning them to park as far away from the beach side as possible.

'You what, love? Well, there's been an accident, you see,' he said to a passing motorist. 'Nothing for you to worry about. All under control. But we've had to rope off the area until we've cleared the scene, OK? Like I say, nothing for you to worry about. Have a good day now.'

Similar responses were given to other motorists, until the police officers had become tired of saying the same thing over and over again.

Down on the beach, Khan was gazing in the direction of Dan Summers' boat. He'd asked the forensic to make a search of it, without Summers, whom he'd sent to the café directly after he'd returned with the plastic sheeting. He still looked weak and pale after his ordeal – and seemed in need of a good hot mug of tea. Khan knew the café owner would be more than happy to oblige.

If they could link the break-in on Dan Summers' boat to the man on the beach, well, at least that was a start. Khan knew that until the CRYPT agents were here and they'd done their testing – whatever that was – he couldn't even get a proper ID on the victim.

Where were they, anyway? he thought. He knew they were supposed to have set off at twelve. Bonati had reckoned it would only take approximately forty minutes, so Khan expected to see them on the horizon soon.

Sure enough, eventually there was the sound of humming in the distance and the assembled group looked up to see the black HT1 Squirrel approaching from the south.

Up in the sky, Jud gazed down at the murky, grey waters of the North Sea and the long strip of pale stones that lined this edge of Suffolk.

'Hardly St Tropez, is it?' he said to Bex.

'Oh, you *can* talk, then,' she said.

'What?'

'Well, that's almost the only thing you've said all flight. I thought you were asleep.'

'No,' he said, nonchalantly.

'Want to talk about it yet?'

'Talk about what?' he said, still looking out of the window with an expressionless face.

'This morning. In the SPA, I mean.'

Jud turned his head and stared at her. His dark hair hung over his forehead with a flick that almost covered one eye, but she could see there was an intense anger in his gaze. He pushed the small microphone from his headset closer to his lips and said quietly, 'Will you just drop it, Bex? *Please.*'

'But why? Look, it's me, Jud. Tell me what's going on.'

He turned away from her and said nothing.

'You looked shaken. Back in that room – when Bonati and I came in. I've never seen you like that before. I'm worried about you.'

Jud still said nothing.

It was Bex's turn to sound impatient. 'Honestly, one day you're going to have to open up, Jud Lester. Maybe not to me, or to Luc, or the professor, but to somebody. I still know almost *nothing* about you. You never talk about home, or school, or friends outside CRYPT. You never talk about—'

'Stop it!' Jud shouted. 'Just stop! I don't need this. I don't want it from anyone. Especially not from *you.*'

Bex paused. What did he mean by that? 'Especially not from you' – why '*especially*'? Had he just confessed unwittingly that she meant something to him?

The atmosphere in the 'copter had soured and the change had not been lost on the pilot. It wasn't Gary, the usual pilot, with whom Jud had become good friends. It was some other guy – CRYPT occasionally hired in ex-military pilots to assist with urgent missions – and this one was keeping his counsel, not saying anything, trying his hardest to focus on the flying and ignore the conversation over the headset, however interesting it was getting.

'What do you mean?' said Bex, more gently now. She couldn't let it lie, not after he'd said something vaguely complimentary like that. She *had* to know more. 'Why am I so different?'

After a few moments Jud finally spoke up. 'Because you . . . *understand* me.'

Bex attempted to hide the smile that was trying to form at the edges of her mouth. He'd actually said something nice about her. And, given his usual secretive self, it was indeed flattering to hear that she understood him. Even if she didn't. 'Then let me in, J,' she said gently.

Bex breathed nervously. She'd called him 'J'. Was she really entitled to do that? She'd heard Bonati and Goode call him 'J'. She watched him for a reaction.

He'd noticed it too, but when she'd said it, it hadn't felt strange. It felt *right*.

He gazed out at the cloudy skies and the remote waters. They seemed to combine to make one foggy mass – disorientating and lonely. Just like his life. There was no doubt his ordeal in the SPA room had affected him deeply. But to explain it now would take hours. And just where would he begin? He'd kept his past locked up for so long it was like he'd lost the key to the floodgates. How on earth could he reveal any part of it without the whole thing cascading out and drowning them both? Denying his past, keeping the floodgates locked, meant he could pretend it hadn't really happened and he was just a normal teenager. It was the best way – the *only* way – to survive.

'One day,' he said quietly. But he saw Bex's face fall. Was that a tear in the corner of her eye? He hated upsetting her like this – none of his past was her fault, after all. He leaned across and placed his hand on hers. 'Soon.'

He found himself breathing in sharply and sucking up his emotion as he returned to look out of the window again at the cluster of houses that clung to the coastline. He coughed and regained his composure. 'Isn't this the place that sunk into the sea years ago, or something like that?'

Bex nodded, miserably. 'Yeah.'

'What do they call it? Coastal something. Coastal . . .'

'Erosion,' said Bex. 'It's when the sea claims the land for itself. It wears away at the coastline, chipping away at the cliffs until they tumble into the water. You can't stop the tide.'

Jud smiled. 'I know. You always have the answers,' he said. 'I bet you were clever at school.' He felt relieved to get her talking again, and for the focus to have switched from him and his emotions to something neutral.

'I should imagine this village has shrunk to a fraction of its original size,' she continued. 'It's all under water now – crumbled into the sea over time.'

'Thanks, Miss,' said Jud, smiling at her.

'You're welcome,' she quipped and he detected a wry smile leaking out of the corners of her mouth.

As the helicopter descended, they could see the buildings and the car park, and eventually a crowd of people standing around some great plastic sheet on the ground. They both knew what was underneath it. To prevent the wind from whipping it up like a balloon, someone had placed large pebbles around its edge, giving an impression from the air of some kind of macabre ritual. Like a fire circle with a sacrificed body in the centre.

But they could both see the stained stones. Nothing could hide those. Blood had haemorrhaged from the body right down the beach towards the water's edge. And that amount of blood usually meant *serious* mutilation.

'Do we have details of exactly what happened to the man?' said Bex.

'Don't think so. Not yet,' replied Jud. 'I'm assuming Khan will brief us as soon as we land. We'll get to examine it, of course. But I don't expect it to be pleasant.'

'So what was Khan doing here in the first place? Bit of a coincidence.'

'Didn't Bonati say it was a holiday or something?'

'A holiday?' said Bex.

'Yeah. I know. Wrong place at the wrong time, I guess, poor bloke.'

'Hmm. If anyone looks like he needs a vacation, it's Khan.'

A few minutes later the helicopter was slowly reaching the ground about a hundred yards further along the beach from the body, on the opposite side from where the jetty was, and where they could see a small boat was moored. The blades caused the white breakers at the water's edge to toss and turn and spiral like miniature whirlpools. The force of the spinning created shapes in the pebbles too, as they shifted and rolled beneath the giant black insect descending on them.

The rotations slowed and eventually the sharp blades came to a stop. Jud thanked the pilot and unlocked the door. They could feel the cold chill from the easterly wind within seconds.

Khan greeted them both with a half smile, which in the circumstances – and given that they knew the DCI was never one for hearty welcomes – was an unexpected bonus. He seemed genuinely pleased to see some familiar faces in this remote place. It had been a while since he'd seen the agents.

'When was it we last met, huh? The Westminster case?' said Khan.

Bex shook her head. 'You're forgetting the case of the masked figures. You know, that jewellery shop in Hatton Gardens, selling the cursed rings.'

Khan smiled. 'How could I forget that? Mind you, several more murders since then, my dear. It's never quiet in the homicide department.'

Jud was impatient to get on with the case in hand. He disliked small talk, always had. And especially with this weasel. They had forged a better working relationship on recent cases, it was true, but he'd never trusted him ever since the first time they met, on the Tyburn case, when Khan had been on the wrong side of the law, taking handouts from entrepreneurs in return for 'favours'. One such favour had been to try to expose Jud for who he really was, and so get the CRYPT closed down.

Things had changed now. Khan had shown great regret over that and had since redeemed himself, at least in the eyes of Professor Bonati. But Jud was less forgiving.

'So?' he said, abruptly. 'The case, Inspector? Nasty one, yeah?'

Khan nodded his head, his expression had turned grave. 'I'm afraid so, Jud. It's not pretty, this one. And it's so bloody weird how the body got here. I'll tell you all about it while we walk. Come on, let's go. You all right, Bex? Good to see you.'

They set off along the water's edge. Bex noticed Khan was hobbling like an injured war veteran. 'What've you done?' she said.

'Twisted my bloody ankle, 'aven't I? Running across the car park. I tell you, I couldn't move it at first. Getting old, you see.'

He explained how he'd seen the man fall to the ground from the café window, and then how he'd watched in disbelief as his limp body had been dragged across the ground and over the dunes towards the beach.

Jud was more interested now. 'So, you actually saw it move . . . by itself . . . across the ground, yes?'

'Well, no, I mean, it wasn't propelling itself. It was being *pulled*. I could see the man's coat – just around the shoulders – it was . . . well, being tugged.'

'But whoever, or whatever, was pulling him was invisible to you, is that what you're saying?' said Bex.

'Correct.'

'So you saw this body being pulled across the ground by an invisible force? Pity we weren't here to see it, Inspector. We might have seen something else,' said Jud, gazing down the long pebble beach in front of them. 'By the way, Inspector, what are you doing in Suffolk, anyway? Don't tell me you're on holiday!'

Khan nodded solemnly. 'It's freezing cold, I'm in the back end of nowhere, I've twisted me ankle and now I've found a mutilated body. Of course I'm on holiday, Lester.'

Eventually they reached the assembled group of officers and paramedics, who cleared the path for the agents to walk through and view the body on the ground.

'Who the hell are these guys?' one local officer whispered to another.

'God knows,' she replied. 'This DCI feller says they're Crime Scene Investigators.'

'Crime Scene Investigators?' said her colleague. 'I thought that's what we did, investigate crimes!'

She just shrugged and backed away, as Khan suggested they take a break up at the café for a much-needed hot drink. He said he'd keep them informed and no one argued. The wind had whipped up again and was blowing an icy chill into their bones – a cuppa, inside the café, sounded good.

Luckily for the agents, the building was obscured by the large dunes on the fringe of the oversized car park, so no one would be able to watch them from its windows; once the officers and paramedics had left, they'd be alone.

'Got your instruments and stuff?' said Khan, when the others had left the beach.

Jud nodded.

'You won't like this,' Khan said quietly, looking particularly at Bex.

Why did everyone always do that? she thought to herself. Why did they have to assume that, just because she was a girl, she was going to be squeamish?

Khan gently rolled the plastic sheeting off the corpse, peeling it off the flesh where it had become stuck and then gazing expectantly in Bex's direction.

'Christ!' said Jud, and he bent over, looking like he was about to throw up.

Bex stared at it and showed no emotion. 'OK,' she said. 'Interesting, Inspector. I've not seen that done before.'

CHAPTER 10

TUESDAY, 1.05 P.M.

GREYFRIARS WOOD, SUFFOLK

'What do you mean, you've lost Lars?' the voice thundered down the line.

Jürgen Møller shuffled in his car seat. He'd been driving for some time before he'd found a decent place for a mobile signal. What was it with these British people? he'd thought to himself. 'Why can you never get a decent signal in this stupid country?' he'd said, whilst negotiating the narrow bends at the same time as tracking the progress of the signal bars on his phone screen. It was always the same: you get a decent signal for a few seconds but find nowhere to park. Then you find a parking place and there's no signal. Eventually, he'd passed a small car park nestled in the trees of Greyfriars Wood and this time the phone signal hadn't been too bad.

'I don't mean we've lost him as in *lost* him, sir,' he said nervously into the phone.

'Well, what the hell do you mean, huh?' The man on the end of the line sounded impatient now. He had reason to be. 'Look, Møller, if Lars has gone AWOL then you just find another stooge, y'understand? Get some other mug who'll work with you and then carry on, OK? We can't let this stop progress, do you hear me? Have you dived yet today?'

'What? Er . . . no, sir.'

'*No?*'

'No, Agnar. I've already told you, we were too busy watching this Summers guy. We've done it, though – I mean, we've made certain he won't dive again, just as you asked.'

'You've killed him, yeah?'

'Not exactly. I mean he won't be using his boat again. He won't be diving any more. It's trashed, Agnar.'

That was it. The man exploded down the line. 'I told you to get rid of this Summers guy! I made it very clear I wanted him removed from the area and *silenced*. That doesn't mean sneak on to his boat and mess up the place a bit. He'll buy new equipment! If he's found anything – anything at all – in that stretch of seabed, then he'll be back. You can bet on it. You know what divers are like – you used to be one, remember?'

'I still am, sir.'

'Well, get into the damn sea then! To hell with Lars.'

'But where am I going to find someone to replace him here, sir? It's impossible doing these dives *and* keeping a look out when you're on your own. I'm never going to find someone to help. It's in the middle of nowhere, sir. If you were here, you'd see that—'

'Ask around.'

'Ask who? Where?' Møller was getting exasperated. 'There's nothing here, Agnar!'

'I don't know, do I?' Agnar thundered at him. 'A student, or someone like that. They're always after making a quick buck. Just get on with it, man, and get the job done out there. I want my prize.'

Møller shook his head in exasperation. Agnar Sigurdsson could be so infuriating. It was all right for him – he didn't have to get his hands dirty. He could stay in his nice, plush office and direct operations from Denmark.

But that was because he was the money behind this entire project, and Møller knew he should sound more grateful than this. Or his boss would simply replace him, never mind Lars.

Sigurdsson was a ruthless employer. You didn't choose to either join or leave his employment. He decided for you. Currently, Møller was on the payroll and as such could be directed, shouted at and ordered to travel to anywhere in the world at the drop of a hat. If he disliked the arrangement, there was nothing he could do about it. It wasn't a voluntary thing. If he complained and tried to leave Sigurdsson's little team, he would be exterminated, just like others in the past had been. You can't be welcomed into Sigurdsson's inner circle and then hope to get out of it once you'd had enough.

Sigurdsson was an extraordinarily wealthy man. Having made his money in property development throughout Denmark, and usually through cutting corners and sweetening planning officials, he had recently turned his attention to his real passion in life: archaeology – Viking remains, to be specific. He was the most patriotic of all Danes, so he often boasted, and his obsession had become quite a costly addiction. He had a small team of dedicated, highly paid people who worked effectively as bounty hunters, sourcing Viking relics wherever they were in the world and bringing them home to the motherland.

Power does things to people. You can become a multi-millionaire, influential, powerful, well connected, persuasive, able to have anything you want, but that isn't enough sometimes. You have to invent weird and wonderful hobbies that capture your passion and rekindle that fire in the belly that once drove you into business in the first place. For some entrepreneurs it's travel, or space exploration, or saving rainforests, or hunting UFOs, or preventing famine. But for Sigurdsson it was history.

And Møller knew well that, once his employer was on the

scent of a significant find, some special prize, he would stop at nothing to get it – nothing. That was why he'd been sent to this remote, rain-soaked corner of England.

He glanced around at the dark, misty woods that bordered the car park on three sides. The ancient trees were bent and twisted like old men. Their bark was wrinkled and blemished with patches of shiny moss and fungus spurs. Some were quite misshapen, with knotty, crooked branches, like giant arthritic hands. It was an unwelcoming place, especially in mist. But Møller had no care for atmospheres and the melancholic mood was lost on him.

'I don't see anyone around here, sir, let alone impoverished students. But I'll try and recruit someone to help. I will try.'

'Look, forget it,' said Agnar.

'What?' Møller sounded nervous. Was he about to be dropped from the project?

'Just get to the airport, instead, OK? What do they call that place?'

'Stansted, you mean?'

'Yes. Get over to Stansted and wait for my next instructions. I'll fly someone over. It shouldn't take long. It'll just be one of the usual team. And make sure you don't lose this one, Møller.'

'But I don't think—'

'Just do it, man! Get over there now to meet them when they arrive. Then the two of you can get into that boat and start diving again tonight. I've thrown too much at this project to let it be stalled now. You have to find the rest of the stuff before someone else finds it. It's *ours*, Møller. Rightfully ours. It's our ancestors'. It belongs here.'

Oh no, thought Møller. He'd heard these rants before and could sense he was about to get another.

'This belongs to us!' Agnar continued. 'You know it does. And I won't let some stranger stumble across it. Some part-time treasure hunter! Some—'

'OK, sir. I get it.'

'No one is going to take that stuff. You hear me? *No one!*'

'All right, all right. Don't worry, Agnar.'

Møller knew only too well how passionate Agnar Sigurdsson was about this project. It wasn't the first assignment his boss had sent him on. Though it was the first time he'd sent Møller so far from the town they both called home, Roskilde in Denmark. A few miles from Copenhagen, it was the place where Agnar had grown up and he rarely left it. Why should he, when instead he could employ stooges like Møller to do his dirty work for him, wherever that may be, while he lounged around in his luxury apartment overlooking the Baltic Sea, glancing over his property portfolio and his stocks and shares in the mornings, perhaps calling his broker or any of his various directors and then excitedly researching where his next archaeological dig might be in the afternoons? It was a good life.

Møller sat in his car, staring out at the cold, damp climate and the dirty woods, and pictured his employer in his pristine, minimalist apartment with its giant glass windows, marble floors and shiny steel worktops. And those views – those incredible vistas across the Roskilde Fjord. The entire building was one of many blocks of apartments he owned in Roskilde and he'd purchased this one especially for the views from the central penthouse number three, now his main residence. It was modest in size, for a wealthy man like Sigurdsson, but he was done with all that luxury. On the rare occasions when they'd met in Agnar's private quarters, Møller had marvelled at how light and spacious it had been, free from the decadent furnishings and luxuries you might expect in a millionaire's home. Why was it so many rich people liked to strip themselves of clutter and live freely in empty rooms once they had indulged themselves enough? It was fashionable, he supposed.

'Please, Agnar. Don't worry. I understand how important this job is to you. It's all under control,' Møller continued, knowing what Agnar's temper could be like when provoked. He was like a Venus flytrap. 'We're doing the best we can. It'll all be found soon and brought back to Denmark. You know it will, Agnar.'

'Enough promises, Møller; it's time to deliver. You need to get out there and comb that seabed. I want my prizes.'

'I just have to be careful with the police, that's all. They may not be patrolling the coast just yet, but they will soon, I know they will.'

'What d'ya mean? Why? What's happened now?' said Agnar, his cold, hard temper rising once again, like the swelling seas of the Baltic through his windowpane.

'After Lars failed to show, I went down to the beach for a closer look. Something's happened down there. We were told to keep away but, with so many police around, I think it must be some kind of accident or maybe even a fatality. I saw an ambulance hurtling down there. I reckon there's a body on the beach.'

'Well, let's hope, for the sake of the project, it's this Summers guy you told me about. That'll stop him meddling. You sure you didn't kill him?'

'I told you, I didn't. I'm worried though, sir. I found the Land Rover. You know, the one Lars collected from the airport? Luckily we each had a set of keys so I was able to claim it was mine. Lars was gone, you know. Gone!'

'So why the hell didn't you go look for him on the beach?' said Agnar.

'I couldn't! The police were stopping anyone from going down there. I'm tellin' you. It was all roped off, see.'

'But they let you take the car?'

'Well, I said it was mine. I had the spare key, like I said.'

'Well, it sounds like it's either Summers they've found on the beach and Lars has done the decent thing and killed him before going into hiding, or it's Lars himself. Either way, this is not convenient, Møller. Not convenient at all. The last thing we need is a police presence there, for God's sake. Where's your boat moored, then? I take it you can still access it?'

'Further along the coast. Yeah, I can still get to it, I think. They've not roped that section off . . . I hope.'

'Well, why don't you reassess the situation when you're back from the airport, huh? It's unlikely they'll be patrolling the coast at night-time, Møller. I mean, what the hell are they going to see? You'll be fine. We must get back on track, before others start sticking their noses in and having a dive themselves. Right, that's all. I've gotta find someone to send over now.' The phone line went dead.

Møller stared through the steamed up windscreen at the gloomy giants outside, still staring at him, their wooden branches curling like twisted arms and fingers.

His boss had seemed to think it was so easy. If you lose a recruit, just send over another. They were all replaceable to him – always had been. But it didn't change the fact that still, in the back of his mind, an ominous sense of foreboding was lingering. He had a strange feeling that it was Lars' body the police officers had found on the beach. Who had done it? Would Møller be next?

He glanced down at the ignition, turned the key clockwise and started the engine again. He began reversing the Land Rover, ready to swing it out towards the car park entrance, its red lights illuminating the dark, damp trees behind him. He flicked the gear lever back into first, turned forwards again and then froze.

What the hell—?

The car juddered and then stalled as he slammed his foot on the brake without depressing the clutch.

Some kind of shape had darted between two giant trees ahead of him, on the other side of the wooden barrier that ran the perimeter of the car park. Had someone been watching him all this time? Was it Lars' killer?

He was sure he'd seen a shape of someone. The face had been hidden in the gloom but he'd definitely made out the head and shoulders. And a glimpse of long blond hair, tied back in a long ponytail, as the figure darted behind some trees. It had had a slight frame, delicate shoulders; it was too small to be Lars' killer, surely. Was it a woman? But out here, alone? Why? And why was it dressed in some kind of pale summer dress – in winter?

The sight had unsettled Møller and he scanned the trees and the undergrowth, looking for any sign of the figure. Nothing.

When he thought about it, the woman hadn't seemed to walk at all. Or run.

It was like she'd almost *glided*. The bracken was deep and it wouldn't have been possible to walk so smoothly, or so fast, through that undergrowth. You'd need to jump or hop like a small deer. But this shape had sashayed across the undergrowth like it was hovering. Its white dress was unmistakable against the dark tree trunks.

He stepped out of the car, closing the door gently. The place was eerily silent now; the wind had dropped and the leaves on the trees had ceased rustling.

'Hello?' he said, nervously. 'Anyone there? Are you all right?'

There was a screech from a sea gull in the distance and it made him jump.

Then silence again.

Loneliness was creeping up on him – a feeling that had always been alien to him until he'd pitched up in this remote corner of England. He was bomb-proof, a machine most of the time. He didn't hold with emotions. They served no purpose.

But what the hell was a woman doing here, in the woods, in cold weather like this? Dog walking, perhaps? In a dress like that? But then why didn't she answer when he called out?

He knew he should turn and leave. Whatever it was he'd seen, it didn't concern him. And it could only mean trouble. But something urged him to stay.

He walked slowly towards the wooden barrier at the fringe of the car park and stood against it, his knees resting against the low, roughly turned pole that lay horizontally across two uprights – part of a long fence that formed a barrier between the car park and the woods. His eyes scanned the vegetation for signs of any solid shapes moving.

Nothing.

Something darted in his direction from behind a giant tree to his right. It caught him unawares and he ducked quickly, knocking the tips of his kneecaps on the hard barrier. The pain ran through his legs down to his ankles.

He staggered backwards, regained his posture and then stood, fixed to the spot, his mouth open and his eyes wide with fear.

The small, sprite-like figure had returned and it swept gently towards him. It was wearing some kind of white robe. He felt a sudden burst of icy cold air as the shape came even closer. He saw the outline of her face. It was cloudy – more like gaseous plasma than a real body – but it was definitely a face. Strikingly beautiful. Her skin was as pale as her hair, pearly white, and she had the most piercing blue eyes that seemed to look straight into him. But the outline of her slender body, wrapped in thin, white cloth, wasn't clear and it blended with her surroundings like a holographic image of some kind.

The wind picked up again as she came closer and closer and then so close it made him stagger backwards again and raise his hands to his face. Between the cracks in his fingers he saw her eyes had widened – great, blue pools in the centre of an aquiline face. Her cheekbones were delicate, like she was made of porcelain. Closer, closer. He blinked. He saw her eyes staring at him – deep into him. They were tearful. The expression on her face was kindly, but tinged with sadness – pity, even.

'Hello,' he said again, fear building inside him like a rumbling earthquake. Was this woman for real? She had come even closer now, so that their faces almost touched, but still she remained mute.

'Who are you? Speak to me!'

The figure gave no response.

Shocked into silence himself, unable to communicate but too scared to move away, he felt another rush of freezing air that seemed to run right through him. She emitted a freezing chill; every nerve in his body tingled and shivered. It was like standing at the door of a giant freezer, or being plunged into cold water for a brief second. He tried to tense the muscles in his fists but his hands fell limp at his sides and he noticed he had begun to shake. He closed his eyes as the figure moved on him. But he felt no pain. Only cold. A final surge of intolerably cold air washed through him and then it stopped.

Møller spun around.

'Hello? Who's there? What the hell—'

He was panting, heavily. He could feel his heart pounding inside his ribcage. He looked around the empty car park, up at the audience of old trees. Nothing. No one.

Was he daydreaming? Or hallucinating? But he'd not taken any drugs; he despised them. He'd not even had a dodgy meal or hit the vodka last night to cause him to have the sweats now. There was no logical reason – none at all – for this situation. And Møller so hated it when things seemed illogical. Most things had a rational explanation. He saw no reason to believe in magic or witchcraft or anything supernatural. He had no religious beliefs either. God seemed illogical to him. He preferred to deal in facts; anything else unsettled him.

But had he really just seen a witch? Had she actually passed through him? What other explanation was there other than witchcraft? He'd seen the woman with his own eyes – a delicate, beautiful vision accompanied by an overwhelming sensation of extreme cold. When he'd opened his eyes again, the figure had gone. But the look in her eyes lingered in his mind and his heart. She'd cursed him, beguiled him. He was scared, he couldn't deny it.

Møller rarely felt fear – it just wasn't rational. His senses were numbed and he was tougher than most. But this had affected him deeply. He felt violated. This was *his* body, after all, *his* space. Like most humans, he felt uncomfortable when someone, or something, invaded his personal space. Yet this girl seemed to have passed right through him. If it *had* been a ghost, so be it – he wasn't altogether closed to the idea of the supernatural – but why here? Why now?

More to the point, why – and how – did it pass through him? His mind was spinning, clutching for theories that would help to explain the experience he'd just endured. But there was no explanation he could find. At least, no rational one. He shivered again. He was used to temperatures far lower than anything this miserable, dank climate could throw at him, but he had felt an extreme drop in temperature – he'd not imagined that. He looked down at his arms; there were goose bumps running across them still. But at least he could make a fist now – his nerve was returning.

He stiffened his body, breathed in deeply and marched back towards the car. There was a palpable sense of someone watching him still as he opened the door, but he tried to dismiss it quickly. Even so, as he climbed in, he found himself locking the doors and windows with an almost frantic feeling that was alien to him. He *never* felt afraid. What the hell had just gone on here?

There was a mysterious mood slowly rising in this remote corner of England – so strong it was even penetrating through Møller's hardened senses now. And somehow he knew this wouldn't be the last time he would feel like this. That pearly white, porcelain face, her long blond hair and the gentle white robes she'd been wearing were printed indelibly on his memory.

The gravel and dirt on the car park floor crunched and squelched as his car swept out of the clearing, on to the road. Behind him, there was a flash of white and the delicate figure glided through the trees further, deeper into the gloom of the forest, sending birds flapping up into the treetops and the rats and the squirrels scurrying for cover.

Then silence returned.

CHAPTER 11

TUESDAY, 1.20 P.M.

WALBERSWICK, SUFFOLK

'Blowin' a gale today, Bett,' said Clive. 'I'm ready for a cuppa.'

'Me too. Come on Sammy! Hurry up.' Bett was waiting for their Border terrier, who'd become distracted, as always, by something on the beach.

'Get a move on, Sam!' shouted Clive.

As locals, Elizabeth and Clive Chadwick knew what the weather could be like on this remote stretch of coastline, but today was especially cold and blustery. A brisk walk along the water's edge had been a daily ritual for as long as they could remember, but neither of them was getting any younger and Elizabeth's hips were not what they were. She never complained, of course, but Clive knew when she was in pain. The icy wind blew into her arthritic joints and her stoical expression belied a growing discomfort that would only get worse in time. Clive was all too aware that these walks, though painful, had become increasingly precious to them both.

'What's he doin' now, love?' said Clive.

Bett shook her head. 'Dunno. Found a dead crab or something?'

They turned round and headed back towards Sammy, who

was still refusing to budge. His tail was wagging frantically and he was pushing his head down into the wet sand, inquisitive as ever. Every so often, he'd stop digging, step back and bark furiously, before heading straight back into the sand again and burrowing with his paws.

'Whatcha got there, boy? Found a bone?'

'I think it's some kind of shell,' said Bett.

'Bloomin' big to be a shell, love,' said Clive, peering down at the ground. 'That's only part of it, I reckon. The rest is buried under the sand. Come 'ere, Sam. Mind out. Let me 'ave a look.'

Clive bent down and pushed the sand away with his hand. The source of Sammy's curiosity was buried quite deep, with just a palm-sized piece of white solid material exposed. As he brushed more sand away, they both could see it wasn't a shell at all.

It was a skull.

'Human?' said Bett.

Clive nodded. 'Think so. It's big enough.'

Sammy started barking furiously.

'Hey, don't be silly, Sam. You've seen one of these before! Don't be daft.'

'Another one from Dunwich, love?'

'I guess so, Bett. Been a while since we've seen one though, eh? And so far up the coast too!'

Having lived in the area for most of their lives, the Chadwicks were no strangers to finding human remains on the beach, dredged up from the remnants of Dunwich graveyards that collapsed into the North Sea over time. They'd found several bones over the years: a thigh bone, part of a foot, even another skull once – though that had been down on Dunwich beach a few miles south of where they were standing.

'Don't tell me,' said Bett, rolling her eyes knowingly. 'Another one for the collection, eh?'

'I'm not leavin' this one behind, Betts. It's a good'un. But I'll take it to Chris at the museum down in Dunwich, all right?

I don't suppose you want this lookin' at you every morning, eh?'

'No. I reckon one ugly face is more than enough, darlin'!'

They chuckled as Clive brushed off the last few handfuls of sand and lifted the skull for a closer look.

Though much of the top of the crown was still intact, the jawbone was incomplete and the back of the skull had worn away considerably. But the eye sockets were still recognisable – deep set, with a pronounced forehead and a long thin ridge running across the top of them where the dead man's eyebrows would once have been.

'Ugly feller,' said Clive.

'Hmm.'

The dog was still growling and showing his teeth.

'Sammy, will you shut up, lad!' shouted Clive. 'Honestly, I don't know what's got into 'im, Bett. I really don't.'

'He's probably just hungry.'

'Well, he ain't havin' this particular bone! Come on, love, let's get back to the car, shall we? I'll call Chris this afternoon. Maybe take it to show him tomorrow.'

They headed back to the car, the delicate skull held gently in Clive's hand. Sammy was still barking as the wind picked up again and rattled around Bett's painful bones.

As they neared the car park, they heard a loud bark in the distance. Sammy was the first to turn towards the sound. He quickly whimpered and scurried to hide behind Clive's legs. 'What's wrong now?' said Clive. 'It's just another dog.'

'Bloody big one, by the sounds of it,' said Bett.

'Where did it come from? Was it over there?' said Clive, pointing back along the beach, in the direction of some large dunes to their left, about twenty metres away.

'I think so. It was quite a bark, wasn't it, love? I reckon it was—'

She stopped.

And stared.

There, on top of the largest dune, was the dark outline of a dog. It was large and black and motionless.

Clive had already turned back towards the car park and was walking away. 'It's just a dog, love. Come on, I'm gettin' cold.'

But Bett wasn't budging. 'Look!' she cried. 'Look at it! It's . . . you know, it's the . . . the . . . whatcha call it?'

Clive stopped. He detected the fear in his wife's voice. 'The black shuck, you mean,' he said, as he came to put his arm around her. 'Don't be silly, love. That's just a myth. A legend. Don't be so superstitious, eh? You'll be telling me it has red eyes next! It's just a story, you know; it's not a real dog – like the one you're looking at over there. Its owner is probably just over the dune. We'll hear him shoutin' in a minute, you wait. I'll admit he's a big'un, yes – looks like some kind of hound; maybe an Irish Wolfhound, I dunno – but you don't need to be so silly, Bett. You've not seen a ghost! Now, come on. Let's get home, shall we?'

He walked her back towards the car. Perhaps it was the skull that had unsettled her, he thought. Not like Bett to be so superstitious.

Before they moved off the beach and into the adjacent gravel car park, Clive turned round and gazed once more towards the sand dunes. The hound was still there. Clive watched as it turned its massive head and looked over in his direction.

Then he saw its eyes.

They were red and glowing.

CHAPTER 12

TUESDAY, 1.31 P.M.

DUNWICH BEACH, SUFFOLK

Jud ran the Geiger probe up and down the deceased's mutilated body, being careful not to let it touch the knotted and bloodied mass of veins and flesh. A series of sharp clicks emitted from the main unit. There was clearly a trace of ionising radiation here. The needle on the electromagnetic field meter, known as a Tri-Axis 333, was fluctuating. The EMF meter was an essential piece of kit for any CRYPT agent, allowing them to detect any surges of electromagnetic energy – a tell-tale sign of paranormal activity. At first the readings were lower, but then the needle rose sharply: 38 mG, 51 mG. After a few more seconds, it settled at 89 mG.

'There's radiation here – no question – all along the outline of the body,' he said. 'Agreed, Bex?'

She nodded. 'The electrostatic locator's the same: high readings again. If this has been done by a paranormal entity, the levels are within the expected range. It's not impossible, given the readings, Inspector.'

'OK. And what about your senses? I mean this ESP malarkey. Do you detect anything unusual?'

Jud and Bex exchanged a quick glance. Khan had always appeared sceptical about agents' powers of extrasensory perception. Like most police officers, he dealt in facts and eyewitness accounts – what was seen and heard. He didn't have much faith in what was detected beyond the usual five senses. So for him to ask if they'd sensed anything 'unusual' was progress indeed. Maybe he was becoming a convert, after all.

But then Khan wasn't the only one who found it hard to believe that CRYPT agents could see and feel things that lay beyond most people's powers of detection. There was always a conflict to be found between the burden of proof needed to get a conviction in the British courts and the kind of evidence a CRYPT agent could produce via their extrasensory perception. The police – from constables on the beat to detective chief inspectors like DCI Khan – required fingerprints, DNA, eye-witness accounts under oath and other kinds of concrete evidence to bring a conviction. What the hell would they do with 'feelings'?

But, as Khan knew well, there were some crimes for which there simply was no reasonable explanation – and no tangible evidence either. A ghost doesn't leave a footprint. And it's not often seen (unless its anger is so intense it creates an ionised plasma so dense that anyone can see it). It was at these times that MI5 called the CRYPT. Not only could they record higher levels of electromagnetic radiation – as they had done here on the beach – they could also sense when a ghost was reaching out to them, connecting with the world, even causing an agent to *hypersense* from time to time. Hypersensing was something every agent both feared and secretly wished would happen to them. It was when their extrasensory perception was so stimulated, so connec-ted to the environment around them, that it played funny tricks on their ordinary senses, allowing them to see, hear and smell scenes from the past, as if they were there themselves. But, incredibly, the evidence an agent was able to gather during a hyper-sense experience was almost always accurate when they later researched the period of history they were seeing. It was astonishing.

And Khan – more than any other officer at the Met – knew that these agents could, and should, be believed. He knew they had to be taken seriously as crime investigators, because the crimes in question were committed by paranormal entities, after all. Khan needed no convincing of that, not any more.

Of course, though many officers (at least the ones who knew about the CRYPT) had ridiculed the idea of teenage ghost hunters, even they were not immune to the kind of fear that paranormal activity could bring. They didn't believe the agents were doing a real job – right up until the moment when they themselves were present at a haunting, or had witnessed the effects of a fatal haunting. Then they became converts, like Khan.

'Well?' he said. 'Do you detect anything, then? I mean, besides this bloody cold?'

Jud looked up and faced the shoreline. He closed his eyes and let the wind whistle around him, blowing his thick, black hair across his forehead.

'There's something under the sea. I can feel it. Some kind of unfinished business, maybe. I don't know. There's a connection . . . to out there.' He was pointing towards the grey waves that stretched to the horizon.

'Jud, it's well known that there's remains of the village under the sea. And that includes the occupants of graveyards now tumbled from the cliffs. The sea's been battering the place for centuries. You don't need ESP to know that; just read your history books.'

'Yes, I know that,' snapped Jud. 'But why now? Why are the souls of old Dunwich energised now, huh? Something's happened out there to cause this. I'm sure of it, Inspector.'

'You really think this killing here is in some way connected to remains lying under the sea? Are you saying the ghosts – if there are some – have come from down there and committed this?'

'Yes, Khan. That is exactly what I'm saying.'

'And you, Rebecca? How about you, huh?'

She was staring at the body. 'We'll know more when we find out who this man is. But Jud's right – there's some kind of link here. This is a protest, maybe. From the disembodied spirits of the deceased lying under the ocean. The ones whose graves fell from the cliffs into the sea.'

'Well, we've been waiting to identify this man but your bloody professor insisted we didn't touch the body until you'd scanned it, or whatever you guys do. Happy now?'

'Yep; I think we're done with the readings. There's a strong trace of electromagnetic and electrostatic energy on the surface of the body, indicating this man has come into contact with a ghost very recently, and the temperature readings show extreme cold spots, particularly around the main wound itself, again suggesting there's been physical contact with a ghost here. Let me just take a few pictures and then we can roll him over.' Jud removed his mobile phone from the front pocket of his rucksack and took three shots.

'Collect 'em do yer?' said Khan. 'Gruesome photos, I mean. Funny hobby.'

'Oh, yeah,' Jud replied, sarcastically. 'Love all this stuff. No, Inspector, I just want to send them to Professor Bonati. He'll need to see them.'

'We can do better than that,' said Khan. 'We're sending him the whole bloody corpse. He's already said he wants to see it himself.'

He fished for a small polythene bag in his coat pocket and took out a bunch of thin plastic gloves too. 'I asked forensics for a handful of these. Figured you probably wouldn't bring any yourselves. But I don't want any fingerprints on this. We do have some interest here, you know. It's not all about what you guys sense. There is still some old-fashioned policing to be done here. You have to get grubby sometimes. Now put these on.'

He handed the thin protective gloves to Jud and Bex and they squeezed them over their fingers and thumbs.

'Right, I'll hold his shoulder and you grab his belt buckle, yeah? We'll try and pull him towards us. Ready?'

'Surely, if we roll him over on to his back, goodness knows what'll come out of him – I mean, look, the back of his chest is still gaping open.'

Khan gazed solemnly at her. 'Bex, by the looks of the ground here, I'd say there's little left inside of this guy still to come out. I'll take my chances, OK?'

They held his body and began pulling it; it was heavier than expected – like a giant piece of meat on a butcher's block. Khan had often heard the expression 'dead weight' and he knew better than most how people always seemed to weigh more when they were dead. He realised it was just because they couldn't support you when you picked them up, but it still felt weird. And this guy was no exception; they had to strain hard to gather his body and roll it over the stones.

'Slowly, slowly!' shouted Khan. 'My guys haven't finished their own tests yet. I mean, you're not the only ones interested in this body. We've still got to carry out more tests on the wounds on his back before he goes off to London, see if we can find traces of a blade or something. Or fingerprints would be nice.'

Khan had seen far too many dead bodies in his line of work – his senses were almost numb these days and they all knew it.

'Unlikely you're going to find fingerprints,' said Jud, shaking his head. 'I mean—' He stopped suddenly as they looked in silence. 'God, look at that,' he said eventually.

They'd rolled him over and his face now stared back at them, still paralysed in a fixed expression of fear. His lips were wide open, dark grey and rigid. It wasn't just his back that had been so brutally attacked – his chest too. But there was something across his chest that had caught their attention.

'What the hell is it?' Khan said, shaking his head and screwing up his face. 'It's not a random wound from a fight, surely. I mean, someone's done that deliberately, 'aven't they?'

There were marks across the man's skin. His assailant – whoever or whatever it was – had used a sharp instrument to carve a set of markings – deep tracks that ran right across his chest, from which dark, browny-red blood was still oozing.

'Thoughts, Bex?' said Jud.

She said nothing at first, but kept staring at the shapes carved deep into the dead man's chest.

'These are letters, aren't they?' she said.

'Looks like it – the first two at least. Then some kind of arrow. Supposed to be "F. S." do you think?' said Khan. 'Someone's initials, perhaps?'

'It's possible,' said Jud. 'But unlikely. Besides, the arms on the F are too long. And what about the arrow?'

'There's no doubt they mean something,' said Bex.

'From what language, though?' said Khan.

Bex shrugged. 'Who knows? It's not one I've seen before, that's for sure.'

'Well, that's what we've got to find out,' said Jud. 'But they're obviously significant. I'll take some more shots.' He picked up his smart phone again and quickly snapped away, being careful to cover every shape in its entirety.

Bex knelt down and traced the lettering with her finger. 'Whatever these markings mean, I think they've been carved into his chest as a kind of protest. They're articulating an anger or maybe a revenge,' said Bex.

'How do you know?' said Khan.

'Trust me, I can feel it. How about you, Jud?'

'Yeah, there's a serious wrong that someone or something is trying to put right here,' said Jud. 'I can sense it too.'

'We were meant to find this, no question,' said Bex, an ominous tone creeping into her voice. 'It's a plea and we have to understand it.'

'We will,' said Jud. 'If it takes us several days of research, we're going to find out what these marks are saying to us. Discover that, and we'll be able to start making some links. I'll send these shots back to the CRYPT now. They can get on with identifying them and hopefully decoding what it says.'

'So, I'll tell the public there's been an incident and we're investigating, yes?' said Khan, glancing up at the dunes and wondering how long he could keep the public at bay. 'But no mention of ghosts, right?'

'Absolutely,' said Jud. 'I reckon you know the routine by now, Inspector. There might be enough evidence to suggest that some kind of paranormal force has been here today. The residue is clear. And you said yourself you saw this man being dragged by something invisible. *But* no one needs to know any of that. Just say there's been an incident and we're on it.'

'Otherwise this place'll be crawling with amateur ghost hunters and reporters,' said Bex. 'You know what can happen, Inspector.'

'Yeah, yeah. Don't remind me,' said Khan. 'I've been with you on enough cases now to know what the bloody public can do when they get a whiff of something ghostly. They go gaga, don't they?'

'It's true, some people are very, very frightened of ghosts,' said Bex. 'And you can't blame them. We humans never like to encounter things we can't explain. It's a human obsession, this idea of *understanding* everything. And when we can't, it seems we're automatically afraid of it.'

'I know, don't tell me. Who do you think's the one who has to give them the phoney stories instead, huh? I can't count the number of times I've had to lie in those press conferences whenever you guys are involved. How many different stories have we conjured up, eh? Remember the Tyburn activists? Protesting against traffic, or something stupid. There were ghosts, good and proper, but we said they were vigilante protestors – students with masks on!'

'Yeah, and imagine the hysteria if we hadn't,' said Jud.

'I seem to remember the whole city was pretty hysterical by the time we'd solved that one,' said Khan.

'Hmm,' said Jud, sneaking a glance at Bex. They both knew Khan had not exactly been helpful on that case, but he'd learned his lesson since then. He'd seen how important the work of the CRYPT was. And, besides, now wasn't the time to go raking up old scores. 'Let's just keep a lid on this for now.'

'Understood. And the body?' said Khan, relieved to be off the subject. 'Can we bag it up? You finished, 'ave you?'

Jud nodded. 'For now. I'm not satisfied we've learned everything we can yet from this corpse, but they'll find out more back at the CRYPT. Give Bonati twenty-four hours, Inspector, you'll see. He'll want to run more tests and see if there're any other traces of radiation or anything else on the body. Then your guys and the coroner can have him, OK?'

'No identity yet, then?' said Bex.

'Nope,' said Khan. 'There was a break-in at the boat along the beach up there. The owner said there was a possibility that this man might have been the burglar, but he wasn't sure. It was hard to identify him face down, Bex, and Bonati said we weren't to touch him until you guys got here. We'll take our own photographs of him too and send the shots on to Scotland Yard – they can get them out to the other constabularies. It won't take long before we get an ID. These things are usually very quick.'

'More than a coincidence, then?' said Jud.

'You what?'

'I mean, there's a connection between this man and the burglary on the boat, I assume? Seems too much of a coincidence, doesn't it?'

Khan shrugged. 'You can ask the guy who owns the boat, if you like. He's in the café over there. He's called Daniel Summers and he's been diving for relics from the old village under the sea, apparently – so he says, anyway.'

'Let's meet him,' said Bex. 'I want to know more about this Dunwich place before we head back to London. It's got a strange vibe. Interesting choice for a holiday, Inspector.'

Khan just glared at her and then replaced the sheeting and made sure the body was well covered – not a task he was expecting to have to do on the first holiday he'd taken in years. Before he covered the man's head, he took a couple of snaps with his iPhone.

They soon set off for the car park.

Khan stopped.

'The Land Rover,' he said.

'What?' said Bex.

'It was there! It's gone. There was a bloody Land Rover there this morning. It was his, I'm sure it was.'

'The dead man's?' said Jud.

'Yeah! I've been stuck on the bloody beach all this time. I didn't know someone had let it go!' He called a police officer over.

'Oi, you! Where's the car gone?' he shouted.

'Which one, sir? The place is full of them now; look around you.' The young officer's attempt at wit was lost on Khan.

'The Land Rover, you damn fool! It was *there*,' he pointed to the corner of the car park near the dunes. 'It was the only damn car in here this morning, apart from a couple near the café. You couldn't have missed it. I think it belonged to the dead man. I saw him click the remote locking and it flashed. It was definitely his!'

The officer signalled to a colleague to come over. He ran across.

'Yeah?'

'The DCI here says there was a Land Rover here this morning. Might have belonged to the dead man on the beach.'

'Not *might*!' thundered Khan. 'It bloody well *did*.'

The officer shrugged and started shaking his head. 'Can't have done, sir. The owner came to collect it, you see. Blond feller. Said he'd been out walking.'

Khan was incredulous. 'You mean to say we have a murder scene, no one about, no suspects, just a dead body – and then up walks a man from nowhere, who says it's his car, and you just let him go?'

The officer had gone red faced. 'Well, he didn't come from the beach side, sir. He came from the village over there. I figured he couldn't have been involved if he was nowhere near the place, could he? He said he hadn't been near the beach this morning. He was asking what all the fuss was about.'

'And you *believed* him?'

'He had his own keys, sir. I watched him unlock it. It *had* to be his.'

'Unbelievable,' said Khan, shaking his head. 'Unbelievable. I tell you, if this was London . . . If you were on my staff, I'd—'

'Inspector?' said Jud. 'The body, remember?'

'Yeah, yeah.' He told the officers to arrange for a police van to take the body to a coroner's address in London, from where CRYPT agents would collect it later. Bonati wanted to see it for himself. The officers nodded obediently and reassured the inspector they'd deal with it straight away.

'Leave it to us,' said one, eagerly.

Khan just raised an eyebrow. 'One of you go and watch the body, while the other one arranges for the van to come and collect it. OK? No need to clear up the blood and mess after you've finished. I'm sure the tide will do that.'

CHAPTER 13

TUESDAY, 2.40 P.M.

STAR INN, DUNWICH

Jud ordered two more Cokes, a cappuccino and an unfeasibly large mug of tea for Khan, and returned to the window seat where Bex and the inspector were gazing out at the dull, grey scene.

'Where's Summers gone now?' said Jud quickly.

'Don't worry,' Bex said. 'Loo.'

The beach café had been far too crowded a venue for any kind of discrete interview with Summers. There were too many interested onlookers, all pretending to drink their tea and appear disinterested – but stealing nosey glances every minute. So Jud had suggested they come to the Star Inn – where he and Bex were due to check in anyway, after CRYPT staff had arranged it for them back in London.

It was a cosy, intimate kind of place. Open fireplaces, mahogany tables, oak panelling on the walls and the very best fish and chips in the area. The agents had not eaten anything since the night before – the furore over Jud's early morning SPA session had put paid to any chance of breakfast – so they had each made short work of a giant piece of battered cod, hand-cut chips, twice fried, and a huge dollop of tartar sauce.

Khan had plumped for 'pie of the day', a small, mostly gravy-filled pot with a loose hat of flaky pastry, which he instantly removed and ignored for the rest of the meal.

'So, what do you make of him?' he said.

'Summers? Nice enough guy, I suppose,' said Jud.

'Yeah,' said Bex, attempting to sound casual. 'He's all right, isn't he?'

'Meaning?' said Jud.

'What? I don't mean anything. I'm just agreeing with you, Jud. He's a nice enough guy, as you say.'

Jud scoffed, 'Oh, come on, Bex, you've not been able to take your eyes off him since he walked in. You couldn't have been more obvious with your affections. You're like a kid at school, ogling some sixth-former.'

'Oh, listen to him,' she said to Khan. 'Anyone would think he's jealous!'

Jud just shook his head, but he could feel a slight burning in his cheeks. Khan was smiling and watching him for a reaction to this teasing.

He couldn't deny it; he was irritated by her obvious interest in this blond beach bum. And the fact that he was allowing himself to be irritated just annoyed him even more. Why should he care if Bex appeared to fancy someone? She wasn't his girlfriend, after all.

Was she?

'But, look, I don't think he's telling us the whole truth,' said Jud.

'What makes you say that, Sherlock Holmes?' said Bex.

'About the break-in on his boat, you mean?' said Khan.

'No. I don't think he knows any more about that than he's already told us. I mean, why he's *here*. He's not being honest about that, I can tell.'

'He's here for diving, Jud, we know that. What's your problem?' said Bex, defensively.

'Yes. But what's he looking for? I mean, why here? Why now?'

'Well, why not?' said Bex abruptly. 'Honestly, Jud, I sometimes wonder if there's anyone you trust.'

'Do you know what?' he said, glaring back at her. 'I don't think there is.'

He still wasn't convinced about Summers. 'I can sense it,' he said. 'There's something about him. Something's he's . . . I dunno . . . *excited* about.'

'Well, you can always ask him,' said Khan.

'I will, don't you worry. I'll ask him as soon— Oh, hi, Mr Summers. You found the toilet, then?'

Summers looked at him oddly. 'No, just went behind a hedge outside.' He raised an eyebrow and gave a wry smile across the table to Bex. She grinned.

Jud felt another tug of irritation.

A waiter came and cleared the plates. Jud continued, 'Anyway, I was just wondering if we could go through it again, Mr Summers – you know, just to get the facts straight and see if—'

'Do you want to see the dessert menu?' said the young man, balancing plates on his left forearm.

'What? Oh, er . . . anyone?'

They each shook their heads and the waiter disappeared.

'Don't you just hate that?' said Jud.

'Hate what?' Bex replied.

'When a waiter completely interrupts you mid sentence. Why can't they wait until you've finished talking, huh? Anyway, Mr Summers, I was wondering if—'

'It's Dan, please,' Summers interrupted, playfully. He smiled at Bex again.

'We'll stick with Mr Summers, if you don't mind,' said Jud. 'Can we go through it again?'

'What, all of it?'

'No, no – just what it was you were diving for. What brings you here in the first place?'

'Why do you ask?' said Summers, and, for the first time, Bex saw a flash of nervousness cross his attractive face. 'I mean, sorry, I was just wondering why you needed to know, that's all. Just curious.'

'Well, then you're the same as us, Mr Summers,' said Jud. 'Just curious. So what's brought you here?'

His eyes darted across the room again, furtively. 'Relics,' he whispered, 'from the old village of Dunwich. Do you know about the old town that's now submerged?'

'Yes, yes. The locals have all been telling us about that,' Khan joined in. 'Anything in particular?'

Summers shot another glance across the hotel bar, scanning to see if anyone else was listening.

'You're sure you're not divers yourselves, yes?'

'Erm, I think so,' said Bex, faking confusion and then smiling.

'I reckon we'd probably know, if we were,' said Jud, attempting to return the sarcasm. 'Why do you ask? You seem . . . nervous.'

It was a few seconds before Summers spoke again. Now he was gazing out of the window. Had he been distracted? Or was he running his answer over in his mind before speaking?

'Look, I can trust you, can't I?'

'Of course you can,' said Bex. 'Shoot.'

'I want you to see something.'

He bent down to his rucksack, hidden under the table, fished around inside the front pocket for a while and then took out a crumpled tissue.

Hunching forward so that others on neighbouring tables were prevented from seeing its contents, Summers unwrapped the tissue on the table.

'Well?' he said.

'It's an old coin and a piece of gravestone, I assume. You found this under the water, yes? Well done, sir,' said Khan.

'No, no.'

'You didn't find it while diving?' said Jud.

'I mean, yes. I did.'

'But you said "no" just then.' Jud sensed he had Summers rattled and he was enjoying it.

'No, I mean . . . What?'

'Just let him speak!' said Bex. 'Carry on, Dan.'

'Well, this coin, first of all: I believe it's very, very old and there are more down there. And other things, too. This may well be just one of a hoard of coins. Occasionally you hear about this – divers uncovering buried treasure troves. There could be hundreds of coins on the seabed – thousands, even.'

'If there are, you'll have to notify the authorities,' said Khan, reaching for it.

'Yes, I know. And I will,' said Summers. 'But I want to be the first to find it. It's fascinating, isn't it?'

Khan studied it carefully. On one side he could just make out the image of a cross in the centre, with letters around it that were difficult to decipher. On the cleaner side, he could see what looked like three words: DOR – ESTΛT – FIT.

He shrugged. 'Looks old to me. Might be Roman?'

'And what about this other piece?' said Bex. 'It just looks like a fragment of gravestone, yes? We know some of the graveyards slipped into the sea when the coast was eroded. There must be hundreds of graves buried in the seabed.'

'Ah, but look at this,' whispered Summers. 'It's got letters on it, but I'm pretty sure they're not English. In fact, I don't recognise them at all.'

'May I?' said Bex, offering an open hand across the table.

He nervously handed it over. 'Be careful with it.' They could see a slight tremble in his hands.

The fragment was small enough to sit in one hand, like a large paperweight, and as heavy, too.

'Been diving here before, have you, Mr Summers?' said Khan.

'No, Inspector. It's my first time in this area. It's a strange place, you know. There's something . . . I dunno . . . kinda mystical?'

Khan looked at Jud, expecting him to respond in agreement, but he wasn't listening. He was fixed on Bex's face.

As he'd watched her take the stone fragment carefully in her fingertips and examine it, he'd noticed her eyebrows rise slightly. She'd seen something. He knew it.

She turned her focus from the stone, now held up level with her nose, and caught Jud's stare. She widened her eyes at him across the table, and he knew there was something significant in that little relic. He also sensed it was sufficiently important to keep it from this Summers guy. Keen to share a secret about the man who moments ago had been the object of Bex's affections, Jud willingly took the piece now offered to him and studied it without any expression. Khan continued to chat to Summers about his exploits, both diving beneath and surfing over the waves in various destinations around the British Isles and beyond.

Summers had been quite correct. There were indeed letters, just a few – or shapes of some kind – etched into the stone about two thirds of the way up, running from left to right. It was clear that the lettering must have continued once, as the line seemed interrupted by the rough edge on the right of the piece.

And then he saw it in the middle of the line of text: the sequence of letters that must've caught Bex's attention.

'Maybe we should borrow this,' said Jud.

'What?' said Summers. 'Borrow it? Why? What's it got to do with the crime scene, huh?'

'Well, look, if you've only just found this and moments after you got it your boat was ransacked, it's entirely possible that whoever paid you a visit was after this.' Jud glanced over in Khan's direction and raised his eyebrows, as if to say, *We need this.*

Khan got the message and continued on his behalf. 'I'm sorry, sir, my colleague is quite correct. There may be a link. We'll take the coin too.'

Summers' face dropped.

'Don't worry, you'll get them back, sir. We just need to discover if they're significant. It might give us some answers as to what the 'ell's been going on here.'

'Then I have no choice?' said Summers.

'No.'

'And I take it I'm stuck here. I can't leave Dunwich?'

'No.'

'Or go diving again?'

'Not if your boat's wrecked.'

'Great. So what am I supposed to do in this place, huh? Who's going to keep me company?' He stole a glance at Bex across the table, who promptly blushed slightly – just enough for Jud to notice.

Jud stood up abruptly. 'Right, I think we're done here, for now. Thank you, Mr Summers. We'll be in touch.'

CHAPTER 14

TUESDAY, 3.11 P.M.

A12 NORTHBOUND,

NEAR IPSWICH

Møller slammed the Land Rover into fourth gear and put his boot to the floor. This thing might have been all right on the rough back-roads of Suffolk, but on a dual carriageway it was slower than he'd have liked.

He was anxious. Not only because of the continued disappearance of Lars, but because of the identity of his replacement, seated in the car next to him.

Why Yolanda? Of all the people his boss could have sent over, why did it have to be her? Møller knew that the man who paid their wages was a shrewd game player. He'd chosen Yolanda for a reason.

Did his employer not know that, up until last year, Jürgen and Yolanda were an item? And a more volatile, stormy relationship it was hard to find.

Now here they were sharing a car together. It hardly seemed believable.

'So . . .' said Møller, deciding to break the stony silence that had consumed them ever since leaving Stansted.

'So, what?' she said.

'What's the plan, Yol?'

She said nothing. She'd forgotten how much she hated him calling her 'Yol'.

'Oh, come on!' he snapped. 'Agnar wouldn't have sent you for no reason. You don't expect me to believe that, do you? He's a shrewd man.'

'Typical,' said Yolanda. 'I mean, you wouldn't be asking these questions if it had been Erik or Hal or Sam, would you? It's because I'm a woman. You've always been a bigot, Jürgen.'

'Don't start,' he said. 'I'm just curious to know the plan. You're obviously not just here to help me dive.'

'Oh, I see,' said Yolanda. 'It's because you think I can't do the work. You think I can't manage the boat, is that it?'

'Just answer the bloody question, Yol. What's the plan? Things are heating up here; you need to know the pressure I'm under. It's getting dangerous and I want to know what Sigurdsson's going to do about it. This guy, Summers, is prowling around. And everyone's asking questions. It doesn't feel right, Yol.'

There was fear in Møller's voice, she could tell. She was disappointed in him. From the moment he'd picked her up from the airport, she could tell he was on edge. It was pathetic how he seemed to have changed since being on this mission. Was it the business over Lars? Or was it her presence there? Or was he getting tired of the orders coming through from Sigurdsson? Either way, he was weakening – she could see that. No wonder Sigurdsson was keen for her to get over here and sort him out.

She smiled cheekily and flicked her long blond hair flirtatiously. 'I think you know what the plan will be,' she said dryly.

'OK. Don't tell me. You've been sent to charm this Summers guy. Yeah? You're going to get friendly with him and then get rid of him, I suppose.'

She didn't need to say anything. They both knew he was right.

'What a way to go,' said Jürgen, half smiling.

'Jealous?'

'You *serious?*' he said, throwing the Land Rover into a tight bend so the tyres squealed beneath them. 'Give me some credit, Yol. We're finished.'

'Hmm,' she said, unconvinced. 'We'll see.'

They drove the last few miles in silence again, but Yolanda could tell from the constant tapping of his hands on the wheel, the anxious glances in his rear-view mirror and the twitching of his eyes that Møller was edgy. Typical man, she thought. If you want something done properly, always ask a woman.

She flipped open the vanity mirror in the sun visor and applied more lipstick and mascara, neatly pursing her full lips and then smacking them together to spread the lipstick evenly. Møller stole frequent looks at her whilst driving. He couldn't help it. Though he hated to admit it, he felt a surge of adrenalin to be near her again. Her vibrant, energetic personality was quite addictive. She could be infuriating, no question, and she loved to boss him around like she did other guys, but he could tolerate that. It was worth it. Besides, she had her gentler moments. There was a vulnerability to her which few people other than Møller had seen. And in moments like this, when she was applying her make-up, it was amusing to see her making all the same facial gestures that any girl made. Behind the tough façade, there was a little girl lurking inside, sat at her mother's dressing table, playing with her make-up. Møller tried hard to keep the car steady so that she didn't smudge her lipstick. Amusing as it might have been to watch, Yolanda's temper could so quickly have been pricked if he'd made her slip. She was most particular about her appearance.

And you could see why. She was such a striking girl – with great looks and enviable blond hair, which she flicked to the side and kept running her fingers through whenever she spoke to someone in that flirtatious way that some girls do.

And she was physically fit too. The many guys who ogled her wherever she went could be forgiven for thinking she was an athlete of some kind, as she had that kind of sporty body, well-toned neck and slender face. She was a sexy girl whom every guy fancied but no one would dare take on in a fight, or compete against in a race. She'd nail you.

Whatever their differences, whatever reasons she'd had for ending their relationship as abruptly as she had done, Møller couldn't deny the fact that he was glad to see her again. And, though he was tougher than most guys and could endure tremendous physical and mental challenges like a true Viking, this girl did something to him. She could reduce him to jelly if she wanted to.

This Dan Summers guy had better get ready. Good luck, Møller thought to himself as he tried to focus more on the road than on the passenger beside him. You're gonna need it.

CHAPTER 15

TUESDAY, 4.00 P.M.

CRYPT, LONDON

Luc and Grace met outside the lifts in Sector Three.

'Ready?' said Luc, smiling. He was pleased to see his partner again. It had been a few days since they'd met up and, though they'd been involved in the odd training session together recently, they'd not been out on a case as a duo for a while now.

Luc enjoyed working with Grace, and the feeling was mutual. She was as cool and sassy as any agent, with her long blond hair and her radiant smile. But she was kooky too. And he liked that. Grace was the kind of girl that would light up a party as much for the funny things she said as for her warmth and good looks. She was brave – you had to be to survive in the CRYPT – but she was able somehow to retain her sense of fun too. And that laugh of hers was infectious.

Anyone could see why Bonati had paired these two agents up together; it was obvious. They were so alike in many ways. Both shared a good sense of humour and a cracking sense of fun, and yet both were able to show that steely determination to get through a case to the end. If there was a difference between their partnership and that of Jud and Bex, it was that neither Luc nor Grace took themselves quite so seriously. Jud was a deep, complex character, and Bex could be pretty intense too. Maybe that was why Luc was Jud's closest friend in the CRYPT and Grace was Bex's too. Socially, the four of them were the perfect match.

'I'm as ready as I'll ever be,' said Grace. 'How're you doin'?'

'I'm OK. I've been waiting for an excuse to get out. You know what I'm like. I don't like being caged up in this place for too long. Let's hope this one takes us miles away, yeah?'

'Yeah, I'm ready to get going too. But Bonati said this one wasn't going to be pretty, Luc. There's some serious injuries for us to examine first.'

'Oh, great,' he said miserably. Grace smiled, as she knew Luc could be pretty squeamish at times. He was fit and strong and probably the most muscular agent in the place but, when it came to blood and guts, he would usually send Grace in first and follow on behind.

They walked down the white-tiled, neon-lit corridor, past rows of laboratories.

'Lab twelve, was it?' said Luc, like a man condemned.

Grace nodded. Soon they paused outside the lab and took turns to gaze into the retina-recognition scanner on the wall. The dark, metallic door slid smoothly across and they were inside. Grace smiled when Luc did the gentlemanly thing and allowed her to go in first. Behind her back she pulled his jumper to make sure he followed her and didn't turn and run.

The professor was already waiting for them, standing the other side of a large table, on which there lay the body from Dunwich. A sheet was covering it, but Luc and Grace could see the tip of his feet poking out of the end, bluish in colour, lifeless.

'OK?' said Bonati, holding the sheet, ready to pull it back.

They nodded.

He pulled gently and they saw the deceased's face revealed. Rigor mortis had set in and the blue lips were fixed open. They could see his stained teeth. His eyes had been respectfully closed, but the expression across the rest of his face was a grimace of pain and horror – that much was obvious.

Then they saw his chest and the marks that had been gouged out with some kind of knife.

'My God,' said Luc.

'Do they know who did this, Professor?' said Grace, moving up close to the body and examining it.

Bonati shook his head. 'We're hoping you can find out what these symbols mean and lead us to the killer.'

'And what about the back?' said Luc. 'You said the body was mutilated, sir.'

The professor nodded his head solemnly and reached for a folder laid on the table next to the body. 'When it was found, the spine had been cracked open at the back and the lungs were pulled out – like wings, Khan said; splayed right out. Here, look at this. Jud sent us these three pictures from his phone. We printed them off, so you can keep these.'

Luc took the photos and grimaced as he passed them on to Grace for a closer look.

'I know; I'm sorry, Luc. I realise this isn't really your thing. But it's important you both see this before you start the research,' said Bonati.

'Obviously some kind of ritual killing?' said Grace. 'Have we scanned the body for radiation, sir? Any signs of the paranormal?'

'Yes. Jud texted to say the readings he took when he scanned the body on the beach were noticeably high. And the temperature was registering extreme lows, apparently, too. He and Bex were sure there were traces of paranormal activity at work.' Bonati returned to the folder. 'That reminds me,' he said. 'He sent us these too.' He showed them two more photos, one of an old coin and the other of the fragment of stone with the symbols across it.

'My God,' said Grace, 'it's the same symbols. These three, at least – look, they're the same as on the body.'

'Exactly,' said Bonati. 'So there's your first clue. Right, I've got to get to a meeting. He's all yours.'

'Gee, thanks!' said Luc. 'By the way, sir?'

Bonati paused at the doorway. 'Yes?'

'Do we know who he is yet?'

The professor nodded. 'Of course, sorry. Only just heard from Scotland Yard actually. They've finally traced him. He's Danish, apparently. Goes by the name of Lars Andersen. God only knows what he was doing on a deserted beach in Suffolk.

'Anyway, good luck. Report to my study first thing tomorrow with some answers, please. Nine o'clock sharp. Have a good evening.'

They watched him leave and waited for the door to slide silently shut.

They were alone with the body, consumed by an eerie silence that weighed heavy on their ears like a gravitational pull. It would be all too easy to feel claustrophobic, or even disorientated down here, in the absence of windows, or any kind of everyday noise.

Grace was staring at Andersen's face. 'He looks terrified,' she said. 'Is that what death is like, do you think?'

Luc was shaking his head. 'No, not always. But I guess it was for him.'

They both stared at his fixed expression and his deathly pallor.

'If only he could speak now,' said Grace. 'I wonder what he'd tell us?'

'He's only just died, so we'll not hear his spirit yet,' said Luc. 'It's too soon. Come on. Let's get the computers up and running. I wanna know all about these symbols. If he can't tell us, we'll find it out ourselves.

'We've got a body, a coin and a piece of stone. Let's do this.'

CHAPTER 16

TUESDAY, 4.41 P.M.

STAR INN, DUNWICH

Jud rolled the coin around in his fingertips. A drop of sticky Coke ran down his wrist. He'd been soaking the coin in the fizzy Coke for twenty minutes, using the small plastic cup he'd found by the sink in the bathroom. He knew well that Coke was a brilliant way of cleaning old, corroded metals. And it was working too. Although it still felt rough in places, encrusted as it was with minerals from years spent on the seabed, the images and lettering were becoming clearer now. He could see flecks of shiny metal where someone had crudely tried to scratch through the crusty layer.

He traced his finger around the letters on one side. They were written over three lines: DOR – ESTΛT – FIT.

What does that mean? he thought. Latin? Was this a Roman coin?

His laptop was in front of him on the dressing table, shoehorned in between the television and the floral tray of instant coffee sachets, tea bags and shortbread biscuits. The mirror directly opposite him was clouded with steam from the kettle, which now boiled. This pleased Jud as it meant, for a few moments at least, he didn't have his own face staring back at him whilst trying to work. It was always the same when you used a hotel dressing table for a desk – you had to contend with your face peering back at you over the laptop.

Jud began researching the letters on the coin. Nothing. He preceded them with various other key words, like *medieval, coin* and others. Eventually he found something. One of the entries on the search engine referred to a coin found in the Netherlands from the medieval mint at somewhere called Dorestad.

The letters, DOR – ESTΛT – FIT, referred to 'Dorestat fit' – which could be translated as 'made in Dorestad'.

Jud kept reading and soon discovered this was once a vast trading centre in medieval times, ideally situated on the banks of the River Rhine, just south of Utrecht. And, most importantly, it had its own mint. So Dorestad coins would have been found right across Europe.

And when was it first made? Jud couldn't find any date on the coin. He turned it over. The Coke on the surface was still doing its magic, but he decided to speed up the process a little and dabbed a flannel into the plastic cup. Soaked in Coke, he rubbed it over the coin's surface, his curiosity building. He *had* to know more about this thing.

As he rubbed, he could see the green crust was wearing away. Eventually, letters became visible on this side too, running around the edge, with an image emerging in the centre, which resembled a cross. He could just make out, LO . . . H . . . R II R . . . X.

It didn't take long for Jud to discover this should have read, 'LOTHAR II REX', meaning 'King Lothar II', who reigned from 855 to 869 over a stretch of territory west of the Rhine, from the North Sea to the Jura Mountains.

So this coin must have originated from the mint at Dorestad in Holland.

But why was it here, in East Anglia of all places? Jud thought to himself. It didn't make sense. One thing was for sure: it couldn't have been just another item belonging to the villagers of

Dunwich before their houses and gardens crumbled into the North Sea. This was *much* older.

And what if there were more? There could be an historic hoard down there – no wonder Dan Summers had seemed secretive downstairs in the bar. And no wonder someone had raided his boat earlier. Perhaps there were other treasure hunters on the coast who were aware of these coins.

But, as exciting as this was, Jud realised it told him nothing about the paranormal. And it told him nothing about these strange letters found on the body down on the beach, and on the broken stone too, which still lay wrapped in the tissue next to his laptop. That was his next research project.

Jud loved this part of the job; some agents didn't. He knew that many preferred the chases and the close encounters with spirits – the more violent the better. Jud was no coward, of course – in fact, he had a reputation for being the steeliest of all agents. Nothing scared him and no one loved a chase, or a scrap, more than he did. But he was bright and intelligent too. And this part of the job – the investigation, the research, the uncovering of historic secrets – was just as enjoyable for him. These were his Indiana Jones moments, when he could discover his own Temple of Doom or Holy Grail. If he'd not been an agent – and he knew, of course, he'd not really had any choice about that – he would have been an archaeologist. Not just for the digging, but for the addictive chase for evidence online.

But time was creeping on and he'd promised he would meet Bex in the bar at five. It was already two minutes to. He wrapped the coin back into the tissue and placed both it and the stone into the inside pocket of his jacket, which he was still wearing. There was no way he was going to leave it behind for someone to come and pilfer.

He leapt down the steps, three at a time, the pocketed stone knocking against his chest as he jumped, and entered the bar area.

Bex was nowhere to be seen, but then it had only just turned five.

He waited. Then ordered a Coke and waited some more. As the cold, fizzy drink ran down his throat, he wondered if it would be cleaning his insides out as it had done for the old coin.

He glanced at the young man who'd served him his Coke. He couldn't have been much more than nineteen or twenty. His thick-rimmed specs and his unmanageable mop of blond hair gave him a studious look. His pale complexion was different to that of his colleagues – he looked like he spent more time indoors than on beaches and boats. Probably a student working here for beer money. Friendly enough – no different to your average barman in a country hotel – but there was something familiar about his face, Jud thought. He had a faint suspicion that he'd seen him before. But he couldn't for the life of him think where, or when.

'Excuse me, have we met before?' Jud said.

'No, don't think so,' said the barman, cheerfully. 'Why do you ask?'

'Oh, nothing. Don't worry. Must be mistaken. I'm sorry.' Jud decided it was best to leave it at that, but there was something in the barman's face that suggested he wasn't telling the truth: perhaps a tiny, wry smile or a slight twinkle in his eye? Jud wasn't sure exactly, but he'd seen something that warranted suspicion. His senses were in overdrive, extending across the bar like antennae.

But he knew, of course, that he should never attract attention to himself like this. He chided himself inside for even raising the issue. They couldn't have ever met before – it was impossible – and this guy just had one of those faces that seemed familiar, like some people do. He flushed at the thought that he'd made himself look foolish, or over friendly. Luckily, the barman just continued serving others and stacking empties into metal trays, ready for the dishwasher.

Jud glanced down at his watch.

Quarter past and still no Bex.

Suddenly, he heard a laugh which he recognised as hers, but it wasn't coming from the staircase or the corridor outside. She wasn't on her way down to meet him, it seemed. The noise had come from the restaurant at the opposite end of the room.

He stepped off the bar stool he'd been perching on and walked to the door. There was Bex, sitting at a window table with Dan Summers opposite her. She was clearly enjoying some comic anecdote from the surfer. Jud saw her tilt her head back and clap her hands in glee as Summers kept reeling off the jokes.

Yeah, funny guy, thought Jud.

He approached the table and stood there for a moment, waiting for Bex to stop laughing and notice him.

Summers saw him first and cheekily said, 'Can I see the wine list, please?'

Bex giggled in an appreciative way; Jud shot her a steely glare, but she missed it.

'Oh, a comedian, eh?' said Jud, flatly. 'Bex, can I have a word?'

'Yeah, sure.'

'No, I meant in private,' said Jud, turning in the direction of the bar behind him. 'Now?'

Summers shrugged his shoulders and looked at her mischievously, as if to say, *You're in trouble now, girl.*

She stood up and brushed past Jud, unimpressed by this apparent summons. She entered the bar area and sat at a free table in the corner.

'What's your problem?' she said sternly. 'I don't appreciate being ordered around like that, especially in front of someone.'

'In front of an admirer, you mean?'

She smiled. 'Oh, I get it. So you *are* jealous, huh? Of course. I'm sorry, I should've realised.'

Jud wasn't going to take the bait. Not here; not now. There was too much to do and he didn't want to give Bex what she was angling for – to see him either lose his rag or confess some undying love for her.

'I'm not going to play this game, OK, Bex? We're here on an investigation. We said we'd meet in the bar area at five o'clock and that's why I came to find you – that's all.' He looked at her as she gazed past him towards the door to the restaurant again, in Summers' direction. 'Have you been drinking?' he whispered.

'No!' she shouted.

'You sure?'

'Jud, firstly it's illegal for someone our age to drink in public, *as you should know*, secondly I wouldn't have got served if I'd tried, and thirdly . . . Well, thirdly, I still think you're jealous. I happen to find Dan funny and charming and you hate it. I'm not *drunk*. I'm just happy in his company . . . Got a problem with that?'

Nothing slipped past this girl, he thought to himself. What was it about her that she could just read his thoughts like that – and be so damned accurate? Still, there was no way he'd let on that she was evenly vaguely correct. Better to ignore the question altogether. 'I've discovered something about the coin,' he said, changing the topic.

'Oh, yeah?'

'Yes. It's from Holland.'

'What?'

Jud nodded. 'Not only that. It's twelve hundred years old.'

Now he had Bex's attention. 'Wow! Really?'

'Yeah, almost. I reckon it dates back to around 850.'

'So what the hell is it doing in Dunwich, then? If it fell into the sea when the old houses crumbled away, then it was here a considerable time before the village was. Buried maybe?'

'That's what we have to find out. Where's Khan, by the way?'

'He's gone back to Dan's boat. Gone to meet some more forensics there. I think they've found fingerprints that match the dead man's. So it must have been him who burgled Dan's boat.'

'And do we know why yet?'

Bex shook her head. Jud could see she was distracted again.

'Bex? You listening?'

She was looking over his shoulder in the direction of the restaurant again. A couple had walked into the bar off the street: she was blonde and very attractive; he was just as fair, but steely faced with a shock of short blond hair, like a military flat-top.

The girl had made straight for the restaurant and had sat down at a table close to Dan's. She was talking to him already. Did they know each other? It looked like they did, the way they were chatting and laughing.

Jud turned round and saw what was happening. 'Hmm . . . who's jealous now then?' he said.

'Shut up,' she whispered. 'I'm more interested in the investigation. If they know each other, we should go and find out who these guys are.'

'Maybe they're just locals – they all seem quite friendly round here.'

'No; they don't look like locals to me.'

'Well, I've no doubt you'll keep an eye on Summers while we're sitting here,' said Jud.

Bex just rolled her eyes.

Chapter 17

TUESDAY, 6.10 P.M.

CRYPT, LONDON

The cold, grey body of Lars Andersen was still laid out on a slab in lab twelve. Luc and Grace were now seated at the computer a few feet away. They'd spent the last hour and a half researching different historic alphabets and symbols, determined to find something that resembled any of the markings across the dead man's chest and on the fragment of stone they'd seen in the picture provided by Bonati. Too much time spent staring at the wretched expression on the man's face had filled them both with pity, which had then turned into determination to find out who – or what – had done this to him. And that meant cracking the code that had been so brutally etched into his skin.

And now they'd had a breakthrough. The system of lettering they'd found which matched the markings most closely was the mystical Norse alphabet of runes, used in Northern Europe more than fifteen hundred years ago. At last, they'd found symbols which resembled the ones here. And they'd even found meanings too.

The ᚨ was believed to represent the 'wisdom of Odin'.

'So who's Odin?' said Luc.

'King of the Norse gods,' said Grace. 'Worshipped by many in

Northern Europe, including the Vikings, no less.'

'The *Vikings?*' said Luc. 'But didn't they invade East Anglia?'

'Yes, I think so. And Northumberland.'

'Coincidence?' said Luc.

'Unlikely. I don't believe in coincidences,' said Grace. 'There's a reason for everything. We just don't know it yet.'

They continued their research and found meanings for the other two symbols: the 🅂 was believed to mean 'guidance for sailors' and the 🅃 meant 'bravery and success in war'.

'So we've got three symbols here, all of which seem to be more than just letters; they're symbolic,' said Luc.

'Good luck charms, you mean?'

'Could be. And they appear on the piece of stone too, which was dredged up from the bottom of the sea.'

'But that doesn't explain at all why the same symbols were carved on to a man's chest, twelve hundred years later, does it?' said Grace.

'No. So what does it tell us?' said Luc. 'Let's think logically.'

'You're beginning to sound like the professor. He loves his logic.'

'Yes, but look at it this way: a piece of stone carrying symbols used by Vikings centuries ago – maybe even the same Vikings who invaded Britain – has been found in the same place they first invaded, and then, moments after it was found at the bottom of the sea, a body is found on the beach with the very same symbols etched across it.'

They looked at each other in silence for a moment, then stared at the corpse. Luc got up and examined the letters again. They were exactly as they appeared on the stone and on the computer screen in front of them.

'So who did this?'

'Someone with an obsession for all things Viking – maybe an allegiance to Odin, even?' said Grace.

'So you think it's some maniac who thinks he's a Viking?'

'Well,' said Grace, 'if it wasn't, then who or what the hell was it? The alternative isn't exactly comforting, is it? I mean, think about it.'

'The ghost of a Viking, back from the dead?'

Grace nodded, an ominous expression on her face. 'If the stone had not been disturbed on the ocean bed, would this ever have happened? That's the question.'

'So there's a connection between the stone and the attack. Someone – or something, maybe – is unhappy that the stone was disturbed.'

'And, if that's the case,' said Grace, staring at the face of Lars Andersen, 'just what lies down there, under the sea?'

CHAPTER 18

TUESDAY, 7.23 P.M.

WALBERSWICK, SUFFOLK

The Chadwicks were enjoying a warming lamb stew in front of the open fire. Clive had completed his daily ritual of sweeping out the hearth (causing ashes to blow around the small snug, as usual, much to the irritation of Bett) and had built a decent fire. He always began with a couple of firelighters, followed by a small mound of dry kindling, then a generous pile of coals. One match was all it ever took, provided he was fast. Half an hour later, he'd placed two good-sized logs on to the burning coals and that was enough. The soles of their slippers were warming nicely as they sat, trays on laps, mopping up the last remains of gravy with some crusty bread.

'Good stew, Bett,' said Clive.

'Not bad. Needed more salt.'

'Aw, no. Mustn't have too much salt, Bett. Bad fer yer.'

'Hmm. Pudding?'

Clive's face lit up. 'You've made a puddin' too?'

'Apple crumble.'

'You're a good'un, Mrs Chadwick. Every sailor's fancy.'

His wife smiled wryly as she picked up his plate, stacked it on hers and trundled out to the small kitchen at the back of the house. Clive could hear her humming something pretty as she went.

He sat back in his armchair and continued gawping at the television. It was a documentary about seabirds on the Channel Islands. Perfect. Footage of a long, blustery beach came into view and Clive was reminded of his bracing walk that morning.

He decided to get up and have another look at that skull he'd found on the beach. He'd placed it on top of the cabinet in the front room – that space so many elderly people reserve for 'special occasions'. They seldom went in there, despite living in a small house with only a kitchen and a snug for alternatives.

As he got up, he could hear the kettle boiling at the back of the house – Bett was preparing a cuppa for them both. Lovely.

His soft slippers padded across the thick carpet, across the tiled hallway and into the front room.

It was dim inside, save for the light from the hall that spilled across the room, and the faint orangey glow from a street lamp down the road. The distant squawks of seabirds and the excited chatter of a keen ornithologist drifted through the wall from the television in the snug, still turned up loud. Bett was humming again in the kitchen, punctuating each trill of hums with a 'la-la-la.' There was the clash of crockery and the clink and scrape of a teaspoon in a cup.

Clive approached the cabinet in the corner and gently raised his hands up towards the skull.

Over in the kitchen, Bett suddenly heard a crash and then a heavy thud, which caused her to drop her tray of cups and saucers and dishes of apple crumble.

'Clive?'

She left everything in the kitchen, staggered quickly down the hall and stood at the doorway to the front room. Clive was on the floor, lying at a strange angle, where he must have fallen. His legs were splayed out awkwardly beneath two spindly dining-room chairs and his chest and head were squeezed down between them.

There were finger marks across the polished dining table top, where he must have grabbed it before sinking to the floor.

And at the other side of the room, still perched on top of the cabinet was the skull.

It had swollen to twice its original size. There was some strange gaseous plasma surrounding it. Its eye sockets were no longer black – they were glowing red, radiating a demonic glow that lit up an otherwise dim corner.

Bett screamed – a piercing screech that filled the room and penetrated through the walls of the terraced house. She wanted to flee the place but she couldn't leave her beloved Clive.

'Darlin'?' She knelt down. 'Can you hear me? Clive! Oh, God!'

No response.

She felt for a pulse.

After a few terrifying seconds, there was a faint tapping at her fingertips as she pressed them further into Clive's wrist. There was life in him – just.

He opened his eyes momentarily.

'Clive?' she whispered.

He put a hand to his chest. 'It's my– ouch. Oh, God, Bett. I can't . . .'

'Don't speak! Don't say anything. Just rest. I'll fetch an ambulance. Stay with me, love. Stay.'

She got up quickly, large tears forming globules in her eyes as she sniffed away the fear. The giant skull in the corner was still swelling. It was beyond the size of a basketball now – its eyes penetrating into the little room like search lights. The swirling gas that enveloped it had swelled too, drifting into the room like a toxic spray.

Bett guessed it must have been the shock of the skull that took Clive by surprise. But it wouldn't take him. No way. She wasn't going to let some old, washed-up relic claim her husband so easily. They were fighters.

Before she went for the phone in the hallway, she turned to

face the skull. Bravely, she raised her hands up towards it – it belonged outside, she thought, by the rubbish. But the red light from the sockets was blinding as radiation poured into the room. The skull was highly charged now, almost fizzing with power.

She clasped her hands either side of the swelling mass and lifted it off the cabinet.

She closed her eyes to protect them, but through her thin eyelids she could tell the light was dimming. She opened them again and shrieked in horror as she found herself face to face with real eyes – staring into her. The sockets and jawline and nose were still skeletal, but the eyes were as real as her own – pearly white with red rings around them, like the watery eyes of an old man with a cold.

Without a moment's thought she hurled the skull across the room. It struck the wall and splintered into a thousand pieces that ricocheted everywhere like shrapnel. She even felt a shard of bone pierce her arm, but ignored it.

She grabbed the phone and pressed 999. It took a few seconds for her to catch her breath enough to tell the operator where she lived.

On the floor in the front room, showered in splinters from the broken skull that had caused the shock to his heart just moments ago, her beloved Clive breathed his final breath.

CHAPTER 19

TUESDAY, 8.19 P.M.

STAR INN, DUNWICH

Dan Summers' day was improving by the minute, but then he always did enjoy the company of women. He'd delighted in meeting and talking to Bex in the bar, and winding up her moody-looking friend, and now here he was talking to yet another attractive female. She called herself Heidi. It turned out he had a lot in common with her. She was a diver too, he'd soon discovered. And he couldn't deny it: she was seriously attractive.

To have found such a kindred spirit here in this little town might have seemed odd – more than a coincidence, perhaps, but Dan wasn't thinking rationally. He was a sucker for good looks and she had it all. He was even happier to discover that the guy who sat next to her, whom he had first thought was her boyfriend, was actually her brother, who she'd introduced as Frederik. Perfect.

When 'Heidi' and 'Frederik' had told him they were taking their boat out that night for a dive, Dan had jumped right into their trap.

And now, here they were, strolling down the beach towards Møller's boat. It had taken only a short while to visit Dan's boat first and collect his belongings. His new friends had expressed concern about the burglary when he'd told them about it. 'You must feel awful,' Heidi had said sympathetically, when she'd seen the mess.

Dan had managed to salvage a spare wetsuit, and another mask, both of which the intruder had missed. The aqualungs he'd brought with him had disappeared, of course, but his new friends had kindly said he could borrow a spare set.

Although it was dark and cold, the weather had eased somewhat and the rain had stopped. It was decent diving conditions. The sea looked calmer than before and Dan was keen to get out there once again, doing what he loved best. To share the expedition with such an attractive diving partner had been an offer too good to resist. If her brother wanted to come too, so be it. The more the merrier.

'So, is this the stretch of beach that was closed off today?' said Heidi.

Dan nodded. 'Pretty much, yeah. It's been a weird day, I can tell you. I'll be glad to get out on the water again – away from this wretched beach.'

His new friends could see he didn't want to talk about it. They'd already tried to chat about the incident back at the hotel, when they'd first met Dan, but it was obvious he had had enough of the whole affair. His eyes had glazed over and he'd changed the subject whenever they'd brought it up. The man who called himself Frederik had kept trying to probe him further, despite the glares from the girl, but to no avail.

'At least it's all over now,' he said.

'Well, it's certainly all over for the victim,' said Dan, as he strolled over the pebbles, remembering with horror his first sight of the body, so badly mutilated.

'Yes, of course. I'm sorry.'

'So, is this your first time over here, Heidi?' Dan said as they continued along the undulating beach, towards the jetty up ahead and the faint glowing light of a boat, bobbing up and down gently on the water.

'Yes,' she said. 'My brother, Frederik, and I have only been diving for a couple of years, you see. We've travelled to England before, of course, several times, but never to dive, and never by boat. It was a great trip over here, wasn't it, Frederik? I tell you, I've been so looking forward to it all! You can show me where all the best dives are. It's so lucky we met you.'

Dan smiled. 'Is Frederik coming too?'

'No, I'll stay on the boat,' he said. 'I'm not as keen as my sister on this diving malarkey. I get a bit claustrophobic, you see. I'll manage things at the surface. We're a good team, aren't we, Heidi?'

'Yes. Of course. But I think you should come, Freddie. Go on.' She gave him a knowing glance, which suggested it wasn't up for negotiation.

'No, I'm fine.' He was wondering what the hell she was playing at now. This wasn't what they'd planned. They'd discussed this in detail on the trip over from Stansted. Møller was going to man the boat while Yolanda dived with Summers. Perhaps she'd got nervous or something?

'You don't need a chaperone! You're safe with me!' laughed Dan, and then promptly wished he hadn't said it.

'Go on, Freddie; come with us, please. You'll get better at it, and more confident, too, the more you practise. Come with us, won't you?' She was glaring at him, now, with a forceful, persuasive look in her eyes. 'The boat will be fine. We can anchor it and the sea's calming now.'

'Very well,' said Møller, taking the hint. She'd obviously got cold feet and didn't want to dive alone with this guy. 'I'll join you.'

Dan had been taken in by Heidi's good looks, it was true, but he had an ulterior motive for agreeing to come on the dive in the first place. He'd already decided, if there were going to be other divers in this area, it was better to work with them – and closely too – so that he could divert them away from the patch of seabed he'd found for himself: the place that would herald more coins and stones and who knew what else, in time. He would never lead them there, of that he was certain. The coastline stretched for miles and there were plenty of other places to explore. He'd soon find a good decoy to distract his new friends.

Sneaking out of the hotel had been more straightforward than he'd expected. Khan had placed a police officer in the lounge and another in the bar area. He had told the hotel manager to keep him informed of Dan's whereabouts.

But what the DCI's officers had not done was double-check the rear of the building, where an old, rusty staircase wound its way up to the top floor, where Dan's room was. Escaping had been easy.

Dan had decided his new friends did not need to know he was under suspicion for anything. He just agreed, casually, to meet them in the car park. He'd got there early so they hadn't seen him sneak out of the building and stand strategically behind a tall vehicle while he waited for them. He was wearing a hoodie, with the hood pulled up over his head. No one asked any questions.

Now they approached a gleaming new boat, moored alongside a jetty that looked smaller than the one Dan had used, but no less secure.

'Wow, nice boat,' said Dan. 'Pretty good for a beginner, eh?'

Yolanda smiled. 'Yes, I'm glad you like it. Our father is very generous, let's say.'

Dan had thought she might have come from wealthy stock and this confirmed it for him. There was something about her – like she'd had a privileged childhood and an expensive education. Her manners and actions were controlled, reserved. Classy lady, he thought.

'Your father must trust you,' said Dan. 'I don't think my dad would have bought me one of these, even if he could have afforded it.'

'Well, I guess we're lucky,' said Møller. 'Father likes us to have hobbies, doesn't he, Heidi?'

'It keeps me out of the discos and the bars – where men are, that's why!' said Yolanda, smiling cheekily in Dan's direction. She was enjoying the role play. It was becoming quite fun. 'My father's always been pretty protective of me,' she said, flirtatiously.

'I'll look after you,' Dan said, just as she'd hoped.

Yolanda smiled sweetly at him as she climbed on to the deck of their boat. Standing on the jetty, Møller was looking nervous.

CHAPTER 20

TUESDAY, 8.31 P.M.

STAR INN, DUNWICH

'So you reckon they're runes?' said Jud.

'Yes,' said Luc. 'No question. They match the symbols on the man's chest perfectly – and on that stone in the picture you sent us. They're letters from an alphabet used in Northern Europe, centuries ago.'

'That's a coincidence,' said Jud.

'What? Why?' said Luc on the end of the phone line.

'Because the coin Summers found originates from Northern Europe too. Holland, in fact. Around the ninth century. Were they using these runes then?'

'It's quite possible, yes,' said Luc. 'So there's a connection. Where exactly is the coin from?'

'Well, I reckon it's from this place called Dorestad. It's near Utrecht. It was a giant trading centre and was raided by the Vikings lots of times.'

'Did you say "Vikings"?'

'Yeah, why?'

'Because these runic letters were often used by Vikings,' said Luc. 'They weren't just a language, either – they had a spiritual significance. Like lucky charms.'

'So, what do they mean?' said Jud.

'One links back to Odin, the Norse god. It's supposed to bring his wisdom. The second means "guidance for sailors".'

'Don't tell me,' said Jud, 'sailors to Britain?'

'It's possible.'

'And the third symbol?'

'It symbolises bravery and success in war,' said Luc. 'The Vikings held strong beliefs in these things – and they worshipped Odin.'

'The same Vikings who raided Dorestad and took all its money.'

'Why Dorestad?' said Luc.

'It had its own mint. It was a prosperous place.'

'So much of the money the Vikings had would have originated from there,' said Luc. 'Jud, this is huge. That Dan Summers guy might have stumbled across a Viking hoard.'

'I think he's done more than that,' said Jud. 'He's disturbed something. This place is weird, I tell you.'

'But there's more,' said Luc. 'Grace has discovered something about the injuries on the body.'

'Go on.'

'The photos you sent showed the lungs had been ripped out, is that right?'

'Yeah,' said Jud. 'It wasn't pretty.'

'Then we're definitely on to something. Grace found out that this kind of thing was sometimes done as a Viking ritual killing.'

'What?'

'Yep. It was a Viking form of torture. It's called blood eagling.'

'You've done well, Luc. There's too much here to be more than coincidence. There're Viking spirits at work – vengeful ones, by the looks of it. This man on the beach—'

'Lars Andersen,' said Luc.

'Yes, this Andersen was killed by ghosts for a reason.'

'Did they think it was Andersen who'd been diving? My guess

is they thought it was him who'd disturbed the graves.'

'No, wait a minute,' said Jud. 'The graves under the sea are from nineteenth-century Dunwich. They're not Viking.'

'But we know, don't we, that the Vikings raided England in the ninth century and East Anglia was one of the first places they came.'

'My God,' said Jud, 'so there could be the remains of a ship under the water? Is that what you're saying? So this has nothing to do with the remains of Dunwich village?'

'It's possible,' said Luc. 'And maybe this Summers guy has disturbed the ship's remains. Stirring up the spirits.'

'Well, they certainly wouldn't thank him for it.' Jud looked at his watch. 'Luc, I've gotta go. I'm supposed to be meeting Bex now. We're going back for a search of the beach. You've done well. *Really* well.'

'Thanks,' said Luc. 'You be careful, yeah?'

'Yeah, yeah,' said Jud, jokingly, though it felt good to have someone who actually cared back at the CRYPT. 'I'll speak to you later. Will you thank Grace for me? You've done great.'

Jud placed the phone back on the receiver, still smiling at Luc's concern. They'd become quite inseparable these days – really good friends. They were like a couple of mischievous school kids sometimes, sat at the back of the lecture rooms, pretending to be rebellious, but everyone knew Jud and Luc were two of the sharpest, most talented members of the agency.

There was no doubt Luc was like the brother Jud never had. And yet even he knew nothing about Jud's past. Jud had had to lie even to his best friend. Whenever they strayed on to the subject of home life – which was rare, as Jud made sure it hardly ever came up – he just said his mother died when he was young (true) and his father was an American (true) who lived in New York and rarely saw anything of him (not quite true). He didn't have to lie about being an only child and he didn't have to lie about being at boarding school, though he did lie about which school. Jud always managed to steer the conversation either away from 'boring old family life' or at least on to Luc's history, which was far more fascinating.

Luc Dubois' parents owned a huge and lucrative vineyard in France. They'd emigrated there from Africa many years before. Luc wouldn't say much about what they were doing in Africa, or why his parents chose to leave, but rumours abounded around the CRYPT that his family had royal connections and had had to flee the continent due to some military coup in their country. Luc wouldn't tell anyone what really happened – not even Jud – so at least they were even on that score; they both had secrets from one another. Perhaps that was why they got on so well.

But where Jud was rugged and hot tempered at times, Luc was cool and composed. He never lost his temper – except whilst playing dual games on the Xbox with Jud. But everyone lost their temper then, so that didn't count.

They made a great team. Jud wondered how they'd managed to stay such close friends even after Bex had arrived on the scene. He'd spent much more time with her than he had with Luc lately, but it hadn't affected their friendship. Maybe Bex deserved some credit there? She'd always got on really well with Luc. She never opposed him or made Jud choose between them like some girlfriends might.

Girlfriends?

He stopped himself. What was he saying?

Whatever she was, she was dear to him. No denying that. And the scene she'd witnessed in the SPA room was unfortunate. She should never have seen that.

As he gazed out of the small bedroom window at the dark clouds outside, for the first time Jud found himself wondering what the consequences would be if he just told her everything. If he offloaded the whole bloody saga – the castle, the night his mother died, the trial in court, the guilty charge and the spell in jail.

They were supposed to be going for a walk tonight – in fact, he was late. It would be the perfect time; away from everyone in London, no one around, just the two of them. He could tell her anything. Maybe everything. Who cared what the consequences were? She wouldn't tell anyone – especially not his father. He could trust her. *Couldn't he?*

But what the hell would his father say if he ever found out Jud had gone and revealed his identity?

And yet there was something about Bex that said *trust me*. Maybe he really would tell her. Maybe tonight.

He grabbed his coat from a chair beside the bed and moved towards the door, his mind whirring with scenarios of what Bex might say, what she might do, if she knew the whole truth about him.

The phone rang as Jud opened the door to leave. He shut it quickly behind him and, before he picked up, whispered to himself, 'Talk of the devil. I'm coming, I'm coming.' He and Bex had arranged to meet in the lobby at eight o'clock and he was running late now. They'd decided a walk along the beach before dinner would do them good. They wanted to get a better feel for the place, now that the crowds of onlookers and police officers and paramedics had all left. Each of them had certainly felt the atmosphere since arriving; it was dark and ominous. And it wasn't just the presence of the body when they'd first arrived that had caused them to feel it. There was a morose feel to this place – a melancholy. With so many remains lying under the ocean, just metres out to sea, there was no wonder there was a residue of emotion that washed over the place like the tide. Locals had been telling them ever since they'd arrived in Dunwich how it was common to find human remains among the pebbles, from the graves now fallen into the sea. But there was an intensity to the atmosphere, which neither Jud nor Bex believed was usual. It was too highly charged. Their sixth senses had been running on overdrive since leaving the helicopter that afternoon.

And desperately they wanted to learn more. An evening's stroll up and down the beach seemed sensible. Knowing what Jud knew now, he felt even more excited to get out there and see if they could spot some Viking ghosts.

'Yes, I know I'm late. I'm coming,' he said, on picking up the receiver. There was no doubt it was going to be Bex.

But there was a slight pause and then a voice said, 'Jud, it's me, Khan. What are you talking about?'

'Oh . . . I'm sorry, Chief Inspector. I thought you were Bex.'

'Yes, she's here with me. We're downstairs.'

'Tell her, I'm coming,' said Jud. 'I know I'm late.'

'No. You wait there. We'll come up to your room.'

'What? Why?'

'Tell you when we get there.'

Jud put the phone down and waited over by the window. He pulled the net curtain to one side and stared out at the gloom. The rain had stopped and the wind had calmed a little, but there was still an eeriness outside. He could see over the village road and the car park in the distance to the beach beyond. He watched the waves as they stormed up the beach. There was only a half moon tonight, but it was enough to catch the tops of the waves and cause them to twinkle.

Jud rested his head on the cold windowpane and fixed his stare on the waves. What lay beneath? What evil had been disturbed down there? Did this fool, Summers, really know what he'd gone and started?

The window was beginning to steam up with Jud's breath. He felt lonely again. And now Khan was here, gone were his chances to talk openly to Bex. Would he ever be able to shift this heavy burden weighing him down?

His mind drifted back to that night again, in the castle. He remembered staring out of the window then too. He'd been in his room for most of the night, just staring out at the gloom, after he and his mother had had another row. It had been a bad one.

He could still hear his mother's shouts and see the disappointment in her face. He couldn't remember what he'd done that night – probably just been cheeky as usual. But he remembered the feeling of loneliness, staring out of that window in the castle tower.

And then what followed on the roof above . . . It was too painful to contemplate again. Not tonight. Not here.

But he couldn't stop it: the image of the tower, the pelting rain in his face, the brutal tugging at his heart and the sickly feeling in the pit of his stomach.

Why had he tried to recreate that all over again in the SPA room? *Why?* Had he not endured enough already? He was just beginning to find some kind of sanity these days – after years of pain. But he *had* to know what happened that fateful night at the castle. That's why he'd simulated it – as best he could. And he would do again. He resolved, as soon as he was back at the CRYPT, he would get into that SPA room and repeat the same simulation. There was something he'd missed that night. Something he hadn't heard or hadn't seen properly. Some clue as to who – or what – had robbed him so cruelly of his mother.

But why did Bex and Bonati have to come barging in? He could have done without that. Why couldn't they have left him alone in his private nightmare?

A sharp knock on the door saved him from the self-destructive thoughts that were seeping into him again. There was something about this place that was causing them to weigh so heavily.

Khan marched in with Bex, who was looking equally as puzzled as Jud.

'What's happened?' said Jud.

'It was important to have some privacy. I didn't want to tell you down in the lobby.'

'Tell us *what?*' said Bex, impatiently.

'There's been another incident.'

'Where?' said Jud. 'Do you mean on the beach?'

'No. Further up the coast at Walberswick. In a house. A woman put a call through to the emergency services. It was her husband. By the time the ambulance arrived he was dead. Heart attack.'

'You're going to tell us something scared him, aren't you?' said Bex. She was all too familiar with the order of events that so often led up to a new investigation.

Khan nodded. 'I'm afraid so. And, believe me, this is a strange one. If this woman can be believed – and apparently the locals say she's as sane as you or I – then I shudder to think what the hell's come over this place.'

'Go on,' said Jud. He was welcoming the distraction of a new case.

Khan relayed the reports he had just received about the Chadwicks.

'We need to get over there, and quickly,' said Jud.

'There's a car outside. Let's go,' said Khan. 'Any word from the CRYPT, by the way? Anything discovered?'

'Plenty,' said Jud. 'I'll tell you both on the way.'

CHAPTER 21

TUESDAY, 9.10 P.M.

NORTH SEA, OFF THE COAST OF

DUNWICH

Jürgen Møller held firmly on to the little wooden wheel and tried to keep a straight course. The wind had picked up steadily since they'd set sail from Dunwich and the boat was now being jolted from side to side like a piece of driftwood. The lights of the village were fading into the distance to their left; on their right was nothingness – no discernible horizon, no surface, just a dark shroud of empty ocean that seemed to stretch up into the sky. There were no stars either – none was bright enough to penetrate through the thick blanket of cloud. But the salty sea air and the howling winds were compensating for the absence of any discernible sights, giving Møller something to focus on in his blindness. He would never normally have felt any kind of trepidation, even here, sailing further into blackness. He was bombproof, after all – impervious to the dark arts of fear or loneliness. But all that had changed since his strange encounter in the woods. He shuddered at the thought of the 'thing' passing through him and leaving him shivering. Whatever it had been, it had accessed a part of his mind closed until now – the part they called fear.

'How much further?' he shouted over to Summers quickly, keen to hear another person's voice. The lights of the coast were shrinking even smaller now. 'I mean, how could the village have slipped this far out, huh? We must have gone too far. Shouldn't we head back inland now? Summers?'

'No, no. We're fine,' said his guest. 'You keep a straight course. We're nearly there.'

'It's getting choppier!' said Yolanda. 'Try and keep straight, Freddie!'

Møller rolled his eyes to the sky. This stupid name of his was beginning to grate. Why the hell did she have to choose Freddie? 'Don't worry,' he said. 'Have I ever let you down . . . Heidi?'

Summers was standing close to the GPS system. He knew where he *didn't* want to go, where he wanted them to avoid – he'd memorised the coordinates – which just left anywhere else. But he needed to sound convincing when telling Frederik to put down anchor. He didn't want to rouse suspicion.

'Where would you like to start?' said Yolanda, sweetly, coming closer, so close Dan could smell her perfume.

Odd to be wearing perfume on a diving expedition, he thought. But still, it was a pleasant addition to the trip.

'Erm . . . I think we're nearly there,' he said. 'Just a few more metres and we can probably drop anchor. There are remains right up and down this coastline. You'll be amazed how far out they are. There's plenty for us to see.'

'Well, I can't wait for us to start exploring together,' said Yolanda, stroking his shoulder.

Møller kept staring straight ahead, a pensive expression on his face and a strange, ominous foreboding at the back of his mind. It didn't feel right.

Was this going to work? Or was it just another of Yolanda's crazy schemes? She'd always thought she was irresistible to men. Perhaps she was. After all, there were only two men on the boat right now: one had succumbed to her charms years ago, and the other was well on the way. But could she live on her charm forever? Would it always work? What if this Summers beach bum realised the whole thing was a scam – before they had a chance to carry out the plan?

He shook away the doubts and focused on the waters ahead. If her plan was going to work, they would soon be rid of this slimy guy, with his blond hair and his good looks. Møller had disliked him as soon as he'd met him. He'd hated the way Summers had taken to 'Heidi' so quickly – he'd made no effort to resist her unsubtle attempts to flirt with him. And, though he hated himself for it, Møller had felt a twinge of jealousy too. Masquerading as her brother 'Freddie' seemed ridiculous. Apart from their blond hair, they looked nothing like one another. How could he possibly be her brother? But Summers had only had eyes for Heidi – he'd barely noticed Freddie, who'd remained pretty quiet from the start. But then Yolanda was enjoying the role play far more than he was. In fact, she was positively loving it.

And the plan was working well so far, Møller had to admit. Their new friend hadn't twigged at all. They'd got him chatting, mostly about diving, proven how much they'd got in common with him and then Heidi invited him for a bit of late-night diving. How could anyone resist?

And he'd come like a puppy to the food bowl. It had been so easy.

And soon, in just a few more minutes, Møller would be watching them tip over the back of the boat, diving gear on, and disappear into the murky depths of the North Sea – from which only one of them would return.

Only now Yolanda wanted him to go too. Why had she bottled it, all of a sudden? he wondered. Perhaps it was seeing how physically strong this guy was. And he was tough, that was obvious. If Møller had to help her, then so be it. The main thing was to get rid of this nuisance as soon as possible. Møller was pleased Sigurdsson had sanctioned the plan. If anything, he'd been surprised when Yolanda had revealed to him what the plan of action was. But he recalled how crazy Sigurdsson had been sounding recently – obsessed with finding and seizing what lay beneath the ocean. He'd stop at nothing to get his hands on what he said belonged in the 'motherland' – even murder.

Møller began rehearsing in his mind how he would impart the good news to his employer when the mission was complete. The Summers worm was gone – dead and buried, once and for all. Lying at the bottom of the ocean, among the forgotten graves of Dunwich. And then the path would be clear for them to carry on with the search. Sigurdsson would be pleased.

Maybe a cash bonus would be in order? It was about time he changed his car and there was a nice Audi RS 5 Coupe he'd seen before leaving for England. Soon it would be his.

'This'll do nicely,' Summers shouted and Møller turned off the engine. This was it then. He began to think how he and Yolanda might celebrate once they'd returned from the depths without Summers.

A few drinks and then – who knows? It could be a good night after all.

CHAPTER 22

TUESDAY, 9.27 P.M.

WALBERSWICK, SUFFOLK

Elizabeth Chadwick looked terrible. The body of her husband still lay in the front room. Khan had insisted that no one should move it until he and the agents arrived. Now she perched on the edge of the floral sofa, a teacup and saucer held precariously in her hand, the teaspoon clinking against the porcelain cup as her hand trembled.

'Drink your tea, Mrs Chadwick,' said the policewoman seated next to her. 'It'll do you good. And you really must eat. You've had such a shock. We don't want you to faint again, do we?'

Bex raised her eyebrows at the police officer, as if to say, *You're right there.* 'So tell me, Mrs Chadwick – and I know it's going to be very hard for you – but how exactly did it all begin?' said Bex. 'You mentioned something about hearing a thud when you were in the kitchen, yes?'

Mrs Chadwick looked up at Bex and Jud, seated on the matching sofa across the room from her. Her eyes were so tired from crying they looked red and puffy. Her bottom lip was still quivering, just like the teacup. Sammy was curled around her feet, resting his head on one of her fluffy slippers, all too aware that she was distraught, but not altogether sure why.

'Yes, dear,' she said. 'I'd only gone out to make us some tea and bring in the pudding. It was his favourite. I'd done a crumble.' She began sobbing again. They waited in silence. Khan was still standing at the window.

A few more minutes and it was clear their hostess was far too distraught to provide any answers yet. They were wasting time.

'Mind if we go next door and conduct an examination of the scene, Mrs Chadwick?'

She nodded her head slowly. 'Of course. But I don't want to go in there. I don't. I mean, I can't. I just—'

'Don't worry yourself, Mrs Chadwick,' said the policewoman. 'You and I can stay right here. We don't have to go in at all. Just take deep breaths – and do try to finish your tea, my love.'

Khan glanced at the agents, who promptly rose and joined him outside in the hallway. 'We'll interview her later. Let's get into the room and see what's what. You brought your equipment, yes?'

'Of course,' said Jud.

Bex led the way. She slowly pushed the door open. There was a light on already in the front room. A police officer was standing near the window, staring out. It was the same man who'd opened the door to them when they'd first arrived.

'How was Mrs Chadwick, sir?' he asked Khan.

'Just as you said: distraught – as you'd expect. So what the hell's been goin' on here then, eh?' He looked around the room. The body of Clive Chadwick was still where he'd fallen, squashed between two dining chairs, with his legs lying awkwardly beneath them. Bex noticed the finger marks on the polished table top. 'He must've tried to steady himself against the table and maybe slumped down to the floor there. You can see where his fingers have slid across the top.'

'Yeah, looks like it,' said Khan. 'And what's all this stuff around him, then? I assume it's the skull she was talking about on the phone, yeah?'

Jud looked at the shards of bone splintered right across the floor, and all over Chadwick's body. 'Yes, this is it. It's completely shattered.'

There was the sound of footsteps outside the door and Mrs Chadwick slowly appeared.

'Look, love, you don't have to come in,' said Khan, gently.

'No, no. I want to. I mean, I *must*. I want you to know how it happened. Clive would want you to know.' She sniffed hard, took a rolled up tissue from beneath the sleeve of her jumper and wiped her nose again. The policewoman appeared just behind her and helped her to approach the scene.

'You don't have to come round this side, love,' said Khan.

'OK, Inspector. I think I just need to—' She went to fall and the police officer caught her. She steadied her down on to a dining chair at the other side of the table from where her husband's body lay.

Jud waited for a few seconds while Mrs Chadwick composed herself, then held a piece of broken bone up and asked, 'Is this the skull you were telling the police about? I gather you had a skull here, yes? Is this it?'

She nodded, but Jud could tell she didn't want to look at it. Not even a piece of it.

'It's evil!' she shrieked. 'I'm tellin' you. I saw its eyes. They were alive.'

'Alive?' said Bex.

'That's what I said. Real eyeballs.' Their hostess glanced at the agents and over at Khan. She knew what they were thinking. 'I'm not mad!' she shouted. 'I'm not. It's true. What do you think killed my husband? It was the shock of it. But I threw it, I did – right across the room. I threw it at that wall and it just splintered everywhere. There was a loud crack and it just shattered.'

'Clearly,' said Khan. 'We can see it's gone everywhere. So where was it before you came in? I mean, when you heard the thud and found your husband, where was it then?'

Mrs Chadwick pointed to the corner where there was a large, mahogany cabinet with glass doors. It housed some glasses, a floral tea set with a gold rim and a couple of coronation mugs. 'On there,' she said. 'Up on the top. Clive had put it there when we got home from the beach.'

'What? So you only found it today?' said Jud, quickly.

'Oh, yes. I thought I said that to the police first of all. Maybe you didn't get the message. My husband and I were out walking, like we always do. We like walks of a morning.' She began to sob at the thought that they'd had their last walk together. She'd never go out alone. She'd be a prisoner in her own home now. She sniffed hard, composed herself and tried to continue. 'And . . . And our dog too. Little Sammy. Well, he found something in the ground. He was digging and barking and, you know, burying his nose and that. He'd obviously found something. Well, Clive went up and found it was this skull, you see, buried in the sand. Quite close to the water's edge.'

Bex and Jud looked at one another.

'Was this at Dunwich?' said Bex.

'No, no. Here at Walberswick. That's the weird thing. We often find bones at Dunwich – I mean, everyone does, from when the old graveyards sank into the sea an' that, but it's unusual to find one up the coast here.'

'So you picked it up and brought it back with you?' said Khan.

Mrs Chadwick suddenly looked worried. 'Yeah, but, I mean, we weren't stealin' it, see. We were just going to give it to the museum, you know, at Dunwich. Clive was going to take it round there tomorrow. You can check with Chris Butcher down at the museum. Clive rang him as soon as we were home. We weren't stealin' it. We weren't.' She began sobbing again and sniffing so hard they thought she was going to give herself a nosebleed.

'Please, Mrs Chadwick. Stay calm,' said Khan. 'No one is accusing you of stealing anything. Not at all. You've done nothing wrong, OK?'

'Was there anything else you found on the beach today?' said Jud. 'Or anything else you noticed . . . I dunno . . . kind of strange? Anything unusual?'

Mrs Chadwick looked up from her tissue and stared wide-eyed at Jud. 'You know about the shuck, don't you love?' She was panting slightly, and Bex could see her hands were shaking again. The policewoman beside her held her hand and told her to take deep breaths again.

'The what?' said Jud, gently.

'The shuck!' said Mrs Chadwick. 'The bloody great hound on the beach. I knew it was real! Clive told me not to worry, but I knew it – I knew we shouldn't have looked at it!'

'Please, calm yourself,' said Bex, 'and tell us what you mean. You saw a dog, yes? It was a big one, was it?'

Mrs Chadwick was shaking her head frantically. 'No! No! You don't understand; it was the ghost dog. Red eyes an' all. They call it the Black Shuck. If you see it – and it looks at you – rumour has it, you'll die.' She looked towards the floor, where she knew her husband's body lay, obscured by the table. And she wailed. 'He saw it. He saw its eyes. They was red, I tell you. They was *red*!'

'What ghost?' said Jud. 'How do you mean, a ghost dog?'

It took a few seconds for Mrs Chadwick to take some deep breaths and compose herself just enough to speak. This was too important; she knew she had to keep a clear head and tell them what she saw.

'It's a legend round 'ere, you see. It's a famous ghost dog – a giant black hound, like. It's got red eyes, you know. And, if it looks at you, well, you're supposed to be cursed – folks say you'll die.' She began to sob again, consumed by an insufferable mix of grief and shock and anger.

'But why is it here?' said Bex, eager to know more but trying to sound as gentle as she could. 'I know this is difficult, Mrs Chadwick. But if you could talk some more about this dog – it may be significant. Why is it haunting this area?'

'I dunno why it's here,' replied Mrs Chadwick. 'I only know who it belongs to.'

'Who?' said Jud and Bex, almost in unison.

'It's Odin's dog. The Viking god. They say it belonged to 'im.'

Jud's eyes widened. Bex knew why. Jud had filled her in on Luc's research whilst travelling to Walberswick. He'd told her and Khan about East Anglia being one of the first places the Vikings invaded. And about the rune alphabet, too, used by the Vikings. And how one of the runes on Summers' stone meant, 'The spirit of Odin.'

And now Mrs Chadwick's words sent a chill down their spines. Someone, or something, had been disturbed under that ocean and, whatever it was, it was enveloping this stretch of the Suffolk coastline in some kind of curse. And the agents knew that, once spirits of the deceased had been disturbed, there was no telling what they would do.

CHAPTER 23

TUESDAY, 9.49 P.M.

(10.49 P.M. LOCAL TIME)

ROSKILDE, DENMARK

Agnar Sigurdsson reclined in a black leather chair near the window of his apartment, sipping a drink and staring out at the dark skies over the Baltic. It had been a trying day. The calls from England had been a nuisance, he couldn't deny, but at least it hadn't taken much to persuade Yolanda to hop on a plane and sort out Jürgen Møller. Sigurdsson knew she would be able to use her charm to effect the plan they'd hatched out together. She was tough and a fast worker. He was proud of her.

As to what had happened to Lars, well, he wouldn't lose any sleep over that. Whether he had gone into hiding or really was lying dead on a beach, no one would miss him. And the chances of the police tracing him all the way back to Sigurdsson were almost nil.

He got up from his chair and wandered over to the exquisitely made sideboard along the far wall, one of only a few pieces of furniture in the room, but of a rare quality. It was a polished cherry-wood piece, with beautifully crafted legs, several draws with ornate handles and a highly polished top, on which a large mahogany drinks tray was placed with a few well-chosen bottles on it and a crystal decanter. He poured himself another glass of mjød, a Danish mead favoured by many of his fellow Danes ever since Viking times. Sigurdsson was nothing if not patriotic. Next to the drinks tray was a small, ornate dish – the size of an ashtray and carved out of wood – filled with ancient coins. Given their age, one might have expected to see them locked up in a safe somewhere, or displayed on red velvet inside the glass cabinet of a museum, but Sigurdsson wasn't worried; he had hundreds of them. And he was soon to have a great deal more. He was excited at the prospect of receiving news of the findings from England – his latest acquisition on behalf of the motherland.

He picked up one of the coins and twirled it around in his fingertips, admiring its craftsmanship. This was a special one – different to the others in the dish – and very precious to Sigurdsson. It was the reason, after all, that his team had been sent to Suffolk.

He'd found it whilst beachcombing over there some years back. Of course, at the time it was just another holiday. He'd spent years making short trips to places synonymous with Vikings, like East Anglia and Northumberland, but it was always for such short periods of time, before he had to return to some business meeting or other. Now that he'd sold off parts of the business and delegated the running of his property empire to his directors, he was fulfilling the promise he'd made to himself when last in England – that he *would* return (or his team of bounty hunters would) to recover more of these beauties. Finally, it really was happening. Soon his loyal divers, provided they didn't get themselves killed like the useless Lars, would be calling him again with news of yet more finds. It was so exciting he could feel the blood pumping around his veins and his heart quickening just to look at this coin now. What a fine piece of craftsmanship! And how heartening it was to have it back in the motherland, where it belonged, in the safe clutches of a true Viking. It just felt right.

He picked up the glass of mjød in his other hand and returned to his chair by the window, still clasping the coin preciously in his fist. Before he sat down, he shot a satisfying glance at the cabinet on the wall behind his chair – a large, immaculate display cabinet, inside which was a selection of ancient artefacts, including hand tools, more coins and an early necklace of coloured jewels. Sigurdsson's dedication to bringing these finds home was beyond question. Since retiring, he'd spent a great deal of money funding digs and dives and expeditions of varying kinds. And, though much of what he had found had been donated to museums across Denmark, he often saved many of the better finds for his own, personal collection. His apartment was fast becoming a museum in its own right: the largest private collection of Viking antiquities in the whole of Denmark.

Sitting down, he slurped the sweet, amber liquid and let it wash around his mouth as he sat back in his chair and looked again at the old coin, now framed by the giant window behind it and the night sky beyond.

It was dark outside, save for the occasional street light. The antique lamp on the sideboard and the crystal chandelier above caused the whole room to be reflected in the dark window, mingling with the view of the ocean below. He could see mirror images of the chair he was sitting on and the cabinet behind. He felt a sense of pride to be sitting in his own museum – a shrine to his passion for archaeology.

He closed his eyes, felt the smooth mjød on his tongue and listened to the ticking of the grandfather clock across the room.

He opened his eyes slowly and smiled.

But what was that?

In the window.

How weird, he thought and got up from his chair. He pocketed the coin and, still clutching his drink, walked closer to the glass, intrigued. Was it his reflection? If it was, he needed a rest, for sure. He looked awful.

As he approached the window, he saw the face was not a mirror image of his own at all.

It was someone else's.

He spun around to look into the room behind him: no one there. He was alone – just the way he liked it. He looked back at the window again and dropped his crystal cut glass. It shattered on the unforgiving marble floor, spilling a dangerous cocktail of mead and glass shards in every direction.

Sigurdsson stood fixed to the spot like a statue and stared deeper into the gruesome reflection that was glancing back at him. It wore an angry, hateful expression, and its glare burned right through him like a blowtorch.

It was a disembodied head.

If he could have moved, he might have fled that place there and then, but he was too intrigued, transfixed. Not exactly fearful – nothing scared Sigurdsson, not even ghosts, it seemed; his senses had numbed years ago – but his curiosity meant he couldn't stop staring at the eerie image at the window. Framed by the lights of his own room, reflected in the window, the face scowled at him with giant eyes that seemed to bulge and pulsate. The edge of the face, its jaw and cheekbones and hair line, were blurred – like they were merging with the night sky somehow. Smoky and translucent at times, the lines around it were indistinct, but its eyes were as solid as his own.

And they were staring straight at Sigurdsson – through him.

Was this an hallucination?

He stared down at the spilled drink on the floor and over at the half-empty bottle on the side. Was it the mjød? A faulty batch, perhaps, that had caused him to have a strange turn and start seeing things? Had someone spiked it, even? But how could they? He'd only opened the bottle today.

Maybe he was asleep and dreaming? Had he dropped off in the chair and this was a dream? Was he actually still sitting there, snoring and dribbling?

But it didn't feel like a dream.

A sudden pain told him he wasn't dreaming – this was real.

It was a sharp stabbing in his left thigh. What the hell was that? He glanced down – nothing there. He put his hand to his thigh – it was hot, *very* hot. The pain was like a burning sensation, focused and isolated, as if someone had extinguished a cigarette on his leg.

He looked down at his trousers and saw a small red glow coming from within the pocket, like a miniature torch shining through the dark material.

He knew there was nothing but the old coin in there, but it was burning right into his leg. Quickly he placed his hand into the pocket, reached down and grabbed the coin. Its extreme heat penetrated into his hand and he shrieked with pain. He fished it out and hurled it across the room. He saw it glowing like a stray coal from the embers of a fire as it spun across the room and landed with a smouldering fizz on the cold floor. His hand was red and blistered where he'd grabbed the coin and his leg was still seething with pain.

What the hell was happening here? He still wasn't fearful – he'd often thought he was incapable of fear, was in some way deficient of that particular sensation, and now this was confirming it. But he was able to feel pain, no question about that. And the burning in his leg was making him angry now.

He looked back again at the face in the window. It was cloudier now – harder to define – but he could see its faint angry expression had altered to something which almost resembled a grin. He thumped his fist on the glass and the image distorted like oil swirling in a puddle, before settling again in the shape of a face.

Sigurdsson heard a scream. He quickly turned to his right, looking along the vast window.

The noise sounded like it had come from outside, on the balcony. He pressed his face against the window, further along from where the ghostly image was, and tried to peer around to see if anyone was standing on the neighbouring balcony.

There was a woman.

He recognised her as the American girlfriend of Ralf, his neighbour. Sigurdsson had only met her a couple of times – she didn't live with him, at least he didn't think she did – but he knew it was her. She was staring back at his own window and screaming wildly. Where the hell was Ralf? he thought. He banged on the glass and tried to attract her attention, but it was too late. She turned and fled indoors.

Sigurdsson glanced down at the pavement – a couple of people had stopped on the pavement and were looking up in the direction of the scream. Shit, he thought, this is not what he needed. His relaxing evening, drinking mead, playing with his treasured coins and staring out at the ocean, was fast becoming a nightmare.

He looked back at the window where the ghostly head had appeared – it had gone; literally vanished into thin air.

But the attention that the girl's screaming had attracted down on the street worried him. Who else had seen this weird image? The last thing he needed was a fuss – people thinking his place was haunted, prowling around, asking questions and hassling him. He lived alone for a reason: he hated other people's company. But the woman's screams had been deafening, even from inside his own apartment. God knows what the people down on the pavement must have thought. This could only lead to hassle.

Quite what the ghost thing was, or why it had haunted him in particular, puzzled rather than scared him. The girl's reaction next door had been different. Her screams would have been heard across the whole building – as well as on the streets below.

Sigurdsson walked across the room and exited, crunching over the broken glass as he went. He ran down the corridor and knocked on the front door of his neighbour's apartment. The door swung open.

Sigurdsson immediately felt the cold breeze on his face and could see the glass doors that led out on to the balcony were still wide open. The lace curtains flapped like sails in the wind. The place had been abandoned. The girl had gone.

He thumped his fist on top of the nearest armchair. 'Damn!' he said.

There was a nagging feeling in the back of his mind that somehow this would lead to something – uninvited visitors, no doubt. You can't have a girl screaming like that and not expect people to attend.

He ran out on to the balcony of the apartment and looked down.

Stupid move.

There was an even bigger swell of people gathered now, all staring up at the balcony.

At him.

He moved back quickly, out of view, but as he did so he caught a quick glimpse of the American girl running from the entrance of the apartment block, into the arms of the people on the pavement outside. She was still crying – seemed inconsolable. Those around her were looking up, and pointing in his direction.

He turned and fled, down the corridor and into his own apartment, then promptly closed and bolted the front door. This wasn't happening. Surely it was a nightmare. What the hell was unfolding here?

He stood the other side of his door and tried to collect his thoughts. He'd been seen on the same balcony from which a girl had just fled, after screaming so loud she'd attracted a huge audience – the same bloody audience who'd then looked up and seen him standing there.

Get a grip. He breathed deeply and then entered his living room, ignoring the broken glass still on the floor. He knew what he had to do before getting out. He made straight for the dish of old coins, emptied them into his pocket and walked into his bedroom, wincing at the pain still soaring in his thigh – wrong pocket to have chosen to stash the coins in.

Once in his bedroom, he made straight for the large oil painting on the wall and lowered it to the ground. A square, metal door, almost the size of the picture frame, was revealed in the wall where the painting had hung: his precious safe. He turned the dial to the left and then to the right for a few measured clicks and eventually it opened.

Inside, there were several large boxes stacked up. He pulled one out and opened the lid. It was filled with hundreds of similar coins. Quickly, he fished into his pocket for the remaining coins from the dish, feeling the sharp pain again from the mysterious burning. He emptied the coins into the metal box, replaced the lid and returned it to the safe. Although he saw it as his duty to bring these coins home to the motherland from wherever he and his team had found them, there were those who might disagree and call it something different – like theft.

He replaced the oil painting on the wall, being careful to straighten it again. Then he ran into the kitchen, grabbed a towel and a dustpan and brush and returned to the living room, where he began frantically clearing up the broken glass and the spilled drink. It had resembled the scene of a fight when he'd first re-entered the room. He knew he had to get it cleaned up – and quickly – before someone came calling, asking questions.

A few moments later, the place looked clean again. The coins were safely locked away out of sight from prying eyes, the mess was cleared up and it looked like nothing had ever happened.

He grabbed his coat and a hat too, which he knew he'd need once outside and on view, and then left the apartment, making for the back stairs instead of the main lifts that led down to the lobby.

Back inside the flat, on the marble floor, just beside a chair leg, the ancient coin that had burned him so badly still lay where he'd hurled it. In his rush to flee the place, Sigurdsson had forgotten to pick it up.

CHAPTER 24

TUESDAY, 10.47 P.M.

CRYPT, LONDON

Luc returned to his large, comfy chair with a second can of Coke from his miniature fridge, picked up the Xbox control from the floor and pressed the pause button again – the frenzied action on screen resumed: a zombie-killing fest.

He knew he should feel slightly guilty: here he was, chilling out in his iPod (the name agents used when referring to their personal rooms, on account of their modest size but the abundance of technical equipment installed in them), while Jud Lester, his Xbox partner in crime and his best buddy, was roughing it in some far-flung stretch of Suffolk without so much as a digital TV, let alone an Xbox. But he didn't. He was, after all, a teenage boy. And this was a particularly engrossing game.

The speed of his thumbs and forefingers was equalled only by the speed of his eyeballs as they darted left to right, following the rapid action on the television screen in front of him. He was a master at this game – even better than Jud at times, which was no mean boast; Jud was the resident king of Xboxing.

The research Luc and Grace had carried out into the incidents at Dunwich had been intriguing and had whetted Luc's appetite for diving again. He was jealous of his friend having the opportunity to dive. He'd enjoyed the sport many times before and had been part of a diving club at his school in France. There was something magical about being under the water; it was like entering an alien world. He'd asked Bonati if he could go and help but was told that two agents was enough for now. If the incident got any bigger then he would be the first to be sent, unless he'd been assigned another mission by then, of course, which was likely.

At any one time the CRYPT might have a dozen separate investigations on the go, with two agents assigned to every case. Ten new recruits were taken on each year and agents were expected to stay at the CRYPT for three years in total. After then it was hoped that they would be moved discretely into a job with either MI5 or MI6, or perhaps up at GCHQ – the Government Communications Headquarters, housed in the famous top-security base near Cheltenham. There were also some possible openings available in research work with various university science faculties. But the CRYPT was still relatively new and no one had yet made that giant step from the agency back into Civvy Street.

Luc's last investigation had seen him and Grace, with whom he was usually partnered, camped out in a giant hangar over at Northolt Airport, where they had gone to investigate the particularly violent ghost of a pilot who'd lost his life in a freak accident on the ground some ten years before. He was not going to leave the airport alone and, not only were passengers getting frightened, but airport staff were refusing to enter the hangar at night.

Luc and Grace had received a special commendation from Professor Bonati for the way they had communicated with the ghost, locked down its strength with the EM neutraliser, and reasoned with it to leave the place alone. It had been a highly successful exorcism, so far.

And now he was allowed at least twenty-four hours R and R.

Most agents, especially the newly recruited zombies, thought that meant 'rest and recreation', but Luc knew very well it often was interpreted by Bonati as 'researching and reviewing' a case. And so he'd found himself in a room with the mutilated body from Dunwich.

Now he was staring at yet more mutilated bodies, only this time they were virtual. His fingers continued to dance rapidly across the sleek, black, wireless controller and his eyes performed a corresponding dance across the screen a few feet away.

CRYPT iPods were snug rooms, fitted out in black and shiny silver, and equipped with every kind of technology, from gaming to music to online surfing to communications. Their name was apt; it really was like living and sleeping inside a giant iPod where every facility was an app.

The noise of gun blasts and engines and cries that blurted from the Xbox and filled the room was suddenly accompanied by the shrill ring of Luc's internal phone.

'Yes?' he said quickly, still intent on finishing this level on his game – he'd never reached this far before.

'It's Bonati. What's that noise? Are you gaming or something? Turn the damn thing off, will you?'

'I'm sorry, sir.' Luc pressed pause – there was no way he was going to lose the progress he'd made so far. 'How can I help?'

'My room; five minutes.'

Bonati ended the call without giving Luc a chance to reply, but then it wasn't a question, after all. It was an order.

Luc cursed him for his untimely interruption. He was so nearly at the end of this stage. He decided to keep the game on pause. Hopefully, he'd be back soon.

He placed the controller carefully on the chair, thrust his sweaty socks into his trainers and rocked them from side to side until his feet were safely inside. The backs of the shoes had almost completely collapsed after so many previous attempts to put them on without bothering with the laces; too much effort to bend, after all.

A few minutes later, he was outside Bonati's office. He heard footsteps in the corridor behind him and turned to see Grace.

'You were called too, huh?'

She nodded. 'Do you know what it's about?'

'No idea.' He pressed the red button and waited. The door slid open and they entered.

'Thank you for coming in,' said Bonati.

Luc and Grace were startled by the other person in the room. They'd not been expecting to see him. 'Hey, guys,' said Jason Goode. 'How's it going?'

'Well, thank you, Mr Goode,' said Luc.

'Yes, I'm fine, thanks, Mr Goode,' said Grace.

Bonati rose from the cherry-wood table where his friend and colleague was sitting and beckoned the agents to come and join them.

They looked nervous as they sat down. Why was Goode here? To have been summoned to the professor's office was not unusual – it's how most cases first began – but to see the man behind the entire CRYPT agency, the owner of Goode Technology PLC, was too much of a surprise to hide. The agents' immediate thoughts were there was something wrong: they were in trouble – serious trouble.

Bonati caught their nervous glances at one another and quickly put their minds at rest.

'Sit down, don't worry,' he began. 'I've not called you here because you're in trouble. I'm sure that's what you think.' He smiled at Goode.

'It's me, ain't it, Giles? Why do people think it's serious when I'm in town, huh? I mean, I'm allowed to drop by every now and again, ain't I?'

'Of course, of course,' said the professor. 'I'm sure Luc and Grace are as pleased to see you as I am. Aren't you?'

They nodded enthusiastically.

'But I think you should come clean, Jason,' said Bonati. 'There is another reason why you're here.'

Luc swallowed hard. This didn't feel right.

'Yes, thank you, Prof. There is indeed.' Goode rose from his chair. Just like his long-time friend, Bonati, Jason Goode liked to pace the floor when he had something important to say. He wandered to the window and then turned sharply to face the gathered group at the table. 'You see, I have this friend, right. She's called Cally.'

'Oh, yes?' said Grace, smiling and listening intently. She and Luc were beginning to feel more relaxed now, privileged even to have this private audience with the legendary millionaire. Their friends would be jealous.

'Yeah, sure. She's a great girl. She works for my company, you see – Goode Technology. She runs my North European branch. She's spends a lot of time in Copenhagen.'

'In Denmark,' said Grace.

Oh, well done, thought Luc – so you know your geography.

'That's right, Gracey. Well, she's in trouble, you see. I don't mean she's injured. Nothing like that. Only she's had a shock. She's seen a ghost.'

Luc and Grace were intrigued. Their faces suddenly wore curious expressions as they sat up and shuffled in their seats. This was getting interesting.

'She was visiting her boyfriend, apparently. I mean, I don't have the exact details, but she was staying in some apartment or other, just outside Copenhagen, in a place called Roskilde. Do you know it?'

They all shook their heads.

'Well, my girl, Cally, claims she saw a ghostly figure hovering outside a window. It wasn't her window – it was the apartment next to hers. On the fourth floor apparently.'

'The fourth?' said Luc, puzzled.

'Yeah, exactly,' said Goode. 'It was just floating there.'

'Must have given her a shock,' said Grace.

'I'm sure. But the thing is, she says it's not the first time she's seen something like this. She reckons the flat next to her boyfriend's is really haunted.'

Luc and Grace knew that a haunting like this was anything but unusual. There were reports like this all over the place. But they knew there was no point in asking why CRYPT was involved. It may have been Denmark, but this was a friend and employee of Mr Goode they were talking about here. There was no doubt they were going to be asked to help. And with Jud and Bex, known to be the best agents in the place, away in Suffolk, they felt flattered to be asked.

'So she doesn't live there, then?' said Grace.

'No, she lives in the States, where she works for my company. She's a good girl, Cally – one of my best. But her boyfriend works in Copenhagen and so she stays with him whenever she can. That's how she knows the place next door to his is haunted, apparently.'

'And you'd like us to go check it out, Mr Goode?' Luc said eagerly.

'Sure I would. I knew you'd wanna help Cally,' he said. 'She's a good employee, you know. The very best. I don't want her in bad shape. She's refusing to go back to that building. Which is bad news for her boyfriend, as you can imagine. Which is bad news for her, which – ultimately – is bad news for me. You see, I don't want her to be unhappy – she's got an important job to do for me. It's vital she gets time to relax.'

'So, what about the owner of the apartment next door to her boyfriend's?' said Bonati. 'What does he say about all this?'

'Well, you know, that's the really strange thing, right. Apparently, she saw him – I mean, they all saw him – in her boyfriend's flat.'

'In her boyfriend's flat? Who did? You said, "they all saw him".'

'The people down on the pavement,' said Goode.

Bonati rolled his eyes and shot a concerned look at the agents across the table. 'So this story is already leaking out, yes? Other people saw the ghost, I assume. And, in any case, why was the neighbour in the flat next door? I don't understand.'

'Like I say, I don't have all the details. Poor Cally was quite upset when I spoke to her on the phone. She said the people down on the ground, the ones who heard her scream from her balcony, told her later that, when they looked up, they saw a man on the balcony where she'd been standing just moments earlier. And someone said they recognised him as the guy from next door, see? His name's Sigurdsson. Some kind of reclusive billionaire, or something.'

'And where is he now?' said Grace.

'I don't know. I've had a very quick call with the police – you know, tried to make some preliminary enquiries – and they've said he's disappeared. He's not in his apartment.'

'So this ghost,' said Luc, 'it was there one moment and then vanished, yes?'

Goode stopped his pacing and came to sit down on the remaining chair at the table. 'Look, I don't really know any more than that, guys. Which is why we've called you in. It's over to you now. I want you to travel there, meet Cally and her boyfriend, let her know we're taking her story seriously, you know. Give her the works. Find out all you can and then get round to this apartment and see what you can find.'

'Can we get access to the flat next door? The haunted one?'

'Sure you can! I have friends. I've already cleared it with MI5, who have cleared it with their friends in Denmark. It helps when you know people.'

Goode wasn't a global billionaire businessman for nothing, Luc thought. It sure helped to be on his side; Luc shuddered at the thought of being his enemy. Goode knew everyone, everywhere.

'Where's the boyfriend?' said Grace. 'I take it he was out at the time when it happened, yes?'

'I guess so,' said Goode. 'He was working late. He's with Cally now, but not in his flat. He's in Copenhagen with Cally. That's where they're waiting for you.'

'And were there other eyewitnesses?' asked Luc. 'I mean, did anyone else see this ghost hovering up at the window? The people on the pavement – why were they there at the time? Or did they arrive afterwards?'

'They heard Cally screaming out on the balcony and they looked up. Some of them must've seen what scared her. Who knows? It could be all round Denmark by now,' said Goode.

'OK. Well, we need to get a story out to the press quickly and try to stop any rumours spreading about a ghost,' said Grace. She knew how investigations usually worked. It was often a case of thinking up some elaborate cover up – maybe a prank, a guy in a mask, or a projection, or a trick of the light. They'd be able to think of something.

'It might be too late for that, I'm afraid,' said Goode, shaking his head. 'Cally says it's already been on the radio. I dunno, perhaps one of the people down on the pavement took a shot of it and called up a radio station. Whatever. But there's a story out there now.'

'But I don't understand why this neighbour guy, Sigurdsson – the one whose flat is supposed to be haunted – has disappeared,' said Grace. 'And why did he go into Cally's flat in the first place?'

'I agree,' said Luc. 'And what does he know about this ghost at the window? Why didn't he report it himself? Who is he?'

'Well,' said the professor, 'that's for you to find out, isn't it? It's why we've assigned you to the case – and why I've already booked you a couple of plane tickets to Copenhagen. You'll be there in the morning. Happy flight.'

CHAPTER 25

TUESDAY, 1 1.08 P.M.

NORTH SEA, OFF THE COAST OF SOUTHWOLD

Dan Summers was back where he loved to be – in the dark, murky depths beneath the sea – foraging. There was something about the secrecy – the quiet solitude – that was so appealing to him. The hassles of the world – unwanted phone calls, noisy neighbours, inane programmes on the telly, junk-mail texts encouraging him to make personal injury claims – there was none of that down here. Just him and the elements. Perfect.

Although, on this particular dive, solitude wasn't needed. He was pleased to have a diving companion – and one so attractive too. Even with her diving mask on, he could see those piercing eyes, that little flick of blond hair across her face, that dainty nose and that slender, shapely body poured into her tight-fitting wetsuit. How could anyone resist the invitation to come and swim with a mermaid? Her brother was keeping a welcome distance from the pair. It almost felt like they were diving alone together, like a couple on a honeymoon.

They had torches fixed to their heads, which was just as well;

it was black as pitch down there – easy to feel disorientated if they weren't careful.

Dan swam on, deeper, punching the blackness with every propulsion of his body. They were close to the very bottom of the North Sea now, some thirty-five metres from the surface, fifteen miles off the coast of Southwold: exactly where he wanted. He'd surprised himself at how well he'd remembered the place from last time. How long had it been now? Four years? Maybe five? Southwold was one of the first places he'd dived. And pretty soon they would both see the reason why he and so many other divers over the years had made the trek.

He knew that what they'd soon see would be a big enough distraction – a red herring, perhaps, when compared to the bounteous finds to be had off the coast of Dunwich itself, but exciting enough to stop his new friends wanting to explore anywhere else.

A few more metres and suddenly Dan's light lit up something. It was a hard, orange plate and it scuttled quickly into the shadows. Other crabs came into view, and sea squirts and lobsters. A long-spined scorpion fish darted past. The place was teeming with life – dahlia anemones, seamats, starfish, a multitude of pink shrimps and an abundance of soft coral known as dead men's fingers.

It was like visiting an underwater exhibition – a zoo for divers. But this one was built in a World War Two submarine. Even Frederik couldn't fail to be impressed. The wreck of the *E30* supported a huge variety of life and it was one of the most visited wrecks along the coast – already a stretch of sea littered with vessels from the Wash all the way down to Felixstowe. The North Sea had claimed countless vessels over the years, but none more intriguing than the ominous shape now resting on the seabed in front of them like a giant whale.

Dan turned to see his fellow divers' faces. Their eyes had lit up with delight and Heidi gave him a big thumbs-up, nodding her head in approval.

He knew it would work. Show them something like this and they'll never return to the seemingly dull waters of Dunwich. This was much more special, especially if you liked wildlife. Which, judging by her obvious pleasure, Heidi did.

Dan felt pleased to have delighted her so. She was cool and sassy and as flirtatious as anyone he had ever met before. He liked it. This short diving trip to Suffolk was unearthing all kinds of treasures.

He swam on, deeper, further into the wreck of the old submarine.

Yolanda decided that here, in the privacy of the old sub, would be the best place to carry out the plan and leave no trace.

She waited for her victim to turn away from her and then released the large metal diving torch from the straps at her side. She quickly brought it down on his head. Before he had a chance to recover, she went for him, from behind, locking her arms across his chest. He was thrashing frantically now, but she held him down, placing her arms around him from behind. Fighting in open water was almost impossible. You had nothing to anchor yourself to, so you couldn't kick or punch properly. And this girl's grip was immense. She folded her legs around his body – she was using him to give herself leverage and was tugging away at the aqualung, trying to loosen the fittings and disconnect the valve. She was still behind him – dodging his random punching and grabbing. She was so elusive – slippery like a dolphin – and she was determined. He could feel her still tugging at his back. The giant aqualung, on which his life depended, was being disconnected.

He bit for dear life on to the mouthpiece inside his mask and breathed deeply. He stretched his feet downwards, down towards the wreck of the submarine, trying desperately to find something – anything – to lock on to, to give him some leverage.

He scrambled around with his boots, just scraping the surface of the old submarine, rusty and encrusted with life. And then his left boot hit something hard. It was a rung from a small, metal ladder that ran up the outside of the submarine's bridge. He quickly lodged his toes under it and held fast. Now he could anchor himself and start hurling proper punches at the woman behind him.

But it was too late.

He felt the paralysis of suffocation.

She'd done it.

He writhed around in blind panic, eyes wide with fear, until she silenced him, perhaps out of mercy, with the solid metal aqualung now freed from the straps. The heavy tank clunked the back of his head and she saw his body go limp. She just couldn't watch his frantic writhing, like a Tyburn jig on a hangman's noose.

As she watched him take his final gulp of water and his body change from terrified spasms to limp inaction, she said a prayer inside. 'Forgive me.' But her whispered words weren't heard down there, deep inside the blackness of the abandoned submarine. She secured the aqualung to his body using a piece of metal twine she'd brought with her and was hiding inside the cuff of her wetsuit. There was enough twine left over to secure his pitiful body to a rung of the small ladder on the submarine. He was going nowhere now.

She gazed at him one last time and then turned, like a dolphin, and darted up towards the surface. Her fellow diver had been no help - no help at all. Where the hell was he, anyway? She spun around and then saw him, high above her, already heading to the surface. No doubt he'd had a ringside seat. What was the point in him being there?

Yolanda was quick to speak first when they reached the surface. She didn't want him to say anything and could see his face was terror struck.

'Don't worry,' she said, soothingly. 'It *was* necessary. Now we can be together, Daniel.'

CHAPTER 26

WEDNESDAY, 12.03 A.M.

GREYFRIARS ABBEY, DUNWICH

Alex and Janey had enjoyed a good night with friends at the Star Inn. As usual, he'd drunk too much and Janey was driving home. She was used to it and she didn't mind. She liked it when Alex had had a few – he didn't take himself so seriously then, even enjoyed a giggle. They'd been visiting the same pub every Tuesday night for a while now, despite only just being officially old enough to drink legally, though they both looked older than their eighteen years. Janey had passed her driving test before Alex – she was older than him by three months, which mattered when you're waiting to drive – and she was usually the one who drove back after the pub. She preferred it that way – it was one of the few times she saw him properly relaxed. His job as a trainee mechanic in Ipswich was hard, especially in winter time, but he was showing promise and had decided he would manage his own branch of Kwik Fit one day. With a modest joint income but very few other outgoings, save the rent on the cottage, they were able to enjoy nights like these regularly – decent food, fine ale and the very best of company, among friends with whom they'd been at school.

The only thing was, when Alex had consumed too much his new-found sense of fun could sometimes spill over into more erratic, daring behaviour. Janey had noticed he was beginning to use his Tuesday nights as a release from what he sometimes called his 'dull life'. Janey worked as a sales assistant for a pharmacy in Walberswick and enjoyed her gardening. She didn't think their life was dull at all, but Alex was a secret dreamer, always hankering for something more.

She pulled out of the car park and headed up Monastery Hill towards home. The road was deserted. Sat in the passenger seat, Alex looked out of the window at the dark night, his usually taught, muscular body now bloated and limp from too much food and drink. The great shadow of Greyfriars Abbey loomed over the hill.

'Hey, shall we go hunt some ghosts?' he said, giggling.

'What?'

He hiccupped a couple of times and then said again, 'Do you wanna go ghost hunting, Janey baby . . .? *Hic!*'

'Where? What're you talking about? Ghost hunting? Don't be stupid; it's cold out there. I wanna get home.'

'Ah, come on,' said Alex. 'You're so boring. What else are we going to do? It's work tomorrow, and the next day, and the next day and the next day.' He paused to hiccup again but this time it merged into a beery belch. 'There's nothing to do round here. Nothing. We're getting old before our time. I dunno if I'm eighteen or fifty-eight. What's the difference . . . ? *Hic!*'

'Well, I suppose I could make it worth your while, if you come home now. You'll soon know you're not fifty-eight.' She looked across the car and raised an eyebrow, flirtatiously. Pointless; he was looking in the other direction, out at the gloom-filled sky and the dark, twisted branches that hung down to the roadside like claws. He was in one of his adventurous moods, she could tell. 'Look, you've got an early start in the morning. It's bedtime, babe.'

'Yeah, I know. I know. I bloody know. That's our life, isn't it? Head down, wait for the weekend. Work, eat, sleep – work, eat, sleep. I mean, is that it? Come on, Janey. Just a quick adventure. You know I love that abbey. It's a brilliant place. I swear it's haunted, Janey. Oh . . . *hic* . . . it's *so* haunted, baby. Come on, stick with me, love; I'll look after you.' He hiccupped again and the window in front of him steamed up.

Janey could see he was in no state to look after anyone, least of all himself, and it was likely she would be doing the defending if anything happened. But she loved him, more than anything in the world, and she hated to see him so frustrated like this.

Besides, if she didn't give in, he'd find his satisfaction through arguments instead. It's what always happened. It was better to go with it, tire him out and then bundle him into bed. Or the cold air might sober him up and they could get that 'early night' she was beginning to hope for. 'What do you wanna do, then?' she said, resigned.

'Park up and we'll go for a stroll. It's cold but it's quite a clear night, I think. We can stargaze. Just a quick walk. Let's do something daring. Come on – live a little!'

Janey brought the car to a halt just beside the old gate into the monastery. 'All right, you big kid. I'll come. But, if we get cold, you promise to warm me up when we get home, yeah?'

'Oh, sounds good,' he said, grinning. 'I think I can oblige.' Then he burped again and Janey got another whiff of stale ale.

As they got out, the wind blew Janey's long hair across her face and her tired, watery eyes started to catch the moonlight.

'Eh, you're a good lookin' broad, yer know,' Alex said, coming around to her side and grabbing her for a quick, restorative cuddle.

'Yeah, whatever, you damn fool. Get off; your breath smells. Come on, let's get this over with, then we can get home and do this properly . . .'

'Patience, my darling.' He released her, grinning again, and ran through the gateway into the darkness of the remote field, laughing as he went.

'Hey, wait!' said Janey. 'Slow down!'

He paused, hiccupped, and together they walked towards the looming silhouette of the ruined abbey. Janey had to admit it was exhilarating to be outside, doing something different for once. The sky was clearing and, as their eyes acclimatised, they began to see a myriad of stars poking through the dark, like needles through silk.

To the east, the waves looked silvery in the moonlight, with rising crests that shifted and shimmered. The moon's magnetic pull on the waters seemed more tangible at this time – like it wasn't the winds pushing the waves at all but only the giant silver ball in the sky, drawing them towards it, like some spell had been cast. Despite the cold wind, Janey had to admit it looked quite beautiful – and she felt like they were young kids again. It was hard even for her to believe that they were both supposed to be adults now. Maybe Alex had been right, after all: this was a good idea.

They walked closer to the abbey ruins. 'I wonder what *he's* thinking?' Alex said.

'Who?'

'Up there,' said Alex, pointing up at the crumbling wall, midway between two open archways. 'The old gargoyle. Look at him. His gaze never changes, does it?'

'Yeah, poor chap. Pretty exposed up here. Looks lonely, doesn't he?'

They found a bench and sat down for another warming hug. They gazed at the water in the distance, their breath swirling in the night air.

'Do you think we'll live here forever?' said Alex.

'On earth, you mean? I don't think we're immortal.'

'No, I mean in Dunwich. Do you think this is where we're supposed to be?'

'Who knows?' said Janey. 'Maybe. Your job's all right, isn't it? I mean, I know it's not the most exciting job in the world, darlin', but it pays well. Maybe it's time to start thinking about a family. What do you think? Alex? Did you hear what I just said?'

He was looking at the edge of the cliff, where it dropped down to the water.

'Look at that.'

'Where? What're you talking about now?'

'Down there. It's weird. Looks like . . . I dunno . . . shapes. Like people.'

'Where?' said Janey. 'What're you talking about? Stop it; you're scaring me! I don't know what you mean.'

'Look,' Alex took Janey's hand and pointed it towards the cliff edge, where the solid earth disappeared, just ahead, on the left. 'See them? Must be trees, but they look like they're moving.'

After a few seconds Janey saw what he meant and her eyes widened. 'Oh, yeah! That's weird. They're . . . Wait a minute. What are they, love?'

Alex felt her body stiffen slightly.

'They *do* look like figures . . . walking towards us.' She stood up. 'Alex, they are. They're *people*. What the hell are they doing out here at this time of night?'

'Don't be stupid!' he said. 'I wasn't being serious, Janey. I was just messing with you. They're trees; it's windy. It looks like they're moving, I know, but they're not. It's a trick of the moonlight. Come and sit down, you fool.'

She was standing behind him now, holding on to his shoulders. 'No, they're not. I'm serious. Come on; let's go.'

The wind had picked up again and was whistling around the old buildings behind them. There was an eerie chill in the air and they both suddenly felt exposed to the elements. Maybe this wasn't such a good idea after all. Their cosy snug and their even cosier bedroom suddenly seemed very appealing.

Alex rose from the bench; even he was beginning to question it now. 'Stop it. You're making me wonder now, Janey. You're getting carried away – it's normally me with the vivid imagination!'

'They're getting closer, Alex! Come on!'

'No way. I'm not going anywhere. I wanna see what this is. If it isn't trees, then what is it, huh? I swear there are shapes down there – and they've moved since we've been standing here. Could be someone on an exercise. Maybe soldiers or scouts on some sort of night hike – or some midnight rambling club!'

'You're drunk!' she said. 'Now, *come on.*'

'No; let's wait on the other side of the abbey. We can watch from there.' Alex set off around the side of the old ruins to find a decent hiding place. Janey ran after him, protesting. It was cold, it was windy, and now they'd seen something that frightened her. Why the hell should they stay? But one thing was for sure: she wasn't going back across the dark field to the car all by herself. Not now.

Alex found a good vantage point, down below one of the remaining arched windows, now open to the elements with a view right across the sea. The ground was damp and their knees felt sodden within seconds, but it would be worth it. They were out of sight here but still had an uninterrupted view of the mysterious shapes that continued to trudge up the hillside from the coast.

Clouds had slowly drifted past, obscuring the moon's light for a few seconds. As the silvery light resumed, they could see the clear outlines of human figures approaching from the cliff. Dozens of them.

'How many are there? Alex, what's going on?' said Janey.

'Like I said, could be people out on exercise. It's not unusual to see soldiers out here. It's pretty barren and exposed – it's probably a good training ground.'

'But they've come from the cliff edge, love! I'm sure it drops off there. What do you think they did, scale the cliff first? This is crazy,' said Janey, holding Alex closer. 'It doesn't feel right. Let's go.'

'Just watch. We can't get back to the car now, anyway – they're too close. We'll be seen. We're better off hiding here.'

'Oh, brilliant,' said Janey. 'So you're saying we're trapped here now.'

They stared in silence as the figures drew closer. In the gloom, it was hard to make out their appearance, but it didn't look like they were wearing soldiers' uniforms. Their clothes weren't tight fitting; they seemed long and flowing.

'What are they wearing?' said Janey. 'They look like . . . Wait a minute . . . What are they, robes or something? Cloaks, maybe?'

'Cloaks!' said Alex. 'Don't be daft; they're just raincoats – maybe a scarf or two. Janey, you really have gone mad tonight. Your imagination is running wild. What did you drink?'

But she wasn't as convinced. There was a growing fear inside her that what they were looking at wasn't normal. 'Is this some kind of cult? Have we intruded on some special festival or something?' she said.

'Well, it's hardly the summer solstice, is it? And this isn't Stonehenge or Glastonbury. I don't know what this is.'

She could tell in his voice that even Alex was beginning to feel confused now. Frightened, even.

As the figures loomed ever closer, edging up to the other side of the abbey, they could make out the furs that seemed draped around their shoulders and small, copper-coloured helmets that glinted in the moonlight. But all thoughts of some cult re-enactment evaporated when they saw their faces.

They were skeletal.

And in the darkness they saw the shiny tips of swords, clasped in skeletal hands.

Janey let out a shriek but Alex quickly silenced her with his hand. 'Ssh! For God's sake, don't say anything.' He cradled her in his arms and stroked her hair. 'Stay still. They won't see us. They've not come for us, Janey. They can't have done. This is bigger than us – it means something else.'

'Look at them!' she whispered. 'They're ghosts, for crying out loud. Walking zombies or something. Oh, God! Alex! We're dead. If they see us, we're dead.' She wriggled out of his grasp and tried to stand up.

He grabbed her quickly and pulled her closer to him. 'Stop it!' he said in a desperate whisper. She could see from his eyes that he was scared now. 'Don't say anything. Just watch.'

'But they're coming this way. They've come for us. Oh, Jesus. This is it.' She began sobbing and buried her head again in the folds of Alex's coat.

He could feel her hands grabbing him tightly and she was now shaking – he knew it wasn't just the cold. He tried to stay strong for her, staring through the open window at the ghosts as they trudged even closer to the building. What were they doing? Why were they here? Questions flashed through his mind as he tried hard to make sense of what his eyes were showing him.

There were two lines of figures – almost like a battle formation. Some at the fringes held long spears, while others brandished giant swords. All wore helmets of tarnished metal, perched loosely above thin, skeletal faces. In the darkness, it was hard to make out their eyes but, as they drew even closer, Alex could see it was because they didn't have any. Just dark, lifeless sockets. These men – if they were men, once – were marching blind. Like automatons programmed to advance, but blind to what they were attacking.

The edges of some of their bodies seemed to merge with the air around them – almost like they weren't solid. Misty. It was still cloudy overhead, so any sharp vision was impossible but, even from here, Alex could see many of them were wispy, cloudy images. They had dark silhouettes, solid enough but, when you saw them up close, they seemed more like projections – holographic images.

And Alex couldn't see their boots. It seemed like their legs disappeared into the earth from below the knee. Like they were walking on a patch of ground that was lower than the one he was standing on.

He blinked hard and rubbed his eyes. He knew he was tired and he knew also that he'd had a skinful, but the spectacle had sobered him up instantly. He wasn't hallucinating. Neither was Janey.

She raised her head from his arms and cried again; the figures were so close now – just the other side of the archway. But they were heading straight for the abbey ruins. At some stage they would be walking around the building, wouldn't they? Or would they pass right through it?

All Alex knew was he didn't want to wait to find out – didn't want to stay and feel a ghost pass right through them. There was only one thing they could do.

'Run!' he said.

He stood up quickly and grabbed Janey by the coat. '*Now!*'

They burst out of the little corner they'd found, like sprinters from the blocks, running past the back of the abbey ruins, keeping the building between them and the ghosts, across the dark fields in the direction of the gateway near the roadside.

'Keep going!' he said. 'Don't look back. Just bloody run!'

They were breathless and their legs were stiff from being hunched up on the ground in the freezing cold. But a strong, insurmountable instinct to flee for their lives had kicked in and they sprinted towards the gateway. Within a few seconds, they'd left the field and were out on the road.

'Keys!' said Alex, who'd instinctively gone to the driver's side of Janey's Fiesta. 'You've got them, haven't you? Quick!'

He looked expectantly over the car's roof at Janey and the fields behind her. 'Come on!' And then he froze. Over her shoulder, back through the gateway in the dark field beyond, he saw the shadows of the figures. They'd changed direction and were now marching towards them.

Janey was crying and fumbling in her pockets. 'I haven't got them, Alex. I can't find them! Oh, God. They must've dropped out of my pocket.'

Alex had already come around to her side and grabbed her. 'Forget them. Come with me! *Run!*'

They turned and fled down the road, in the direction of Dunwich village. Their footsteps were hard and loud on the solid tarmac, save for the splashes they made when they hit puddles, but they'd given up trying to sneak away. This was a desperate sprint, right down the centre of the road. If a car came around the corner now, they knew they'd be dead, but it was worth the risk.

Neither of them stopped to look over their shoulders until they'd reached the car park of the pub, where they collapsed on the ground, their chests heaving and wheezing. Their legs were jelly-like. Luckily, behind them, the road was quiet; there was no one following them; they'd made it.

Without hesitating or even considering the time of night, they ran up to the giant, oak door and began to knock furiously on it until their knuckles were raw.

CHAPTER 27

WEDNESDAY, 2.14 A.M.

STAR INN, DUNWICH

Daniel stood at the window in his boxer shorts and thin, white T-shirt. His blond hair was tousled from hours spent shifting the pillows around, tossing and turning, trying to find sleep. The extraordinary events of the evening had removed all chance of sleeping now; his head was whirring with it all. And the night had been filled with strange noises, anyway – some couple talking in the car park until very late and the sound of someone yelling to be let in: a marital argument, no doubt.

He couldn't erase the memory of watching Heidi – or Yolanda, as she eventually confessed to being called – do away with the other guy under water. It was harrowing. Then the desperate swim to the surface, convinced that he would be next, having witnessed the brutal killing.

Little did he know when he'd agreed to go diving with this couple that one of them had planned all along to kill the other. And he was right there, in the thick of it, watching as it took place. He shuddered again and tried hard to wipe the image from his mind: the desperate writhing around as Yolanda took away Møller's air supply and the sight of him gulping his last breath before the water washed into his lungs. Dan knew he'd never get over that – never be able to forget such a sight.

Then he thought of Yolanda, the blonde bombshell with the tight body and the persuasive eyes. Did she really say what she said on the voyage back to Dunwich? It was incredible. Or did he dream it? He looked at the bed; it had been slept in – so did he dream that? Or was he dreaming still?

Disorientation was seeping into him, leaving him confused and unable to grasp reality. The cold air leaking through gaps in the window frame beside him made him shiver and it brought him out of his trance-like state.

He returned to the bed again, lay down, closed his eyes and began to relive his conversation with Yolanda, for the tenth time. Perhaps he had missed something – some clue to suggest that it had indeed been fantasy all along; some impossible event, or incredible sight that proved it could not have happened and it was indeed in his imagination, a stress-filled nightmare.

'You've killed your brother,' he distinctly remembered saying to her, gazing out across the dark, ominous coastline on their return trip to the jetty, the cold wind blowing on their faces. 'You've dragged me out here. You've now made me an accomplice.'

'He's not my brother,' she'd said.

'What?'

'I *said*, he's not my brother; he was my boyfriend.'

'Jesus. Thanks for the warning,' Dan had replied.

Then Yolanda had come closer to Dan and he'd braced himself. Though he hated to admit it, and would fight hard not to show it to this woman, he was undeniably afraid of her. Would she do away with him just as easily as she had the other guy, whoever he was? He glanced around the boat – there could be a gun somewhere, maybe several. He decided to play it cool – avoid provoking her anger.

'I mean, you must have had your reasons,' he said. 'Did he knock you around or something? Did he beat you, this boyfriend of yours?'

Yolanda laughed. 'Hell, no. I'd like to have seen him try. He was . . . how do you say it? Surplus, that's all. He was surplus to the plan. We didn't need him any more. My instructions were to dispatch him.'

'*We?* You said "we" then. And what *instructions?*' said Dan, intrigued. 'From whom?'

'Sigurdsson.'

'And who the hell is Sigurdsson?'

'Agnar Sigurdsson: the man behind this whole operation. He funds the search. He pays for the dive; he buys the boats; he pulls the strings.'

'You're going to have to slow down,' said Dan, holding the boat's wheel and trying valiantly to focus on the tiny jetty and the lights in the distance. 'I don't know what you're talking about.'

Yolanda decided to fill him in – from the beginning: the operation to find the Viking hoards beneath the sea; the reason why she and Møller had met up with him at the hotel; how Sigurdsson had wanted, at first, to do away with Dan. That was why she'd been sent to England, after all, to get rid of the opposition so that she and Møller could continue to search the seabed.

But then she told him how she found him attractive; it was his courage, his sense of adventure – all the surfing and diving and living life on the edge. She said she found it all so alluring.

And Dan was listening intently.

But behind his smile he wasn't so sure. It was all too convenient a story. No one fell in love that quickly, and so much so that they felt ready to do away with their old boyfriend – that was just madness, wasn't it? He knew he couldn't – shouldn't – believe this story that Yolanda had developed strong feelings for him already. But he so wanted it to be true. She was beguiling. There was something about her, something electrifying – something that allowed you to forgive her actions and the consequences of her vicious temper. But he knew this was insane. She was just using him to get to the treasure. She must have planned to do away with this other guy all along – how could Dan have been the reason for that murder?

And who the hell was this Sigurdsson guy, pulling her strings from Denmark?

When Dan had probed her more, to find out who was behind this operation and what kind of a man he was, Yolanda's tone had changed. He'd noticed a melancholy washing over her, the only time he'd been able to see some kind of emotion from this killer. Her face had dropped and she'd stared out over the ocean before answering him. How, after all, could you sum up a man like Sigurdsson to someone who didn't know him? After all these years, it seemed incredible he wasn't known the world over; he had such influence over Yolanda's life. But that was how he liked it – powerful, controlling, but from the shadows: the secret puppeteer.

'He's a loveless man,' she had said, mournfully. 'And I should know . . . He's my father.'

Now, lying on the bed, still turning the events over in his mind, Dan could feel temptation calling again. He wanted to believe her. He hated himself for feeling like this – for even considering her offer instead of going straight to the police, as he knew very well he should. But it was an offer wilder than any of his dreams. Beyond imagination. And she was so damn good looking.

She'd asked him to join her – to join her father's team, spend his life diving across the world, searching for treasure and being paid handsomely for it. Millions of Danish kroners. A luxury apartment overlooking the Baltic. His own boat, own sports car and a salary the like of which he'd never achieve elsewhere.

And, more importantly, he could have *her*.

The stakes could not have been higher. Here he was, a beach bum, scrabbling around for pennies for his next feeble expedition – working in bars and restaurants and cleaning jobs between dives, just to save for the next trip out. He had no roots to speak of – only a circle of fellow nomads he called friends. No family, no girlfriend. Few prospects.

And now this. Surely he could be forgiven for giving it just a little consideration . . . couldn't he? But was it all just a fantasy to string him along long enough to show her the site of the treasure and then do away with him just as she had the other guy? Was she really going to take him back to Denmark with her and allow him to live like a king?

It was bullshit. Surely it was.

He glanced over at the clock on the bedside cabinet: 2.24 a.m. In less than ten hours she would expect his decision. If he wasn't back at her boat by midday, she'd know he wasn't interested. And she'd leave him alone – or so she'd said.

But at the back of his mind there was a fear growing. And it was festering like rotten fruit in a bowl, discolouring everything else.

Daniel knew, deep down, that all this careful thinking and deciding and weighing it over in his mind was pointless.

He had no choice.

She wouldn't accept no for an answer, would she? He knew everything now. And, after all, he had just witnessed her killing someone. There was no chance of her allowing him to wander off into the sunset, was there, really? Back to his old life, as if nothing had ever happened.

Everything had changed now. And he knew too much.

If he failed to show up, would she just shrug her shoulders and go back to Denmark alone? Would she let him off, just like that, and say, 'Never mind; I'll find another boyfriend'? Unlikely. She'd come straight after him. The blonde assassin would pronounce judgement again. This Sigurdsson would deploy his men to help her, if need be. She'd be joined by whole armies of killers, all searching to silence him.

The simple truth was he could either go along with her plan, accept her invitation – however fantastical it really was – and allow himself to be strung along, or he could turn her down and wait for her to kill him. Death now or death later, after a few more days of diving with this beauty – that was the real choice.

Maybe that was why she was quite happy to tell him about the operation, and Sigurdsson, and everything else – because she'd do away with him soon, and dead men don't talk.

He felt his heart beginning to race again and stood up quickly to pace the floor. He moved to the window and pulled the curtains back slightly. It was a partial moon, but still bright enough to send silver light cascading over the bay. He gazed out of the little window like a condemned man, stealing a last glimpse of the moon before the dawn brought the hangman's noose. His quick breaths steamed up the windowpane. He thought of Frederik, or Jürgen, or whatever he was called, lying tethered to the submarine beneath the waves. Dead.

He glanced again at the small alarm clock by his bed: 2.30 a.m. She'd be sleeping.

What if he just ran now? Made a bolt for it? Fled the hotel, cranked up the boat and got the hell out of there? He could be long gone by the morning. She'd never find him.

Would she?

CHAPTER 28

WEDNESDAY, 7.30 A.M.

STAR INN, DUNWICH

Jud and Bex were enjoying a hearty breakfast. 'Anything and everything the chef can throw at us, please,' was what DCI Khan had said when asked if he would like anything from the cooked menu.

And the chef had delivered, too; their plates were bursting with bacon, sausages, eggs, hash browns, mushrooms, tomatoes, beans, black pudding and two thick slices of fried bread. Bex had not enjoyed watching Khan tuck into it like a wild dog, runny egg dribbling down his chin. And he had an irritating way of clanking his knife and fork unnecessarily loudly on the bottom of the plate every time he gathered up more food to shovel in. And then he'd give a loud exhale and a lick of the lips just after he swallowed as he prepared himself for the next offering on his fork.

Jud was no better. What was it about some men and how they became almost primeval when you placed a hot breakfast in front of them first thing in the morning? she wondered. They weren't dining, they were 'feasting'.

'Did you hear the noise last night, then?' said Khan.

'Nope,' said Jud. 'Why? What happened?'

'I didn't hear any noise. What was it?' said Bex.

'Well, it's hard to say – people are being tight-lipped about it, to be honest,' said Khan. 'But my room's at the front, just above the door. I heard somebody clattering on the door about one o'clock this morning. I got out of bed and looked out of the window but couldn't see down to the front step. There was definitely someone there, though. I reckon it was either a member of the landlord's family – maybe an argument, I thought – or a drunken resident, forgotten his key, probably.'

'So what happened?' said Bex, intrigued.

'Well, nothing else. I stuck my head out of my room to see if I could hear anything, but nothing. I assume the landlord must've let whoever it was in, because I'm sure I heard the door open and close, after which there was no more noise.'

'And no reports from the local police?' said Jud.

'No. Nothing,' said Khan. 'I've already checked. But, whoever it was who was knocking on that door, they were in a right old state. They were shouting for someone to open up – sounded very impatient. Kept knocking like there was no tomorrow.'

They looked around the restaurant now. There was nothing out of the ordinary, just a few other diners, a couple of waitresses darting in and out of the door leading to the kitchen, someone cleaning the bar.

'Do you think there's any connection to the current investigation, Inspector?' said Bex.

'I don't think so, no. Like I say, probably just a family squabble, or someone forgetting their key. Either way, they seem to have hushed it up now, don't they?'

A waitress breezed past their table and Jud saw his opportunity. He was as intrigued as Bex to know more about the incident and wasn't content with Khan's explanation.

'Excuse me?'

'Yes, sir.'

'My friends and I heard a disturbance in the night – someone was trying to get in. About one o'clock, I think. Do you know what happened?'

The waitress shook her head. 'I don't live in the hotel – I only got here this morning. I've not heard anything, though. You could ask the landlord. I'm sorry if it kept you awake.'

Khan shot a glance at Jud once she'd gone. 'What was that for? You should let it go. We've got more important things to think about.'

'Just curious,' said Jud, smiling.

'Nosey, more like,' said Bex.

'Well, you know. Anything out of the ordinary may be significant. It might have been Summers.'

Bex shrugged. 'Maybe.'

The young barman whom Jud had seen the previous night – with the thick-rimmed specs and ginger stubble – entered the restaurant carrying a bundle of newspapers. Even now, looking at him, Jud felt the same niggling feeling in the back of his mind that he knew his face. But from where? And when? He dismissed it. There was no way he was going to ask him again, risk making yet another fool of himself and give the impression he was some kind of secret admirer of this guy. Especially not in front of the others.

But he had to know more about what happened outside. He and Bex both felt frustrated that Khan had been the only one to hear the commotion – but then his room was above the door, so no wonder he'd heard the shouting. Jud waited to catch the barman's eye and then signalled for him to come over to the table.

'Hello, again,' he said cheerfully.

'Sorry to bother you,' said Jud. 'My friends and I were just wondering what the noise was in the middle of the night. Someone forgot their key, did they?'

The young man's expression had altered. He glanced around the room furtively before quickly pulling up a chair to the table.

'Funny you should ask,' he said in a hushed tone. 'My Dad – I mean, the landlord – says I'm not supposed to tell anyone about it, but I can't help it. It was, like, *so weird.*'

He regaled them with what he'd seen during the night – Alex and Janey racing back to the pub, looking terrified and with some bizarre tale of being chased by ghosts. He spoke in a hushed whisper, but as dramatically as he could, buoyed up by the fact that something out of the ordinary was finally happening in this sleepy little village. Something that appeared to interest him greatly. He told them how his father had eventually allowed them back in and given them a room for the night, provided they kept silent about what they'd seen and were gone first thing in the morning. He'd said he would drive them home himself, if he had to.

'And your father told you to keep silent too, yes? Why was that, do you think?' said Khan, looking concerned. 'I mean, why the secrecy?'

'Don't tell me,' said Jud before the guy had had time to answer. 'Your father didn't want to scare the hotel guests, I suppose. Bad for business?'

'Yes, exactly,' said the landlord's son. 'It's amazing what fear of the paranormal can do to people, to a whole village, sometimes. It spreads quickly, doesn't it?' He looked at them with a sly smile and said, 'But I suppose you know that, don't you?'

Jud and Bex glanced at one another. What the hell did he mean by that? They both knew it was best not to pick up on such a comment – not here, at least, in a public restaurant. They chose to keep silent and just smile back at him, but each had made a mental note to investigate what he'd meant by his last comment, later in the day.

'But these regulars,' he continued, 'well, I reckon they were on to something. It's not the first time I've—' He stopped suddenly.

'Pat!' a middle-aged man had entered the room and came straight over to the table. His belly was as large as you'd expect for a landlord with a penchant for his own beer. His face was leathery and lined, like a weather-beaten fisherman's. This was clearly a guy who liked sea air. 'What're you doing?' he said, rhetorically. 'Let these people get on with their breakfasts, Pat. Now, come on, there's work to be done.' He was agitated and was doing a poor job of hiding it.

'Sorry, Dad,' said Pat ruefully, as he got up from his chair and followed his father obediently out of the restaurant.

Khan and the two agents watched them leave, surprised at the young man's submissive manner. Jud tried to imagine himself showing such obedience to his own father – not likely.

As the two men went through the doors in the corner of the room, the agents saw the landlord push his son into the corridor and jab his finger into his chest. They listened intently and heard raised voices, but the words were indistinguishable. Whatever was being said, there was little doubt the young man was in trouble.

'So, what do you make of that, then?' said Khan.

'A hell of a lot more than you first thought, eh, Inspector?'

Khan nodded and rolled his eyes. 'OK, Sherlock Holmes. So I was wrong, but that doesn't mean to say this kid was telling the truth, does it? I mean, he may have an axe to grind against his father. We dunno. He may hate working here. He may have a vivid imagination. These might be lies, for all we know, dreamed up by a bored teenager with a grudge.'

'Judging by the way his father reacted when he saw him whispering to us, I'd say he was telling the truth,' said Bex. 'And you can see why his father wouldn't want the whole world to know the place was haunted. He'd scare everyone.'

'They're already scared,' said Jud. 'Think about the body on the beach. The car park was packed by the time we arrived here. It'll be all up the coast now.'

'Glad you mentioned the body on the beach at last,' said Khan, his mouth crammed full of bacon. 'That's what we're supposed to be discussing, isn't it? We've got enough to deal with, without another bloody ghost story. I'll have a word with the landlord later – find out what happened last night. He won't be able to hide anything from me. He knows who I am by now.'

'Look forward to hearing how you get on,' said Jud, cheekily.

'In the meantime, what have you guys found out about the way this Lars Andersen feller was killed, eh? Did you say your friend, Luc, had found out that the markings on his body – and the ones on that little bit of stone, too – were from some kind of . . . what did you say? Runic alphabet, was that it? Used by the Vikings, you said. Seriously?'

'Yes,' said Jud. It certainly sounded strange when put like that – even far-fetched – but then Khan had a habit of saying everything in a cold, matter-of-fact way so that it often made theories seem fantastical. But this was true; Jud knew it.

'And you said you've found out that the coin which Summers found is of Dutch origin, yes? What was the place you said?'

'Dorestad,' said Bex. 'It was a very wealthy place, especially in Viking times – had its own mint, apparently.'

'So the Vikings would have invaded it, yeah?'

Jud nodded. 'Guess so.'

'So, all this begs the very obvious question, what the hell has this Summers guy started here?'

Bex finished her plate and gently placed the knife and fork together. 'We have reason to believe Dan Summers has disturbed a Viking hoard.'

'Of coins, you mean?' said Khan.

'Well, yes.'

'And how did they get there?' said Khan.

'We think maybe a Viking ship got into trouble and sank off the coast of Dunwich,' said Jud. 'It's possible. You know this stretch of coastline is littered with wrecks, so the websites say. Why not a Viking one?'

Bex was nodding. 'I don't disagree with that. It also explains how the rune stone got there.'

'Ah, yes. What did the letters on that stone actually mean?' said Khan. 'Did Luc manage to find that out?'

Jud filled him in about the significance of the shapes and their meanings – the wisdom of Odin, guidance for sailors and bravery in war. It all pointed to the theory that it was a rune stone carried by Viking sailors for good luck on a voyage.

'And what about the couple in Walberswick? Mrs Chadwick talked about the black dog. What was that all about?'

'The Black Shuck,' said Jud, nodding. 'I know. She said there's a local legend that it's the dog of Odin, the famous Viking god. Apparently, it's supposed to bring a curse on whoever it looks directly at.'

'This is a strange place and no mistake,' said Khan, stirring his tea. 'I mean, it's got an atmosphere, hasn't it? Don't you think?'

Jud and Bex sneaked a look at one another and smiled. Here was DCI Khan, the hardened cynic who only dealt in facts, talking to them about the 'atmosphere' in a location. How times had changed since their first meeting, when he'd been scathing about the agents' powers of extrasensory perception.

'I agree,' said Bex. 'It feels unsettling. Like the air when a storm is brewing – heavy and thick.'

'Yeah, with an air of anticipation,' added Jud.

'All right, all right. Let's not get poetical, shall we? Let's focus on the facts, please. And then there's the injuries on the body up at the beach. What did you call it, "blood eagle", or something?'

'Yes, Inspector. "Blood eagling" – a brutal way of dispatching your enemy, used by the Vikings,' said Bex.

'It's those bloody Vikings again,' said Khan.

'I know,' said Jud. 'There's no question, in my view, that there are too many connections to the Vikings here for it to be any kind of coincidence. There may well be the remains of a Viking ship down on that seabed. If it went down in a storm or something, then we can assume there may have been men on board – many of them. So their souls lie on the bottom of the ocean.'

'And Summers has disturbed them,' said Bex.

'Yeah, but it wasn't Summers who was blood eagled, was it?' said Khan. 'So that doesn't fit, does it?'

'No, but if you think about it,' said Jud, 'Summers' boat was raided by someone. It's reasonable to think it was Andersen.'

'So he was seen leaving the boat and was mistaken for Summers, you mean?' said Bex.

'Exactly.'

'Let me get this straight,' said Khan. 'The dead man, Lars Andersen, was killed by the ghost of a Viking, who mistook him for Summers, the man who had just disturbed the souls of dead Vikings under the sea.'

'Yes,' Bex and Jud said in unison. He was doing it again, speaking in that matter-of-fact way, exposing their theory as some kind of fantasy – but it was true.

Khan pulled a face to express his cynicism.

'I know it sounds hard to believe,' said Bex, 'but when have you ever found the cases we're involved in to be anything other than weird? We're talking about the supernatural here, Inspector. You should know by now that these cases are rarely predictable.' She looked around the hotel restaurant at the other diners. 'Hey, where *is* Summers, by the way?'

'What?' said Jud.

'Summers. Where is he? Why's he not having breakfast?'

'He's a surfing bum, for God's sake. He'll still be in bed, Bex.'

'And what about that couple he was seen talking to last night? Where are they now?'

'Probably in bed, too. It's still early, Bex. Jud's right,' said Khan. 'But I'd certainly like to speak to them all today.'

'And what about the people you heard last night? Where are they?' said Bex.

'Patience, my dear,' said Khan. 'I'll speak to the landlord, like

I said, and find out what happened and who visited in the night. Now, let's think about that skull in Walberswick, shall we? The woman said she saw it glow. Its eyes were red, or something. Is that possible? Really? Do you think the old woman's losing her marbles?'

'It's possible the skull itself was Viking,' said Jud. 'And, if so, then the disembodied spirit of the deceased could well have been stirred, just like the others under the ocean. Besides, she also said they'd seen the Black Shuck, so they were doubly cursed, you might say.'

DCI Khan was looking puzzled. 'You know, I just don't understand it; really, I don't. I mean, why should a skull that has washed up on the beach at Walberswick suddenly come to life because of something this stupid diver has disturbed under the ocean, huh? I mean, it just doesn't make sense, does it?'

'I'm fed up of hearing that phrase "make sense",' said Jud. 'When we can't understand something because it hasn't come to us through the usual five senses, we say it doesn't "make sense". Why can't people understand we have hundreds of bloody senses? And besides, just because something seems strange or improbable to us, doesn't mean it can't happen. We humans think we know it all. Most people have this tiny, narrow view of the world through just the five senses they recognise. Unless they can see something, or hear it, or whatever, then they don't believe it can happen. It's bullshit. When something comes along that challenges this view, we say it doesn't make sense so it can't happen. Why does everything have to "make sense", huh?'

'All right. Easy, tiger!' said Khan, smiling. 'Someone got out of the wrong side of the bed this morning!'

Bex was smiling at Jud. She loved it when he went off on one like this. His passion for what he did was infectious.

'I'm sorry, Inspector,' said Jud. 'It just frustrates me how humans are obsessed with logic and rational thinking and sensible reasons for everything. Life is so much more complex than that.

We think of time as a single line moving from past to future. That's rubbish. Then we think dead people are behind us, forgotten about, in the past, never to come back. That's bullshit too. The souls of dead people don't get left behind like driftwood on a beach. They don't stay frozen in time as the rest of us march onwards. They're still here, living amongst us. They've not gone anywhere; how could they? We're not all running in a single race, with people falling behind and vanishing; we're all in the same space, all mingling together. Only some of us are alive and some of us are dead.'

'You mean, the world is not defined by how we humans perceive it,' said Bex. She always had that uncanny knack of saying in a few words what Jud was trying to articulate in a lengthy rant.

'Exactly!' said Jud. 'That's exactly it.'

Bex detected a surge of excitement inside as she felt Jud's approval.

Khan finished his last mouthful of breakfast, straightened his knife and fork and then leaned back in his chair. 'Well, that's a very philosophical discussion, thank you, I'm sure. Descartes would be very proud of you.'

'*Cognito ergo sum,*' said Bex.

'You what?'

'I think, therefore I am,' said Jud. 'Descartes' sixth mediation. He sat in his armchair and reflected on the nature of reality.'

'And the fact that he could sit and consider whether he existed or not,' continued Bex, 'was proof enough that he existed.'

'Hmm, if you say so,' said Khan. 'Anyway. Shall we get back to these bloody ghosts, yeah?'

'Keep your voice down, Inspector!' whispered Bex.

'Sorry. So this stretch of coastline is being invaded, you say, just like it was centuries ago,' said Khan, quietly, 'only this time the Viking marauders are *ghosts.*'

'Seems that way, doesn't it?' said Jud. 'But we're going to have to keep a tight lid on this. Fear could go viral within hours. Like I say, news of the attack on the beach is probably already in the towns and villages up and down the coast. People are already asking questions. It's going to be hard to contain this. Especially if what this Pat kid was saying is true, and the ghosts are now coming en masse. It'll be hard to keep this from the public if there's been other sightings.'

'Hmm, funny you should talk about keeping it from the public,' said Khan, beginning to sound impatient. 'Guess who's got a press conference this morning, eh? Who's the one who has to face the public every time? Old muggins, here. It's all right for you guys; you can hide away, but I have to go out there and face the public every bloody time.'

If Khan was waiting for some kind of sympathetic nod, he wasn't going to get it. The agents showed little emotion. The inspector had his job and they had theirs.

'So what're you going to say, then?' said Jud coolly.

'You tell me,' said Khan, glancing down at his watch. 'You've got an hour to think of something. I'm on at nine.'

CHAPTER 29

WEDNESDAY, 8.19 A.M.

(9.19 A.M. LOCAL TIME)

FLIGHT 3095CPH TO

COPENHAGEN

Somehow, Luc and Grace knew they weren't flying over a British city. It was hard to put your finger on what it was that was so different, but it just didn't look like anything they'd seen in England. The buildings were quite tightly packed together and there were fewer high-rise buildings than in your average capital city. It looked so clean too. Some of the roofs were a brilliant red in colour; others were a deep turquoise, like that of the striking Christiansborg Palace, seat of the Danish Parliament, which could be seen for miles, and the equally conspicuous turquoise turrets of the Rådhustårnet, the City Hall Tower. The city resembled a model village, especially out of an aeroplane window. The scale seemed wrong for it to be full size and the buildings seemed too polished and clean.

'It looks like a Lego town,' said Grace.

'Well, you'd expect it to, wouldn't you?' said Luc. 'This is where Lego was invented, after all. It's a Danish company.'

'Oh, yeah! Duh!'

The aeroplane began its descent and soon they had even clearer views of the architecture. Many of the smaller buildings were painted in cheerful colours, especially on the waterfront, where rows of tall, tightly-packed terraced houses snuggled together, each one painted in a different pastel shade of blue, green, pink or peach.

Luc and Grace saw a great expanse of tarmac and recognised it as Copenhagen Airport, spread across the island of Amager, south of the city, connected by several bridges that ran across the water like giant arteries. Luc and Grace had spent the last hour gazing down at different islands and peninsulas, all interconnected by vast suspension bridges, huge feats of engineering in this cold landscape. As the aeroplane approached the runway, they caught a glimpse to the east of the longest bridge of them all, the Øresund: a sixteen-kilometre masterpiece of engineering, connecting Sweden to Denmark.

'Look at that!' said Grace.

'Yeah, not so miniature now,' said Luc. 'Incredible, isn't it? I'd like to have seen the Lego instructions for that!'

The aeroplane eventually found terra firma with an almost imperceptible judder and soon the engines were silenced. The flight had not been long – just under two hours – but after a fairly sleepless night, an early morning spent frantically packing and then a speedy dash to Stansted Airport, the CRYPT agents were feeling stale and weary.

'Need a good coffee,' said Luc, standing up and stretching. His tall frame seemed accentuated in the modest-sized cabin.

'Yeah, me too,' said Grace. 'But let's get to the railway station first, OK? Don't want to miss the train.' She gathered her long blond hair together in a neat ponytail and fished in her pocket for a scrunchy. She liked to wear her hair back when working – though her long hair on this occasion had helped to hide her tired eyes during the flight. She looked tired. She wore little make-up, but rarely needed to. Her fair complexion and piercing blue eyes were the envy of many agents at the CRYPT.

'Yes, boss, coffee can wait, then,' said Luc, grinning that attractive grin that made him such a pleasure to be with. He was charming, there was no denying it, and there were few back at the CRYPT who failed to enjoy his company. Grace had always felt so lucky to be paired up with Luc for most assignments. And this one was turning out to be more exciting than most. Little did they know a few days before that they would be flying into the airport of what looked like a giant Lego set.

Their itinerary had already been set by the staff at the CRYPT, who organised everything for them: a short taxi ride over the bridge into the main city and to the railway station, where they would meet their contacts, Cally and her boyfriend, Ralf; then a train ride together of some twenty minutes to Roskilde; check into the Hotel Prindsen and then straight round to Ralf's apartment block. The trip was officially a social one, if anyone asked. People on aeroplanes were often chatty and it was important they had a cover story if any person asked what brought them to Denmark. They were catching up with their 'good friends' in Roskilde. Jason Goode had briefed his employee, Cally, on how he and his guys would take care of things from here on, and he'd told her that she must stop worrying. Everything would be fine, he'd see to that.

Her partner, Ralf, had said he was happy to host the agents – anything to stop Cally from worrying so much (Ralf had been allowed in on the secret – 'How could I keep it from him?' Cally'd asked Goode when they'd first talked) – but Goode had said a hotel would be fine. He never liked his agents to stay over with civilians, even if they were employees of his. It was essential they had some privacy to conduct their research and report back to the CRYPT without people eavesdropping. But they would certainly appreciate full access to the flat – and especially the balcony.

Goode had pulled some strings at MI5, who'd talked to their

counterparts in Denmark and given the CRYPT agents access to the apartment next door to Ralf's, abandoned since the incident last night. The police had already visited the place, entering the apartment via the balcony next door, and found no one there. But perhaps the CRYPT agents would be able to find more evidence – especially of a paranormal kind: traces of electro-magnetic energy, not to mention traces of a spiritual or emotional kind. Though a select few officers in Denmark had been made aware of the real identities of Luc and Grace, as far as the public were concerned – and especially the other residents of the apart-ment block – they were just friends of Ralf's. Secrecy was key. No one else needed to know they'd be exploring the flat next door most of the time.

Luc and Grace had briefly researched Roskilde the night before, as soon as the briefing with Bonati and Goode had been wrapped up – and they'd been shocked to find news reports of the 'ghostly head' seen in Roskilde. News travelled fast in Denmark, clearly – especially where ghosts were concerned. Several news websites had talked of an apparition being seen hovering outside the fourth floor windows of an apartment in the old part of the city. There were rumours that the apartment belonged to a multi-millionaire recluse – but neither Luc nor Grace had been able to find out anything about this guy, not even his name. Perhaps Cally's boyfriend would be able to shed more light on it. The fact that his neighbour had suddenly upped and left was beyond coincidence. The hunt was on.

Eventually, Luc and Grace left Arrivals and made their way to the taxi rank outside the airport lobby. The drive was brief but scenic, through the streets and over the canals of the fashionable district of Christianshavn, a labyrinth of waterways and backstreets dating back to the 1600s.

'It feels like Venice,' said Grace.

'Yeah, only colder,' Luc replied, grinning.

The weather had improved slightly since the day before their arrival and the views across the waterfront were as picturesque on the ground as they were from the air, but there was a cold, blustery wind that rattled and flapped the coloured bunting on the waterside buildings.

In front of the multi-coloured houses, small market stalls were jostling for position, their striped tarpaulins flapping in the breeze. As the taxi crossed the main bridge into Copenhagen, they saw boats of all shapes and sizes moored at various jetties dotted along the banks: fishing trawlers, smaller dinghies, passenger boats and the occasional yacht. In the distance, they saw what looked just like a Viking longship.

'Look at that!' said Grace. 'The Vikings are here, then!'

'Yeah, I suppose there'll be plenty of replicas like that all over Denmark. Roskilde is supposed to have quite a few – it was a massive Viking settlement, I think,' said Luc.

'There are so many connections,' said Grace. 'The runic letters, the Viking rituals; we're in the right place – there's a reason something's kicked off here too.'

'I know,' said Luc. 'This ghost that's been seen in Roskilde – it has to be linked to what's going on in Suffolk. And something tells me we're going to find out soon. It might be a pretty place now but there's more to it than meets the eye, I'm sensing.'

'But how is it linked? Why did a ghost appear at the apartment block in Roskilde last night? I mean, why now? Why here specifically?'

Luc shrugged as he gazed out of the taxi window, beyond the pretty buildings and the boats and the flags, further downstream, to where the river widened into the grey waters of the Baltic. There the water was choppier, the winds were picking up and the clouds in the distance were slowly darkening.

CHAPTER 30

WEDNESDAY, 8.50 A.M.

STAR INN, DUNWICH

Yolanda Sigurdsson stared up at the ceiling and contemplated the course of events that had led to her taking her ex-boyfriend's life. Had it been the right call? Had she let her own feelings dominate all reason? It wasn't the first time she'd dispatched someone, of course. She was a trained assassin, just like the rest of her father's team, and she'd been called upon twice before to dispose of people who were judged to be either surplus to requirements or a threat to the operation. Life was cheap in the Sigurdsson house, or so it seemed at times. Nothing was more precious than the motherland, nothing more important. When people showed signs of doubt or fear or selfishness, they had to be dealt with. When a man, or woman for that matter, put their own interests above those of the motherland, or jeopardised the mission to bring historical antiquities back to their rightful home, then the orders would come from her father to 'end them'.

But had Jürgen Møller failed in this way? Had he really become a threat to the operation's success? Did he deserve his watery grave?

Yes, yes and yes! she told herself. He had failed to complete the mission. Even worse, he had allowed Lars Andersen to go and get himself murdered, thus attracting the attention of the police, the media and the countless locals who had now turned up in droves to see what was going on. It could not have gone worse for the mission. And Møller had been showing distinct signs of weakness too. She remembered her father's words as she left him in Denmark only the day before: 'Get this Møller to do his job properly, or get rid of him. Either way, don't come back until this is sorted, right?'

And now she had sorted it. Møller had weakened, no question – she could tell it from the moment she'd seen him at the airport. He was whining about the dangers involved. He was close to cracking, that was obvious. Who knew what he might have said or done if left alone in this wild, remote place? He had become a liability to the mission, to Sigurdsson and to the motherland.

She knew her father wouldn't object. After all, he'd never really liked Møller, and Sigurdsson had already shared his concern with her about the calls he'd been receiving from Møller over the last twenty-four hours. They had confirmed in his mind too that he was indeed weakening. Something had happened in Suffolk that had brought about this change in Møller.

What was it about this place? On the drive from the airport, she'd noticed he'd been a shadow of his usual self – all nervous and worried about the mission. They'd been on many missions before, some of them just as dangerous, but he'd never been so nervous. No, she'd done the right thing, hadn't she?

Guys like that were ten a penny, anyway.

But this Summers kid was different.

Yolanda lay there, thinking how strange it was how history repeats itself. She remembered meeting Møller for the first time, all those years ago. How his charm and his looks and his courage had impressed her. And so it was with Summers. Though the task was to charm him enough to get him out there and show her the treasure sites, then maybe get rid of him too, she couldn't deny that she was beginning to feel something for him. She'd not banked on actually liking this guy. That was not in the plan.

But she'd not even contemplated his not turning up at midday. Of course he would. How could he resist? How could he refuse such an offer? Riches beyond his wildest dreams and enough adventure and challenge to last him a lifetime.

She shook away the niggling doubts that were seeping into her brain. She'd been right to get rid of Møller. And today would herald a new start for her, for the mission and for the motherland. Though Summers had denied it when she'd asked him, she felt sure that deep down he was a Viking too. He looked it, with his fair complexion, rippling muscles and hardy skin. He had some Danish blood in him, there was no doubt. She may have to go back generations and generations, but she'd find it all right. He was a worthy recipient of the mission, a worthy challenger. And, if she could prove he was of Danish origins (even if she had to fake the evidence), then who knows? Maybe even her father would like him.

She dressed quickly, applied some subtle make-up – she didn't want to appear too keen for Daniel – and then picked up the phone. It was time to make the call to her father. She hoped and prayed he'd understand.

'Papa, it's me,' she began.

At the end of the line there was a slight pause. It had been a while since she'd called him 'Papa'. Working as part of his team, she could rarely let on that they were related and so she usually called him either 'Sir' or 'Agnar', like the rest. She resented the idea that others might see her merely as the boss's daughter and thus beyond criticism. She'd earned her place in his operation on her own merits, not because of her surname – at least, so she thought. Others would see it differently, no doubt, and so she'd confined her private conversations with him to a minimum. These days it hardly felt like they were father and daughter at all.

'What's happened?' Sigurdsson said, cutting straight to the

chase. There was a reason she'd opened with 'Papa' and he knew it.

'What do you mean? Why do you ask that?'

'Oh, come on, I'm busy. I don't have time for games, Yol. What's happened?'

She felt disappointed to hear this abrupt tone. He sounded seriously stressed.

'Perhaps I should ask you the same, Papa. You sound stressed.'

'Stressed? You think so? I'm beyond stress, Yolanda. My apartment is haunted, I have reporters and police officers prowling around and now I'm hiding in a hotel in Copenhagen. You bet I'm stressed. The entire operation is at risk.'

'Haunted?' she said quickly. 'Are you serious?'

'No, I'm joking. Ha ha. It's all a big joke. I'm feeling in humorous mood. Look, when was the last time I joked, huh? *Huh?*'

He did have a point. Yolanda could not remember her father ever cracking a joke or even laughing much. He was a serious man, with a functional attitude to life. You work hard, you reap the rewards and, above all, you stay loyal to the motherland.

'I'm sorry. I do believe you. So do you want to talk about it? I mean, is that why you hardly ever leave the flat? Because of some *ghost?*' She could hardly believe she was saying it. 'I hate to think of you living in some hotel by yourself. Can't you go back home?'

'There's not time to talk of it now,' Sigurdsson snapped back. He didn't need anyone's sympathy and didn't much care for the direction this conversation was taking. 'So what do you want?'

'Well, I have some news for you.'

'You got rid of the Summers guy, yes? You can carry on diving now? Please give me some good news.'

Yolanda hesitated. 'The dive can continue, yes. We can get out there and start retrieving the find.' She was struggling to know how to tell him the truth, given the mood he was in. 'There's no reason why we can't have most of the hoard safely stowed in the boat by the end of the week. Then we'll be home. You'll have it, Father; you'll have the biggest hoard of them all to add to your collection – safely in the motherland. It'll be yours, you'll see.'

'Good. Well, get going then. And don't call me until you've got some good news.' The line went dead. Yolanda was spared the frustration of having to tell him the real truth – at least for now.

She figured it was better to do exactly as he said – get down there again as soon as possible, and preferably with Daniel, and then contact her father with great news of hoards of coins uncovered, and anything else she could find from the Viking site. Then he wouldn't care who was alive and who wasn't.

She placed the receiver back and walked towards the door. The events of the night before had brought a deep hunger within her and she needed to satisfy it soon. Breakfast.

She left the hotel room and moved swiftly down the corridor to the staircase. She hoped she'd find Daniel having breakfast too, though she knew it was too risky to acknowledge him. Maybe just a sneaky glance in his direction would be enough. She could feel the adrenalin pumping around her body as she descended the stairs, high on the romance and the intrigue. Two apparent strangers exchanging glances across a restaurant: it was thrilling.

The noise in the lobby was audible from halfway down the stairs and it made Yolanda pause for a moment.

What was that?

Had they found Møller's body?

Had she not secured it well enough to the seabed and it had washed up somewhere? Had the police come prowling around again?

For a second, she wondered if she should turn and run – find a fire exit and leg it. But hunger was playing havoc with her insides and she needed food. Besides, Daniel might be waiting for her. She couldn't bear the thought of disappointing him and not showing. He might think she was the one who had fled. She had to go in there, if only to see if he was up yet – see if he'd made a decision.

And, in any case, the commotion downstairs may not have anything to do with Møller at all. Why should it? She'd fastened his lifeless body well enough to the old wreck down there. She thought it unlikely he'd been washed up, and why should his body have landed here particularly? Maybe this was nothing to do with it at all. Perhaps it was a coach party of tourists or something. It certainly sounded like there were a lot of people down there, but there was no reason why it should affect her – provided they weren't all after breakfasts too. Then she'd be stressed. She continued down the staircase, turned left at the end of the corridor and entered the lobby.

It was in chaos. At least twenty people were queuing up to get into a small room next to the restaurant. They had cameras strapped to them and recording equipment.

She saw a waiter squeezing through the crowd, on his way to the kitchens. 'Excuse me,' said Yolanda, 'what's going on? Is it a wedding party or something?'

The young man shook his head. 'No, it's a press conference. To do with this body on the beach, I guess. The police are talking about it now. People want to know what's going on, I suppose.'

She knew, or at least she hoped she knew, what he was talking about, since Møller had filled her in on the journey from the airport. She hoped to God this was the body of Lars and not Møller after all. This couldn't have been a new body already, could it?

'There's a lot of interest in one body,' she said. 'Is it the same one, found yesterday? I thought they were saying that was some kind of accident, no?'

The waiter shook his head. 'Not what I heard. People are saying it was murder – brutal, if the rumours are true. Someone said they saw the body – said it was ripped open, or something. Horrible.'

'What do you mean, "ripped open"? Like some kind of . . . ritual killing, you mean?'

'That's what they're saying. Just rumours, though. We'll know more when the police start talking. Look, I must get on. Why don't you squeeze into the room yourself, if you're so interested?'

'Yes, I will, thanks.' Yolanda suddenly caught sight of Daniel's face at the doorway to the restaurant. He looked tired – probably slept as little as she did. She raised her eyebrows at him and flashed her eyes wide. He looked in the direction of the little conference room, suggesting they should go in there and listen. It was risky, but she felt high on the thrill of it all. To be in such close proximity to so many police just hours after the incident under water was exhilarating. Besides, she needed to know what this danger was all about. If it had been Lars, then she wanted answers. They joined the queue to get into the room.

A few moments later, they were sitting at the back of the small function room, usually reserved for private parties. There was a makeshift lectern at the front – a small table with a box on it, on to which a microphone had been strapped with black tape. The room was buzzing with anticipation as reporters from local newspapers and radio stations all waited eagerly for word on what some were calling the 'Suffolk sacrifice'. Yolanda saw a scruffy-looking gent with a worn face and a creased suit walk to the front of the room, followed by two younger-looking officers – if they were officers – who surreptitiously moved into the shadows once the man in the centre had found his position at the box.

'Ladies and gentlemen,' said DCI Khan, 'thank you for coming this morning. I know there's been a lot of speculation about what occurred yesterday and I'm sorry it's taken this long to put out a statement.' He cleared his throat. 'Thank you for your patience. Let me begin.'

CHAPTER 31

WEDNESDAY, 9.02 A.M.

ORFORD, SUFFOLK

It was a bright, optimistic morning, full of possibilities. The early mist was clearing in the tiny lanes that wove their way from the old village up the hill, slowly revealing the first glimpses of the great stone keep at Orford Castle. The gently rolling mounds that surrounded the castle were wet with dew.

Brian Jenkins was beginning to like retirement; it had taken long enough. He'd finished his job on the docks down in Felixstowe more than a year ago but it had taken this long for him to finally relax, slow down and enjoy the simple things, like a pint with his mates in the pub, picking fresh peas and digging up carrots on his allotment, and taking his beloved Jack Russell, Sally, for early morning walks, like today. It was cold and wintery but he was still up bright and early. He'd resolved to give in to his wife's nagging and finally do what she'd been asking for months now: he was going to clear out the shed. Years of hoarding had left it jam-packed full of junk and today was the day he was going to attack it.

But it was too nice a morning to begin straight away. He'd decided to steal a quick walk up the hill to the castle with Sally. It woke him up, recharged his batteries and made him feel human again. Standing here on the hilltop, gazing down at the village, he felt at peace. He looked down the steep slope to the roof-tops of the terraces on the old street that wound its way to the coast. He saw his own smart little terrace – but then all the houses were smart in Orford. It was a reputable retreat. Luckily, his wife was a local girl and she'd lived in the house before they'd married – and that was a million years ago, or so it felt – long before the place had become so fashionable. He gazed at the freshly painted white windows and the gloss black door with its polished brass handle and letter box. His wife had always looked after the place well.

Margaret would be up now, putting the kettle on, emptying the kitten's litter tray. Bloody animals – Brian hated them and they made him sneeze, but Margaret said she loved them and he figured a few sinus problems and a wheezy chest were worth enduring if it meant his wife was happy and he could get out and play on his allotment (or in the pub, truth be told). She wasn't that keen on cats, either, if she was honest, but it got him out of the house, which was a result.

He turned to face the castle again: deserted – just the way he liked it. He'd been here so many times over the years, he felt proprietorial about it, like he was the guardian of the many memories that still haunted this place. No one knew the grounds as well as he did and yet he never tired of coming up here. There was a certain peace to be found, unlike anywhere else he'd been. At one stage in his life – maybe it had been a mid-life crisis, looking back – he'd felt sure he'd been a resident of the castle in a previous existence, so connected was he to the building. He'd read up on the place incessantly and researched how the castle owners and their army of workers had lived over the centuries. Margaret had only ever rolled her eyes whenever he'd mentioned it. All little boys loved their castles.

The wind was whipping up, as it usually did up here on the top, but Brian was used to it. He just zipped up the collar of his fleece, tight around his neck, and strolled on up the steep slope towards the main keep. As a man of sixty-one he was fitter than most guys ten years younger, largely due to these early morning sorties up the hill.

He got into a decent stride, legs pounding, heart beating steadily, breath exhaling like a dragon's, and then he paused for a moment.

'Huh?'

Down at his feet, the grass was stained – dark brown. Foxes? He knew from his own garden that they had a nasty habit of urinating on the grass and discolouring it in patches. But there was too much here. Bloody big fox, he thought.

He looked further up the slope and saw that the stain continued up towards the east wall of the old stone keep ahead of him.

Tentatively, with a burgeoning sense that this was not going to end well, he stepped closer. As he approached the abbey wall, he caught a glimpse of something on the other side of the open archway.

It was a body, lying face up to the sky and, as Brian drew nearer, he could see it was the most tragic and disgusting thing he'd ever seen in his life. He went pale and clutched his stomach. Within seconds the bile rose from his gut and made him heave. Great groans bellowed out into the wind as he threw up like a drunkard after closing time. Strings of vomit dangled perilously from his paling lips before he was able to wipe them away with a screwed up handkerchief that had been living in his fleece pocket since the last time he'd worn it.

He slowly gathered himself together, gulped several long draughts of fresh air and walked around the wall to where the corpse lay. It was a man – in his thirties, maybe – brown hair, stubble and a grisly look of fear etched permanently on his face. The expression he'll now wear forever, until the flesh decays from his skull, thought Brian, as he stared, transfixed.

But there was no chance of the flesh decaying from this guy's chest; it had already been gouged out. There was a gaping hole of red and pink and blue. Two syrupy lungs lay outside of his broken ribcage, fanned out like wings and covered in congealed blood. Pearly white bones poked up through too much flesh. How had all this once fitted inside this man? thought Brian. Is that what's inside of all of us? It was like a tin of sardines opened and spewed out, twice the volume. Only this wasn't sardines, was it? It was a *real* person. A human being. Someone's relative. Brian retched again at the sight – it was too much.

He wiped his own mouth for the second time with the stinking handkerchief and started looking around him, nervously. The place was still deserted. OK, so this was getting scary now. He could feel himself beginning to shake, and he knew it wasn't the cold. Whoever did this could still be close by. He might be the next victim. He rubbed his brow with trembling hands and accidentally knocked his specs. Before he could catch them, they fell – deep into the soggy mess on the ground. He let out a shriek and quickly stooped to pick them up, without thinking. He hurriedly wiped them on his trousers.

Idiot. The tips of his fingers were now drenched in blood, and there was a guilty-looking stain on the side of his trousers. He wasn't wearing his usual dark jeans; they were in the washing basket that morning so he'd had to put on his pale ones. And they now resembled the boiler suit of a man at an abattoir.

'Oh, Jesus! Oh, God!'

He looked around again – still no one there. He was alone on the hillside, but he wouldn't be for long, that was for sure. The place was a favourite for dog walkers, even at this time of year, and Brian had been surprised not to have seen anyone yet.

No one to see him pitch up unawares and stumble across this corpse. No one to see how he accidentally dropped his specs and had to pick them up from the bloody ground.

Just a man, standing next to a mutilated corpse, freshly killed by the looks of it, and now with the dead guy's blood all over his hands.

What had started as a bright, optimistic morning had rapidly descended into a nightmare.

CHAPTER 32

WEDNESDAY, 9.21 A.M.

(10.21 A.M. LOCAL TIME)

ROSKILDE, DENMARK

Cally led the way through the large, revolving doors constructed of shiny chrome and tinted glass, with Grace, while Luc and Ralf carried the bags in the next revolve behind them. They walked across the polished wooden floor and waited for the lift. It was fast and efficient and they were soon rising to the floor that housed Ralf's flat. All four of them were relieved to have left the public street, where, at the rear entrance to the building, they'd been disappointed to see a collection of reporters and anxious-looking locals and even a small van with a television satellite dish fixed to its roof. Ralf had said, 'You should see it round the front entrance – even worse!' Now, in the solitude of the lift, they were able to reflect and prepare for the work to be done in the apartment next to Ralf's. The agents had already checked into the hotel nearby, while Ralf and Cally had waited for them in the taxi, and then they all headed straight round to the apartment block in question. Goode had continued to pull strings, ably assisted by Bonati, and they'd cleared them for some private time in Sigurdsson's flat, free of interference from the Danish police – at least for a short while.

Soon there was a pleasing *ting* sound and the lift doors slid smoothly open to reveal a gaping view of the Baltic Sea through the glass walls opposite. From up here you could see for miles and, now that the morning fog was lifting, they had uninterrupted views of the icy ocean. There were few ships on it, just a couple of tiny dots in the distance – oil tankers that moved slowly across the horizon's sweep like seeds on a pond.

'It's impressive up here,' said Luc. 'Nice place.'

'Yeah, it works for us,' said Cally, smiling, as if she lived there all year round. It was Ralf's bachelor pad, but he was perfectly happy for her to give others the impression that she shared it. The truth was they didn't see enough of each other these days, and this recent visit of Cally's was all too rare. How tragic that it had been so marred by the events of the night before. It was not turning out to be the romantic visit they'd both counted the days for.

'Ralf works over in Copenhagen, but he prefers the relative quiet of Roskilde, don't you, darling? At least, it *was* quiet until I arrived and started screaming from the balcony! Now look at it!'

Luc moved closer to the window and saw an even larger swell of people down on the ground, outside the main entrance to the apartment block.

'News travels fast in these parts,' he said.

'Yes, and I'm sorry for that,' said Ralf. 'It seems the people of Roskilde are easily spooked.'

'It's the same anywhere,' said Grace. 'It's what the paranormal does to people. Panic sets in and it's hard to shift sometimes. It can spread like wild fire.'

They opened the door to Ralf's flat and entered. It was a clean and orderly bachelor pad, decorated in a minimalist style, with chrome fittings, pine floors and black leather furniture that contrasted well against the plain white walls.

'Tea?' said Cally. She knew all too well the Brit's penchant for the drink and was perfectly able to navigate her way around Ralf's sparsely equipped kitchen.

'No, thanks,' said Luc. 'Do you mind if we get straight out to the balcony and take some readings? Then perhaps round to next door, if we can?'

'Yes, of course,' said Cally. 'Let me show you round. I understand that Mr Goode has managed to get you access for a while.'

'Yes, he pulls strings like a puppeteer,' said Luc, smiling cheekily.

Easy there, thought Grace. Perhaps Luc had not realised he was speaking to one of Goode's most trusted senior staff. Cally was one of his 'go-to people'. She was smart, elegant and sassy. She got things done. Even after spending such a short time with her, Grace could see why Goode relied on her. She was indispensible, especially since he had decided to spend so much of his time in London these days. She ran things for him back in the States, which was why Ralf saw so little of her these days.

They moved swiftly through the apartment to the living room that led out to the balcony at the front of the building. The cold air wafted in as Ralf slid the heavy glass door open.

Out on the balcony, it was fresh and bracing. The weather was clearing still and the skies over the Baltic were pale blue, with faint wisps of cloud that drifted quickly in the sea breeze.

'So that's your neighbour's apartment, yes?' said Grace, pointing to the left. 'And that's the window where you saw the apparition?'

Cally nodded. 'That's right.' She shuddered slightly and Grace noticed Ralf move towards his partner and gently take her hand in his. It was obvious that yesterday's incident had shaken Cally. The agents had heard from Bonati how Goode had been 'very concerned about her', when he'd first received her call from Roskilde. That was, after all, why the agents had been instructed to drop everything and get over there as soon as possible. When ghosts spooked one of Goode's own people, it became a top priority for the agency.

'Can you talk us through it? I mean, if that's OK?' said Luc, as he took out various instruments and began taking readings. The EMF meter registered high radiation within just a few seconds, and the Geiger counter confirmed there was radiation here too.

Cally began to recount what she'd seen the day before: how she'd screamed when the head had first come into her peripheral vision and she'd turned to see what it was; the shock of it; the horror of the disembodied head, floating, the edges of its skull somehow merging with the air around it. It had been truly abhorrent.

'No wonder you screamed, darling,' Ralf said once she'd finished her story.

'We need to get into next door,' said Luc. It was hard to see inside the neighbour's flat as the bright sky reflected off the windows and obscured the darker room behind the glass.

'Yes, of course. Follow me,' said Ralf.

He led them out of the apartment, along the hallway and up to the adjacent apartment. Ralf knocked firmly on the door and a police officer opened it.

'We've been expecting you,' he said. 'You are officers from England, yes?'

Luc nodded his head and he and Grace entered.

'You have half an hour or so, is that OK?' said the officer. 'I shall be in the lobby downstairs if you need me.'

'Thank you,' said Grace, as she watched the officer leave with Ralf and Cally, who returned to their flat down the corridor. She turned to Luc. 'Goode has friends in high places, it seems.'

'It helps having MI5 on your side,' said Luc, 'and Whitehall too. Let's get the instruments set up. Come on; we don't have long.'

They moved into the kitchen and then into the main living room at the front of the building. It was a mirror image of Ralf's own flat – same layout – except it was clear that the resident of this place had expensive tastes. The room was by no means crowded with furniture, but what there was was clearly of supreme quality, suggesting this guy had serious money to spend. The wooden sideboard with crystal decanter, the oil paintings on the wall, the tasteful leather chair positioned for the very best views across the Baltic . . . This man knew how to live, it seemed. And the strange cabinets dotted everywhere, inside which there were artefacts from history – what was all that about? Luc and Grace's curiosity was pricked.

'Are you thinking what I'm thinking?' said Grace.

'That these artefacts are Viking, by any chance?' said Luc, staring into the largest cabinet on the wall behind the leather chair.

'Yep. I think you could say this man is proud of his Danish roots.'

'Proud enough to go digging for them and stir up ghosts?' said Luc.

'It's possible. What do you feel here?' asked Grace, standing by the window, looking out.

'It's an unwelcoming place, for sure. There's no love in this room. No warmth. Only memories.'

'Memories?'

'Yeah. You know, history. These old artefacts are important to this guy, that's obvious. It's like a museum. But it's weird. It's like the people who used to own these things are still here somehow. Do you know what I mean?'

'Exactly. That's what I feel too. It's strange. You set up the instruments in here and I'll have a wander around, see what else he's got. I'm beginning to see why the place has attracted the attention of ghosts. It feels alive with them.' She disappeared back into the kitchen and then out to the hallway, from which two bedrooms were visible.

Luc took out the Tri-Axis EMF meter and his laptop. He

connected them up wirelessly and began taking readings. Within seconds, the meter was reading 43 mG. He knew this was incredibly high already – especially as the place seemed to be devoid of electrical equipment, save his own laptop. There was no television, which Luc thought unusual. Neither was there any kind of CD player or iPod speakers. What did this guy do for entertainment? Luc thought to himself.

As he continued taking other instruments from his bag, the EMF meter soared to 89 mG. There was no question that the place was alive with radiation. He picked up the electrostatic locator and held it near the cabinet behind the chair. The needle went crazy.

He returned to his bag and removed the Geiger counter. He held the probe in his hand and was about to move over to the cabinet when the machine started emitting loud beeps already. He was standing near the leather chair.

Why should it display this kind of energy?

He bent to look under the chair and lowered the probe to the floor as he did so. It went crazy. Then he noticed the coin, apparently discarded by the chair legs, and he pointed the probe towards it. The Geiger counter went ballistic. An old coin? Why the hell should an old coin do this? he thought.

He picked up the handheld EMF meter and brought it over to where the coin lay. The needle soared and then rested at 128 mG. With so much radiation, Luc was amazed the coin wasn't glowing.

He picked it up and immediately felt a burning sensation in the palm of his hand.

'That's incredible,' he said aloud. 'Grace! Come here, quick. Grace?'

There was no noise from the other room.

'Grace?' He left the living room and went into the kitchen: no one there. He went into the small, square hallway and saw two doors leading into what he presumed were bedrooms. 'Grace, where are you? You must come and see this.'

He opened one door – just an empty bedroom, sparsely furnished. He shut the door again and made for the second door, which was left ajar.

'Grace?'

He pushed the door wide open, causing light from the hall to spill into the dark room. Luc fell against the door frame in shock.

There, in the centre of the room, was an apparition. Surrounded by a strange gaseous plasma stood the huge frame of a man, its wide shoulders draped with what looked like some kind of animal fur.

In the corner of the room, facing Luc, Grace crouched beside a wardrobe. She stared back at him, wide-eyed with fear. He'd never seen her like that. He knew now why she'd remained silent – perhaps the ghost had not even seen her yet. Until now.

The figure turned around to see where the light was coming from and Luc saw its face. He almost wretched in disgust at the skeletal cheek bones, eyeless sockets and pursed black lips. Luc saw the remains of a beard – loose, wiry hairs protruding from its wide, skinless jawbone. It was one of the most startling visions he'd seen since joining the CRYPT. Not in any SPA session had he seen anything like this before.

Though the face was devoid of skin, it was framed with long, straggly blond hair, matted and filthy, which stuck to its cheekbones and across its large, protruding forehead.

He knew he was staring at a Viking warrior.

Grace had been determined not to move, so as to avoid its glare. But it was too late. The light from the hallway illuminated the entire room and there was no hiding place now.

The ghost lunged at Luc, who was still standing, frozen in the doorway. He retaliated by thrusting his foot into its belly, hard. The ghost bent over, but did not topple. Instead, it rose to its full height and made for Luc again. He threw punches at it, his arms raining fists down on the figure, but to no avail.

'Get the neutralisers!' he yelled to Grace, who was moving out of the corner and was about to leap at the ghost from behind. 'Don't attack it! Get them now and switch them on, for God's sake.'

She grabbed her bag and fled into the living room, where she found Luc's own bag and his neutraliser inside.

By the time she'd returned to the bedroom, Luc was pinned to the wall in the opposite corner. The ghost was going for his throat. Long, wiry fingers were at his neck, and they started applying pressure, piercing Luc's thin flesh. The ghost's bony face was as menacing as it was hideous, and a foul stench, like rotting flesh, emitted from its jaws. Luc heard the ominous sound of clicking – that familiar but evil sound often heard in the presence of a ghost as it attempts to speak. It was insect-like: a series of whispered, high-pitched clicks that burst from its mouth.

'Hurry!' Luc shouted, half choking. He kicked and punched the ghostly figure in front of him, trying to ignore the clicks that rose in volume now and penetrated his ears like needles. His boots crunched into bone.

Grace switched on the neutralisers, set them on the bed, then flew at the ghost. She grabbed it from behind and tried to squeeze her arms together to trap it, while Luc kept lashing out from his side. But its back was broad and strong; Grace could feel its spine and ribcage pressing into her own chest. But it was enough – it gave Luc a moment to compose himself, to take a couple of large gulps of air to shake off the queasiness brought on by the stranglehold, and then grab a large, heavy-framed oil painting from the wall. He jabbed one of its corners into the ghost's forehead. The hard, brass frame thudded against the ghost's skull, Grace quickly released her grip and the figure went down, catching the edge of the wooden bed as it fell, causing its skull to splinter and crack, and then slumping to the floor.

Luc stood on it and heard the crunch of bone beneath his heavy boots. As they both kicked at it, they could feel the resistance against their feet was slowly weakening. The edges of the ghost's body were becoming more cloudy, blending with the air around it.

The combination of the EM neutralisers, reducing the electromagnetic energy which the ghost had been drawing on, and the physical blows, which the agents continued to rain down on it, had worked. They watched in silent shock as the figure slowly faded from view. The plasma that had become solid enough to produce a physical representation of this Viking ghost was now becoming translucent again, until eventually Grace and Luc could see it fade into the air.

And it was gone.

CHAPTER 33

WEDNESDAY, 9.43 A.M.

STAR INN, DUNWICH

It had looked like they'd bought it. The reporters' questions, once a battery of frenzied shouts and cries, had almost ceased. DCI Khan's sense of relief was shared by Jud and Bex, who were still standing a few feet away from him in the corner of the room, where they could keep an eye on proceedings without attracting too much attention to themselves. This was Khan's show, after all – his gig. They had no intention of stealing the limelight, especially when so much of what had been said in the last twenty minutes was garbage.

The story they'd concocted had been as detailed as usual – it was always the little inconsistencies which the journalists were trained to sniff out like hunting dogs, and so you had to be thorough before you went into a press conference. Khan knew this better than most, for it was invariably him who found himself presenting stories to the public that were designed to cover up the paranormal activity that was really happening. He'd become a smokescreen for the CRYPT these days.

But even the inspector thought this press statement was a belter – one of their best. The man found on the beach was a tourist to the area. They were still waiting to ID him, but they had good reason to suspect he was of Danish extraction. He'd been seen in the evening the night before by a late-night dog-walker. And apparently she'd seen him swimming, fully clothed. Tests from a post-mortem would soon confirm their suspicions that he had consumed large quantities of alcohol. So it was assumed that he'd been in a reckless mood and had decided to enjoy a late-night swim.

Tragedy had struck when he had become entangled in what the police now believe was a disused fishing net, which must have been ripped from a trawler some time ago and was drifting perilously close to the land. The net had hard, plastic fixings and thick twine and the man had become badly entangled. Unable to move, they believed he'd been swept towards rocks further down the beach and then eventually washed up here. This was why his body was so badly injured. (Onlookers had seen the bloodstains on the pebbles, so there was no point in denying a brutal injury had been sustained.)

Witnesses? Well, no call was put out to the local lifeboat, and no one had come forward with any more evidence other than that provided by the dog walker, but traces of fishing net and plastic hooks were found on the man's body, some deeply embedded in his chest. And there was severe bruising on his head and shoulders, which would be consistent with a blow against something hard, like rocks.

The important point, as Khan had been determined to press home, was that there was no suspicion of anyone else being involved in this death – though, of course, the police would continue their investigation in earnest and consider all options.

There were two people seated at the back of the room who had not been convinced by the story – not the comments about the accident, at least. It had seemed too incredible to them and, besides, Lars didn't drink. Yolanda knew that. But, when Khan had uttered the words 'Danish man' just moments earlier, Yolanda knew it was Lars. So why were they making this up?

And Daniel Summers knew, better than anyone, of the brutal injuries sustained on the man's body. They just didn't seem the kind of injuries caused by stray fishing nets, or jagged rocks even. This had been much more deliberate.

Yolanda turned to Daniel, both their faces ashen pale. 'Why is he lying?' she whispered. 'I don't get it. What the hell happened out there?'

'Who knows?' said Dan. 'But it certainly wasn't an accident, that's for sure. Whoever this poor guy was, he was killed deliberately.'

'How come you're so sure?'

'Because I was the one who found him, wasn't I?'

'And can you describe his face?' Yolanda said, anxiously.

Dan shook his head slowly. 'He was lying face down. I only saw his back, but it was a mess, I tell you.' She saw his eyes glaze over. 'Why do you ask?' he said eventually.

'Because I think I know who he was,' Yolanda whispered.

'You *what?*'

'Yeah. He worked for my father. He was helping Møller. And Møller was supposed to be keeping an eye on him – watching him from the cliff, to tell him when the coast was clear. How the hell this happened, I don't know. Møller said he didn't see anything, when I asked him. Bloody fool.'

Dan was taken aback at how she spoke about someone whom, just hours earlier, she'd dispatched so cruelly. He reminded himself never to upset this girl. That's if he chose to go with her – and he still hadn't decided. He had plenty more questions for her yet and had intended on grilling her over breakfast – until they'd seen the crowds of reporters gathering for the press conference, of course. His questions would have to wait for now.

He looked at her as she flicked her eyes furtively across the crowded room, scanning for anyone else she knew or suspected. It seemed her default setting was permanently on the offence. She trusted no one and expressed her true feelings to no one, so she was rarely let down. But that gaze of hers – those piercing blue eyes and the casual, flirtatious flick of her blond hair across to one side whenever she wanted to attract his attention – it certainly worked.

'So what do we do now?' said Dan.

'We carry on. Agnar will be calling tonight for another update. We have to get out there and continue the search, I guess. He's panicking already, you see. We have to give him some good news, and soon, or I swear he'll go crazy.'

'Go out there again now? Are you kidding?' said Dan. 'When the police learn that Møller is missing, they'll close off this entire stretch of coastline. Any boat will be spotted and they'll send us away, or haul us in for questioning.'

'Why should they learn Møller is missing?' snapped Yolanda. 'They don't even know he's here. He didn't exactly come through customs, Daniel. He didn't fly here, like me; he sailed here with Lars. The same way we'll leave. And no one will miss him, trust me.'

Dan couldn't believe her coldness. She was something else, this girl.

'But what if he's . . .' Dan looked around and huddled closer to Yolanda at the very back of the room, out of earshot. 'What if he's . . . washed up? What if they find his body?'

'They *won't*. No one will know about him, will they?' She was staring at him now, her glare penetrating into his eyes, willing him to keep his mouth shut and do as he's told. '*Will they?*' she said knowingly.

Dan understood perfectly what she was saying: keep your mouth shut or you'll end up at the bottom of the ocean.

Great start to a relationship, he thought. But he was beginning to realise he was in so deep he had little choice. The deliberations of last night - the tossing and turning, the pacing the floor, the hours spent staring out of the window, trying to decide whether he should go with Yolanda - were a waste of time. He had no choice. This Sigurdsson would have 'friends' all over the world, no doubt. There was little chance of escaping him forever. Or his daughter.

'No, they won't,' he whispered.

'So, we get out there as soon as possible. We find whatever is left beneath the sea and then we disappear with it. And live with the riches you couldn't even dream of. My father pays well – you'll see.'

'But the place will be overrun with police, surely.'

'Not so much now,' said Yolanda. 'There'll be some, maybe, but the body has been moved. And if they are lying and someone is responsible for this, then they know he won't be coming back here in a hurry, will he? Lars' body has already washed up. They won't be looking for another. Besides, they won't connect it to any divers out there. Why should they, huh?' She looked at his fearful face. 'You worry too much, that's your problem,' she whispered, smiling. 'Come on, let's go.'

She took his hand and led him from the room and straight out of the hotel, ahead of the rush of reporters and police officers.

But one person saw them leave. She'd been studying them from the other side of the room ever since they'd entered. She'd noticed their furtive looks and hushed whispering. And now she too grabbed her partner and made for the door.

'Come on,' said Bex. 'Follow me.'

As the two of them headed for the door, Jud caught a glimpse of the landlord – the father of the young man, Pat, who'd tried to tell them about the shouting heard last night. He quickly seized his opportunity and went over to him.

'Where're you going?' said Bex.

'Just a minute.'

He approached the landlord. 'Excuse me; can I have a quick word?'

The large man looked harassed. 'I hope it is quick. You can see I've got a lot of people here, and they'll all be wanting coffee now that the detective inspector's finished his cabaret act. So what is it, sir?' He tried to force a smile but there was a hurried, impatient tone in his voice.

'Oh, it was just about last night,' said Jud, casually. 'I was wondering what the noise was all about, that was all. I had the impression at breakfast that your son knew what happened, but he was called away, wasn't he? So he was unable to tell us. Could you shed any light?'

Jud saw the landlord's forced smile vanish and his lips went thin. 'I'm sorry, sir. I really am very busy. I don't know of any noise. There was a couple having a row outside last night – is that what you mean? It was no big deal. It's not unusual; it's what alcohol does, isn't it? Especially with them. They're a local couple – everyone knows them – and they're always rowing. He drinks too much, see? So I invited them in, gave them a coffee and allowed them to stay in one of my spare rooms. I didn't want them going home together, not in the mood he was in. They'd had too much to be able to drive, anyway. But they've gone now.'

'Oh,' said Jud, unconvinced. 'That's funny, you see, because your son started to give us quite a different story at breakfast.'

'He's got an imagination, that boy!' The landlord forced a chuckle. 'Do excuse me, I must get on – lots to do, you know.'

'Jud, come on!' said Bex from the doorway. 'They're getting away!'

'Who are?' Jud returned to where she was waiting. 'Who are we supposed to be chasing, Bex? You didn't say.'

'The girl who was in the bar last night – you know. She was talking to Daniel; she had a guy with her but he's gone now.'

'But you said, "they're getting away". Who's she with now?'

'Daniel! Come on!'

'Oh, for God's sake, Bex. Will you let this guy go?'

'There's something fishy here, Jud. I swear it. Why has she hooked up with Daniel now? And where's the other man? They looked guilty in that press conference; there was something about the way they were whispering to each other. I didn't like it.'

'I know why you didn't like it, Bex,' said Jud.

'Oh, will you get over it!' she snapped at him. 'I'm serious. Something's up. Now, come on. Quick!'

Jud looked back into the hotel but the landlord had already seized his chance and promptly vanished into a back room somewhere.

'Damn!' said Jud. 'Now look what you've done. I could've grilled him then, Bex. I reckon I'd got him rattled. I could have found out whether his son really was dreaming or not. I wanna know if that couple outside last night, the ones making the noise, whether they really did see something paranormal.'

But Bex had already gone. He ran after her, out of the door and across the hotel car park.

Daniel and his mysterious companion had vanished. Bex spun around, her eyes searching over the sand dunes in the distance, up the road into the village, back towards the beach car park and the café.

No sign of them.

'Oh, great,' said Jud. 'So now we've both lost everyone. Great morning, Bex. What the hell do we do now?'

Bex was about to answer but she caught sight of someone over Jud's shoulder. She'd seen him sneak out of a back door of the hotel and he was now running across the car park towards them, stooping low like some sniper.

'Come with me,' said the landlord's son in a furtive whisper. 'I've got a half-hour break and then my dad'll notice I'm gone. There're some people I need you to see. Hurry!'

They followed him at speed out of the car park and up the lane, which wound its way behind the hotel, up past a few more houses and then into the wide, Suffolk countryside. The skies opened up into a wide arc, but the wind still rattled their clothes and swept down their necks.

'Where are we going?' shouted Bex, getting colder by the minute. She and Jud had to run to keep pace with their anxious-looking tour guide.

'It's just up here. Not far. You'll see.'

They approached a bend in the road and then saw a lay-by further up on the left, near the grounds of the abbey ruins. There was a parked Ford Fiesta. Jud could see the backs of two people seated in the front.

'The people who we heard last night, yeah?' he said to Pat.

'That's right. They caught a taxi home this morning but I knew they were coming back with the spare keys, so I called them quickly and told them to wait for us before they drove home again. I knew you'd want to speak to them, you see.'

'How did you know that?'

'Oh, just a hunch.'

'What?' said Bex, stopping in the road. Jud paused too.

Pat smiled cheekily. 'Don't worry. I won't say anything. I've always admired what you do. If I was a couple of years younger, I might even have applied to join you guys. Who knows? We could've been on the same team.'

Jud and Bex looked at each other, silently. This could be a bluff – albeit a cunning one. Did this guy *really* know about the CRYPT?

'I'm not stupid, you know,' Pat continued. 'I might be working in my father's hotel in a sleepy village in the middle of nowhere, but I've got a computer, and that's all you need.' There was jealousy in his voice and it had not been lost on them.

'We've met before, haven't we?' said Jud. He'd known there was something familiar about this guy the moment he'd seen him behind the bar and he knew he had to confront him sooner or later.

Pat just nodded silently, raised an eyebrow and gave a knowing smile. He wasn't going to divulge anything else here. And, from the look on his face, Jud knew he shouldn't have raised it here –

not in front of Bex. It was just too dangerous. If this guy was from Jud's past, then who knows what he might say? He could know everything. And he really did look familiar. If only he could place that face. Jud hated the fact that so many of his childhood memories seemed out of reach since the nightmare incident at the castle. It was almost like he'd spent so long trying to deny anything like that had ever happened, that his life to date fell into two halves: pre-Mum and post-Mum; Jamie and then Jud. If this guy arose from the Jamie years, then he was buried beneath the years of guilt and heartache that cluttered Jud's mind. No wonder he couldn't recall him easily. And that made Jud worry even more. Did this man know his real identity? It was impossible!

'Well,' said Jud, 'that sounds intriguing, but let's save it for another day, shall we? You've got twenty-six minutes and counting before you lose your job and your home.'

But Bex hadn't missed the exchange. She'd seen the knowing glances and resolved to find out more as soon as she could. Was this someone from Jud's past? Someone who could reveal something, anything, about his secretive life? She certainly hoped so.

Two people got out of the car – they'd seen the visitors approaching in their rear-view mirror and knew one of them was Pat.

'So, here they are,' he said to the young man. 'Tell them what you saw.'

'And you are?' said Jud to the guy, who seemed to have been glancing around the hedges and fields since getting out of the car, and wore a nervous expression.

'Alex – Alex Fetcher. And this is my wife, Janey. Pat said you were police officers, yeah?'

Jud's eyes flicked across to Pat, who gave him a knowing wink.

'Yes, indeed – crime scene investigators. We tend to be assigned the unusual investigations. This is my partner, Bex De Verre.'

Bex felt a tiny surge of excitement at the description. 'Hello,' she said. 'So what happened last night?'

Alex and Janey recounted the sights of the evening before: the two lines of figures, approaching in the dark, some carrying spears, others holding giant swords. When Jud asked why they thought this wasn't a re-enactment by some bloodthirsty volunteers, out for an adventure, Alex said sharply that their faces were skeletal. 'Coz they were Zombies!' he said. 'That's why. Walking dead, they were.'

Janey shook with fear and Alex held her close. The wind was whipping up again and the dark clouds, which seemed to have sat belligerently in the sky ever since the agents' arrival in Suffolk, hung inhospitably low. There was an unwelcoming mood in the air that was not lost on the agents. Bex had sensed it as soon as she'd started walking up the road after Pat.

Jud spoke first. 'So you are saying you saw dozens – was it dozens?'

'Yeah. There were loads of them,' said Alex.

'OK. Dozens of ghosts, all heading inland, towards you, dressed in some kind of primitive battle dress and carrying ancient weapons, you say?'

'Yeah. I know it sounds stupid. I'm sorry, but that's what I saw.'

Bex reassured him, 'You don't need to feel embarrassed. But I'm concerned about where they were heading. What happened after you fled? Did you see where they went next?'

Alex and Janey shook their heads. 'We ran so fast from the place, there wasn't time to see where they were marching to,' said Janey.

'When we got back to the car, we didn't hang about, I can tell you,' said Alex. 'I dunno, maybe the abbey was important to them?'

Jud shook his head. He knew that the abbey would not have even been built at the time when Vikings invaded this stretch of coastline, though there may have been some kind of church on the site back then. But he was sure that what this couple had seen were the ghosts of ninth-century Viking soldiers – although he had no intention of explaining that to them. He was still keen to promote the possibility of their being eccentric, part-time historians, out on a re-enactment. Strange, but plausible. This was Britain, after all, with more than its fair share of history buffs and people who liked to dress in old costumes and pretend to be someone else at weekends.

He could see these eyewitnesses were still distressed – fear was written across their faces and it was terror like this which could spread right across the county in no time at all. He had to attempt to keep it under wraps for as long as possible.

He spoke calmly and respectfully. 'I think the most likely explanation, Mr and Mrs Fetcher, is that you stumbled across a group of historians – eccentrics, I've no doubt, especially given the odd masks you've described, but humans all the same. This is an historic place, filled with ancient traditions and customs stretching back centuries. No wonder people like to visit it and, at times, escape into another era. The country is full of historical re-enactment societies, I'm sure you know – some of them more fanatical than others.'

'What?' said Alex. 'You're not serious, surely! Are you mad, mate?'

Jud approached him and looked him straight in the eye. Bex held her breath and prayed her partner's temper had not yet been pricked. 'I don't joke about these matters, sir,' he said calmly and respectfully. 'The alternatives are far harder to believe, are they not?'

'But . . . But Pat here said that you'd believe me. He said you'd listen. Didn't you, Pat? Eh? Tell them *you* believe us, at least.'

'Oh, yes, I believe you all right,' said Pat, standing behind Jud and giving him a disappointed glare. 'And so do the officers here.

Don't you, huh? I know you don't believe they were historians, any more than I do, do you?'

Jud turned and stared at Pat; he was bugging him now. Enough was enough. He'd been odd from the start, this guy, claiming to know all about what they did, but refusing to expand on where and when they'd met before.

And then Pat did something that both startled and disappointed Jud. He said, 'Re-enactment societies? Ha!' And it was the laugh that followed which brought memories flooding back for Jud. He'd recognised it. He knew who he was, when they'd met and where.

It was Hartwell – scrawny, annoying Paddy Hartwell. They'd been at boarding school together. Hartwell was a couple of years above Jud, but he remembered him – remembered that laugh. Well, you would. It was as irritating as it was unique, like the gurgling sound water makes going down a plughole, but recorded and then played back at twice the speed. He recalled how this kid used to hang around with the bigger guys and hover like a fly on the fringe of the action, laughing in his own stupid, gurgling way whenever his brutal friends chose to pick on some unsuspecting little first year. This kid was not much bigger than the first years himself at the time – and he'd not grown much since then, either – but he had friends, powerful ones too. Jud never knew why the bigger guys should allow him to stick around with them. Probably just enjoyed having a sycophantic fan following them around – it made them feel good. They treated him no better than they treated their victims, but Hartwell was always seen with them.

Jud had never thought to ask him his surname back at the hotel. And he'd not recalled his Christian name at first; everyone just called each other by their surname at school.

He was still giggling. 'Middle-aged men in Viking costumes and skeleton masks! Come on; you can do better than that, really!'

Jud clenched his teeth and glanced at Bex. Hartwell giggled again. That sound used to drive Jud to distraction, especially when it was the soundtrack to one of his own friends getting picked on by Hartwell's bigger mates. No one, not even the older guys, tried picking on Jud at school. Jamie Goode could look after himself, but he often saw his friends getting roughed up a bit, and there was always that constant gurgling laugh in the background whenever it happened.

Enough. He'd seen red.

Before Bex could stop him, he grabbed Hartwell and pulled him towards the hedge, away from the car and the dazed-looking couple. Hartwell tried to resist and pull back, but Jud's grip was vice-like. He was going nowhere, not until Jud had finished with him. He kept walking further down the road, out of earshot, and then stopped, still gripping his arm tight.

Hartwell was smiling. His penchant for winding up his peers had clearly not changed. He loved the reaction his laugh had provoked from this pompous kid who thought he was the business, dressed in his black agent clothes and wearing his fixed, moody expression. Who the hell did he think he was?

Of course, Hartwell knew the answer to that question better than anyone. And if Jud didn't take his hand off him soon, he would start spilling the beans.

'It's been a while, Jamie, hasn't it?' he whispered, gleefully.

Jud couldn't hide his anger. This was moving too quickly. 'What did you just call me?'

'Oh, come on,' said Hartwell. 'Let's not pretend, shall we?'

Jud pushed his chest hard and Hartwell fell backwards towards the hedge, which was spiky and uncomfortable. Jud wasn't a kid any more. He'd grown and was now considerably taller and stockier than Hartwell. Everything soon balances out once kids grow up, he thought.

'I don't know what you're talking about,' he said flatly.

Bex was running towards them, anxious that the eyewitnesses were about to witness something else – a CRYPT agent beating up a civilian.

'Go away!' Jud shouted at her. 'This is between *us!*'

She stopped where she was, but she didn't go back to the couple. She stayed there, on the roadside, hoping to block their view of what was happening down in the ditch.

'You can push me around, punch my lights out if you like, but you can't erase what I know, Goode. And I know it all.'

Jud stood there, frozen to the spot. For the first time in ages, he was speechless.

'I know where you've been. I know what happened. I *know what they said you did.*'

That was it. Nothing could hold him back now. He flew at Hartwell like a wild animal, venting his frustration, his guilt, his heartache, his anger in one fell swoop. He picked him up by the scruff of his neck and threw him, literally, to the floor. When Hartwell refused to get up, he dragged him up by his shoulders and pushed him backwards, towards the nearest tree trunk, where he slammed him against it and held his arms tight. He pulled him up close and whispered very slowly, 'You continue and I will break you. Understand? I will *break you.*'

Hartwell's grin had finally disappeared. The message had got through, at last. There were no bigger friends around to help him now – no one to hide and giggle behind. Just him and this raging kid in front of him, who was bigger, stronger, quicker than he'd ever be.

'Hey, it's OK,' he said, gently now, pursuing a different tack. 'It's me! Harty! I'm just saying I know you, that's all. I know what you've been through. No need to get angry, mate. We go back a long way. And I can help you.'

Jud released his arms and Hartwell rubbed his left shoulder, wincing in pain. Jud quickly glanced back at Bex. She was up beyond the car now, ushering the couple across the road and into the abbey grounds on the other side. She'd saved his skin. She must've realised he was going to blow his top, and quickly moved his audience the hell away – probably on some pretext of showing her where they'd seen the figures approaching over the hill the night before. Anything to prevent them seeing – and reporting – what Jud might do next. She knew better than most what his temper was like when provoked. She'd deal with him later, Jud was sure of that. But she couldn't have heard anything important . . . he hoped.

'But . . . how? How do you know all this?' Jud didn't know what else to say. There was no point in denying it. But how and why should this guy know any more than what happened at school? He could accept that he'd recognised Hartwell, but how the hell did it work the other way around? Jud's hair was different, even his eyes were now a different colour; he had a different identity from Jamie Goode. Why should Hartwell make the connection? He gave the impression that he knew *everything*; maybe he wasn't lying.

Hartwell watched Jud thinking it through – the cogs whirring inside his head, faster than ever, trying to keep pace with what was unfolding here. The magnitude of it all. The fact that someone could potentially blow the whole thing – forever.

'It's OK,' he said gently. 'I'm not gonna talk. But don't hit me. Please don't do that. I'd hate you to lose your job, but you will if they see you hit me again. I won't be able to help you then.'

Jud looked surprised. 'Help me? Why should you help me? I've just pushed you into a hedge and threatened you.'

Hartwell's words, 'if they see you hit me', had served as a chilling reminder that people were watching this – or had been. He'd lost his temper once again and he knew he'd have to face the consequences. But the words, 'I know what you did', ran deep for Jud and struck a nerve buried far within him. His actions had been inevitable.

He looked again up the road, in the direction of Bex, and was relieved to see she had disappeared through the gate into the abbey grounds and was gone.

'But *how*?' he said again, incredulously. 'How did you know?'

'You may not remember, but your father will. Ask him about Pat Hartwell. He'll tell you.'

'Tell me *what*?' Jud could feel his temper rising again, clenching his fists, gritting his teeth. This weasel was secretive and sneaky, just like he'd been at school.

Hartwell could see he wasn't going to get away from Jud without some kind of explanation. 'OK. So I followed you when I left school, right. I mean, I followed everyone. I like to know what others are getting up to; nothing wrong with that. I searched for you online and found where you were living. I knew what your parents did, because you used to tell everyone at school. Everyone knows Goode Technology, Jamie. It's hardly a secret, is it? And . . .' He dropped his voice and tried his level best to sound more caring this time. 'I know about what happened at the castle. I know about your mother, Goode.'

Jud took a deep breath and tried to stay calm. 'You said you know what I *did*.'

'No. I didn't say that at all. I said I know what they *said* you did. That's different, isn't it, Jamie? I don't believe you did it, see? I knew you at school, for God's sake. And I knew you wouldn't have done something like that. You were a rebel, yes, but you had good values. I can't deny you that.'

'But you said I should ask my father – he'll tell me. What will he tell me?'

'That I applied to join the PIT. I wanted to be a part of his early attempts at paranormal investigating. Don't you see? I had the skills. I can see ghosts just as well as you can. But he didn't take me on. I never even got a reply from him. Nothing.'

Jud was struggling to keep up again. 'So, let me get this straight. You researched me. You found out where I lived and you applied to work for my father?'

'Exactly.'

'Why? You can't see ghosts!'

Hartwell looked at him with a disappointed expression on his face. 'Goode, what is it about you, huh? Why do you agents all think that you're the only people who can see ghosts? You think you're the only ones interested in this kind of stuff? Well, you're not. You might be the chosen few who get to ride the Fireblades and fly in the 'copters and chase about town dressed in your little black suits, thinking you're it, but meanwhile there are plenty of us who've been investigating the paranormal for years. I've been seeing ghosts since I was tiny.'

'Really?' Jud was going to take some convincing here. This guy was just a jealous person from his past – bitter and resentful that he'd ended up working in a sleepy bar in the middle of nowhere while Jud and his team had the adventures. He'd just admitted as much. Why should Jud believe that he had similar powers of ESP? It was all too convenient.

'Yes! You're not the only one to live in an historic house, Goode! My folks' place in Berkshire was haunted. I regularly saw ghosts there. And at other places too. I've always been interested in the paranormal. How do you think I saw the advert for joining the PIT in the first place? It was in one of my ghost-hunting magazines. I applied as soon as I saw it.'

'Look, I'm sorry you didn't hear anything, OK. I'm sorry that I ended up as an agent and you didn't. I'm sorry you're working in your father's pub. Life is full of disappointments, yeah? Get over it.' Jud had had enough of this guy's whinging. As far as he could see, he had a decent life. He had his family, a regular job and, most importantly, he had his identity – the one thing Jud didn't have any more, and never could. There was no reason for Hartwell's pathetic moaning. There was nothing Jud hated more than jealousy – especially when it came from slugs like Hartwell. He'd wasted enough time with this guy already. To hell with the consequences – it was only Hartwell's word over Jud's. If anyone listened to this slug then he'd deny everything and explain it was all just fantasy fuelled by jealousy.

He turned and began to head up the road after Bex.

'So what're you gonna do, huh?' Hartwell followed him, his voice sounding less confident now.

'About what?' said Jud. 'You? Or this couple?'

'Both.'

Jud wanted rid of this nauseating little man. He stopped and turned back to him. 'I'll take a look at where they saw these figures coming and then reassure them they weren't ghosts. As for you: *nothing*. I don't care what you say. Have a nice life.'

He set off into the abbey grounds at a brisk walk. But somehow he knew it was not going to be the last time he'd see Hartwell.

And, sure enough, like an unwanted stray dog, Hartwell followed after him.

CHAPTER 34

WEDNESDAY, 12.02 P.M.

PENTHOUSE SUITE,

GOODE TOWER, LONDON

Professor Bonati walked smartly to the first available chair and sat down before his knees gave way. They felt tense and trembled and his heart was kicking on a pace. It didn't matter how many times he came up here to Jason's penthouse on the thirty-eighth floor of the Goode Tower, he was never able to escape the jaws of vertigo. It engulfed him – consumed him. It left every sinew in his body taught, with the exception of the muscles in his knees, which went to jelly as soon as the lift set off skywards. By the time the *ping* sounded to herald his arrival in the heavens, the nightmare was well under way and the delirium had started.

Averting the glare of the vast floor-to-ceiling windows that ran around most of the giant, circular office, he wiped the sweaty palms of his hands on the legs of his suit, then took out a handkerchief and mopped the little beads of sweat from his forehead. Taking deep breaths, he tried consciously to steady the beat of his heart with mental counting down from ten. Dr Vorzek, Bonati's trusted assistant at the CRYPT and the brains behind the agency's technology, was seated across the room from the professor. She watched and waited for him to glance over in her direction so she could offer him a sympathetic smile. She knew all too well how he felt up here and, though she didn't suffer with vertigo, or any kind of phobia for that matter, she knew how much he struggled with coming up to see Goode. And she also knew how little sympathy Bonati received from him. She'd been working alongside the two men long enough to know how Goode liked to tease him.

'You all right, old bean?' Goode said, smiling cheekily. He was well versed in eccentric English greetings and enjoyed mimicking those friends with whom he and Bonati had studied at Cambridge all those years ago. 'I say, pip pip.'

'Yes, I'm fine,' the professor snapped back. 'Can you get to the point? I'm quite busy, Jason.' He resumed his mental countdown again, trying to relax the muscles in his body and avert his gaze from the great abyss behind the windows.

Goode eased back in his chair, swung away from his desk and looked philosophically out of the window. 'Well, you see, I just don't get it. What is it with Suffolk? The place seems riddled with bodies. Are you guys doin' anything about it, huh?'

'I might suggest that's a slight exaggeration, if I may, Mr Goode,' said Dr Vorzek. 'It is hardly "riddled", as you suggest.' She found his melodramatic language irritating. He would be away from the place for days, sometimes weeks on end, and then return, ready to 'stir fry' everyone into action, creating the illusion that he was somehow in charge. Vorzek knew that it irritated the professor too, but somehow he'd always been able to hide it better than she could.

'So what's the story, Prof?' said Goode, smiling at Vorzek and then turning to Bonati.

'Kim has told you, there's been another body found in the same condition as the one in Dunwich. This time at Orford – not far away. The police are saying it is presenting the same injuries.'

'Any eyewitness accounts?'

'Yes, they're slowly coming in,' said Vorzek. 'Apparently there was a man found at the scene, with blood all over his hands. But it is unlikely that he did it.'

'Why so sure?' said Goode.

'He was an elderly gent; the victim was a young man, fit and healthy, by all accounts.'

'Kim's quite right,' said Bonati. 'And the brutal injuries found on the body – which were far too violent for the elderly man found at the scene to have caused – are consistent with those found on the body in Dunwich. Exactly the same, in fact.'

'And you think it's this . . . What did you call it? Blood eagle thing?'

'Well, all I'm saying at this stage is the injuries are similar to a Viking ritual, in which the victim's ribcage is cracked open and his lungs are fanned out, much like an eagle's wings.'

'OK. So that's where the connection to the Vikings is, yeah?'

'Not just that, Mr Goode,' said Vorzek, 'not by any means. There's plenty more.' She went on to brief Goode on the case so far: the strange sighting by DCI Khan in the car park that led to the body being found on the beach – the same body that was now lying in a research room in Sector Three; the runic symbols on the fragment of stone found by Summers, which matched the symbols carved into the body; the skull up at Walberswick; and the strange reports just coming in from Jud of the couple he had met who'd claimed to have seen Viking ghosts coming over the cliffs.

Bonati had spoken to Jud on the phone and noticed that he sounded odd – more cautious than he had for a long time. When the professor asked if he was all right, he'd seemed withdrawn and then had made an unusual request: he wanted to meet up with his father as soon he returned from Dunwich – that's if his father was in the country, of course. When Bonati had probed him further and asked him if he was in trouble and if there was anything he could do to help, Jud had remained tight-lipped. He'd promised to raise it with Goode – and now was the time.

'Look,' said Bonati. 'We really need to talk about J.'

'Oh yeah?'

'Do you want me to leave?' said Vorzek. Though she, like a handful of staff at the CRYPT, knew all about Jud's background, she knew this was a sensitive subject for the two men and she was beginning to feel out of her depth.

'No, no,' they both replied.

'I want you here,' said Bonati. 'It's important you hear this, Kim. When Jud was filling me in on the progress up in Suffolk, he sounded . . . well, I don't know . . . withdrawn, you see.'

'That's not unusual,' said Vorzek. 'What made you worry this time?'

'Well, he asked to see you, Jason.'

'He what? He asked to see *me*?' Goode knew as well as Bonati that Jud never asked to see his father. He'd built up an independence, a survival instinct, these days – well, he'd had to, hadn't he?

Bonati could never recall a time when Jud had asked to see his father. 'Has he ever asked *you* that before, Kim?' said the professor.

She shook her head and looked concerned.

'So, why?' Goode said, and there was a flicker of nervousness in his eyes, which was not lost on his guests. 'I mean, what's it about, Giles? Tell me, has something happened I should know about? Huh? Vorzek?'

They shrugged. 'Search me,' said Bonati. 'He wouldn't tell me anything. Just said he wanted to see you, that's all. He wouldn't say why. I'm sorry, Jason.'

'How did he sound? Apart from "withdrawn"?'

'Worried, if I'm honest. But, look, we do need to talk about J, anyway. I've been worried about him for a while now. And I know you have too, Kim, haven't you?'

'Yes, I have. He seems, well . . . you know . . . preoccupied.'

'He's always been like that! Hell, you know he has. There's a lot going on in that little head of his. Poor kid.'

'No, but he's different at the moment,' said Bonati. 'He seems even more distant than usual.'

'Yes, and even Bex has mentioned it to me, a couple of times,' said Vorzek. 'Like his mind is always on something else.'

'That's because it always is. He's a bright kid, my son. You know he's always thinkin' and worryin' and lookin' over his shoulder. Hell, I mean, wouldn't you, in his position?'

'I found him in the SPA the other day,' Bonati cut to the chase. 'He'd gone in there unscheduled, you know. He was constructing his own simulations, Jason. I mean it. His *own* tests.'

Goode sat up in his chair, swung back towards his desk and leaned across it, earnestly. This was serious now. 'Go on,' he said.

'Well, from what I could see when I walked in on him, there was a . . .' He paused, unsure whether to go on, hesitant as to what his next sentence might do to his old and dearest friend.

'What? Tell me; *what?*'

'Well, it looked like the simulation of a . . . castle turret.'

Goode raised a hand to his mouth. Now the professor had worried him. He didn't want to hear any more. He knew exactly where this was heading. He stood up quickly and paced the large office.

'When will he let it go, Giles?' he said. 'When will he get over it, huh? Tell me he will, one day, please. What happened that night – it wasn't his fault. We know that, don't we, Giles? I believed him then and I believe him now.'

'I know, I know,' Bonati said, sympathetically. 'Me, too; no question. But I don't think he's just trying to clear his name, Jason. He's trying to find out what happened that night. He really is.'

Goode walked to one of the giant windows that overlooked the entire city and leaned his head on the glass. Bonati gripped the sides of his chair and felt his knees weaken again; just watching his friend stand so close to the edge was enough to set his vertigo spinning. Vorzek smiled at him.

'Well, I admire him for that,' said Goode, 'but he mustn't do this to himself. Creating simulations like that – ones in which we are ourselves emotionally involved – can only bring us problems. They're exhausting at the best of times and, when we're emotionally attached to them, they can finish us off sometimes. Giles, you know that!'

Bonati heard his friend's voice rise in anger. He braced himself for another of his rants. They were always so quick to start. Only, this time, perhaps it was justified.

'So what do you think you're doin' lettin' J get access like that, huh? I mean, what kinda operation are you runnin' here, the both of you? Can all the agents go and use the SPAs whenever they like, Vorzek? Can they, huh? Talk to me!'

'I know you're angry, and I'm sorry for that.' Vorzek spoke in a calm, measured tone. 'I'm sorry that he found a way in. We have strict systems in place – very strict security – designed to prevent agents from doing just this, but he's persistent. And so clever, too. If he wants to do something, there's no stopping him; you know that as well as I do, Mr Goode.'

'Hmm . . . and just where does he get that from, do you think?' said Bonati to his old friend. 'You can't blame him for being so inquisitive, or driven, Giles. You really can't.'

Goode allowed a momentary smile to pass his lips, before he gazed ruefully across the city skyline. The morning mist had shifted and there was some sunshine trying to break through the clouds to the east.

'So maybe he's found something we've missed, my friends.'

CHAPTER 35

WEDNESDAY, 12.19 P.M.

DUNWICH BEACH, SUFFOLK

Daniel took Yolanda's hand and helped her carefully from the jetty on to his boat.

'Proper gentleman, aren't you?' she said.

He just smiled. He was beginning to wonder whether this was indeed the right thing to do. As if he'd had a choice. He knew full well that, if he turned and fled, pretty soon either Yolanda or any number of her father's henchmen would catch up with him. One day.

And her whispered threats at the back of that press conference – the looks that said, *Keep your trap shut or you'll end up like Møller, at the bottom of the ocean* – had been quite enough to persuade him it was better to keep on the right side of this girl. Besides, he fancied her. And he was just an ordinary guy; looks overruled everything. He had no choice. He was already smitten.

And now, here she was, on his boat. They were alone. Somehow, showing Yolanda around his own boat made him feel more powerful – like a bachelor in his bachelor pad. This was his place, his territory, and she was his guest now. He felt a twinge of excitement when he thought about what he was about to present to her.

It was still stowed away, with the other items, inside an old life jacket, into which he'd made a small incision and then stuffed the secret finds. He'd then scrunched up the jacket and squashed it into the old plastic box with other life jackets and safety equipment. No one would ever find it.

'Not quite the same boat as yours, I realise,' he said apologetically.

'It's not a bad boat. You have all you need. But, hell, Daniel, why don't you tidy up now and again?'

He'd only sneaked back to the boat a couple of times after the police had finished with it – once to hide the secret items, and once to salvage what gear he could for the night dive with 'Heidi' and 'Frederik'. He'd not tried to tidy up much, save for a few discarded things lying on the floor, which he'd picked up. It was still a mess.

'No, it doesn't usually look like this!' he said. 'I was burgled, remember?'

'Of course,' said Yolanda, looking around at the mess. 'How awful. So, what exactly happened?'

'Someone broke into the boat when I was out having breakfast. I must have only been gone a short time. They wrecked some of my equipment. Left the place like this. Didn't take anything, as far as I know, just trashed whatever they saw.'

'They were looking for something specific?' said Yolanda. 'Or just trying to scare you, or something?'

This was a ridiculous conversation and she knew it. She'd told Daniel almost everything, save for the fact that one of her men wrecked his boat. She thought she'd spare him that little piece of news. She was trying so hard to hide the fact that she knew exactly who had broken in, and why. She knew it was Lars and that he had disabled as much of Dan's diving and navigation equipment as possible – then got the hell out of there. Only, she knew from Møller that it had gone wrong somehow. Something had happened to him. For some reason – and she would find out, no question about that – Lars must have been attacked on his return. She still harboured a slight suspicion that it could have been Daniel himself. But she admired him for that – she'd done the same thing, dispensing with Møller, after all.

'You poor guy,' she said. 'You didn't deserve this.'

'Yeah, I know. One of your guys, was it?'

'Huh?'

'Oh, come on, Yolanda. You've told me just about everything else. I know about Møller – I was there when you . . .' He trailed off. He couldn't bring himself to admit that he'd invited a murderer on to his boat – and was now alone with her. 'When we were diving, I mean. And you've told me about Sigurdsson, your father. I know I'm not the only one interested in what's out there. Hell, that's why we're going out there again isn't it?'

'Yes, and this time do you think you can take me to the right place?' She gave him a knowing smile.

Daniel grinned. He deserved that. She'd seen right through his decoy plan when they'd gone out with Møller, but she was more preoccupied with other things at the time. Like getting rid of her partner.

'Well, if my father ordered your boat to be ransacked, then I didn't know about it,' she lied.

Daniel smiled. 'Well, that's good enough for me,' he said. He walked over to the white plastic box that contained the stash of old life jackets and buoyancy aids. 'Grab a seat,' he said. 'I've got something to show you.'

'What're you looking for?'

'Oh, just some equipment to take with us.' He pulled out the life jacket and turned away from Yolanda so she couldn't see what he was fishing from the lining.

He couldn't quite believe he was doing this. What was he thinking of, showing this perfect stranger his treasured prize? But there was something so beguiling about this girl, he just couldn't resist trying to please her. She had that kind of face – that kind of body, too – that made you want to shower her with gifts and impress her. As reckless as he knew it was, he was going to do it – she was going to have it.

The old coin and the broken rune stone with the curious lettering on it were still with the investigators, but he'd kept the third and most precious find. The one he'd not unwrapped in the café the day before. The one he was so careful not to reveal to that nosy woman who'd been clearing his table.

Carefully he unwrapped it now and turned to show Yolanda.

'Oh my God,' she said, eyes wide.

CHAPTER 36

WEDNESDAY, 12.30 P.M.

(1.30 P.M. LOCAL TIME)

HOTEL PRINDSEN, ROSKILDE,

DENMARK

Luc collapsed into a large, leather chair in the hotel lounge. The room was lavishly furnished and the lighting was dimmed, bringing a warm, intimate feel to what was an otherwise large, open space. The agents had been impressed by the luxurious surroundings of one of Denmark's most famous hotels. The extravagant chandeliers, the gold-leaf decorations, the imposing pillars, the painted, panelled ceilings all brought a welcome change after the minimalist décor of Ralf's flat, and the brutal haunting next door.

They had chosen a secluded corner of the lounge, away from prying eyes. The furniture was grand, with a range of impressive armchairs that seemed to dwarf the silent guests occupying them. The concierge at the door had boasted how the Prindsen was one of the oldest and most treasured hotels in the country, dating back to 1695. Certainly, you only had to look at the grand façade on the street to know it was going to be good.

They were ready for a respite; the events at the apartment block had taken their toll, they couldn't deny it. It was by no means the first fight with a hostile ghost for either of them, but it had been a gruelling one. The decision to grab the giant oil painting and smash its frame into the ghost had been the right one, not least because it crunched into its bones and weakened it while the EM neutralisers did their work, but also because of what it had revealed to them.

Luc and Grace had been surprised to see the door of a safe built into the wall where the painting had hung. Further probing with the instruments had revealed an electromagnetic radiation higher than the two agents had ever recorded before. It was virtually off the scale. What was in that safe? They'd been impatient to find out.

Twenty minutes of fiddling and code cracking and listening intently to the sound of the little wheel turning and clicking inside its housing had come to nothing (as Grace had warned it would) but then the police had provided the essential electronic listening device and the safe door was eventually opened to reveal prizes that exceeded everyone's expectations. The police agreed to leave them alone for a further twenty minutes, but that was it. No more.

Inside, Luc and Grace had found more coins – ancient ones, by the looks of it – assorted jewellery, gem stones and a couple of large, plain-looking stones which, much to the agents' delight, displayed runic lettering on them, quite similar to the letters they'd seen on the body and on the rune stone back in England.

'So, at least we now know there is a definite connection between this guy's apartment and the hauntings in Suffolk. I mean, there has to be,' said Grace, as she too reclined in a large chair, opposite Luc. The polished wooden coffee table was adorned with plates of open sandwiches, salad bowls, baskets of fries and two large glasses of Coke. Luc was balancing a large bowl of mussels in his lap and hurling empty shells into a small side dish perched precariously on the arm of his chair. As a Frenchman, he could never resist seafood whenever it was on the menu and these mussels were particularly good. Bonati always said that investigations required stamina, and that meant eating properly. Never neglect lunch, was his regular mantra – and they had certainly obliged.

'So?' said Luc, a tear-shaped drop of garlic sauce clinging to his lips. 'What does it all mean, huh?'

Grace was pensive. 'Well, that's the question, isn't it? I just can't believe that all this has arisen because someone has unearthed some Viking treasure.'

'But that's exactly why, isn't it?' said Luc.

'I'm not sure. I mean, think about it. This guy, Sigurdsson – his place was full of Viking memorabilia. He's obviously been collecting coins and stuff for years, and yet there's been no paranormal activity, no fatal hauntings, until now.'

'None that we know about,' said Luc. 'There could easily have been some here in Denmark, or anywhere else. We don't attend all the paranormal incidents in the world, Grace! This guy might have been stirring up trouble every time he's gone digging, and we'd never know about it. Or maybe some of these coins come from the same place – you know, Suffolk. It's perfectly possible he's been over there on some expedition. I mean, this guy's got enough artefacts to fill a museum, and they can't all have come from Roskilde, can they?'

Grace knew that what Luc was saying made sense, of course, but she still believed there was something more to this, something they weren't considering. 'Look,' she said, 'I don't believe these things would be enough to stir up the souls of Viking warriors – or, at least, not just the coins themselves – even if they are from the same beach in Suffolk. Or the jewellery. Unless . . .' She trailed off, deep in thought.

'Yes?' said Luc, anxiously. 'Unless what?'

'Well, unless the things uncovered had some kind of emotional significance to the people who once owned them.'

'Brilliant, Holmes,' said Luc, sarcastically. 'I mean, what would we do without you? That may have been one of the most obvious things you've said so far,' he teased. 'These things are valuable in their own right, Grace. Of course their owners would have been attached to them – why wouldn't they?'

'Look, I know these items would have been important, of course they would, so I don't think they would have been dropped or lost, would they? They're too important for that.'

'And?'

'So . . . I reckon they were placed in the ground rather than dropped accidentally.'

'Placed?'

'Yeah, like a burial: a Viking burial. They were different to other burials, weren't they? Especially if the deceased was someone significant, like a war hero or leader of some kind. And there are burial sites in England, aren't there?'

'That's true,' said Luc. 'I know they used to bury various things along with the dead, ready for their journey to Valhalla.'

'To *where*?' said Grace.

'Valhalla. You know, in Norse mythology it was this kind of hall where the dead were sent – dead heroes who died in battle – presided over by the god, Odin. I remember it from when we studied the Vikings at school. Don't you ever learn history in England?'

'I did, but I didn't always listen,' said Grace. 'So you think the dead were packed off with their precious belongings, for when they arrived at their Viking heaven?' said Grace.

'Exactly. And that would certainly have included jewellery and coins.'

'Weren't the Vikings often buried in ships?' said Grace. 'I'm sure I heard that there were these famous ship burials?'

'Yes, they were. Some were placed in ships and set alight, then pushed into the sea. But there were others, I think, that were placed in ships that were buried on the land.'

'Really?'

'Yeah, of course. It's only like a giant coffin, isn't it?'

'Well, if we want to find out more about Viking burials and rituals, we couldn't have come to a better place. This is where it all started,' said Grace. 'Time for a trip to the Viking museum, yeah?'

'I think so,' said Luc, picking up his Coke glass and draining it.

'I'll tell you what,' said Grace, 'they may be used to finding remains wash up on the beach at Dunwich from the old village that sank into the sea, but, one thing's for sure, this diver – you know, the Summers guy Bex was telling me about? – I reckon he's found more than he bargained for, don't you?'

They agreed and tucked heartily into their fries, which Luc promptly dipped into the last remnants of his moules marinière, licking his lips.

Across the lounge, a man in a dark suit was watching them. The lighting was dim but his camera needed no flash. He clicked several times and then sent a text with the latest update. He couldn't believe how quickly that guy had demolished his bowl of mussels.

But he couldn't begrudge a kid his last meal, could he?

CHAPTER 37

WEDNESDAY, 1.38 P.M.

DUNWICH BEACH, SUFFOLK

The wind was picking up again. Bex's long, dark hair was rasping around her neck and blowing across her face as she stared out to the murky horizon.

The Fetchers had gone home to recover. Hartwell had returned to his little job in his father's little hotel behind them. Summers had disappeared with this new woman, whoever she was. And the man with whom the woman had originally entered the hotel yesterday had not been seen that morning. Even DCI Khan had had to return to London where other investigations were demanding his attention.

She was alone with Jud. At last. Just them, the wind, the sea and the occasional lonely seabird, calling out from the grey skies high above them.

They'd been walking for several minutes now and Jud had not yet said anything. The purpose of venturing out and the reason why Bex had suggested it – to get some fresh air and talk through the investigation so they could somehow get a handle on the pace of events that were unfolding – had clearly backfired, since Jud was in one of his silent moods.

That was OK, she thought to herself. She had been partnered

up with him for some time now and was well versed in how to read the signs. Patience was a virtue when dealing with Jud Lester and she had all the patience in the world. But they'd never get another opportunity like this. Such privacy. Such solitude. And the vast expanse of sky and sea and miles of sprawling, flat beach seemed to bring a better perspective out here. At least, Bex hoped it would.

She stopped in the sand and looked at Jud. 'You ready?'

He raised his face from the stones below and gave her a reticent, belligerent kind of look. 'What?'

'I said, are you ready?'

'For what?' The wind was blowing Jud's dark locks across his stubbly jaw, giving him a rustic, windswept look, which was not unattractive to Bex. But the expression he wore was a hostile one. His default setting these days was melancholic, withdrawn. But here, in the seclusion of the wild Suffolk coast, he would open up to her. If it took all day and night, he would; she knew it. Bonati had already been on the phone to her, asking them both to report back to CRYPT immediately for a debriefing, so that he and Goode could get a handle on this investigation, which was escalating. Goode had told the professor to get them back as soon as possible, before he had to fly out once again on business.

But Bex had chosen not to pass this little message on to Jud. Not yet. Bonati could wait a short while. She'd never get an opportunity like this again.

'Are you ready to talk to me?' she said, staring him in the face. 'No,' she said, 'don't look away. Look at me. Talk to me.'

'About the case?'

'Yes, in time. But first I want to talk about you, Jud.'

'Me?'

'Oh, stop playing games, will you?' She was beginning to feel the first spots of rain on her face and she pulled her collar tight up to her neck, as the wind rattled around them both. 'Tell me what's on your mind. There is nothing – *nothing* – you can't say to me. I can keep secrets. I won't talk to anyone. I don't want to. There's no one else I want to talk to, or be with. I only want to be with you.' She could feel droplets on her cheek and knew inside it wasn't only the rain.

He looked at her, with her hair dampening, her body shivering and that imploring, desperate look in her eyes, pleading to be let into the private fortress of his mind: a place where no one – not even his father or the professor – was ever allowed now.

He'd not looked away yet, but stared into her eyes and it both unsettled and excited her. Was she about to crack him? She was flicking through her mind, desperately trying to choose the right words now – on the very edge of him opening up. Should she shut up and wait? It had been a few seconds and he'd still not said anything. Was he about to look away, turn and start walking off again?

'Please?' she said gently.

He smiled. He could see her eyes were watching his lips as she struggled to interpret what the smile meant. She looked up again and their eyes met.

And then he kissed her.

A slow, gentle kiss. He watched her eyes close and he felt her body go limp against his. He quickly put his arms around her and held her tight. They kissed again. Then hugged each other. As she looked over his shoulder at the ocean beyond, she began to feel his body moving. Was he shivering? His shoulders began to jerk and she could feel the breath leaving him in great sighs, only to be sucked back in again sharply.

He was sobbing.

She held him tighter and squeezed the misery out of him, releasing each time he gulped for air and then holding him tight again. She didn't need to say anything; she just hung on, tightly. He was coughing now, and spluttering – sniffing hard and trying to compose himself. Still she hugged him. She stood on tiptoes, clasped the back of his head and drew his face deep into her shoulder. Whatever it was that had consumed him for so long, whatever had hijacked his mind and frozen his emotions all this time, it seemed as though it was leaving him.

A few moments passed and then he pulled away from her. She grabbed his hands before he went and wouldn't let go. His face was tear-stained, his nose was running and his eyes were red and blotchy. But she knew right then how much she loved him and how she could never be parted from him.

He was pulling at her hands, trying to be released, staring past her to the sand dunes and his escape route beyond. She could feel his body trying to pull back from hers. 'Don't go,' she said. 'Don't run. Not now. Stay. Talk to me.'

He sniffed and then smiled. 'But it's raining,' he said.

She shrugged her shoulders to show how little she cared.

'OK,' he said. 'You're a determined agent, Rebecca De Verre. I'm not gonna win, am I? So I give up. I can't do this any more. I can't do it alone.'

She released one of his hands but held tightly on to the other and began leading him further down the beach, further into the dark storm that lay ahead of them. The rain became heavier but still they walked on, and slowly Jud began to talk.

CHAPTER 38

WEDNESDAY, 2.00 P.M.

STAR INN, DUNWICH

Pat Hartwell was sitting in his small bedroom, scheming. Jud's reaction to seeing him again had been disappointing to say the least, but not unexpected. It wasn't as if they'd been best mates at school. And when Hartwell revealed that he knew everything about Jud – or Jamie – then he knew he'd be angry. But, if he was honest, he'd always hoped that one day he really would join the CRYPT. He'd followed their work so closely over the years that he almost felt like one of the agents already. And to see them, here, in his father's hotel . . . Well, he just couldn't believe his luck.

He'd handled it badly and he was angry with himself for it. When he'd returned from his altercation with Jud up on the road, his father had questioned where he'd been and shouted at him to get back behind the bar and start setting up for the evening shift. Pat had told him to 'go to hell' and had been sent to his room.

Sent to his room? How old did his father think he was?

His life was going nowhere, and he knew it. While Jud and his annoyingly attractive partner had the adventures, what did he do? He served breakfasts and pulled pints for bored, boring tourists, who all asked the same stupid questions like, 'How long have you been here?' and 'What's it like living next to a ghost town under the sea?' Some actually thought the village was still preserved beneath the waves, like there had been some giant flood or something, covering the village as it stood. They didn't have the sense to realise the ground beneath the buildings had crumbled over time, so there were no houses still intact under the ocean – just a pile of rubble.

He gazed out of his window. This was a depressing place – a cold, remote hideaway; a lay-by in which life had dumped him, like some discarded litter, while others sped past on their more exciting journeys.

He wanted adventure. And he'd already decided how he was going to find it. He turned back to look at the rucksack on his bed. There was precious little left in his room that he hadn't already packed. But then, he didn't own much. He could travel light.

The journey to London was going to be arduous but he knew it would be worth it. He had to keep out of sight. He knew the surrounding area like the back of his hand and had already planned the route he was going to take across the fields, through the woods and up, eventually, on to the main road that led towards Ipswich. It would be dark and cold – and spooky as hell – but he loved the challenge. Besides, nothing scared him. Not any more. Once on the main road, he was sure he'd be able to thumb a lift. And then a direct train from Ipswich to Liverpool Street, and he'd be nearly there: at CRYPT HQ. Oh, boy, did he have some news for them. It would be fun.

The plan was cunning. The knowledge he had on Jud presented an opportunity. He had bargaining power, and he knew it. To simply tell the first stranger he met, or ring up and tell a newspaper journalist or start tweeting and blogging about it would be a wasted opportunity. This was worth something to someone. Blackmail was the key.

You let me join the agency or I'll expose the whole thing – and your star agent too.

It was worth a try. What else did he have? Nothing – just a monotonous life, pulling pints and clearing dishes. But now he felt high on the thrill of it all. The altercation with Jud had confirmed it for him. Whatever the consequences, whatever was about to happen to him, it would be better than the sentence he'd been given of serving bacon and eggs to overweight, docile tourists in a sleepy corner of Suffolk. London beckoned. It would be dangerous – he doubted that Jason Goode would accept him with open arms and give him a job, just like that – but he knew it was worth a try. Anything was worth a try if it meant an escape from here.

He picked up his bag and grabbed his mobile phone and wallet from the small desk. He packed a torch too, for the dark walk through the woods en route to the main road. The laptop was already safely tucked away in his bag – his only treasured possession. He'd need that if the plan didn't go well. He'd have a lot of emails and blogs to write. The world would soon know about the CRYPT if Jason Goode didn't want to play ball.

He felt a surge of excitement and adrenalin at the thought of the adventure that awaited him. Next stop: the Goode Tower, London.

CHAPTER 39

WEDNESDAY, 2.39 P.M.

(3.39 P.M. LOCAL TIME)

VIKING SHIP MUSEUM,

ROSKILDE

They were looking at one of the strangest buildings they had seen for a long while; built on to the water's edge, overlooking the Baltic Sea, Roskilde's famous museum was long and low and built of square slabs of concrete and wood, balanced on top of each other like some random Lego house built by a toddler. As they approached it, Luc wasn't sure if he was looking at a museum, a multi-storey car park or some giant defence post. It seemed too solid, too impregnable to be anything so cultural or artistic as a museum.

'It's built on the exact site where they found five Viking ships,' said Grace, remembering what she'd read in the taxi, coming to the site. 'And they're all here, inside, I think.'

'OK,' said Luc. 'Well, they obviously didn't think this place had to be pretty.'

'Supposed to be amazing when you get inside, though,' said Grace.

They reached the main doors and entered. Though the exterior of the building was dark and solid and forbidding, the inside could not have been more different: spacious, airy and washed with light from the many windows that ran along the water's edge. The reason for the bright viewing conditions was to show off to their best advantage its precious finds: the ships.

Luc and Grace couldn't fail to be impressed. The museum boasted five Skuldelev ships – large, oak-built longboats – the same five that were found on the site in the 1960s. Each one was displayed in its own bright corner of the Great Hall, flooded with natural light. The timbers were dark and worn and contrasted sharply with the clean, pale walls and beams. But it was the shape of each vessel that impressed – sleek, streamline, as sharp as a dagger. Though many of the timbers were missing, metal skeletons of each ship had been made and they provided an outline of the vessel, within which the surviving timbers could be carefully placed, creating the illusion of a whole Viking ship. They were perched precariously on thin, iron legs, so thin you could hardly see them. It seemed like these vast, dark giants were somehow floating in an otherwise plain, white mausoleum.

'Eerie, isn't it?' said Grace.

'Yes. It's like each ship has a character of its own – like they're alive.'

They proceeded down the long viewing gallery, stopping to peer over the sides, down into the Great Hall, at each ship. They looked at rows and rows of display boards, each showing paintings and annotated diagrams of how the ships were used in their heyday.

And then Grace found a series of boards that depicted the rituals often adopted for Viking burials. It was clear that they were often quite grand affairs. If the deceased were held in high regard, then many of their belongings would be buried with them in a ship just like the ones on display. Jewellery, tools and weapons were all stowed away either side of the body, which was placed in the centre of the longboat. And rune stones; large or small, these were stones on to which lettering was engraved.

'With all these artefacts found in one place under the North Sea, it's got to be a burial ship they've found,' said Luc.

'Agreed. Some ships were pushed out to sea, unmanned, as a burial at sea. Others were buried inland, weren't they?' Grace said.

'Yeah, but the ones sent out to sea – so it says here – were most often set alight as they left. There was no one on them; they just drifted out in flames. So very little would have survived. The ship they've found in Suffolk might have been buried.'

'Yes!' said Grace. 'That's how it got there with so much of its contents still intact. It was buried at Dunwich centuries before, and then, in the nineteenth century, it collapsed into the sea like everything else in Dunwich.'

'It's possible, isn't it?' said Luc. 'And if that's the case, and it really is a ship burial, I wonder who was in it. We know it was usually important Vikings who received a send off like this; so, whoever it was, they were obviously admired by their fellow Vikings.'

'Because they're coming back?' said Grace.

Luc nodded. 'Looks like it.'

Grace was leaning over the wall of the viewing gallery, staring at the largest of the warships at the other side of the Great Hall. 'If this diver guy really has found the remains of a Viking burial ship then God knows how many others are going to be interested in it, if word gets out. We'll have the whole diving community out there, uncovering everything. Disturbing the whole site.'

'And the ghosts too,' said Luc, gazing past the remains of the ship to the sea beyond, through the giant, square windows.

They'd not noticed who was standing behind them; probably just another tourist, anyway. There were a handful of others who'd braved the cold and the wind to visit the same day; neither Luc nor Grace had paid much attention to them since arriving –

they'd been far too distracted by the great Viking ships in the place.

But behind them now, standing just a few feet away, pretending to show interest in the same ships, was the guy from the hotel. And this time he'd been close enough to record their conversation.

Sigurdsson would be happy with this. He felt pleased not to have silenced them just yet. This was one conversation he was glad to have overheard. But time was ticking on. His employer would soon be phoning to see if the job was yet done. It was time. And he knew exactly the place to do it: the shipyard outside. The wind was loud out there, and the flapping of the flags and the rattling of the safety fencing would drown out the sound of the bullets.

Luc was still gazing out of the window. 'What's out there, Grace? Can you see? Is that a replica ship or something?'

'Oh, yeah,' said Grace. 'Didn't you know? They've built a series of replicas of the ships in here, so you can see what they actually looked like. We can go and see them if you want.'

'Of course! Let's go.'

'We'll have to be quick, though,' said Grace. 'Bonati will want to know about the ship burial soon. It explains everything about what's happened at Dunwich – and maybe here, too.'

'Yeah, we'll call him when we go. Don't worry about it,' said Luc. 'Come on. I've got to see these ships!'

They moved along the gallery and out towards the exit in the far corner that led to the jetty outside. They passed yet more display boards and cabinets, each one showing the kinds of artefacts carried in ships, and buried in them too. It was all too much of a coincidence. They knew for certain this was what was lying under the North Sea at Dunwich. But was the haunting in Ralf's apartment building linked to the hauntings in Suffolk? Whose burial ship was it? And why the brutal revenge killings by the ghosts?

These questions would be answered in time. But they couldn't resist a quick peek at the replica ships outside.

The wind hit them as soon as the door was opened. It had picked up while they'd been inside the great, solid museum. Although the building had let so much light in and, with windows everywhere, had felt almost like they were outside, it was only when they came out for real that they realised the difference. The cold, biting wind rattled around their ears, bringing a chilling pain quickly and causing them to pull their coats tight around themselves.

But it was worth the excursion outdoors. The ships were magnificent. Giant, oak timbers created a beautiful curve, along which lines of red and yellow were painted, matching the stripes on the single, vast, square sail above. They were like huge toy ships – too clean and pristine to be real.

Grace was further up the jetty, around the corner of the building; she always found it frustrating when people spent too long on any exhibits in a museum. She was the kind of girl who sped in and out of places: quick glance, quick read of a few displays and then out. Besides, it was freezing out here now, exposed as it was to the wind that swept off the Baltic and battered this side of the museum.

But Luc stood, leaning into the chained safety fence for a closer look at the nearest ship. He studied the gorgeous, streamlined designs; so sleek. He imagined these ships cutting right through the waves like a bullet.

And then he suddenly felt something in the small of his back. It was a sharp, painful dig.

He quickly spun around and came face to face with a tall, stocky man with blond hair. His expression gave nothing away, and he just whispered two words to him: 'Keep walking.' Before he turned around again, Luc glanced down and saw the top of a gun. The man saw him looking at it and pressed the gun even deeper, this time into his kidneys. Luc winced in pain and the man spoke coldly: 'Move.'

It couldn't have worked out better for the assassin. He'd hoped to pick them off one by one, but the problem with these kids was they were always together. Here, outside, the girl had seemed impatient and he'd watched her walk off, around the corner of the building. It was the perfect time to strike. He was going to march the male target to the opposite corner of the jetty, away from the giant windows, put a bullet in him and then throw him into the water. He had twine in his pocket and knew there were plenty of heavy things around that he could tie to the body to make sure it sank quickly, and stood little chance of bobbing to the surface again: the chains from the fencing, the metal posts, the small metal signs dotted around the place – plenty to choose from. He just needed to get this kid quickly away from this side of the building, where anyone inside could see them.

They turned back the way the agents had just come and started walking away. Luc was unable to signal to Grace – and where was she, anyway? Quickly, his mind was whirring for options, problem solving, scanning the area for anything sharp, searching for anyone he could shout to. But he knew that if he so much as raised his voice the sharp barrel in his kidneys would deliver him a bullet. Given how far away from Luc's body the man's hand had been, it was either a very long barrel or, more likely, a silencer. So he meant business, this guy.

They walked on.

Around the other side of the giant building, Grace was getting bored with looking at ships. Her face was cold and her lips felt chapped. She turned to assess how dry they looked in the giant panes of glass, built into the museum wall behind her. And then she saw Luc. Right through the building, on the other side, she could see him walking slowly, purposefully along the jetty. There was a large, burly man walking right behind him. Why was he walking so close? She felt a wave of concern come over her; something wasn't right. Why was Luc leaving? And who the hell was this guy, walking so close to him? Was he a security guard?

Oh, don't tell me, she thought. He's gone and got into trouble for climbing on the fence or something – trying to get on to one of the boats, probably.

And then she saw something that made her stop and catch her breath. Though they were some distance away now, at the opposite side of the building, she could still see them under the bright lights that spilled on to the jetty outside, and she saw his arm. It was jabbing into Luc's back.

She caught a quick, fleeting glimpse of the barrel of a gun. She sprinted down the jetty. She reached the corner of the building, in between the windows and paused for a second, breathing heavily now. She couldn't be seen from here; she was OK. Then she moved again. Closer.

What the hell was she going to do? she kept thinking to herself. She had no weapon, nothing to use to hit the guy with. What help would she be? Though the agents had all learned the art of self-defence, this guy had a gun – end of story.

On the other side of the building, Luc heard the man speak again: 'Stop,' he said quietly. 'Just here.'

Luc could see he'd chosen a place obscured from view. There were no windows here, just dirty, concrete walls. No boats, either; just the edge of the jetty.

'On your knees,' said the stranger. 'Don't turn round.'

This was it. It had all happened so quickly, Luc was struggling to believe this was real. A few moments ago, he and Grace were gazing over the Viking ships and the Baltic Sea beyond. There was no one here – just them. They'd solved the case – or at least had made headway into what the hell had been found in Suffolk – and they were about to call Bonati and report in.

Now he was down on his knees, facing the water, with a gun to his back.

He closed his eyes. He knew if he tried even the slightest movement, the gun would go off. He had to freeze and wait for the next instruction. But, as he gazed out over the grey sea and the darkening clouds above, he felt the sinking, sickening feeling that there would be no more instructions. Had he spoken his last words? Would the next, and last, sound he heard be the ominous thud of the bullet racing out of the silencer?

And then he felt it. It knocked him over on to his face, just inches away from the edge of the jetty. The man's body was heavy, like a lead weight, and it overpowered even Luc's considerable strength.

'That was too close,' Grace said, standing over them both. 'You could at least try to get him off you, Luc. I'm pulling as hard as I can! I can't lift him by myself!'

Luc began wriggling out from under the pressure of the giant man, now unconscious, slumped over him. He saw Grace standing there, smiling, with a giant fire extinguisher at her feet. There was blood dribbling from the end of it on to the jetty. He turned and saw a severe gash on the back of the man's head. At the crown of his head, his blond hair was red and matted.

'Thank you?' said Grace.

Luc was drawing large gulps of fresh air into his lungs and trying to steady his heartbeat. 'Sorry, Grace. Thank you.'

'So who the hell is this guy?'

Luc shook his head. 'Dunno. But I'm guessing, whoever he is, he's carrying out someone else's orders.' He gazed at the gun in the man's hand. 'That's a serious piece of kit; professional job. He'll be a hired killer. Neat; quick; discreet. He'll be working for someone, I've no doubt.'

'The man in the apartment next to Ralf?'

'Could be,' said Luc. 'I suspect we've been trailed since we pitched up at that place. Someone was probably watching the apartment block, seeing who was there stirring up trouble for its owner. We should've been more careful.'

Luc got to his feet and looked down at the man, sprawled on the floor. He checked for a pulse.

'I've not killed him, have I?' said Grace, her voice choking. 'Oh, God. Tell me I've not killed him!'

'No, no. But he'll have a headache when he comes round, you can bet on that. Come on; let's go. We'll call the police from the museum. We've done nothing wrong, but it doesn't exactly look like that. Come on – before people start coming out.'

CHAPTER 40

WEDNESDAY, 4.19 P.M.

NORTH SEA, OFF THE COAST OF

DUNWICH

Daniel held the wheel steady on Yolanda's boat; the swell was building again and the vessel rocked from side to side. Rain had picked up and it rattled against the windows like gunfire.

'Have you found it yet?' Yolanda said, not for the first time.

'No. Have patience! We will. We're close to the spot now. I promise you. I'm not lying this time! We're nearly at the place where I dived before and found it.'

'You're a talented diver, Mr Summers,' said Yolanda, as she played with the precious item in her hand. It was a beautiful silver amulet, hanging on a silver chain. In the centre of the pendant was the figure of a woman; her hair was tied back and she was bearing what looked like a drinking horn. Neither Yolanda nor Dan could believe the amulet's condition. It had clearly been buried in the sand for all this time – up until the moment Dan had stumbled on it whilst digging for coins down in the depths.

When the light from his head torch had first shone on the edge of the amulet and he'd pulled it gently from the silt, his eyes had widened, like jewels themselves.

He'd thought at the time it was Victorian. He'd assumed it had belonged to someone in the old village up on the cliff top. Perhaps they'd dropped it on to the ground, it had become buried and then, when the cliffs had crumbled into the sea, it had found itself dropping to the seabed with so much else from the old village.

But when Daniel had unearthed the other items – the old coin and the fragment of stone with the runic lettering on it – he'd wondered if the necklace could be older.

Seeing Yolanda's face when he'd first shown the amulet to her confirmed his suspicions. She'd not been able to hide her excitement. This was indeed a necklace of Danish origins – and the picture on the front of it was the intricate engraving of a Valkyrie. What they were holding was a precious pendant that gave the wearer protection – in battle, in life, even in the afterlife. Yolanda could tell that Daniel had no idea – no idea at all – of its real significance. She tried hard to hide her excitement, but she just couldn't. She had only ever seen one other of these before – and it was one of her father's most prized possessions. Of all the artefacts and relics he and his team had unearthed over the years, his Valkyrie amulet was surely his most precious.

He'd never let her put it on, though. That was always the rule. Once, as a little girl, she'd stumbled into her father's office when a desk drawer had been left open. She'd found his amulet, wrapped in tissue paper. She unwrapped it and was about to put it on over her head, when her father had appeared at the door and bellowed at her to drop it. She could recall the day as clear as if it were yesterday. She'd not known then – or now, really – why her father had been so very angry. It was something they just didn't talk about afterwards. At the time, he'd said that the pendant was once her mother's, a family heirloom from generations ago – which may have been true – and that it was disrespectful to put it on. He wanted his late wife to have been the last person to wear it. He always said that, when Yolanda was old enough, he would consider giving it to her. But he still hadn't and, if she was honest, she'd forgotten about it, anyway.

Until this. The amulet in her hand had brought it all back. Now she was as eager and excitable as she'd been as a girl. She just *had* to wear it.

'So what did you call them? Valkyries, was it?' said Dan. 'The woman on the front was a Valkyrie, you said?'

'Yes, like an angel, I suppose you'd call her,' said Yolanda. 'In my motherland, we saw them as heroines who had the power to choose who died and who survived in battle, you see. The Valkyrie leads the chosen ones who die as heroes to the place we call Valhalla, the afterlife presided over by our great god, Odin.'

'So, let me get this straight,' said Dan, unconvinced, 'the Valkyrie is a mythical woman, like an angel, who hovers over the battle, choosing who's going to die and who's going to live. Is that right?'

'Yes, pretty much.' Yolanda could tell Dan was not taking this as seriously as he should have been. She gave him a look to say the same – and he registered it.

Quickly, he added, 'That's an incredible thing, Yolanda. I mean, really interesting. And you think the figure engraved on to this amulet is one of these Valkyries, then?'

'Definitely. They were usually shown with their hair scraped back and holding up a drinking horn, which they would offer to the heroes on the battlefield, you see. Who knows? There may be a Valkyrie waiting at the gates of Valhalla just for you,' said Yolanda, smiling at him across the boat.

Dan felt nervous again. Only the day before, he had watched this woman choose the fate of Jürgen Møller, so he was not sure how to take this comment. Was she his very own Valkyrie? Had she already decided that he would survive and Møller would die?

Would she decide in his favour again? Did he have any say in the matter?

He reminded himself never to ask her to wear her hair back or come to him bearing a drink in the future.

'So?' she said, carefully placing the amulet and chain into a small drawer to the side of the wheel, near where Daniel was standing. He caught a glimpse of the contents of the drawer and was alarmed to see what looked like the handle of a revolver. She shut the drawer again quickly.

'Nice boat,' he said politely.

'Yeah, it's OK; one of my father's fleet. At any one time, he has up to six boats and their crew out searching for buried Viking sites.'

'That's some investment,' said Dan.

'I told you: he's got too much money, my father. He needs to spend it on something, doesn't he? Why shouldn't he invest in historical dives and digs? I mean, what's wrong with that?'

Dan could detect mild anger in her voice. He didn't want to be the one to criticise her father, whatever she thought of him – and it was hard to know, she was so fickle with her moods. Change the subject, quickly, he thought.

'It shouldn't take too long,' he said, glancing through the windows at the rough seas outside. 'It's not the best night for it, though. Shame.'

'We'll have plenty of cruises in the future, in better weather than this, don't you worry,' said Yolanda. 'Once we've cleared the rest of the site, we'll live like royalty, you'll see. My father might buy you a new boat . . . if you're a good boy, of course.' She smiled and flashed her piercing eyes in his direction.

God, she's so hot, Dan thought to himself. Her looks had overshadowed her violent tendencies and allowed him to forgive and quickly forget what she'd done to this Møller guy only the day before. How could he refuse her anything? She had him, hook, line and sinker. If a Valkyrie was a beautiful goddess who held men's fate in the palm of her hand, then Yolanda was one, for sure. And, in a short while, he would know what his fate would be.

Would he be led back to the boat with more Viking riches? Or was this Valkyrie leading him closer to Valhalla?

CHAPTER 41

WEDNESDAY, 6.18 P.M.

CRYPT, LONDON

'So you've still not located him?' said Jason Goode, pacing the floor again, this time in the less spacious office of his old friend, Professor Bonati. He disliked being cooped up in the subterranean room and preferred being up in the penthouse where it was light and spacious and offered views right across the city: all the reasons why the professor hated it.

Bonati shook his head slowly. His face showed the same concern that was written across his old friend's. 'I've told you, *I don't know.*'

'And you, Khan? Your guys haven't found him yet?'

The DCI shook his head solemnly. 'We've only just been notified by the professor, here. You've gotta give me time. But we will find him. And Bex. They can't have gone far. They've no bikes with them, and there are no trains around for miles. We've no reports of a taxi being requested from Dunwich in the last few hours, so they must be on foot.'

'So, let me get this straight, Giles. You told Rebecca to get back here with him – after we spoke. You told her I've gotta go back to the States soon. You said Jud had asked to *see me*; I mean, we both know he's never done that before. There's clearly something wrong for him to ask out of the blue like this, Prof. And then the next we know, he's gone AWOL. You don't need me to tell you how worried that makes me feel. What the hell's going on, huh?'

Bonati was trying desperately to find some positives. 'At least he's not alone, Jason. I mean, Bex is probably with him. So, at least he's safe with her. She's a got a level head, that girl; don't you worry.'

'I know that. And you're right, we should be grateful. But I've got a real bad feelin' about this. I don't like it, Giles. He's not answering his phone, and neither is she. For God's sake, man, I thought you were able to manage these agents. Now I'm beginning to wonder.'

They both knew this was unfair – it was impossible to account for an agent's every move, twenty-four seven, and least of all Jud. He was his own man. They both also knew that this wasn't the first time he'd gone, or at least tried to go, missing. There were times in the past when Bonati had caught him trying to leave with no explanation as to where he was going or why. But he'd managed to talk him down on those occasions. This time was different. They had no trail for him beyond Suffolk. The hotel owner had said both he and Bex had checked out earlier that day. Khan had already called the local police in Suffolk and they had no answers either. The helicopter pilot had set off to collect them from Dunwich, as they'd arranged, but he'd found no one at the rendezvous place and had no choice but to fly back alone. Khan had sent out a request to the local force to start combing the beach again. This time, they were looking for the agents, not a body. At least, they all hoped and prayed it wouldn't be bodies they'd find.

'It's not as if the damn investigation is even over yet. We still don't have any real answers, other than somebody's stirred up trouble under the sea. That's not enough. People are digging up historic finds all the time and it don't mean ghosts will come outta nowhere. There's gotta be something else going on here, and yet we are *still* in the dark.'

'Well, that's not entirely true, is it, Jason?' said the professor. 'Since we last spoke, there's been a report in from Luc and Grace in Copenhagen. Apparently they've found more Viking coins in an apartment over there. And maybe even fragments of rune stone too. And while they–'

'So?' interrupted Goode. 'They're not the only Viking coins in the world.'

'If you'll let me finish,' said Bonati, calmly. 'Whilst there they disturbed what they think was the ghost of a Viking warrior, which they had to neutralise. It looks like there is indeed a link between what happened there and what's been happening in Suffolk. Luc and Grace have been doing more research and they are certain that what this diver guy disturbed under the sea in Dunwich was some kind of funeral ship – the remains of some Viking burial site that may have fallen into the sea. The burial may have been on the site where the village was then built centuries later, so when Dunwich crumbled into the sea, the Viking remains would have fallen with it. And, if that's true, there are plenty of reasons why spirits might have been disturbed.'

'So who's God damn grave was it, huh? Some powerful Viking, I guess?'

'We don't yet know; but we will, Jason. We will.'

Goode approached Bonati's large, mahogany desk and thumped his fist down on it, shaking the three whisky tumblers they'd been steadily draining since they'd first entered his office. 'Listen, Giles, people have been savagely, brutally killed up and down the damn country, there's been Viking ghosts seen from here to Denmark, and you're still giving me "maybe" and "might". You don't know for sure.' He went to the drinks table near the window and poured himself another bourbon. 'Besides,' he said, spinning around again, 'none of this is helping us locate my son, is it? His disappearance may not have anything to do with the case he's been working on – nothing at all. There might be something else that's happened and we don't even know about it. Now *think*. There must be something we've missed here.'

Khan took a deep breath. He knew what he had to say would shock Goode into a further rage. His temper was no different to his son's, it seemed. He was relieved to have Bonati in the room with him. Khan was older and weaker than Goode, who prided himself on his strength and agility. He wasn't just powerful in business; he was physically fit too. Khan spoke calmly and slowly. 'There was one strange thing I heard, Mr Goode. It was when I was speaking to the owner of the hotel where the agents were staying in Dunwich.'

'Go on,' said Goode, nervously.

'Well, he said that *his* son had gone missing too.'

'So? What do I care? There's no connection, is there? I mean, it's not as if they know each other, is it? Probably had a row with his father, or somethin'. God knows, Khan, I know how that feels. So what's that got to do with us?'

'Well, that's just it, you see,' interrupted Bonati. 'Khan, here, asked the landlord for his son's name, didn't you? And . . . well . . . Do you want to tell him or shall I?' The professor looked at the DCI in silence.

Goode came and sat in the chair opposite Bonati's desk. He looked even more anxious now. 'What? Tell me, what, guys? Who is he?'

'His name is Hartwell – Pat Hartwell.' Khan waited for the name to register in Goode's mind, as Bonati had said it would.

Nothing. They glanced at each other again, quickly.

'So, who the hell's Pat Hartwell? I mean, what the hell—?' And then he stopped. The words had pricked something in his memory as he'd mouthed them. Bonati could see his eyes widening and his mouth fell open.

'Oh, Jesus. I remember. He was the kid who tried to join us before, wasn't he, Giles? In those early days. He's the one who—'

'Kept on writing to us.' Bonati nodded his head with an ominous expression written across his face. 'Exactly. The boy was obsessed. How many letters did he send us? Perhaps we should have taken him on, after all.'

'The guy was a loony, Giles. Come on! He kept sayin' he had gifts we could use. Sayin' he'd be our best ghost hunter yet. Only problem was he kept tellin' us every God damn day. Hundreds of letters.'

'That's right. Eventually, if you remember, we started throwing his post away unopened. God knows what some of his later letters said. He might have been threatening us; who knows? I guess he would have got angry for not receiving a reply to every one.'

'And now,' said Goode, 'years later, in some sleepy little village in the middle of nowhere, he turns up. So his dad runs the hotel there? The same place where Jud was staying. But how did he make the connection? Why should he know anything about Jud and Bex? I mean, J is unrecognisable now, isn't he?'

Bonati looked across his desk. His face was deadly serious, but he tried to speak gently. This was getting sensitive and he couldn't predict what effect his next words would have on his oldest and dearest friend. 'Perhaps you didn't read those early letters of his, Jason? I guess not.'

'Go on.'

'Well, I did. And I remember clearly one of the reasons why we had to reject him. You see, he was at school with . . . Jamie. He *knew* him before.'

Goode placed his whisky glass down on the desk, bent over and put his head in his hands. 'Oh, God. So he knew J. Don't tell me he recognised him now, did he? Please, Giles. Please don't say that.'

'Well, we don't know that for sure,' said DCI Khan. 'But we can't pretend it's not possible. He might have done. And if he did—'

'Then J would've lost the plot completely. Hell, he must be

scared out of his mind right now.' Goode stood up and began moving quickly from one side of the room to the next, pausing occasionally, all the time shaking his head and trying to think it all through. The enormity of the situation was sinking in now. 'And you say he's gone missing, Khan?'

He nodded.

'Since when?'

'This afternoon, apparently. My guys are on it.'

I tell you, Inspector. You've gotta find that kid. You've gotta find him now. God knows what he could do to J. To all of us.'

Khan nodded. 'I know. We're on it. We'll find him. He may be with Jud, we don't know.'

'Don't tell me. He went missing around the same time as Jud and Bex, yeah?'

Bonati nodded again and looked ruefully at the floor. 'I'm sorry, Jason. I'm so sorry. There was just no way we could ever have guessed this would happen.'

'Not today, perhaps.'

'What do you mean?'

'Oh, come on, Giles. Maybe not today, but we knew it was gonna happen sooner or later. We've been taking too many risks. You know we have. We should never have sent him outta London. Never. It's too risky. We should've kept him near us, all the time. It's safer in London. So many people here; he can blend in easily. Less chance of being seen and . . . well . . . recognised. We've done this to him.' Goode's voice was choked. 'I tell you, Giles, we're—'

'Stop it,' snapped Bonati. 'We can't blame ourselves. Jason, listen to me. You just can't keep him locked up like some prized pet. He's got to make his own way, out there. I know there's the court order; we know all about that – how we're responsible for him – but you can't lock him up or keep him on a tight leash in one city. The conditions of his early release stated that we're responsible for his whereabouts, but that doesn't mean we have to imprison him again. After all, it's Jud we're talking about here. *Your son.* He's his own man, Jason – a grown man, now. And you've got to let him be—'

'Responsible for his whereabouts, huh? Are we? *So where the hell is he?*' Goode walked around to the professor's side of the desk and perched on the edge of it. Bonati felt uncomfortable all of a sudden. He hated it when his friend was explosive like this. He felt just as relieved as Khan to have someone else in the room. There was no telling what Goode might do next. He felt an acute sense of responsibility for Jud, especially with his father out of the country for most of the time, and now he couldn't even account for his whereabouts. His son was lost – in every sense of the word.

'Look, I'm sorry, Giles. I'm sure we'll—'

'Shut up. You hear me?' Goode pushed past Bonati's chair, towards the window again. 'Shut the hell up. You caused this, not me. I wasn't the one who sanctioned this mission. I'm always nervous when he's out of the city. This was *your* call.' He turned to face the professor and there were tears in his eyes now. Anger was quickly being replaced by despair – a sickening, frightening feeling that he was not going to see his son again. Khan felt acutely embarrassed to be there, at this private time. He'd only known these men a short while and, though he was privy to Jud's chequered past – because one day, not so long ago, he'd snooped around and found it out for himself – it didn't seem right to be here now, watching this great man slowly dismantle.

'OK,' said Goode quietly. 'Is the 'copter here, yeah? I mean, it's back from Suffolk now?'

The professor nodded.

'Tell Gary to get the engine started again. I wanna go there for myself.'

'Where? Dunwich?'

'Yeah. Jud and Bex don't have bikes with them. Hell, there's nothing much out there, from what you told me. They can't have gotten far. I wanna comb that place myself and find them, before this Hartwell kid does any more damage, OK? We've gotta reassure J that we'll put a lid on this kid. We'll zip him up and keep the past where it is. It'll be fine. Khan, you search for him, and the professor here and I will find agents Jud and Bex.'

He moved to the door.

'So, what're you waitin' for? Come on. I wanna find my son.'

Chapter 42

WEDNESDAY, 6.54 P.M.

(7.54 P.M. LOCAL TIME)

TRAIN BOUND FOR

COPENHAGEN, DENMARK

The race was on. Luc and Grace had to get back to the hotel, pack up their belongings, catch the train to Copenhagen and then get on the first flight back to London – before Sigurdsson, if indeed it was him who'd sent the assassin, found out that his man had failed and the agents were still at large. Those were Bonati's instructions. This case was spiralling out of control and the professor wanted everyone back at the CRYPT, at least long enough to hold a summit meeting and agree the next plan of action.

Bonati had been horrified to hear that there was someone after them – someone jabbing a gun in Luc's back and asking him to kneel. It just didn't bear thinking about. He wanted them all home, and he wanted it to happen now.

The agents were happy to oblige, after all. No complaints from them. They were eager to show the others back at the CRYPT that they had managed to find out more on the case – they'd located the very roots of it. The apartment in Roskilde, home to Agnar Sigurdsson, had been the place where this Viking obsession had begun, so it seemed.

Besides, their trip to Denmark had suddenly lost its appeal. But, sitting on the train now, bound for Copenhagen airport, neither of them felt certain they would even make it back. The experience at the museum had shaken them both and reminded them sharply that neither was invincible. As CRYPT agents, they were so used to operating in secrecy, that perhaps they'd taken their anonymity for granted. It seemed they were able to go about their work under a permanent veil of secrecy. But that veil had just been lifted. Someone had really, honestly, been assigned to follow and kill them – and it scared them, there was no denying it. Somewhere out there, out of the windows, was a man looking for them – a man with a gun, and bullets with their names on. They felt sick at the thought of it.

Ever since they'd boarded the train at Roskilde station, they'd both been more vigilant than ever. They'd spent a while walking through the carriages, trying to select an empty one. They just couldn't be too careful. They wanted to keep everyone at arm's length and had stolen surreptitious glances at passengers as they swept down the train, and had watched the people waiting on the platforms every time the train passed through a station on the main line.

They'd chosen a pair of seats at the very end of an empty carriage. Luc had sat with his back to the wall, observing the whole carriage ahead of him, and Grace had sat opposite him, with her eyes on the doorway that led into the next carriage along. Anything suspicious, and they'd press the emergency button without hesitation, stopping the train and alerting the guard. This was no time for heroics. They *had* to make it back to London, and not in a body bag.

After making an anonymous call to the Danish police, using a telephone at the museum, and informing them (in hushed tones) of the man lying unconscious on the jetty, they had decided it was advisable to get the hell out of the place and not wait for them to arrive. You just never knew who was listening, or being paid as an informant, or working for this Sigurdsson. The only people they could rely on now was each other.

'So where did this guy go? Do we know?' said Grace.

'Who? Sigurdsson, you mean?'

'Yes. The man who owns the apartment. Surely the police have found him now and questioned him?'

'Why? What has he done wrong? It's not a crime to see a ghost, and it's not a crime to collect antiques, either – unless they're stolen.'

'No, but I think it's still a crime to arrange to have somebody killed, isn't it?' said Grace.

'We've no proof that it was Sigurdsson behind the attempt, Grace. None at all.'

'Makes sense, though, doesn't it? He's the only one who could have a problem with us being here, I'd say. We were there at his apartment. If someone's been trailing us from there, then they might know what we've seen – the relics and all that.'

'Yes, that's true. But we've no proof,' said Luc. 'In any case, this is a matter for the police. I'm sure they're trying to track him down as we speak.'

'I doubt they're the only ones,' said Grace, staring out of the window, a thoughtful expression across her face. She was remembering the scenes in Sigurdsson's apartment – the ghost in the bedroom; Luc's face when he came in and saw it moving towards her.

'What do you mean?' asked Luc.

'I mean, the Viking ghosts. With so many of their belongings lying in that man's apartment, no wonder we saw a ghost there. I'd say he's a marked man now. You can hide from the police, but you can't hide from ghosts.'

'No; well, maybe he'll get what he deserves. If he is behind the raiding of the Viking hoards under the North Sea – if that's what is there – then he'll have much to answer for. No question. I wouldn't want to be in his shoes.'

Though they were speaking quietly, someone could hear their words. He was standing in the small, narrow space between the carriages, next to the luggage rack and the toilet door. He'd seen them get on the train early – watched them from the platform. He'd traced their movements once inside and seen which carriage they'd chosen. Just as the guard blew his whistle and the train's engines struck up, he'd jumped on and navigated his way to the best vantage point of all: here, out of sight but in earshot – just.

He glanced out of the window at the passing buildings. He knew this line like the back of his hand and could tell from the types of buildings and the names of the factories and shops in the retail parks approaching from his left that they were already on the outskirts of Copenhagen. It would be seven or eight minutes from here, with no hold-ups. He didn't have much time.

He was still reeling from hearing the mention of his name – not once, but several times – but he breathed deeply and steadied his heart, ready for action. The agents looked young and athletic, just as his man had described. He would need all his strength. But he was more cunning than he was strong. He knew how to get their attention. Now was the time to strike.

As the train shook and the windows rattled, he pushed his way to a place where he could be seen by the girl facing the door, then he grabbed his chest to give the impression his heart was failing him, fell to the floor and let out a cry for help. Inside his coat pocket, his other hand rested on the handle of a revolver.

CHAPTER 43

WEDNESDAY, 6.59 P.M.

DUNWICH BEACH, SUFFOLK

They were feeling cold and damp and their bodies were stiffening. Neither of them could recall how long they'd been lying in the sheltered corner of the dunes. The sky was darkening and the wind had whipped up, but they'd lost track of their surroundings. There was just too much to say. Bex had sat and listened and nodded and stroked Jud's arm occasionally. She was a good listener – he knew that. It was one of the things he loved about her. She might be tough – tougher than anyone else at the CRYPT; probably tougher than him, too – and she was confident, but, when it came to listening to him, she was happy to just absorb it all, let him get it off his chest and not interrupt – like his father always did. He knew he could talk to Bex. And now he had.

That fateful night, up in the tower at his father's castle home, when he'd seen his mother so cruelly taken from him . . . But it was so damn hard to recall. That was just the problem. And it was what had been eating him up inside all this time. He knew, because he'd been convinced the castle was haunted, that ghosts had been responsible for pushing his beloved mother from the tower. He'd seen shapes around her. He'd called out from his window but she'd not heard him.

But what were they? And why? Why should they have done that to her? Bex knew as soon as she'd heard this that it was the reason for the SPA session both she and the professor had walked in on. She knew now Jud had been trying to recreate the conditions that led up to the tragic end.

And then the arrest and the look on his grief-stricken father's face when the police told him they suspected his son of pushing her off himself.

And then his father's early attempts – those desperate attempts – to establish the existence of ghosts, if only to justify Jud's pitiful pleas in the court room at his trial: 'The ghosts did it; the ghosts did it!'

After his exhausting recounting, Jud had fallen silent eventually. They'd sat in quiet contemplation for a period – hours, who knows? – just staring out at the sea, watching the sun set on the horizon, huddling close for warmth. Bex hadn't cared if they would sit there all night until the morning. She didn't want this intimate, private moment to end. She had Jud all to herself, at last.

But the strain of revisiting his past in such graphic detail had taken its toll. She knew it was freezing cold and the ground was damp – so damp it had soaked through to their bones – but she had wanted him to rest. She'd stroked his wet forehead as he'd slept and watched his chest as it slowly rose and fell.

When he'd opened his eyes, she'd kissed him on the lips.

Now they stared out at the darker skies. The world was different now – and it would never be the same again. How could it? Neither of them was certain of what would happen with Hartwell on the loose.

'We'd better be getting on,' said Jud, sleepily. 'I'm soaked; I'm cold; I don't even know what time it is, but I guess someone will be looking for us. Have you checked your phone lately?'

'Battery's gone. There's hardly any reception out here, anyway.'

Jud smiled. The conditions were bracing, but the peace and

solitude warmed his thoughts. 'We'll come back here one day. No matter what happens now, we will come back one day – in the summer, when it's warm. And we'll sit here, together, and we'll talk about tonight. How we sat and we watched the . . .'

He fell silent.

'What's wrong?' said Bex. She felt his body jolt and it startled her. 'What are you looking at?'

He was staring over to his left. They were sheltering in a small dip in the sand dunes, where the wind was kinder and the grass was softer, but he'd seen something over the grassy tops of the dunes as they swayed in the wind.

'Tell me, what?'

He stood up slowly. 'Bex, look. Slowly, stand up.'

She edged upwards, her legs were stiff and her back was hurting, but she strained her neck to see over the tops of the dunes to where Jud was now pointing.

'Where?'

'Not on the beach; in the sea,' said Jud. 'Can you see it?'

'Yeah, there's a boat out there, I know,' said Bex. 'I was watching while you were asleep. It's been there for ages.'

'No. Not the boat – closer to the shore. Look again.'

And then she saw them: several darker shapes, rising from the waters. At first they'd looked like waves, the heavy swells that rise before the white crests break. But they weren't waves. They were solid figures. And they were growing in size and number.

'Oh my God,' whispered Bex. 'Is that what I think it is?'

'Looks like that couple up by the abbey weren't lying, were they? These are ghosts. Just like they told us.'

'They're creeping out of the sea,' said Bex. 'They're coming.' She went to move, but Jud grabbed her.

'Get down,' said Jud. 'Let's watch them first.'

CHAPTER 44

WEDNESDAY, 7.03 P.M.

(8.03 P.M. LOCAL TIME)

TRAIN BOUND FOR

COPENHAGEN, DENMARK

'Are you all right?' Grace said slowly and gently.

The man on the floor was groaning. Luc glanced back down the aisle into the carriage they had been sitting in – there was no one around.

'We've got to find someone who speaks Danish!' he said, desperately. 'Or this guy's not going to make it. Do you think it's his heart?'

'Must be,' said Grace. 'Can you hear us?' She was bending down, close to his face. He was making noises that suggested he was choking in pain.

He grimaced and grabbed his chest. '*Hjælp mig.*'

'What's he saying? Go and get someone, quick!' said Grace. 'Someone who understands him. And find an alarm button to press to stop the train.'

Luc set off down the carriage.

But then he stopped. The groans from the old man had suddenly been drowned out by a second noise.

Grace was screaming.

He turned sharply and saw her being held down by the man. He'd grabbed her and wrestled her to the floor. Luc couldn't believe what he was seeing. Had this guy been faking it?

He ran to them. Grace was wriggling and shoving and kicking him now, desperate to be free of his iron-like grip.

'Hey! Get off her!' Luc demanded as he reached the little gap between the carriages where the man had fallen. 'What the hell are you doing?'

He stepped on the man's arm, just as he was going to swing for Grace. The man tried to get to his feet but Luc pounded into him, his fist meeting the guy's cheekbone and his heavy boot connecting with his stomach. Grace wrestled herself free and then joined Luc in trying to flip the guy over on to his stomach so they could secure his arms behind his back. Whoever he was, he'd be answering to the police when they arrived. But where the hell was the guard?

'Did you find the alarm?' said Grace.

'No. You screamed and I came straight back! Hey, get off her, I said!' The man was still coming after Grace, so Luc put his full weight behind his punch and landed one into the man's solar plexus. He coughed and was instantly winded.

'Get out, Grace!' yelled Luc. 'Go and get help, now!'

'I'm not leaving you,' she said. 'We shut this guy up together.'

Luc now had him in a kind of bear hug, both of them on their knees. The man was flailing his arms around, trying to land punches wherever he could. Luc was taking a beating but was not defeated – he knew he'd be too much for this older man eventually. He was strong and athletic – one of the strongest agents at the CRYPT. If he wanted an unarmed fight, this guy had chosen the wrong person. And Grace had been able to get some kicks and punches in, too. He was clearly weakening, for all his size.

But, throughout the assault, he said nothing.

Then Luc saw him reaching for something inside his coat. Luc pulled his arm away but the man went for the same place with his other arm so quickly that Luc didn't have time to grab it.

Grace was running through the aisle, reaching the end. As she kept tapping her fingers on the electric button to open the door, she heard a gunshot behind her and it took her breath away.

She turned around.

'Luc!'

There, at the other end of the carriage, he was kneeling on the floor, clutching his stomach.

She watched his assailant stagger to his feet and run straight through the open door into the next carriage along. He sprinted down the aisle in the opposite direction and within seconds was out of sight.

She ran to Luc. 'Oh my God. Where did he shoot you? Luc? Talk to me.'

He was bending over further now, still grabbing his stomach but coughing uncontrollably. It was like he was going to be sick. She knelt down to see his face. 'Luc! Did you get a bullet? Where? In your stomach? Talk to me. Please. You're OK, yes? Oh God. You'll be OK; I know you'll be all right. I'll get help.'

Though she hardly ever lost her cool, Grace was surely panicking now. Tears were welling up. Still Luc made no sound, save for the coughing and spluttering that was incessant now.

'Get someone,' he managed in a choking voice. 'It's my stomach. It went in. Oh, Grace.' He collapsed to the floor.

She stood up and spun around. People were entering the carriage they'd been in. They'd heard the gunshot and quickly ran to her aid.

'*Hvad er der sket?*' said the first man to reach them. '*Var, at en pistol?*'

'What? English, please! Help us. Please, help!'

'What's happened?' he said more slowly. 'Was that a gun I heard? Has this man really been shot?'

'Yes. Yes, I think so. It's his stomach.'

'Where did the attacker go? That way?' the man asked.

Grace nodded. The man signalled to two others to come and help Grace while he and another ran off down the train in the direction of the assailant. The buildings of central Copenhagen were coming into view and the train was slowing down as it approached its destination.

Luc had gone quiet. Grace checked his pulse – he was still alive, but critical. She loosened the shirt around his neck and laid him in a recovery position with the help of those around her.

'Luc?' she kept saying. 'Stay with us! Come on.'

The two passengers with her kept speaking his name too and telling him he would be OK.

He started to shake uncontrollably and continued to cough and retch.

Grace's face went ashen. It had all happened so quickly. Her head was light, dizziness was setting in and the whole carriage began to spin. Moments before she keeled over, a woman grabbed her and set her down on the first seat in the carriage, through the open door. Then she returned to Luc, who was bent double on the floor, crippled with agony.

No words came from his lips, only coughing and spluttering as blood began to trickle slowly out of his mouth.

Three carriages on, Sigurdsson sat down and tried hard to hide his panting. He grabbed a discarded newspaper and held it up to his face to read. He'd timed it just right: any second now the train would reach the station and he'd be off before the alarm was raised. Soon his beloved Denmark would be free of these inquisitive agents, digging into its precious past as if they were on some school history trip.

One down; one to go.

CHAPTER 45

WEDNESDAY, 7.12 P.M.

NORTH SEA, OFF THE COAST OF

DUNWICH

Daniel watched the navigation system on the boat. It was far more technical than anything he'd seen before. His own equipment, and that of his fellow diving friends, was nothing like as advanced. This girl really did have money, if the boat was anything to go by: sophisticated and powerful, with a sleek body that was fast and nimble – just like Yolanda.

'So, do you think we're there, yet?' she said, approaching Daniel from behind and placing her hands around his waist as he stood at the wheel.

'Yeah, sure. I think this is it. Let's put down anchor and steady the boat. Then we'll get down there. It's quiet out here tonight; I can't see anyone else. The boat will be fine here.'

'Yes. I'm surprised there's no police out,' said Yolanda.

'Nothing left to investigate, at least not until the morning when it's light again,' said Dan. 'The night is ours.'

She smiled and moved towards the little drawer, which housed the beautiful gift he had given her. She took out the amulet and chain and twirled it around her fingers again.

'There'll be plenty more where that came from,' said Daniel.

Yolanda looked unconvinced. 'We might find some old coins, perhaps even some other Viking ornaments or jewellery, but it's unlikely we'll find another one of these, trust me. My father and I have been searching for years. You don't see these every day.'

'No?'

'Once in a lifetime, I'd say.'

'Well, I'm glad to have been of service,' Dan said, smiling. 'We make a good team, don't you think?' His attempts to prove indispensible to Yolanda and her father were poorly hidden. But he didn't care. He knew how quickly this girl could change and now that he had decided to come on board with her, there was no going back. He *had* to stay alive and see it through. The promises of riches and luxury and many more nights spent with this beautiful girl were enough to make any man want to stay alive. And so far she had been good to him.

He looked out of the window at the dark waves that rocked the boat as the engines fell silent. He thought of Møller's body, lying at the bottom of the ocean, in its submarine grave.

'Let's go and get the gear on,' he said.

'No rush, my darling,' said Yolanda, taking his hand and leading him towards the open cabin door that led out on to the deck. 'You just said there's no one around. We have all night. My father isn't expecting a call from me until the morning. Slow down, Dan. Feel the rocking; smell the air. Don't you just love night sailing?'

He was beginning to feel nervous again. It was whenever she smiled: she looked her most beautiful and yet her most deadly when she grinned at him. Her face was pale and pure and her teeth were immaculate. Her eyes were shining tonight and, as they moved on to the open deck, the moon brought a twinkle to them. Her long, blond hair was blowing around her face wildly. Out here, in the moonlight, her windswept features were ravishing. He just wanted to kiss her.

Was it too soon? Would he anger her if he moved in too close? He decided it was better to wait until she made the first move. Focus on the job in hand – to get the diving gear ready. If he looked at her too long, he felt vulnerable – like most guys did in her presence.

She was still clutching something in her hand.

'Is that the amulet? Don't lose it, whatever you do,' he said, nervously. 'I'm sure your father wouldn't thank you.'

'Relax,' she said. 'You worry too much, that's your problem. I won't be letting go of this just yet. The wind can blow and the boat can bounce around all it likes, but nothing will take this from me. It's safe with me.'

She moved to the rail that ran around the boat. The waves were turbulent now and Dan felt nervous when she stood too close to the edge.

'Hold on!' he said, clinging to the rail beside him. 'We don't want you falling overboard, especially not with that in your hand!'

She ignored him and turned to face the driving wind and the seas below her. He watched her hair sweep past her face, blown horizontal by the gale.

'Aren't you cold?' he said. He'd suddenly noticed that she wasn't wearing a thick jacket like he was. Her thin fleece seemed inadequate protection against the wild elements out here on the North Sea, but she wasn't shivering at all. She looked relaxed and warm. They really do breed them tough in Scandinavia, he thought.

He watched her from behind. She raised her hands up to her neck. He knew exactly what she was doing. In fact, he was amazed she'd resisted the temptation this long.

She was placing the amulet and chain around her neck.

'Here, let me help you,' he said. He moved in closer towards her. She could feel his warm body pressing against her back. He took the chain from her and placed it around her neck, as she swept her hair to one side to make it easier for him.

'Thanks,' she said.

He closed the clasp on the chain and leaned in closer to give her a gentle peck on the nape of her neck – it was too much to resist. Wisps of her blond hair tickled his face as his lips met her soft skin. He could feel her body relax gently in his arms. The boat rocked them for a while as they moved in unison to the rise and fall of the waves.

She looked down at the amulet and whispered, 'It's beautiful, Daniel. Really beautiful.'

'You what, my love?' Daniel said. It was hard to hear her whisper against the wind. 'What was that?'

'It's beautiful. Really beautiful,' she whispered again.

Daniel looked up from where he had settled into the back of her neck. That's odd, he thought. She was emitting a strange, low whisper, unlike her usual delicate tone. This was hushed, deeper, more smoky.

She spoke again, in a tone almost unrecognisable to him. And her words were different, too. Danish, he guessed. It wasn't as romantic as French or Italian, but the way she spoke was seductive still.

'*Dens smukke, min kærlighed.*'

He stood back. It was like someone else was speaking. Weird, he thought, how different she sounded compared to when she spoke English to him.

'I don't know what that means, but I hope it's good,' he said, as her windswept hair blew on to his cheek and she gradually turned to face him.

'Whoa! Jesus. Oh, God!' he stumbled backwards and tripped over a fastening, screwed into the wooden deck. A giant shiver ran right up his spine and sent tingles across his scalp. His heart began to pound and there was a nausea rising from deep within him. He staggered to his feet again.

'What the hell . . . ?'

The transformation was sudden and chilling. He could still

see Yolanda's eyes – her hair, her body – but her face and neck had become almost translucent; thin, bluish skin covered her cheekbones and jaw, so thin you could see veins through it. Her lips were thinner, darker too. And when she parted them to speak, they cracked, as though they were chapped and dry.

She smiled.

And then she rose upwards. She seemed taller than Daniel. He quickly glanced at the deck – her feet were leaving the floor; she was levitating. She brought her arms up and splayed them, like wings.

'Yolanda? Please. No, no.' He fell to his knees in front of her. What was happening was too much for him to take in. It made no sense and out here, in the cold winds and under the dark skies, it was terrifying. Though they had been in blackness, save for the small light spilling from the cabin behind him, it now seemed like Yolanda was emitting light herself. She moved towards Daniel, who was cowering on the deck, shielding his face from the sight.

As he peered through his hands, he saw the tips of wings protruding from behind Yolanda's shoulders.

She emitted a whisper – a low, guttural rasp, but the words were indecipherable to Daniel, '*Du er den udvalgte! Kom med mig.*'

If he had understood the Valkyrie's message, he would have collapsed there and then, but ignorance protected him. She was telling him he was the chosen one, bidding him to come with her.

To Valhalla.

Her body was floating on the wind, rising up from the deck. And it was becoming more and more like a holographic image, illuminated against the black sky, but translucent, like a projection.

And locked in its clasp around her thin neck lay the chain with its amulet, glowing.

Her hair was scraped back from her forehead by the strong wind that was building to a gale, pounding the boat. Yolanda's clothes were concealed now in some kind of lacy veil. As she rose above him, above the whole boat, Daniel could see the wings in full stretch now.

'*Du er den udvalgte!*' she continued to whisper, and her words blended with the roar of the wind. '*Kom med mig.*'

Daniel froze. He screwed himself into a ball – on his knees, head in his hands – and closed his eyes. The motion of the boat was more violent now as the waves took hold. And the light was cascading down on to the deck.

A sound was rising, cutting through the wind and the roar of the seas. It was different now, like an engine of some kind. Daniel quickly looked up. Lights blinded him from the south-east. Was someone approaching?

Up in the air, Jason Goode signalled to the pilot to draw in closer. He and Khan had seen the boat in the distance and the strange light emanating from its deck. The 'copter had been just moments from beginning its descent, approaching the Suffolk coastline and the fields above Dunwich, where Gary had landed before, but when Goode spotted the boat out to the east, he urged him to move in nearer. Banking around and approaching it now, they couldn't quite believe what they were seeing.

'What the hell is that?' said Goode. 'Is it some kind of trick? It looks like a figure of some kind. Khan, can you see that too?' he said excitedly. 'My God, what is that?' The inspector nodded to indicate he could see it too, though he just stared in silence, a quizzical look etched on his face. 'What about you, Giles? Can you see it?'

Bonati had been trying very hard not to 'see' anything for the duration of the flight here. His vertigo was crippling him and there were few things worse than a helicopter ride for someone so afraid of heights – windows everywhere, an eerie sense of floating and the deafening sound of the rotary blades in his ears. But he looked down at the sea in the direction Goode was pointing.

He stared at the scene, his fears subsiding as the incredible sight came into view.

'Giles, what do you reckon?' said Goode, excitedly. 'A spirit, yeah?'

'If what the agents are saying is true, and some Viking remains have been disturbed down there, then my guess is that's a spirit, yes. And a particular kind, I'd say. It's a Valkyrie.'

'Yeah, I've heard of those. Some kind of Viking angel, huh? Wow; that's a new one for me, Giles. We've never seen one of those, have we? You can add that to the CRYPT portfolio.'

Khan rolled his eyes and prayed that the helicopter would soon find terra firma. Though he wasn't crippled with Bonati's fear of heights, there were better things to be doing in the evening than hovering above a boat in a violent storm, trying to get a glimpse of a ghost.

'Hey, but look closer, Giles – on the boat. What's that on deck?'

'It's a body,' said Khan. 'Someone's down there, on the boat. Poor sod.'

'My God. Is that J?' said Goode. 'Do we need to get down there?'

Bonati's face looked grave. 'Let's hope not. I'm not sure we can get close enough and, although we've got a winch on board, in this wind it's anybody's guess whether we could get it to him.'

'Are you saying we shouldn't try, Bonati? Is that what you're sayin'?'

'Er . . . no; of course not. If you want to try and save whoever that is then be my guest. I'm staying right here.'

Khan was leaning close to the window, trying to make out the identity of the man on his knees on the deck. He looked up briefly, shielding his eyes from the 'copter's lights. And then Khan saw his face.

'No, it's not Jud! I know that guy. It's Summers – Daniel Summers. You know, the diver who started this whole bloody thing.'

They watched out of their windows as the extraordinary sight of the Valkyrie rose above the terrified man on deck.

And then it happened.

Without any warning, the man climbed on to the railings that ran around the edge of the deck and plunged, head first, into the freezing waters.

'Crazy bastard!' shouted Goode. He leaned over towards the pilot. 'Gary, get the winch going. He won't last any longer than a few minutes in that freezing water. Drop it now!'

The helicopter lowered towards the dark, ominous waters. From this level, its passengers were able to get a clearer view of the strange, angel-like being that was still hovering just above the deck of the boat.

It was emitting a light from its body, and from its back protruded large, feathery wings. They could see its face was female – strikingly beautiful, but almost translucent.

'My God,' said Khan. 'Look at that. It's beautiful.'

'No!' shouted Bonati. 'Don't fall for it. Don't even look at it. The Valkyries were known for them charms. Don't fall for it, Khan. Even a hardened old copper like you could fall for something like that.'

'He's right,' said Goode. 'Next thing you know, you'll be leaping out of the God damn 'copter, joining her on the boat. And we'll be back to where we started. Look away. Don't watch her. She's looking for someone else to have. If she can't have that Summers guy, it could be one of us.'

The winch was lowering into the water and Goode slid open the heavy door so that he could get a better look and use the giant torch that was kept inside the 'copter. Freezing winds blasted into the interior and rattled around the passengers within.

'God; this English weather!' shouted Goode over the noise of the gales and the roaring seas just below them. 'Welcome to hell.'

He gripped on to the torch and pointed it down at the sea. There was nothing there, and then, just below them and to the left, he saw Summers. He was treading water and waving desperately. The cold had almost completely taken his breath away but the violent writhing around of his limbs was keeping his blood pumping, at least for now. He knew he'd not last long. Would his beautiful Valkyrie get her way, after all?

'Quick; grab my other arm, Khan. Come on! I wanna lean out and make sure he's got the winch. Do it!'

Khan moved over to where Goode was dangling out of the door. He grabbed him firmly, allowing him to lower himself half out of the door. The wind was rasping him, turning his face instantly numb.

It worked.

Summers managed to grab the metal hook at the end of the winch. He held it firmly in both hands as Goode turned towards the 'copter and signalled with his thumb for Gary to start winding in again.

Just as the winch was reaching the base of the 'copter, the Valkyrie swooped up towards them. Goode could see right through her as she flew to him. Her hands were outstretched and she scratched his face. Though his skin was numb, the shock of it made him scream so loud Bonati could hear it from where he had tucked himself up behind the seats, trying to hide his eyes from the drop below. The professor stood up quickly and came to help Khan pull both Goode and their new passenger inside.

Summers was now dangling like a fish on the end of a rod. Though Goode had a firm grasp on his arms, his legs were still fully exposed and the Valkyrie was on him. Her fingernails sank into his flesh.

'Aagh!' he yelled. 'Get it off me! Get it off! Aagh!' She was lacerating his legs; the pain was unbearable. She climbed up his body as an insect climbs a stem. Goode, Khan and Bonati all came face to face with her.

'Don't look at her eyes!' yelled Bonati.

Together they gave Summers one last pull and he landed on the floor of the 'copter, shivering and wriggling around like a herring.

'Close the door!' shouted Khan. 'Close it!'

But Goode was transfixed. The Valkyrie was beguiling – enchanting. He couldn't take his eyes off her: that pale skin, those dark lips and the chillingly beautiful, blue eyes that seemed to glow in the darkness like orbs.

Bonati went for Goode. He pulled him backwards, right on top of where Summers was still lying, and, with an almighty shove, Khan closed the door of the 'copter.

They'd done it. Summers began to catch his breath and the warmth of the 'copter's sophisticated heating system started to thaw his bones. His legs were bleeding badly, but they would heal. It was a relief to close the door and silence the deafening gales outside.

But it wasn't over.

Goode had seen something whilst hanging on to the 'copter's frame outside. As he'd waited for Summers to grab hold of the winch, he'd allowed his eyes to momentarily flick towards the coastline again. Hovering so close to the waves, he'd been able to see something that startled him further – down on the pebble beach, away to his left.

'Swing the 'copter round!' said Goode, anxiously. 'Quick! I wanna see what's on the beach up there.' He signalled for Gary to manoeuvre towards where he was pointing.

If the figure rising up from the boat had frightened them, it was nothing compared to what Goode had seen through the gloom. The moon had provided just enough silvery light to illuminate the pebble beach and the grassy dunes that ran along its fringe, up to the place where the crumbling cliffs began again.

'There! Look!' he shouted.

They saw figures moving along the sand, each rising out of the water, gaining full height and walking like some ghostly pilgrimage up the coastline.

'See them?' said Goode through his headset. He was speaking so loud now he nearly deafened his flying partners.

'Yes, sure; I see them,' said Bonati.

'So what are they, Professor?' said Khan, equally transfixed by the growing hoards of dark figures marching together. 'Don't tell me. They're not accountants and lawyers out on some weekend re-enactment, right? I mean, these aren't local volunteers, are they? You're gonna say these are ghosts too, yeah?'

Summers winced in pain as he sat up and tried to see out of the window, to where everyone was now gazing.

The professor nodded. 'It's possible. There's something rank in this place. Like when you prick a wound – it bleeds and the pain starts all over again. Someone, or something, has disturbed this place and it's fighting back. The Valkyrie is proof of that.'

'Well, I tell you what, gentlemen,' said Goode, in a hushed voice now. 'If Jud and Bex really are down there, then God help them both. The place is under siege.'

CHAPTER 46

WEDNESDAY, 7.20 P.M.

(8.20 P.M. LOCAL TIME)

AMBULANCE, COPENHAGEN,

DENMARK

'Stay with me, Luc. Come on. You can do it. Stay with me. Hang on.' Grace was talking continuously to him, partly to let him know she was with him and partly to ease her own nerves. Constant talking prevented her from dwelling on what might be happening to her fellow agent.

This was serious now.

The medic at the other side of Luc's stretcher was monitoring his progress, connecting up his drip and checking his mask was working. There was machinery throughout the ambulance's interior and it seemed like it was all in use tonight. Grace was scared.

The train had stopped, as it was scheduled to, in Copenhagen's central station, but the scene that unfolded took the guard on the platform by surprise. The passengers spilled out on to the platform as they would normally do, but then the train staff rallied round and secured a stretcher to get the injured passenger off. Within minutes, the paramedics were at the scene.

And now, here they were, racing through the evening traffic, sirens blaring.

Sigurdsson had escaped unnoticed. He'd been one of the first people off the train and sailed through the barriers before the guard had even been informed there had been an incident. He'd timed it to perfection – if the gun had gone off any earlier, there would have been a welcome party of police for him on platform six as the train rolled in.

'He's going to be all right, though, isn't he?' said Grace, her voice choking with emotion. 'I mean, it's only his stomach. It's not like his chest or anything. They'll find the bullet. He'll be fine, won't he? I mean, he'll be—'

'Shh,' the medic interrupted her. 'Keep calm, miss. We're doing all we can. He's been shot and we won't know the extent of the internal damage until we get him into theatre. There will be bleeding. It's a question of where the bullet went. But we're doing all we can. He's in safe hands now.'

'Yeah. But, I mean, he's still alive now, you know. I mean . . . Well, if the shot had been fatal, he wouldn't . . . Well, you know . . . It's good that he's still with us. That means he's gonna be OK, yeah? He's gonna be—'

'Please, miss. Calm yourself. We're doing all we can.'

Grace fell silent and stared miserably at Luc's face, behind the mask. His eyes were closed now and his body was still.

Grace's head was pounding and her eyes were itchy and tired from all the crying. She felt sick. She really didn't know if she could do this. She didn't want to be in the ambulance any more. She felt trapped. She wanted to be somewhere else – somewhere she could hide away and not face the reality that was unfolding around her, like the worst nightmare anyone could ever have.

They'd grown into such a good partnership. How the hell was she going to cope without him? Everyone loved Luc, back at the agency, mostly for his sense of humour and sense of fun, but Grace knew him better than most. She knew that behind that jokey exterior lay someone who really cared. She was surprised at how close they'd been getting. And now, just looking at him, lying there, helpless, she could hardly take it in.

Stop it, Lord, she said inside. Wake me up. I want it to stop now.

She slumped back on the bench, closed her eyes and felt the vibrations of the speeding tyres in the metal walls of the ambulance behind her, running through her spine. The sirens wailed again and the vehicle lurched left and right as it weaved between the cars. Grace screwed her eyes up tighter, brought her hands up to her face and began to pray.

CHAPTER 47

WEDNESDAY, 7.38 P.M.

DUNWICH BEACH, SUFFOLK

'There're dozens of them,' whispered Bex, sitting close to Jud, sheltering from the gale that was now battering the dunes and cliffs right along the coast.

'I know. Whatever they're coming for, it's going to happen tonight,' said Jud. 'You can feel it, can't you?'

'Oh, yeah. The air is thick with tension. There's been some brutal damage here and it needs to heal, like any wound. Someone's disturbed the very place that should have remained hidden.'

'Well, you know who started this bloody mess: your friend, that Summers guy.'

'I know. And I do wish you wouldn't keep calling him *my* friend. Besides, I don't like blond hair.' She smiled wryly at him through the gloom.

Down on the beach, the rows of figures were still rising from the ocean and walking up the steep banks of pebbles that rolled down to the water's edge. Each time the waves broke over the stones, it seemed there was another tide of ghosts, marching up on to land.

It was hard to see how each one was formed, as the night had now enveloped the landscape, but the moon provided just enough light to see their cloaks and the silvery glistening of their metal helmets. These were Viking warriors – had to be. It struck the agents that nothing else in the vicinity had changed much since the first time these invaders hit Suffolk shores. There was nothing to orientate them to the current century – no buildings, no boats, nothing but the ancient pebbles, which pre-dated the Vikings by millions of years – so it could have been any time in history. The only thing that anchored them to the present was each other.

Jud was struck by how much he was beginning to depend on Bex as his anchor, not just here, now, but always. She was his rock. He'd admitted to himself now that he needed a close relationship – he couldn't lock up his emotions in solitary confinement forever. He needed someone to understand what he was going through. And here, in the remoteness of the wild Suffolk coast, he felt closer to Bex than he'd ever done in the past. Not even in the romantic city of Venice, where they had investigated a case together not that long ago, had he been drawn to her in the same way. It was like it was safe to tell her everything here, let her into his world at last. It didn't seem to matter what he told her here. Of course, he knew that sooner or later they would have to return to London and face the music together. But here, they were cocooned from the outside world: from the CRYPT and from the truth.

But he couldn't escape the harsh reality of the moment. What the hell were they going to do about the armies of ghosts marching steadily towards the old, surviving buildings of Dunwich village? Pretty soon the walking dead would hit civilisation. And then all hell would break. The villagers, the tourists, the late-night dog walkers, the drinkers in the pubs and the workers coming home from neighbouring towns and cities would all see the ghosts for themselves. And they were as vulnerable as anyone could be. The agents had already seen just what these Vikings were capable of – the image of the blood-eagled body on the beach just a short walk from where they sat was still very real in their minds. Soon there'd be other fatalities. Who could tell what the ghosts' intentions were?

'Why have we not heard anything from Grace and Luc? That's what I want to know,' said Jud. 'I mean, Luc told me they'd research the history for us, since they were going to Denmark, anyway, while we stuck it out here, in the cold. What's happened?'

'I don't know,' said Bex. 'I'm worried about that. It's unlike Grace not to call me. Something's happened over there, I can feel it.'

'In Denmark?'

'Yes. It's unusual for her not to call and keep me posted with how it's going. And you've not heard from Luc, have you?'

Jud shook his head slowly. 'I've got the same bad feeling about this too. He's in distress, Bex. I can *feel* it.'

'Let's hope we're wrong – we have been before. But we do need to know if they've found any stronger links between that haunting in Roskilde and the events over here, so that we can communicate with these figures – reason with them; give them what they want. There are far too many ghosts for the neutralisers to have any effect on them. We have no choice but to communicate with them. Like we did in Tyburn. We have to tell them what they want to hear.'

'Which is what?' said Jud. 'That we're sorry someone's disturbed their things under the sea? You're right, there has to be more to it than that, hasn't there? I mean, whatever has been disturbed, it *has* to have extra special significance. And right now, we still don't know what that is.'

As the troops marched past them, down on the pebble beach, Jud and Bex saw a light in the sky approaching from the east, over the sea.

'Is that what I think it is?' said Bex.

'It's a 'copter, isn't it? You can hear the blades. Is it ours, do you think?'

'Could be. Reinforcements? Have you called CRYPT? Coz I haven't.'

They looked at each other with guilty expressions. The last few hours had been so emotional for them both – an outpouring of honesty. They'd lost track of all communications. When they'd checked their phones earlier, neither of them had any battery left, and besides, they knew the reception out here was almost non-existent, even for the top-of-the-range smartphones Goode Technology provided them with. They were alone.

'If that is a CRYPT 'copter, then God help us if it's Bonati or Goode. We're in for some trouble, I can tell you,' said Bex.

'Why?'

Bex was ashamed to admit it, but she knew he'd find out sooner or later. 'The last time I used my phone, I spoke to Bonati. We agreed we should come back to London straight away. The professor wanted us all back for a debriefing before this thing got out of hand.'

'And you didn't tell me?' said Jud.

Bex shook her head furtively. 'I know, I know. I should've told you. But when you started to open up to me, do you think I was going to tell you to stop, huh? No way! I figured London could wait. This was more important.'

'I don't blame you, Bex. We're as bad as each other.'

'As good as each other, you mean.'

'The light's getting stronger. It's definitely a 'copter and it's heading straight for the beach. They must've seen the ghosts now. At least it'll be reinforcements.'

They watched the lights approach them. Soon they could see the black, insect-like Squirrel helicopter reach the edge of the beach. It roared over their heads and began to descend on to a large, open field behind them, not far from the car park down near the café. They quickly ran towards the noise. The black paint of the 'copter rendered it almost invisible in the night sky. Only

291

the windows gave away its position as they reflected the moon's gaze.

Jud and Bex heard the blades come to a final halt as they ran towards the place where it had set down. The grass was long in patches, and soaking too, but their clothes were already so drenched they hardly noticed. It was a black HT1 Squirrel – they knew it had to be the CRYPT's. The doors of the 'copter swung open and three dark figures slowly climbed out on to the grass.

'Professor?' shouted Jud. 'Is that you?'

'Hello, Jud,' came the reply.

He recognised it instantly – it wasn't Bonati. It was his father. Jud hesitated. After the emotional outpouring to Bex, he felt tempted to embrace him like any son would his own father. But he wasn't sure of the response he'd get, especially in front of Bex. His father would have no idea of how much Bex now knew. He spoke as nonchalantly as he could manage, mindful of the time that had elapsed since they last spoke, but aware too of the artificial roles they were supposed to be playing in this constant fiction. 'Hello, Mr Goode. Funny meeting you here. Long time no see.'

'Where the hell have you been?' came his typically direct response.

Jud had expected nothing more. He knew, from what Bex had told him, that the CRYPT had been expecting them both in London. And he also knew that his father was not someone who liked to be kept waiting. But there was an emotion in his father's voice that was different to plain anger – he was concerned too, Jud could tell, though he knew also that there was little chance of him admitting so, either here or in private.

'Oh, you know – cinema, a bit of shopping. Thought we'd check out the casinos later.'

DCI Khan smirked. Bex winced behind Jud and braced herself for a fight. Goode just glared at his son through the gloom. He tried his hardest not to show any kind of smile, though his son's mischievous humour had always slightly impressed him. This was just the kind of sarcastic comment he himself would have given his own father. It was a stupid question, after all. Where else could the agents have got to in this remote place?

Bonati interjected, 'Can we have an assessment of what's going on down there, on the beach? Thoughts please; either of you?'

'We have good reason to believe they are the ghosts of Viking invaders, who could well have been here before, centuries ago,' said Bex.

'And the cause?' said Goode. 'We know there's always a cause. Luc and Grace in Denmark have suggested it's to do with some kind of burial mound, yeah?'

'Yes,' said Jud. 'We would agree with that. If someone significant was buried in this area in the ninth century, maybe, then it's possible the remains could have shifted into the sea when the cliffs crumbled away. This place is famous for its coastal erosion . . . Wait a minute. Who the hell's that coming out of the 'copter? Who's with you?'

'This is Daniel Summers. I think you know him, yes?' said Bonati, as they watched Summers stagger out on to the grass. He'd been told to rest and recuperate inside the 'copter for a while, but he was far too curious to just sit there, talking to the pilot. His body was wrapped in a blanket, taken from the emergency kit stowed away inside. His hair was still soaked and his face was deathly pale. But he was alive.

Bex glanced at him, though suddenly she felt less inclined to smile. She saw no need to wind up Jud further, or make him jealous like before. He'd been through enough and, besides, Summers was no match for Jud. Never had been, really.

'I think I may have caused all this,' he said, gloomily. 'I have, haven't I?'

Bex spoke sympathetically: 'No, no, don't be—'

'Yes,' interrupted Jud. 'You have.'

'And just what do you think you've unearthed, then? That's the ten million dollar question,' said Goode. 'Talk to us. Because, unless we find some answers soon, those ghosts down there are gonna keep rising outta the sea and scaring people right along the God damn coast. Come on, everybody; *think*, will you?'

'It's the necklace, isn't it?' said Summers.

'What?' said Jud. He knew about the fragment of rune stone and the old coin. He knew about the crazy legend of the black dog, too; but, so far, there'd been no mention of a necklace.

Summers filled them in on the significance of the amulet and chain that he'd presented to Yolanda on the boat – and the consequences of her putting it around her neck.

'So that ghost – the Valkyrie we saw hovering above you – that was this Yolanda girl?' asked DCI Khan. 'Is that what you're saying? Seriously? I mean, is that possible, Jud? Huh? Professor?'

Jud nodded his head, deep in thought. 'Some items, especially precious ones, can be so highly charged with radiation that they can physically affect the actions and even appearance of the living, not just the dead. There's a synergy that takes place – like a melding of the elements that make up both the item itself and the body around it. So, in this case, the amulet acts like a catalyst. It's rare, though, isn't it, Professor?'

'Yes, indeed it is rare,' said Bonati. 'I tell you, I'd be fascinated to get that Valkyrie girl into the CRYPT labs and run some tests. Where did she go, Jason? Is she still out at sea? I can't see any light now.'

Goode shrugged. 'When I pulled Summers up into the 'copter, she went for us both, like you saw, but then she swept down beneath the 'copter. I shut the door damn quick. You know I hate to say it, but she could have become caught up in the rotary blades – we'll never know. She was thin, like a projection.'

Bonati nodded. 'Maybe. Her state had looked more like non-conflict plasma – translucent, wasn't she? – but it's possible the blades could have struck her if she was partly solid.'

Summers' face fell as he gazed out to the dark sea and was unable to see any flicker of light out there.

Nothing. Where was she? Was that to be the last he'd see of Yolanda? He was finding it difficult to keep up with the strange events that had unfolded in this remote place. He felt dizzy and freezing cold.

Khan grabbed him as his body went limp. 'You OK?' the inspector said. 'Do you wanna go back inside the 'copter, yeah?'

'No,' said Summers. 'I want to stay here and find out what the hell is happening.'

'Good,' said Bex. 'So, you found the amulet under the sea, yes?'

Summers nodded slowly.

'In the same place as the stone fragment and the old coin? And you think there may be more?'

'Yes. That's why I wanted to come back. And that's why Yolanda was so keen too. Her father's an archaeology enthusiast, or something. He hunts down treasure belonging to his motherland.'

'Denmark?' said Bonati.

Summers nodded again.

'His name is Sigurdsson?'

'Yes. I believe so. But how did you know?' said Summers.

'The Danish police informed me he was the owner of an apartment in Denmark where another haunting took place,' Bonati said. 'My agents found a stash of relics there. It was packed with evidence of archaeological digs.'

'What haunting?' said Summers. 'So there's been something going on in Denmark too? Yolanda never said.'

'Don't worry about that now,' said Goode. 'What the hell are we going to do about the ghosts? Or had you all forgotten?'

They stared down, over the edge of the mound where the helicopter had landed, and saw dark, shadowy figures still rising from the sea.

'Come on; *think!*' said Goode.

There was a sudden ringing, followed by a shout from the pilot, Gary. 'Mr Goode? It's for you.'

'So, at least someone can get a signal round here,' said Jud.

'Do you know how much these things cost?' said Goode. 'Of course it's got a damn phone signal!' He ran off to the helicopter and disappeared inside.

'We've got to get down there and try to stop them,' said Bex.

'How?' said Jud. 'Have you seen how many ghosts there are? There may be dozens now. Our neutralisers would be useless. And we can't take them on physically – there're far too many.'

'So we distract them?' said Bex.

'That might work. Or we light a fire?'

'Where are we going to find enough dry wood round here?' They looked around the gloomy, barren field. It was a stupid suggestion and Jud knew it. But things were becoming desperate.

'Hey! Come here!' Goode was shouting from the helicopter – and Jud could tell from his tone that something was seriously wrong. The wind was whipping up, blowing horizontally across the open field and rattling the blades on the 'copter.

'What? What's happened? Tell us.'

Goode ran towards them. Jud could see straight away that his face wore a grave expression.

'It was Grace. She's still in Denmark.'

'What? Come on; what?' said Jud. There was a growing pain in his stomach and a feeling of indigestion in his chest. 'It's Luc, isn't it?'

Goode nodded his head. 'I'm afraid he's been injured. Grace is with him now. They're in the hospital in Copenhagen.'

'Oh, God.' Jud stood frozen to the spot. 'What happened?'

'Well, it seems he's been shot.'

'*Shot?*' said Jud.

Bex moved closer to him and grabbed his hand. 'I'm sure he's fine,' she said.

'No, he's not fine,' said Goode. 'Look, I'm really sorry. He's in intensive care, but there's a lot of bleeding. He was shot in the stomach.'

Goode flicked a glance at Bonati. The professor knew exactly what he was saying. There was no need for any words. 'Let's go,' he said calmly. 'We need to be there for him.'

'What?' said Jud, looking around. 'What're you doing? I'm coming, for God's sake. You can't stop me. I wanna be there.'

'No,' said Goode, firmly. 'He will recover, I'm sure. And we'll help him to come back home. You'll see him in London. You need to listen to me. That wasn't all Grace said. *Listen.* They were being tailed, she thinks – probably this Sigurdsson guy – and it's because of what they've found out over there. They've researched everything. I told her what's happening here and she's explained it.'

'Go on,' said Bex.

'You know they think it was a burial here, on the land, and it slipped into the sea, right? Well, I told her about the Valkyrie and the amulet. She thinks she knows who it belonged to. And, if she's right, it makes sense of everything.'

'Really?' said Summers, equally transfixed by the news unfolding. 'Who? Tell us!'

'Ragnar Lodbrok: probably the most famous Viking of them all.'

'I read about him,' said Bex. 'He came to England about 850, if I remember rightly. But why would he have had an amulet – a piece of women's jewellery?'

'Well, accounts of his life are real patchy, you know. I mean, Viking history is half myth, half truth at times. But we think he was married to a Swedish princess named Thora. So it's perfectly possible that he brought her with him, right? And there are those that suggest she died over here.'

'My God. So, if that's true,' said Bex, 'then she would probably have had a ship burial – I mean, the works. She would have had everything buried with her – including her jewellery, which means she'd have been buried with the amulet.'

Bonati nodded his head in agreement. 'If Grace is right, and this Thora was buried around these parts, then there's every chance her grave collapsed into the sea.'

'And everything with it,' said Summers.

'Wait a minute,' said Bex, 'Ragnar Lodbrok famously believed he was the son of Odin, didn't he? And that black dog – you remember, Jud, the one that couple saw? She said it was the Black Shuck – the dog belonging to the Viking God, Odin. It explains everything.'

'So do you think that Yolanda took on the life of Thora when she wore the amulet?' said Summers. 'Is that what you're saying?'

Bex nodded. 'It's possible that she's displaying the appearance of a Valkyrie while embodying Thora's spirit, since Thora was the amulet's rightful owner. And, if that's the case, we have *got* to find her. If we can present her to the ghosts on the beach, they'll be silenced. No wonder there is unrest in this area. The remains of a seriously important Viking grave have been disturbed. They should never have been touched.'

'So you think Ragnar Lodbrok is invading again? Is that what you're saying?' said Summers.

'Looks like it,' said Bex. 'We've got to speak to him and his followers. We've got to reunite him with his wife.'

'Grace said that Lodbrok was eventually killed over here and when his sons found out about it, they returned and blood eagled the man who did it, King Aella. It explains a lot, doesn't it?' Goode said.

They nodded. Jud had fallen silent again and was staring out to sea. 'Sorry, you'll have to deal with this, Bex. I can't. I've gotta see Luc. I've gotta be there for him. I've gotta—'

'No,' interrupted Bonati. 'Listen to me, Jud. Your place is here, helping Bex to end this whole saga. You know what to do. You'll think of something together – you're a team.' He approached him, up close. 'Look at me. She needs you here. Leave Luc to us; we'll sort it. Trust me. He'll be fine. Now, go! Get down there and end this, before it's too late.'

The professor turned and ran to the helicopter with Goode. They leapt in, the doors were closed and within a few moments the giant blades had begun turning again.

CHAPTER 48

WEDNESDAY, 9.23 P.M.

DUNWICH BEACH, SUFFOLK

'Over here!' shouted Bex, as the wind rattled around them and made her words almost inaudible in the din. 'Here!' she shouted again. 'It's another body!'

They'd walked further over the dark field, in the direction of the village. Concerned that the ghosts would soon approach the place, it was better to catch them where they were heading than try to stem the flow of them rising out of the sea. It was too late for that now.

Bex was up ahead, impatient as ever; Jud was walking by himself, his extrasensory perception on red alert. Khan was walking behind, helping Summers, who had clearly not recovered from his ordeal out at sea but was determined to be with them rather than by himself right now.

Up ahead, in the middle of the boggy field, Bex had stumbled over something that had almost made her sick.

It was a mutilated body, lying face down, its back and ribcage split open, just like before. The soft, pulpy mess of organs and veins and blood vessels, reaching out of the pale bones was abhorrent to look on. The face was obscured from view and it was impossible, especially in the darkness, to identify it.

'Here!' she shouted again. 'Come on!'

Jud, Khan and Summers ran over to her.

But they soon stopped in their tracks.

'No. Not again,' said Summers. 'I can't do this again.' He grabbed his mouth as if he were about to throw up and ran a few feet away, where he knelt down and tried to catch his breath.

'Shall we roll him over?' said Jud. 'We have to know who it is. Come around to this side and we'll roll him from here.'

They fed their hands underneath the deceased's left arm and shoulder and then pulled up and over, as quickly as possible, neither of them wishing to be completely stained with congealed blood.

'I don't believe it!' said Jud. 'It's Hartwell. Poor bastard.'

Bex was equally shocked as they rolled him over and saw his startled face, eyes wide, terror etched into every muscle. Though Khan had seen more than his fair share of murder victims, this was one of the worst he'd seen – perhaps worse than the first blood eagling down on the beach.

'So, where was he off to?' said Khan. 'The direction of his body, with his feet towards the pub and his head pointing towards the field, suggests he was struck down as he was leaving for somewhere in this direction.' He looked behind him, the way they had come. 'But where? There's nothing up here; only fields. And at this time of night? These injuries look fresh to me. I reckon he's not been here long.'

'Was he looking for us, do you think? Maybe he was spying on us, or something?' said Bex. 'He could have been leaving the hotel to find us.'

'It's possible,' said Jud. 'You never know with this guy. He was trouble. But I'd never have wished for this.' Jud felt bad now for bullying him earlier. He was, after all, one of a rare group of people with whom he could say he shared a past. And, for that, he felt aggrieved to have been robbed of him already. They'd only just seen each other again and, although their reunion had been acrimonious and the need to silence this kid had been immense at the time, now that Jud had shared everything with Bex, he felt less angry or afraid of the damage Hartwell could have wreaked. His secret was already out; at least, it felt that way, having confessed all to Bex. He knew, of course, that Hartwell could have done much to damage both his reputation and that of the CRYPT. Had that been where he was heading? Jud wondered.

'At least he won't talk now,' said Bex, with a callousness that surprised Jud.

'Yeah, I guess so. Still – poor kid. Could've made an agent, after all; you never know.'

'I don't want to see this any more. Let's go,' said Bex. 'We've got to get to the ghosts before it's too late. Inspector, will you stay with the body and inform the authorities?'

'Yeah, of course. It wasn't much of a holiday, anyway. Leave him with me. I'll stay here.' Though his tone was sarcastic, in truth, he felt relieved to have a reason not to go any further with the agents. All this running about in the dark, hunting for ghosts, was not exactly what he'd been built for, or was expecting to do when this whole sorry holiday had begun. Though he had often teased the agents, like the few other police officers at the Met who knew they existed, Khan was beginning to develop a quiet respect for what they did – especially out here, where the evidence of what ghosts could really do to humans was just about everywhere.

'You go,' he said. 'I'll stay here and keep the body company. You staying too, Summers?'

He looked confused. 'Er . . . I dunno.' He turned to Jud. 'Should I come with you?'

'No. You stay with the inspector. You've done enough already. And we can't risk anyone else getting injured. We'll take it from here.'

'No, I'm coming with you,' he said. 'Please.'

'He could be useful,' said Bex.

'Whatever,' Jud snapped at them. 'Just don't hold us up.'

He shot one last look at the lifeless body of Pat Hartwell. No one, not even he, could feel anything but pity for him. And it fuelled his own determination to end this haunting now. He felt a twinge of guilt. He knew, if he hadn't been so preoccupied with his own misery and stress, he would have focused more on the investigation and – who knows? – he could've saved Hartwell's life. He stared at his terrified eyes, the last expression he would ever make. How tragic it was that the very thing he'd been obsessed with – the paranormal – was the thing that brought about his end. It wasn't right and Jud knew very well he and Bex should've worked harder to prevent it.

He sucked in a long gulp of cold, night air, tensed his muscles and resolved to carry on, for Hartwell's sake. Though it was too late for him, it was time to end the ghosts and avoid any more atrocities. This place had consumed Jud's thoughts and brought about a woeful sense of loneliness that had affected him deeply for the last twenty-four hours. But it was time to buck up and get on with what he was best at – working as a paranormal agent. It was what Hartwell would have wanted.

Khan wished them good luck and said he would take on the unenviable task of informing the landlord at the hotel about the tragedy. Looking at the state of the poor guy on the ground by his feet, he'd already decided to get his fellow officers or paramedics here before he approached the deceased's parents back in the hotel. He wouldn't want them to see their son in this state. They could make the official identification once the body was taken away and cleaned up.

Free from the aging Khan, the agents were able to pick up the pace now, and they darted across the field, looking for signs of the paranormal, always shooting glances in the direction of the sea, hoping to get a glimpse of the Valkyrie. Summers ran on, gaining strength now and reluctant to stay behind with the brutally injured body. He too was keen to see where his Yolanda had gone.

They were going to need her, if their plan to appease the ghosts would work. Neither Jud nor Bex actually believed it was likely she could have been sucked up into the rotary blades of the helicopter. She may have disappeared momentarily but, as they knew from experience, ghosts don't suddenly die. She'd be back and they'd need to be there when she returned.

The plan, so hurriedly put together, was to entice the Valkyrie down towards the beach somehow, probably using Daniel Summers himself, since he was still the object of her affections – or Yolanda's, at least. Once they had her close, they'd try to communicate with the marching Vikings on the beach. If their theory that Yolanda, in wearing the amulet with the image of the Valkyrie, had taken on the characteristics of a Valkyrie from the afterlife but had, at the same time, summoned up the spirit of the amulet's rightful owner – Thora – was true, then that may – just may – be enough to appease the ghosts and allow them to rest in peace once again.

If it didn't work, then the disturbances Summers had made under the ocean could send a tidal wave of Viking ghosts, attacking the shores of England just like before, seeking revenge.

But where the hell was the Valkyrie?

The three of them stood on the edge of the field and scanned the sea below them. There was a strange smell in the air – a rank mixture of salty sea and rotting flesh. The ghosts were marching, slowly, purposefully towards them. But there was no sign of the Valkyrie's illuminated, sprite-like body.

And then Summers let out a shriek. 'There!' he shouted. 'Look! Down there!'

Jud and Bex traced the line he was making with his arm and saw a small shaft of light emanating from below the cliff edges. It was darting about like a feather in the wind, but radiated a silvery light.

'That's it. That's her,' said Summers. 'I know it. Let's go!'

Jud was cautious. 'Be careful,' he said. 'The ground is uneven here. We need to find a way down. You don't know where—'

But it was too late. Summers was gone. There was something about the dancing light ahead of him that had an hypnotic effect on the young surfer. He was drawn to it like a moth to a light bulb. Transfixed. He was running now, stumbling over the undulating ground. His feet gave way a couple of times and caused him to stumble, but still he pressed on, closer to the perilous drop at the end of the field. Below them, the lines of ghosts marched past, their skeletal faces catching the moonlight.

'Wait!' yelled Bex, but her words were lost on the driving wind that howled around the cliffs and blended with the waves that broke over the stones below them. 'Come back, for God's sake. Wait!'

The agents took off after Summers, but they were determined not to lose their bearings and to keep a track of where the crumbling cliffs dropped away.

'Come back!' shouted Jud. 'Summers, don't be stupid, man! Wait for us!'

They saw the light of the Valkyrie rising towards them, getting bigger, brighter. Then they saw the dark silhouette of Summers. He was heading straight for it, like a man possessed.

'Yolanda!' they heard him cry.

Then they saw him drop, like a stone, over the edge of the cliff. They heard his cries for a few seconds and then an ominous deathly thud as his body hit the impregnable stones below.

'Oh, God!' cried Bex, as she ran to Jud and grabbed him.

He enveloped her in his arms and kissed her head. 'Keep it together,' he said. Now he was the strong one, hugging her, urging her on, just like she'd done for him, hours earlier. He was resolute, ready to take control of the situation, after too long spent moping and crying in this barren place. He was ready for a fight.

'This way,' he said, leading her by the hand towards a safer path that wound its way gently down towards the pebble beach below. They could see the Valkyrie still hovering around below them and then they saw it rest near some stones to their right. Its light was fading.

As they approached it, they saw it was hovering over the body of Summers, who was slumped awkwardly on the stones, lifeless.

'Quick,' said Jud. 'Now's the time. Come with me.'

They ran on to the beach and approached the Valkyrie. She turned to face them and it made them pause. Her eyes were bright, like cat's eyes on a black road, but there were tears forming around them. Her translucent wings were as still as a butterfly resting on a flower, but she was staring at Jud – through him, almost. He shivered – and knew it wasn't just the cold.

'Don't look at her!' said Bex, grabbing his face in her hand and turning it towards her.

'OK, OK,' he said. 'She's beautiful.'

'So am I!' Bex shouted at him. 'Come on! What's the plan?'

They saw, over the Valkyrie's shoulders, that the Viking ghosts were approaching them. There must have been fifty or more, each one trudging slowly over the uneven ground. Stumbling, hobbling, but always moving forwards, like some unstoppable tide.

'They're marching for you,' shouted Jud, over the din of the waves and the wind.

'What?' said Bex.

'For her,' he said, pointing to the Valkyrie. 'I'm trying to tell her. It's why they've come. If this is the ghost of Thora, then they've come to protect her. They want the amulet. We've got to get her to take it off and show them it's safe.'

Bex moved towards the Valkyrie.

'Wait!' shouted Jud. 'What're you doing?'

'It won't get me,' said Bex. 'It wants Summers.'

Jud watched as Bex drew even closer towards the ghost. Its eyes were following her but Bex was careful not to make any sudden movements.

Gently, gently, she told herself.

'Yolanda, Yolanda,' she whispered. 'It's OK. I know you're there, Yolanda. Can you hear me?'

The Valkyrie gave Bex a strange, sad look.

She was listening. Her wings and her gentle, almost translucent body were shivering now, twitching like an insect, but not fleeing.

Somewhere inside the feathery frame of the ghost, Yolanda's spirit lurked. She was still there.

'Yolanda, hold up the chain. Yolanda? Listen to me. The amulet: take it off.'

There was no response. Jud moved in closer. If this ghost was about to scratch, or grab, or do anything to Bex, he'd be on it like a shot. He saw the Viking soldiers marching ever closer.

'Quick,' he whispered. 'We don't have long. Hurry.'

'Thora?' Bex said gently.

The Valkyrie jolted. Its expression changed and, without warning, it flew at Bex's face.

'Aagh! Get it off!' Bex cried, trying to fumble for something to swat and punch, but her eyes were closed to protect them from the Valkyrie's razor-like fingers and she was stabbing around blindly.

Jud moved in closer and grabbed the ghost. He held it in a vice-like grip, his hands clasped together around its feeble frame. Though you could see through its body in places, there was some resistance there; he could feel he was holding something.

'Thora, you're safe,' he whispered. 'They've come for you. Give them the amulet.'

The ghost turned to face him. He jolted his head backwards to get away from the strange stench that emanated from its mouth. But he held on.

The Vikings were almost on them. The agents could see their bony faces, each one wearing a fixed expression of horror and anger and revenge.

In trying to appease them by bringing them the Valkyrie, the ghost of Thora, they had inadvertently given the impression they were attacking her, imprisoning her in Jud's arms.

'Release her!' shouted Bex. 'Let her go. Now!'

Jud dropped her from his arms and Bex pulled him away sharply. She led him by the hand up to the edge of the beach where they could get a safer vantage point.

'What're you doing?' said Jud. 'We need to go and get the amul—'

But he stopped, open mouthed.

The Vikings surrounded the ghostly angel. There was a large, menacing figure at the front of the group, fiercer, heavier than the others. It had a prominent forehead and a wider skull than most. Unlike some of the other eyeless faces around it, this figure had large, piercing eyes that were beginning to shine now. A dark red glow was growing in intensity, deep inside each eyeball.

The giant ghost was closing in. The agents, watching in silent shock from a short distance away, saw the figure soon embrace the Valkyrie. It raised it up towards the skies. Jud and Bex saw it turn to face the rest of the ghosts that were now swarming around the scene, each one emitting some kind of rattling noise from its skeletal jaws.

'It's Lodbrok,' whispered Bex.

'Do you think so?'

'It has to be. Watch him.'

They saw the ghost raise the Valkyrie up further with both arms. Then it let out a deathly kind of cry, half choking, half screaming, but a sound distinct from anything human.

It set the angelic-like figure back down on the ground again and then, carefully, lifted the amulet from around its neck. Within seconds, the body of the Valkyrie slumped to the ground.

The Vikings rallied around their leader, jostling to see the amulet and raising their fists towards the sky.

'Look, there,' whispered Bex. She was pointing to the pebbles where the Valkyrie's fragile body had slumped. 'Look at that.'

And they watched as the figure began to change form. The light that had been emitting from its body was fading and, as it did so, the translucent parts of its frame were becoming more solid, darker, stronger.

Yolanda was returning. Her blond hair, which had been burning bright gold before, was now dull and limp on her head, darkening as the rain fell on her.

The ghosts that had been jostling around the Valkyrie were fading too. Their leader had turned away from the girl, still lying motionless on the pebbles, and had begun to trudge back towards the sea, the amulet clasped securely in his hand. His fellow ghosts turned, too, and obediently followed.

'No one will dive here again,' said Bex. 'They mustn't. There's too much history here – too much beneath the waves. And when it's stirred up we see the spirits of the past come back with such vengeance, such anger. Viking burials cannot be disturbed.'

'Just like any burial site,' said Jud. 'Better to leave them in peace.'

'Thora was here tonight. She came back from the dead to show them, maybe to show us, she mattered once. She was important then – and we mustn't forget her.'

'But there have been too many victims, Bex, too much death. Too many innocent people.'

'But we stopped it, Jud. We did. We caught the Valkyrie and we returned the amulet to the ghosts.'

'Did we? Really?'

'Yes! Don't give up on me, will you? This is an important job we do. We're there when it matters.' She looked up at the dark night and felt the rain on her face. 'And when it happens again – which it will, somewhere, soon – then we'll be there again, protecting the public. Luc too. You know he'll be fine.'

Jud shrugged his shoulders. They saw Yolanda's body move. Bex went to her. She spoke gently but firmly. 'Hello? Can you hear me?'

Yolanda opened her eyes and nodded. 'Yeah,' she whispered.

'I'm glad you're alive. I can't imagine what you've been through. But you've got to come with us. The police will need to see you. You're going to have to answer some questions. Come, let me help you up.'

They pulled her gently to her feet and helped her across the pebbles towards the village buildings in the distance. Blue flashing lights appeared over the dunes as the police cars and ambulances poured into the rain-soaked car park, once again.

CHAPTER 49

FRIDAY, 2.19 P.M.

CRYPT, LONDON

Jud ran from the briefing room. Panic was rising through his veins like water boiling in a pan. He didn't want the embarrassment of losing it in front of his fellow agents, or even Bex. This was one crisis only he could deal with, in his own time, in his own space. And if he was going to cope with the fallout that would run long and deep, he was going to have to do it alone. He knew that.

He ran down the corridor of Sector Two and found the lifts at the end. Luckily one arrived quickly and it was empty. He slipped in and pressed the close button instantly.

'Come on! Come on!' he shouted at the doors as they slowly joined again, bringing a veil of privacy that he was so needing. He could feel the tears were welling up now.

It wasn't until the doors had kissed that Bex appeared at the end of the corridor. She looked down towards the lifts and saw nothing, no one.

'Jud!' she yelled at the top of her voice.

Silence.

Up in the lift, Jud did not have time to sit on the floor, bury his head in his lap and try to breathe, as he'd have liked to. He was at Sector One within seconds and the *ting* sounded. He waited for the doors to part again and then checked the corridor for anyone. It was empty just now – perfect timing. He ran towards his room. Moments later, he was inside.

He fell on to the bed and allowed the mounting pressure of grief to explode out of him, through his puffy eyes, his nose, his choking mouth. It had to come out; he knew that. He wouldn't bottle it up this time. But anger was rising just as strongly, conflicting with the sad grief. He rose from the bed and looked around him, in desperate need of punching something. Anything.

He grabbed his coat and some shoes on the floor, and hurled them at the wall. Then he ripped the duvet from his bed and threw that too. He was becoming wild now, he knew it, but he couldn't help himself, finding anything to hurl around, ripping posters from walls, smashing plates that were still on his desk with congealed tomato sauce stuck to them. Anything he could find.

There was a beep from outside, which suggested he had a visitor. He heard a voice.

'Jud? Let me in, *please.*'

It was Bex. He couldn't face her now. He was too embarrassed. He had to man up. But not yet. He didn't want her to see him like this. He ignored her.

'I know you're in there,' she said. 'Let me talk to you. Let me hold you. We can get through this together.'

Still nothing from inside.

'He was my friend too, you know.'

Jud paused inside but still said nothing. He was listening now, but incapable of saying anything.

'You're not the only one who's going to miss Luc. You're not the only one who feels it. The briefing room is a mess. Everyone's crying in there. You're no different, Jud Lester. You should've been there with us – helping us. You should've–'

'Go!' yelled Jud from inside. 'Get away from me! I don't want any lectures! Go away. *Now!*'

Outside, in the corridor, Bex rested her head on the door and closed her eyes. It felt like they were right back to where they started again: him shutting her out every time he could feel emotion rising; locking out the world and, in so doing, claiming somehow that he was the only one who could feel grief – the only one with problems.

When Professor Bonati had announced Luc's death in the hospital in Copenhagen, there was not a single agent in the room who'd not felt sick.

He'd not survived the gunshot.

Disbelief, anger, confusion, fear – everyone's emotions had run riot. But Jud had quietly got up from his chair and slunk out of the room, his face ashen white. Bex had noticed him, as had Bonati, and his glance over to her and his tilt of the head had said, *Go and get him.*

She sloped off down the corridor. She knew he needed time – everyone did. But this private, self-indulgent wallowing in self-pity was beginning to bug her. She thought they'd made progress in the wilds of Suffolk. Maybe not.

She'd come back and see him later, when he was in a mood to talk. And then she'd hold him, hug him hard, cradle him like she had in Dunwich, and reassure him that it really was OK to share emotions. In fact, it was essential.

Inside his room, Jud had finished venting his anger against anything he could find. He collapsed on to the bed again, the mess around him a reflection of the mess his mind was in right now. Like Bex, he'd thought he'd made progress. He was on the road to rehabilitation at last, able to share his history with a friend. But just as he'd opened the door to one, another soul mate – the guy he shared everything else with, all the usual guy stuff – had been taken from him.

The barriers were going to come up again, just like before. Self-preservation is a potent force. When his mother died, the gates were locked to his emotions – for good, or so he thought. They'll be locked again now, he thought.

He lay back on the place where his pillow should have been and closed his eyes. They were itchy from crying and rubbing them. He'd been stabbing them with his fingers out of frustration, trying to push the tears away.

There was another beep from outside.

Not another visitor? he thought. 'Go away!' he yelled.

'I beg your pardon?' said Bonati.

Jud sat upright. 'Er . . . I'm sorry. I didn't realise it was you.'

'Get up right now and come with me.'

Jud waited for a few seconds. He hadn't expected Bonati to sound so angry. But he didn't want his pity, either.

'Now!' the professor shouted through the door.

There was little in Bonati's voice that suggested this was an option. Jud rose and unlocked the door. Bonati was standing there, just staring at him.

'Come this way,' was all he said, and he set off towards the lifts at a pace that even Jud struggled to keep up with.

They entered the first available lift in silence. Jud was damned if he was going to start the conversation – why should he? The professor had ordered him out of his room just at a time when he wanted to be alone. He'd intruded on him, so why should Jud be polite now? But he was curious about where they were going – he'd assumed to Bonati's office for a telling off.

'Where are you taking me?' he said, miserably.

'You'll see.'

They watched the large, blue number displayed on the black screen at the top of the lift change to '2'. A few seconds later, it changed to '3'. Odd, thought Jud; why are we going into Sector Three? The lift stopped but the doors failed to open. Panic rose inside Jud again. No one liked being stuck in a lift. Especially not right now, when all he really wanted to do was escape the whole place and find some space for a while. Being stuck in a lift with the professor was the opposite of what he needed. No doubt he'd use the opportunity to lecture him, like usual.

The professor took out a small, white credit card and swiped the scanner next to the door. You could unlock the doors manually in this way and Jud moved towards the doors, ready. But they didn't open. Instead, the lift lurched again and began descending.

Descending? Jud was open mouthed. Everyone knew Sector Three was the very deepest part of the CRYPT. There was no Sector Four.

He glanced at Bonati. 'Professor?' was all he could say.

Bonati smiled at him. 'Wait.'

The steely blue number '3' on the black screen above remained the same and then . . . '4'.

Jud stared at the number, wide-eyed. 'What?' He couldn't believe what he was seeing. The CRYPT had a fourth sector? How could this possibly be true? Was he dreaming this? Had he fallen asleep on the bed in his room and was now in the land of dreams? It felt like that.

The doors slid aside once again and Bonati walked out into the darkness.

'Come on,' he said. 'I'll explain.'

Jud stepped out into a dark, cold corridor and the lift door closed behind them. Bonati flicked a switch to his right and small, halogen spotlights came on, running all the way down a long, straight corridor in front of them. Jud's face was still incredulous.

'Before we go on, I think I'd better explain,' said Bonati. 'Your father and I have been working on this sector for some time now, ever since the CRYPT was established, really. The provision for a fourth level was put in by the planners right from the start – you just didn't know about it. But it's finished now. And that's just as well.'

'Why? What's it for?' asked Jud, eagerly. This place was baffling – such a shock to the system. For the lift to have descended further into what Jud had assumed would be soil and rubble and rock was difficult to comprehend. And now, to find a whole floor of pristine, white corridors, spotlights and ominous metal doors firmly shut was too exciting for words. If only they'd shown him at a happier moment. Why now, for God's sake?

But, if he thought about it, Jud could guess why Bonati had brought him down here now. Like so often before, the professor would have been worried that he was about to go AWOL again. Maybe Bex had been to see him and warned him that Jud was taking Luc's death very, very badly. Maybe this secret trip underground was a ploy to distract him – prevent him from making a run for it like he'd done before, grabbing his bike helmet and keys and escaping for a while. If he was honest, that was precisely what he would have done, had the professor not arrived when he did.

And he may still decide to do that after this weird trip. Once he was back upstairs – and this small distraction was over – his grief would return and he would have to get away.

'Your father and I have been researching something.'

'So? You're always researching things, sir. My father never stands still. What's different this time? What is it that requires its own floor, for God's sake? Why won't you tell me?'

'Calm down,' said the professor, as they set off at a slow pace down the white, tiled corridor. The heels of his shoes clicked evenly as he walked and sent miniature echoes rattling around the impregnable walls. This could have been any place in the CRYPT: same lights, same sparse décor. But it was hard to comprehend that it was even deeper underground. 'All in good time.'

They reached the fourth door on the right – Jud had been counting – and then the professor stopped. He went to open it via the card scanner to the right, but paused and turned to Jud. 'Listen,' he said, 'this is really important. I want you to concentrate. Wake up, get a grip of yourself and get ready.'

Jud's heart was speeding up now and he was getting breathless. His hands were feeling sweaty and Bonati could see his red, blotchy eyes were beginning to blink rapidly. He was uncharacteristically nervous, but given his current emotional state that was to be expected, thought Bonati. It'd soon be over.

'Your father and I have been conducting research into an area of paranormal science no one has investigated before, at least not that we know of. We've been conducting experiments that have been highly controversial and would, if leaked, cause this whole place to be closed down. The terms laid down by MI5 at the beginning of this project did not allow for the work we have been doing. It's not in the rule book, so to speak, but you know your father – always pushing boundaries.'

'What?' said Jud, impatiently. 'Tell me what the hell you've been doing, please!'

'There was a reason your father and I had to jet off to Copenhagen immediately after we heard the news about Luc. We wanted to be with him, of course, but there was another reason why we had to get there . . . I mean, in time.'

'*In time?*' said Jud, incredulously. 'In time for what? You mean before he . . . ?'

'Yes,' said Bonati, gently. 'It was essential we were there *before* he died.'

'Why?' Jud had gone pale now. 'Tell me what's going on, sir.'

He scanned the card along the machine, pressed his face up to the pupil-recognition system and the door eventually slid slowly open. Dim, red lights set into the ceiling flashed on automatically as they entered. The room was small, not much bigger than Jud's own dormitory, but it was sparsely furnished with only a couple of metal tables, each with computer screens on. There was an odd-looking cabinet in the centre – tall enough to stand in, with glass walls, like a modern shower cubicle.

'What the hell's going on?' said Jud. 'What have you been doing?'

Bonati told Jud to sit down next to him at one of the long, metal tables. He turned to Jud and clasped his arm, gently. 'Listen to me. Your father and I have, we think, discovered how to make contact with the deceased once they have passed over. Not like some psychic circus act, or some pretend medium in a theatre or at a fairground, OK? This is *real*.'

Jud's eyes were wide now. He sat there, silent, trying valiantly to steady his heart before it exploded out of his chest and bounced out of the room.

'We've designed a tracer system – electromagnetic – you might think of it as a tracking device. But it's not a physical microchip attached to someone's ankle. It's in their mind – their spirit. When someone dies, if they are fitted with the EM tracer then there's a chance we don't lose them, not forever. We can trace the activity of their disembodied spirit – the part of us that leaves our body when we die. We can track it. And we can contact it. We can encourage the spirit of a deceased person to return – to draw on the electromagnetic energy he or she once emitted, and to return as plasma that is attracted to the electromagnetic radiation, like any ghost does, as you know. But we can get a ghost to do this on demand – if we can trace them.'

'This isn't real,' said Jud. 'You're joking. My father's finally flipped. This is in the realms of fantasy.' He stared at the cubicle in the centre of the room. 'Is that where . . . you know . . . ?'

Bonati shook his head. 'Not yet. We've had no success in enticing a disembodied spirit to take form here. But, in principle, we think it will work. It depends on whether the spirit wishes to be contacted, after all.'

'So how do you know it works? You're not finished yet. You've found nothing.' Jud was about to stand, but the professor held him back.

'Wait,' he said. 'We've done it. Don't you see? We fitted Luc with the EM tracer. He has it. And, just before he died, he said something to us. Jason and I both heard it. He said, "Tell Jud, I'll be back." That's what he said, J. Honest.'

Jud was finding it hard to stem the flow of tears again. His voice was faltering as he spoke. 'And you want me to summon him?'

The professor slowly nodded his head. 'We might not see him appear yet, it's early days, after all, but it's worth a try. We've been perfecting this for months, J. Your father and I really think we've done it. And Luc is the one to help us. Even if we don't see him yet, we'll hear him – I'm certain of that. You've got to believe, Jud.' As he spoke, he was switching computers on, setting up scanners and running tests. The two screens in front of them sprung into life and Jud could see rows of gauges and graphs and LED screens and dials, like being in some hi-tech rocket.

He sat back in his chair, trying hard to take this in. Bonati dimmed the lights further using one of the buttons on the bank of controls in front of him. The room was dimly lit with a wash of red. The place was eerily quiet, save for the faint whirring of the computers and the electromagnetic hum from the giant cabinet in the centre of the room.

'Ready?' said Bonati.

Crypt:
The Gallows Curse

Andrew Hammond

When a brutal crime is committed . . . but there's no human explanation . . . who can the police turn to?

CRYPT:
Covert Response Youth Paranormal Team

Terror has seized London. People are dying in vicious attacks. But those who survive agree: the killers, bearing the scars of the hangman's noose, materialised out of thin air.

CRYPT has been dispatched.

The hunt is on . . .

978 0 7553 7821 0

headline

Crypt:
Traitor's Revenge

Andrew Hammond

When a brutal crime is committed . . . but there's no human explanation . . . who can the police turn to?

CRYPT:
Covert Response Youth Paranormal Team

A security breach at the Houses of Parliament fuels bizarre rumours, whilst reports of horrific sightings ignite panic in York . . .

CRYPT has just landed its most explosive case yet!

978 0 7553 7822 7

headline

Crypt:
Mask of Death

Andrew Hammond

When a brutal crime is committed . . . but there's no human explanation . . . who can the police turn to?

CRYPT:
Covert Response Youth Paranormal Team

A figure in a white mask swoops down a deserted hospital corridor towards a quarantined patient. Covered in black sores the man can't be saved by modern medicine. But then, the masked figure is not a modern doctor . . .

Only CRYPT has the skills to respond to this emergency call!

978 0 7553 7823 4

headline